JAMES LEE BURKE

BLACK CHERRY BLUES

PHOENIX

A PHOENIX PAPERBACK

First published in Great Britain in 1990
by Century
This paperback edition published in 2005
by Phoenix,
an imprint of Orion Books Ltd,
Orion House, 5 Upper St Martin's Lane,
London WC2H 9EA

An Hachette Livre UK company

A CIP catalogue record for this book is available from the British Library.

Typeset at The Spartan Press Ltd,
Lymington, Hants

Printed in Great Britain by
Clays Ltd, St Ives plc

The Orion Publishing Group's policy is to use papers that are natural, renewable and recyclable products and made from wood grown in sustainable forests. The logging and manufacturing processes are expected to conform to the environmental regulations of the country of origin.

www.orionbooks.co.uk

For John and Flavia McBride

I would like to thank the John Simon Guggenheim Foundation for its generous assistance, and I also would like to thank the National Endowment for the Arts for its past support.

chapter one

Her hair is curly and gold on the pillow, her skin white in the heat lightning that trembles beyond the pecan trees outside the bedroom window. The night is hot and breathless, the clouds painted like horsetails against the sky; a peal of thunder rumbles out on the Gulf like an apple rolling around in the bottom of a wood barrel, and the first raindrops ping against the window fan. She sleeps on her side, and the sheet molds her thigh, the curve of her hip, her breast. In the flicker of the heat lightning the sun freckles on her bare shoulder look like brown flaws in sculpted marble.

Then a prizing bar splinters the front door out of the jamb, and two men burst inside the house in heavy shoes, their pump shotguns at port arms. One is a tall Haitian, the other a Latin whose hair hangs off his head in oiled ringlets. They stand at the foot of the double bed in which she sleeps alone, and do not speak. She awakes with her mouth open, her eyes wide and empty of meaning. Her face is still warm from a dream, and she cannot separate sleep from the two men who stare at her without speaking. Then she sees them looking at each other and aiming their shotguns point-blank at her chest. Her eyes film and she calls out my name like a wet bubble bursting in her throat. The sheet is twisted in her hands; she holds it against her breasts as though it could protect her from twelve-gauge deer slugs and double-aught buckshot.

They begin shooting, and the room seems to explode with smoke and flame from their shotgun barrels, with shell wadding, mattress stuffing, splinters gouged out of the bedstead, torn lampshades, flying glass. The two killers are methodical. They have taken out the sportsman's plug in their shotguns so they can load five rounds in the magazine, and they keep firing and ejecting the smoking hulls on the floor until their firing pins snap empty. Then they reload with the calmness of men who might have just stood up in a blind and fired at a formation of ducks overhead.

The sheet is torn, drenched with her blood, embedded in her wounds. The men have gone now, and I sink to my knees by my wife and kiss her sightless eyes, run my hand over her hair and wan face, put her fingers in my mouth. A solitary drop of her blood runs down the shattered headboard and pools on my skin. A bolt of lightning explodes in an empty field behind the house. The inside of my head is filled with a wet, sulphurous smell, and again I hear my name rise like muffled, trapped air released from the sandy bottom of a pond.

It was four in the morning on a Saturday and raining hard when I awoke from the dream in a West Baton Rouge motel. I sat on the side of the bed in my underwear and tried to rub the dream out of my face, then I used the bathroom and came back and sat on the side of the bed again in the dark.

First light was still two hours away, but I knew I would not sleep again. I put on my raincoat and hat and drove in my pickup truck to an all-night café that occupied one side of a clapboard roadhouse. The rain clattered on my truck cab, and the wind was blowing strong out of the southwest, across the Atchafalaya swamp, whipping the palm and oak trees by the highway. West Baton Rouge, which begins at the Mississippi River, has always been a seedy area of truck stops, marginal gambling joints, Negro and blue-collar bars. To the east you can see the lighted girders of the Earl K. Long Bridge, plumes of smoke rising from the oil refineries, the state capital building silhouetted in the rain. Baton Rouge is a green town full of oak trees, parks, and lakes, and the thousands of lights on the refineries and chemical plants are regarded as a testimony to financial security rather than a sign of industrial blight. But once you drive west across the metal grid of the bridge and thump down on the old cracked four-lane, you're in a world that caters to the people of the Atchafalaya basin – Cajuns, redbones, roustabouts, pipeliners, rednecks whose shrinking piece of American geography is identified only by a battered pickup, a tape deck playing Waylon, and a twelve-pack of Jax.

The rain spun in the yellow arc lights over the café parking lot. It was empty inside, except for a fat Negro woman whom I could see through the service window in the kitchen, and a pretty, redheaded waitress in her early twenties, dressed in a pink uniform with her hair tied up on her freckled neck. She was obviously tired, but she was polite and smiled at me when she took my order, and I felt a sense of guilt, almost shame, at my susceptibility and easy fondness for a young woman's smile. Because if you're forty-nine and unmarried or a widower or if you've simply chosen to live alone, you're easily flattered by a young woman's seeming attention to you, and you forget that it is often simply a deference to your age.

I ordered a chicken-fried steak and a cup of coffee and listened to Jimmy Clanton's recording of 'Just a Dream' that came from the jukebox next door. Through the open doorway that gave on to the empty dance floor, I could see a half-dozen people at the bar against the far wall. I watched a man my age, with waved blond hair, drink his whiskey down to the ice, point to the glass for the bartender to refill it, then rise from his stool and walk across the dance floor into the café.

He wore gray slacks, a green sport shirt with blue flowers on it, shined loafers, white socks, a gold watch, and gold clip-on ballpoint pens in his shirt pocket. He wore his shirt outside his slacks to hide his paunch and love handles.

'Hey, hon, let me have a cheeseburger and bring it up to the bar, will you?' he said.

Then his eyes adjusted to the light and he looked at me more carefully.

'Great God Almighty,' he said. 'Dave Robicheaux. You son of a buck.'

A voice and a face out of the past, not simply mine but from an era. Dixie Lee Pugh, my freshman roommate at Southwestern Louisiana Institute in 1956: a peckerwood kid from a river town north of Baton Rouge, with an accent more Mississippi than Louisiana, who flunked out his first semester, then went to Memphis and cut two records at the same studio where Carl

Perkins, Johnny Cash, and Elvis began their careers. The second record put him on New York television, and we watched in awe while he played his sunburst rhythm-and-blues guitar or hammered his fingers on the piano keyboard while an audience of thousands went insane and danced in the aisles.

He was one of the biggest in the early rock ’n’ roll era. But he had something more going for him than many of the others did. He was the real article, an honest-to-God white blues singer. He learned his music in the Baptist church, but somebody in that little cotton and pecan-orchard town rubbed a lot of pain into him, too, because it was in everything he sang and it wasn’t manufactured for the moment, either.

Then we read and heard other stories about him: the four or five failed marriages, the death of one of his children in a fire, a hit-and-run accident and DWI in Texas that put him in Huntsville pen.

‘Dave, I don’t believe it,’ he said, grinning. ‘I saw you ten or twelve years ago in New Orleans. You were a cop.’

I remembered it. It had been in a low-rent bar off Canal, the kind of place that featured yesterday’s celebrities, where the clientele made noise during the performances and insulted the entertainers.

He sat down next to me and shook hands, almost as an afterthought.

‘We got to drink some mash and talk some trash,’ he said, then told the waitress to bring me a beer or a highball.

‘No, thanks, Dixie,’ I said.

‘You mean like it’s too late or too early in the day or like you’re off the jug?’ he said.

'I go to meetings now. You know what I mean?'

'Heck yeah. That takes guts, man. I admire it.' His eyes were green and filled with an alcohol shine. He looked at me directly a moment, then his eyes blinked and he looked momentarily embarrassed.

'I read in the newspaper about your wife, man. I'm sorry.'

'Thank you.'

'They caught the guys that did it?'

'More or less.'

'Huh,' he said, and studied me for a moment. I could see that he was becoming uncomfortable with the knowledge that a chance meeting with an old friend is no guarantee that you can reclaim pleasant moments out of the past. Then he smiled again.

'You still a cop?' he asked.

'I own a bait and boat-rental business south of New Iberia. I came up here last night to pick up some refrigeration equipment and got stuck in the storm.'

He nodded. We were both silent.

'Are you playing here, Dixie?' I said.

Mistake.

'No, I don't do that anymore. I never really got back to it after that trouble in Texas.'

He cleared his throat and took a cigarette out of the pack in his shirt pocket.

'Say, hon, how about getting me my drink out of the bar?'

The waitress smiled, put down the rag she had been using to clean the counter, and went into the nightclub next door.

'You know about that stuff in Texas?' he asked.

'Yes, I think so.'

'I was DWI, all right, and I ran away from the accident. But the guy run that stop sign. There wasn't no way I could have avoided it. But it killed his little boy, man. That's some hard shit to live with. I got out in eighteen months with good time.' He made lines on a napkin with his thumbnail. 'A lot of people just don't want to forget, though.'

I didn't know what to say. I felt sorry for him. He seemed little different from the kid I used to know, except he was probably ninety-proof most of the time now. I remembered a quote in a *Newsweek* story about Dixie Lee that seemed to define him better than anything else I had ever seen written about him. The reporter had asked him if any of his band members could read music. He replied, 'Yeah, some of them can, but it don't hurt their playing any.'

So I asked him what he was doing now, because I had to say something.

'Leaseman,' he said. 'Like Hank Snow used to say, "From old Montana down to Alabam'." I cover it all. Anyplace there's oil and coal. The money's right, too, podna.'

The waitress put his bourbon and water down in front of him. He drank from it and winked at her over his glass.

'I'm glad you're doing okay, Dixie,' I said.

'Yeah, it's a good life. A Caddy convertible, a new address every week, it beats collard greens and grits.' He hit me on the arm. 'Heck, it's all rock 'n' roll, anyway, man.'

I nodded good-naturedly and looked through the service window at the Negro woman who was scraping my hash browns and chicken-fried steak on to a plate. I was about to tell the waitress that I had meant the order to go.

'Well, I got some people waiting on me,' Dixie Lee said. 'Like, some of the sweet young things still come around, you know what I mean? Take it easy, buddy. You look good.'

I shook hands with him, ate my steak, bought a second cup of coffee for the road, and walked out into the rain.

The wind buffeted my truck all the way across the Atchafalaya basin. When the sun came up the light was gray and wet, and ducks and herons were flying low over the dead cypress in the marsh. The water in the bays was the color of lead and capping in the wind. A gas flare burned on a drilling rig set back in a flooded stand of willow trees. Each morning I began the day with a prayer, thanking my Higher Power for my sobriety of yesterday and asking Him to help me keep it today. This morning I included Dixie Lee in my prayer.

I drove back to New Iberia through St Martinville. The sun was above the oaks on Bayou Teche now, but in the deep, early morning shadows the mist still hung like clouds of smoke among the cattails and damp tree trunks. It was only March, but spring was roaring into southern Louisiana, as it always does after the long gray rains of February. Along East Main in New Iberia the yards were filled with blooming azalea, roses, and yellow and red hibiscus, and the trellises and gazebos were covered with trumpet vine and clumps of purple wisteria. I rumbled over the drawbridge and followed the dirt road along the bayou south of town, where I operated a fish dock and lived with a six-year-old El

Salvadorean refugee girl named Alafair in the old home my father had built out of cypress and oak during the Depression.

The wood had never been painted, was dark and hard as iron, and the beams had been notched and joined with pegs. The pecan trees in my front yard were thick with leaf and still dripping with rainwater, which tinked on the tin roof of the gallery. The yard always stayed in shadow and was covered with layers of blackened leaves. The elderly mulatto woman who baby-sat Alafair for me was in the side yard, pulling the vinyl storm covers off my rabbit hutches. She was the color of a copper penny and had turquoise eyes, like many South Louisiana Negroes who are part French. Her body looked put together out of sticks, and her skin was covered with serpentine lines. She dipped snuff and smoked hand-rolled cigarettes constantly, and bossed me around in my own home, but she could work harder than anyone I had ever known, and she had been fiercely loyal to my family since I was a child.

My boat dock was in full sunlight now, and I could see Batist, the other black person who worked for me, loading an ice chest for two white men in their outboard. He was shirtless and bald, and the weight of the ice chest made his wide back and shoulders ridge with muscle. He broke up kindling for my barbecue pit with his bare hands, and once I saw him jerk a six-foot alligator out of the water by its tail and throw it up on a sandbar.

I stepped around the puddles in the yard to the gallery.

'What you gonna do this coon?' Clarise, the mulatto woman, said.

She had put my three-legged raccoon, Tripod, on his chain, which was attached to a wire clothesline so he could run up and down in the side yard. She pulled him up in the air by the chain. His body danced and curled as though he were being garroted.

'Clarise, don't do that.'

'Ax him what he done, him,' she said. 'Go look my wash basket. Go look your shirts. They blue yesterday. They brown now. Go smell you.'

'I'll take him down to the dock.'

'Tell Batist not to bring him back, no.' She dropped Tripod, half strangled, to the ground. 'He come in my house again, you gonna see him cooking with the sweet potato.'

I unsnapped his chain from the clothesline and walked him down to the bait shop and café on the dock. I was always amazed at the illusion of white supremacy in southern society, since more often than not our homes were dominated and run by people of color.

Batist and I bailed the rainwater from the previous night's storm out of my rental boats, filled the cigarette and candy machines, seined dead shiners out of the live-bait tanks, drained the water out of the ice bins and put fresh ice on top of the soda pop and beer, and started the barbecue fire for the lunch that we prepared for midday fishermen. Then I opened up the beach umbrellas that were set in the holes of the huge wooden telephone spools that I used as tables, and went back up to the house.

It had turned out to be a beautiful morning. The sky was blue, the grass in the fields a deeper green from the rain; the wind was cool on the gallery, the backyard still deep in shadow under the mimosa tree, and my redwood flower boxes were streaked with water and thick with petunias and Indian paintbrush. Alafair was at the kitchen table in her pajama bottoms, coloring in the Mickey Mouse book I had bought her the day before. Her black hair was cut in bangs; her eyes were big and brown, her face as round as a pie plate, and her skin had already started to grow darker with tan. If there was any physical imperfection in her, it was her wide-set front teeth, which only made her smile look larger than it actually was. It was hard to believe that less than a year ago I had pulled her from a downed plane out at Southwest Pass just off the Gulf, a drowning little girl whose bones had felt hollow as a bird's, whose gasping mouth had looked like a guppy's in my wife's lap.

I brushed her fine black hair under my palm.

'How you doing, little guy?' I said.

'Where you went, Dave?'

'I got caught in the storm and had to stay in Baton Rouge.'

'Oh.'

Her hand went back to coloring. Then she stopped and grinned at me, full of glee.

'Tripod went ca-ca in Clarise basket,' she said.

'I heard about it. Look, don't say "ca-ca." Say "He went to the bathroom." '

'No ca-ca?'

'That's right. "He went to the bathroom." '

She repeated it after me, both of our heads nodding up and down.

She was in the first grade at the Catholic school in New Iberia, but she seemed to learn more English from Clarise and Batist and his wife than she did from me and the nuns. (A few lines you might hear from those three on any particular day: 'What time it is?' 'For how come you burn them leafs under my window, you?' 'While I was driving your truck, me, somebody pass a nail under the wheel and give it a big flat.')

I hugged Alafair, kissed her on top of the head, and went into the bedroom to undress and take a shower. The breeze through the window smelled of wet earth and trees and the gentle hint of four-o'clocks that were still open in the shade. I should have been bursting with the spring morning, but I felt listless and spent, traveling on the outer edge of my envelope, and it wasn't simply because of bad dreams and insomnia the previous night. These moments would descend upon me at peculiar times, as though my heart's blood were fouled, and suddenly my mind would light with images and ring with sounds I wasn't ready to deal with.

It could happen anywhere. But right now it was happening in my bedroom. I had replaced several boards in the wall, or filled the twelve-gauge buckshot and deer-slug holes with liquid wood, and sanded them smooth. The gouged and splintered headboard, stained brown with my wife's blood as though it had been flung there by a paintbrush, lay in a corner of the old collapsed bar at the foot of my property. But when I closed my eyes I saw the streaks of shotgun fire in the darkness, heard the explosions that were as loud as the lightning outside, heard her screams as she cowered under a sheet and tried to shield herself with her hands while I ran frantically toward the house in the rain, my own screams lost in the thunder rolling across the land.

As always when these moments of dark reverie occurred in my waking day, there was no way I could think my way out of them. Instead, I put on my gym trunks and running shoes and pumped iron in the backyard. I did dread lifts, curls, and military presses with a ninety-pound bar in sets of ten and repeated the sets six times. Then I ran four miles along the dirt road by the bayou, the sunlight spinning like smoke through the canopy of oak and cypress trees overhead. Bream were still feeding on insects among the cattails and lily pads, and sometimes in a shady cut between two cypress trees I would see the back of a largemouth bass roll just under the surface.

I turned around at the drawbridge, waved to the bridgetender, and hit it hard all the way home. My wind was good, the blood sang in my chest, my stomach felt flat and hard, yet I wondered how long I would keep mortality and memory at bay.

Always the racetrack gambler, trying to intuit and control the future with only the morning line to operate on.

Three days later I was using a broomstick to push the rainwater out of the folds of the canvas awning over my dock when the telephone rang inside the bait shop. It was Dixie Lee Pugh.

'I'll take you to lunch,' he said.

'Thanks but I'm working.'

'I want to talk to you.'

'Go ahead.'

'I want to talk to you alone.'

'Where are you?'

'Lafayette.'

'Drive on over. Go out East Main, then take the

bayou road south of town. You'll run right into my place.'

'Give me an hour.'

'You sound a little gray, podna.'

'Yeah, I probably need to get married again or something. Dangle loose.'

Every morning Batist and I grilled chickens and links on the barbecue pit that I had made by splitting an oil drum horizontally with an acetylene torch and welding hinges and metal legs on it. I sold paper-plate lunches of barbecue and dirty rice for three-fifty apiece, and I usually cleared thirty dollars or so from the fishermen who were either coming in for the day or about to go out. Then after we had cleaned the cable-spool tables, Batist and I would fix ourselves plates and open bottles of Dr Pepper and eat under one of the umbrellas by the water's edge.

It was a warm, bright afternoon, and the wind was lifting the moss on the dead cypress trees in the marsh. The sky was as blue and perfect as the inside of a teacup.

'That man drive like he don't know the road got holes in it,' Batist said. His sun-faded denim shirt was open on his chest. He wore a dime on a string around his neck to keep away the *gris-gris*, an evil spell, and his black chest looked like it was made of boiler-plate.

The pink Cadillac convertible, with its top down, was streaked with mud and rippled and dented along the fenders. I watched the front end dip into a chuckhole and shower yellow water all over the windshield.

'Dixie Lee never did things in moderation,' I said.

'You ain't renting him our boat?'

'He's just coming out to talk about something. He used to be a famous country and rock 'n' roll star.'

Batist kept chewing and looked at me flatly, obviously unimpressed.

'I'm serious. He used to be big stuff up in Nashville,' I said.

His eyes narrowed, as they always did when he heard words that he didn't recognize.

'It's in Tennessee. That's where they make a lot of country records.'

No help.

'I'll get us another Dr Pepper. Did you feed Tripod?' I said.

'You t'ink that coon don't know where the food at?'

I didn't understand.

'He ain't lost his nose, no.'

'What are you saying, Batist?'

'He ate all your fried pies. Go look your fried pies.'

Dixie Lee cut his engine, slammed the car door behind him, and lumbered down the dock into the bait shop, flipping one hand at us in recognition. His face was bloodless, the skin stretched tight on the bone, beaded with perspiration like drops of water on a pumpkin. His charcoal shirt, which was covered with roses, was damp along the buttons and under the armpits.

I followed him inside the bait shop. He dropped a five-dollar bill on the counter, opened a long-necked Jax on the side of the beer box, and upended it into his mouth. He kept swallowing until it was almost empty, then he took a breath of air and opened and closed his eyes.

'Boy, do I got one,' he said. 'I mean wicked, son,

like somebody screwed a brace and bit through both temples.'

He tilted the bottle up again, one hand on his hip, and emptied it.

'A mellow start, but it don't keep the snakes in their basket very long, do it?'

'Nope.'

'What we're talking about here is the need for more serious fluids. You got any JD or Beam lying around?'

'I'm afraid not, Dixie,' I rang up his sale and put his change on the counter.

'These babies will have to do, then.' He opened another Jax, took a long pull, and blew out his breath. 'A preacher once asked me, "Son, can you take two drinks and walk away from it?" I said, "I can't tell you the answer to that sir, 'cause I never tried." That ought to be funny, but I guess it's downright pathetic, ain't it?'

'What's up, partner?'

He looked around the empty bait shop.

'How about taking me for a boat ride?' he said.

'I'm kind of tied up right now.'

'I'll pay you for your time. It's important, man.'

His green eyes looked directly into mine. I walked to the bait-shop door.

'I'll be back in a half-hour,' I called to Batist, who was still eating his lunch under the umbrella.

'I appreciate it, Dave. You're righteous people,' Dixie Lee popped open a paper bag and put four bottles of Jax inside.

I took him in an outboard down the bayou, past the four-corners, where the old flaking general store with its wide gallery sat in the shade of an enormous oak tree. Some old men and several Negroes from a road-maintenance crew were drinking soda pop on the gallery.

The wake from the outboard swelled up through the lily pads and cattails and slapped against the cypress roots along the bank. Dixie Lee lay back against the bow, the beer bottle in his hand filled with amber sunlight, his eyes narrowing wistfully in the sun's refraction off the brown water. I cut the engine and let us float on our own wake into an overhang of willow trees. In the sudden quiet we could hear a car radio playing an old Hank Williams song in the shell parking lot of the general store.

'Good God Almighty, is that inside my head or outside it?' he asked.

'It's from the four-corners,' I said, and smiled at him. I took out my Puma pocketknife and shaved the bark off a wet willow stick.

'Boy, it takes me back, though. When I started out, they said if you don't play it like Hank or Lefty, it ain't worth diddly-squat on a rock. They were right, too. Hey, you know the biggest moment I ever had in my career? It wasn't them two gold records, and it sure wasn't marrying some movie actress with douche water for brains. It was when I got to cut a live album with the Fat Man down in New Orleans. I was the only white artist he ever recorded with. Man, he was beautiful. He looked like a little fat baby pig up on that piano bench, with a silver shirt on and rhinestone coat and rings all over his fingers. He was grinning and rocking and pounding the keys with those little sausage fingers, sweat flying off his face, and the whole auditorium going apeshit. I mean with white broads trying to climb on the stage and people doing the dirty boogie in front of the cops. I mean it was his show, he owned them, man, but each time he finished a ride he'd point at me so the spotlight would swing over on my guitar and I'd get half of all that yelling out there. That cat had a generous heart, man.'

Dixie Lee shook his head and opened another Jax with his pocketknife. I looked at my watch.

'Yeah, I'm sorry,' he said. 'It's a problem I got, getting wrapped up in yesterday's scrapbook. Look, I got something bad on my mind. In fact, it's crazy. I don't even know how to explain it. Maybe there's nothing to it. Hell, I don't know.'

'How about just telling me?'

'Star Drilling sent me and a couple of other leasemen up to Montana. On the eastern slope of the Rockies, what they call the East Front up there. Big gas domes, son. Virgin country. We're talking hundreds of millions of dollars. Except there's a problem with some wilderness area and the Blackfeet Indian Reservation.

'But that don't concern me. I'm just a leaseman, right? Fooling around with the Forest Service or Indians or these crazy bastards spiking trees—'

'Doing what?'

'A bunch of cult people or something don't want anybody cutting down trees, so they hammer nails and railroad spikes way down in the trunk. Then some lumberjack comes along with a McCullough and almost rips his face off. But I don't have any beef with these people. Everybody's got their own scene, right? Let Star Drilling take care of the PR and the politics, and Dixie Lee will get through the day with a little JD and God's good grace.

'But we came back for six weeks of deals and

meetings at the Oil Center in Lafayette. So I'm staying at the motel with these two other lease guys. The company picks up all the bills, the bar's always open, and a black guy serves us Bloody Marys and chilled shrimp by the pool every morning. It should have been a nice vacation before I go back to wheeling and dealing among the Indians and the crazies.

'Except two nights ago one of the other lease guys has a party in his rooms. Actually it's more like a geek show. Broads ripping off their bras, people spitting ice and tonic on each other. Then I guess I got romantic and went into the bedroom with this big blond gal that looked like she could throw a hog over a fence.'

His eyes shifted away from me, and his cheeks colored slightly. He drank again from the Jax without looking back at me.

'But I was deep into the jug that night, definitely not up to her level of bumping uglies,' he said. 'I must have passed out and rolled off the side of the bed between the bed and the wall, because that's where I woke up about five in the morning. The snakes were starting to clatter around in their basket, then I heard the two other lease guys talking by themselves in the other room.

'One guy – I ain't using his name – says, "Don't worry about it. We did what we had to do." Then the other guy says, "Yeah, but we should have taken more time. We should have put rocks on top of them or something. Animals are always digging up stuff in the woods, then a hunter comes along."

'Then the first guy says, "Nobody's going to find them. Nobody cares about them. They were both troublemakers. Right or wrong?"

'Then the second guy says, "I guess you're right."

'And the first guy says, "It's like a war. You make up the rules when it's over."

'I stayed quiet in the bedroom till I heard them call room service for breakfast and a couple of bottles of Champale, then I walked into the living room in my skivvies, looking like I'd just popped out of my momma's womb. I thought both of them was going to brown their britches right there.'

'You think they killed some people?'

He touched his fingers nervously to his forehead.

'Good God, man, I don't know,' he said. 'What's it sound like to you?'

'It sounds bad.'

'What d'you think I ought to do?'

I rubbed my palm on the knee of my khaki work trousers, then clicked my nails on the metal housing of the outboard engine. The dappled sunlight fell through the willows on Dixie's flushed face.

'I can introduce you to the Iberia sheriff or a pretty good DEA agent over in Lafayette,' I said.

'Are you kidding, man? I need a drug agent in my life like a henhouse needs an egg-sucking dog.'

'Well, there's still the sheriff.'

He drank the foam out of the Jax bottle and looked at me with one eye squinted shut against the light.

'I'm getting the impression you think I'd just be playing with my swizzle stick,' he said.

I raised my eyebrows and didn't answer.

'Come on, Dave. I need some help. I can't handle worry. It eats my lunch.'

'Where do you think this happened?'

'Up in Montana, I guess. That's where we been the last three months.'

'We can talk to the FBI, but I don't think it's going anywhere. You just don't have enough information, Dixie.' I paused for a moment. 'There's another bump in the road, too.'

He looked at me as a child might if he was about to be brought to task.

'When I was on the grog, I had a hard time convincing people about some things I heard and saw,' I said. 'It's unfair, but it goes with the territory.'

He stared at the water and pinched his eyes with his fingers.

'My advice is to get away from these guys,' I said.

'I work with them.'

'There're other companies.'

'Be serious. I was in Huntsville. The Texas parole office don't give you the best letters of recommendation.'

'I don't know what to tell you, then.'

'It's a mess of grief, huh?'

I began pulling in the anchor rope.

'You're gonna turn to stone on me?' he said.

'I wish I could help. I don't think I can. That's the way it is.'

'Before you crank that engine, let me ask you a question. Your father was killed on a rig out in the Gulf, wasn't he?'

'That's right.'

'It was a Star rig, wasn't it?'

'Yep.'

'They didn't have a blowout preventer on. It killed a couple of dozen guys when it blew.'

'You've got a good memory, Dixie.' I twisted the throttle to open the gas feed and yanked the starter rope. It didn't catch.

'It don't matter to you that I'm talking about Star Drilling Company?' he said.

I kept yanking the rope while oil and gas bled away from the engine into the water. Then I put one knee on the plank seat, held the engine housing firm with my palm, and ripped the starter handle past my ear. The engine roared, the propeller churned a cloud of yellow mud and dead hyacinth vines out of the bottom, and I turned us back into the full sunlight, the slap of water under the bow, the wind that smelled of jasmine and wisteria. On the way back Dixie sat on the bow with his forearms lying loosely between his legs, his face listless and empty now, his rose-emblazoned shirt puffing with warm air.

Late that afternoon the wind shifted out of the south and you could smell the wetlands and just a hint of salt in the air. Then a bank of thunderheads slid across the sky from the Gulf, tumbling across the sun like cannon smoke, and the light gathered in the oaks and cypress and willow trees and took on a strange green cast as though you were looking at the world through water. It rained hard, dancing on the bayou and the lily pads in the shallows, clattering on my gallery and rabbit hutches, lighting the freshly plowed fields with a black sheen.

Then suddenly it was over, and the sky cleared and the western horizon was streaked with fire. Usually on a spring evening like this, when the breeze was cool and flecked with rain, Batist and I headed for Evangeline Downs in Lafayette. But the bottom had dropped out of the oil business in Louisiana, the state had the highest rate of unemployment in the country and the worst credit rating, and the racetrack had closed.

I boiled crawfish for supper, and Alafair and I shelled and ate them on the redwood picnic table under the mimosa tree in the backyard. That night I dreamed of a bubble of fire burning under the Gulf's green surface. The water boiled and hissed, geysers of steam and dirty smoke rose into the air, and an enormous blue-green oil slick floated all the way to the western horizon. Somewhere far down below among the twisted spars and drill pipe and cables and the flooded wreckage of the quarter boat were the bodies of my father and nineteen other men who went down with the rig when the drill bit punched into a pay sand and the wellhead blew.

The company's public relations men said that they didn't have a blowout preventer on because they had never hit an oil sand at that depth in that part of the Gulf before. I wondered what my father thought in those last moments of his life. I never saw fear in him. No matter how badly he was hurt by circumstances or my mother's unfaithfulness, and eventually by drunken brawls in bars and the time she was locked up in the parish jail, he could always grin and wink at me and my brother and convincingly pretend to us that misfortune was not even worthy of mention.

But what did he feel in those last moments, high up on the monkeyboard in the dark, when the rig started to shake and groan and he saw the roughnecks on the platform floor dropping tongs and chain and running from the eruption of sand, salt water, gas oil, and cascading drill pipe that in seconds would explode into an orange and yellow flame that melted steel spars like licorice? Did he think of me and my brother, Jimmie?

I bet he did. Even when he clipped his safety belt on to the Geronimo wire and jumped into the black, even as the rig caved with him on top of the quarter boat, I bet his thoughts were of us.

They never found his body, but even now, almost twenty-two years later, he visited me in my sleep and sometimes I thought he spoke to me during my waking day. In my dream I saw him walking out of the surf, the green waves and foam sliding around the knees of his overalls, his powerful body strung with rust-coloured seaweed. His wind-burned skin was as dark as a mulatto's, his teeth white, his thick, curly hair black as an Indian's. His tin hat was cocked at an angle on his head, and when he popped a wet kitchen match on his thumbnail and lit a cigar stub in the corner of his mouth and then crinkled his eyes at me, a shaft of morning sunlight struck his hat and flashed as bright as a heliograph. I could feel the salt water surge over my legs as I walked toward him.

But it's the stuff of dreams. My father was dead. My wife was, too. The false dawn, with its illusions and mist-wrapped softness, can be as inadequate and fleeting as Morpheus' gifts.

chapter two

The days became warmer the first week in April, and on some mornings I went out on the salt at dawn and seined for shrimp in the red sunrise. In the afternoon I helped Batist in the bait shop, then worked in my flower beds, pruning the trellises of purple and yellow roses that I grew on the south side of the house. I pumped iron and did three miles along the dirt road by the bayou. At four o'clock I would hear the school bus stop, and five minutes later I would hear Alafair's lunch box clatter on the kitchen table, the icebox open; then she would come looking for me in the backyard.

I sometimes wondered if perhaps she were simply fascinated with me as she would be by a strange and interesting animal that had come unexpectedly into her life. Her mother had drowned while holding her up in a wobbling bubble of air inside a crashed and sunken plane flown out of El Salvador by a Sanctuary priest. Her father had either been killed by the army in the mountains or he had been 'disappeared' inside a military prison. Now through chance and accident she lived with me in my rural Cajun world on the edge of the Louisiana wetlands.

One afternoon I had moved the picnic table out in the

sunlight and had gone to sleep on top of it in my running shorts. I heard her bang the screen door, then when I didn't open my eyes she found a duck feather by the pond and began to touch peculiar places on my body with it: the white patch in my hair, my mustache, the curled pungi-stick scar on my stomach. Then I felt her tickle the thick, raised welts on my thigh, which looked like small arrowheads embedded under the skin, where I still carried shrapnel from a mine and sometimes set off airport metal detectors.

When I still refused to respond I heard her walk across the grass to the clothesline, unsnap Tripod from his chain, and suddenly he was sitting on my chest, his whiskers and wet nose and masked beady eyes pointed into my face. Alafair's giggles soared into the mimosa tree.

That evening while I was closing the bait shop and folding up the umbrellas over the tables on the dock, a man parked a new Plymouth that looked like a rental or a company car by my shale boat ramp and walked down the dock toward me. Because of his erect, almost fierce posture, he looked taller than he actually was. In reality he probably wasn't over five and a half feet tall, but his neck was thick and corded with vein, his shoulders wide and sloping like a weight lifter's, his eyebrows one dark, uninterrupted line. His muscles seemed so tightly strung together that one muscular motion seemed to activate a half-dozen others, like pulling on the center of a cobweb with your finger. If anything, he reminded me of a pile of bricks.

He wore his slacks high up on his hips, and the collar of his short-sleeved white shirt was unbuttoned and his tie pulled loose. He didn't smile. Instead, his eyes flicked over the bait shop and the empty tables, then he opened a badge on me.

'I'm Special Agent Dan Nygurski, Mr Robicheaux,' he said. 'Drug Enforcement Administration. Do you mind if I talk with you a little bit?'

The accent didn't go with the name of the man. It was hillbilly, nasal, southern mountains, a bobby pin twanging in your ear.

'I'm closing up for the day and we're about to go to a crawfish boil in the park,' I said.

'This won't take long. I talked with the sheriff in New Iberia and he said you could probably help me out. You used to be a deputy in his department, didn't you?'

'For a little while.'

His face was seamed and coarse, the eyes slightly red around the rims. He flexed his mouth in a peculiar way when he talked, and it caused the muscles to jump in his neck, as though they were attached to a string.

'Before that you were on the force in New Orleans a long time? A lieutenant in homicide?'

'That's right.'

'I'll be,' he said, and looked at the red sun through the cypress trees and the empty boats tied to the dock.

My experience with federal agents of any kind has always been the same. They take a long time to get to it.

'Could I rent a boat from you? Or maybe could you go with me and show me some of these canals that lead into Vermilion Bay?' he asked. His thinning dark hair was cut GI, and he brushed his fingers back through it and widened his eyes and looked around again.

'I'll rent you a boat in the morning. But you'll have to

go out by yourself. What is it exactly I can help you with, Mr Nygurski?'

'I'm just messing around, really.' He flexed his mouth again. 'I heard some guys were off-loading some bales down around Vermilion Bay. I just like to check out the geography sometimes.'

'Are you out of New Orleans?'

'No, no, this is my first trip down here. It's nice country. I've got to try some of this crawfish while I'm here.'

'Wait a minute. I'm not following you. You're interested in some dope smugglers operating around Vermilion Bay but you're from somewhere else?'

'It's just an idle interest. I think they might be the same guys I was after a few years ago in Florida. They were unloading a cigarette boat at night outside of Fort Myers, and some neckers out in the dunes stumbled right into the middle of the operation. These guys killed all four of them. The girls were both nineteen. It's not my case anymore, though.'

The twang, the high-pitched voice, just would not go with the subject matter nor the short, thick-bodied dark man who I now noticed was slew-footed and walked a bit sideways like a crab.

'So you're out of Florida?' I said.

'No, no, you got me all wrong. I'm out of Great Falls, Montana, now, and I wanted to talk with you about—'

I shook my head.

'Dixie Lee Pugh,' I said.

We walked up the dock, across the dirt road and through the shadows of the pecan trees in my front yard. When I asked him how he had connected me with

Dixie Lee, he said that one of his people had written down my tag number the morning I had met Dixie in the café outside Baton Rouge. I went inside the house, brought out two cold cans of Dr Pepper, and we sat on the porch steps. Through the trunks of the pecan trees I could see the shadows lengthening on the bayou.

'I don't mean any disrespect toward your investigation, Mr Nygurski, but I don't think he's a major drug dealer. I think y'all are firing in the well.'

'Why?'

'I believe he has a conscience. He might be a user, but that doesn't mean he's dealing.'

'You want to tell me why he came out to see you?'

'He's in some trouble. But it doesn't have anything to do with drugs, and he'll have to be the one to tell you about it.'

'Did he tell you he celled with Sal the Duck in Huntsville?'

'With who?'

'Sal the Duck. Also known as Sally Dio or Sally Dee. You think that's funny?'

'I'm sorry,' I said. I wiped my mouth with my hand. 'But am I supposed to be impressed?'

'A lot of people would be. His family used to run Galveston. Slots, whores, every floating crap game, dope, you name it. Then they moved out to Vegas and Tahoe and about two years ago they showed up in Montana. Sal came back to visit his cousins in Galveston and got nailed with some hot credit cards. I hear he didn't like Huntsville at all.'

'I bet he didn't. It's worse than Angola.'

'But he still managed to turn a dollar or two. He was

the connection for the whole joint, and I think he was piecing off part of his action to Pugh.'

'Well, you have your opinion. But I think Dixie's basically an alcoholic and a sick man.'

Nygurski took a newspaper clipping out of his shirt pocket and handed it to me.

'Read this,' he said. 'I guess the reporters thought this was funny.'

The headline read 'CURIOSITY KILLED THE BEAR.' The dateline was Polson, Montana, and the lead paragraph described how a duffel bag containing forty packages of cocaine had been dropped by parachute into a heavily wooded area east of Flathead Lake and was then found by a black bear who strung powder and wrappers all over a hillside before he OD'd.

'That parachute came down on national forestland. But guess who has a hunting lease right next door?'

'I don't know.'

'Sally Dio and his old man. Guess who acted as their leasing agent?'

'Dixie Lee.'

'But maybe he's just a sick guy.'

I looked away at the softness of the light on the bayou. Out of the corner of my eye I could see the knuckles on his hand as he clenched the soda can.

'Come on, what do you think?' he said.

'I think you're in overdrive.'

'You're right. I don't like these cocksuckers—'

'Nobody does. But I'm out of the business. You're tilting with the wrong windmill.'

'I don't think killing bears is funny, either. I don't like to see these guys bring their dirt and greed into a beautiful country. Your friend Pugh is standing up to his bottom lip in a lake of shit and the motorboat is just about to pass.'

'Then tell him that,' I said, and looked at my watch. The breeze dented the leaves in the pecan trees.

'Believe me, I will. But right now I'm *fiigmo* here.'

'What?'

'It means "Fuck it, I got my orders." In three days I go back to Great Falls.' He drained his soda can, crushed it in his palm, and set it gently on the porch step. He stood up and handed me his card.

'My motel number in Lafayette is on the back. Or later you can call me collect in Montana if you ever want to share any of your thoughts.'

'I've got nothing worth sharing.'

'It sounds depressing.' His mouth made that peculiar jerking motion again. 'Tell me, do you find something strange about my face?'

'No, I wouldn't say that.'

'Come on, I'm not sensitive.'

'I meant you no offense,' I said.

'Boy, you're a careful one. A woman once told me my face looked like soil erosion. I think it was my wife. Watch out for Dixie Pugh, Robicheaux. He'll sell you a bowl of rat turds and call it chocolate chip.'

'I changed my mind. I'll share one thought with you, Mr Nygurski. You didn't come all the way down here to follow a guy like Dixie Lee around. No matter how you cut it, he's not a long-ball hitter.'

'Maybe he is, maybe he isn't.'

'What's really going on up there?'

'Everything that's going on in the rest of the country, except accelerated. It's a real zoo story. All the big players are there, nosing up to the trough. Keep fooling around with that rock 'n' roller and you'll meet some of them.'

He walked off through the trees, his feet loud on the dead leaves and dried pecan husks.

The moon was down that night, the sky black, and trees of lightning trembled on the southern horizon. At four in the morning I was awakened by the rumble of dry thunder and the flickering patterns of light on the wall. A tuning fork was vibrating in my chest, but I couldn't explain why, and my skin was hot and dry to the touch even though the breeze was cool though the window. I heard sounds that were not there: a car engine dying on the road, the footsteps of two men coming through the trees, a board squeaking on the porch, the scrape of a prizing bar being inserted between the front door and the jamb. They were the sounds of ghosts, because one man had been electrocuted in his bathtub with his radio in his lap and the other had died in an attic off St Charles when five hollow-point rounds from my .45 had exploded up through the floor into the middle of his life.

But fear is an irrational emotion that floats from object to object like a helium balloon that you touch with your fingertips. I opened my dresser drawer, took my .45 from under my work shirts, slipped the heavy clip into the magazine, and lay back down in the dark. The flat of the barrel felt hot against my thigh. I put my arm across my eyes and tried to fall asleep again. It was no use.

I put on my sandals and khakis and walked through the dark trunks of the pecan trees in the front yard, across the road and down to the dock and the bait shop.

Then the moon rose from behind a cloud and turned the willow trees to silver and illuminated the black shape of a nutria swimming across the bayou toward the cattails. What was I doing here? I told myself that I would get a head start on the day. Yes, yes, certainly that was it.

I opened the cooler in which I kept the soda pop and the long-necked bottles of Jax, Dixie, and Pearl beer. Yesterday's ice had melted, and some of the beer labels floated in the water. I propped my arms on the lip of the cooler and shut my eyes. In the marsh I heard a nutria cry out to its mate, which always sounds like the hysterical scream of a woman. I plunged my hands into the water, dipped it into my face, and breathed deeply with the shock of the cold. Then I wiped my face on a towel and flung it across the counter on to the duckboards.

I went back up to the house, sat at the kitchen table in the dark, and put my head on my forearms.

Annie, Annie.

I heard bare feet shuffle on the linoleum behind me. I raised my head and looked up at Alafair, who was standing in a square of moonlight, dressed in her pajamas that were covered with smiling clocks. Her face was filled with sleep and puzzlement. She kept blinking at me as though she were waking from a dream, then she walked to me, put her arms around my neck, and pressed her head against my chest. I could smell baby shampoo in her hair. Her hand touched my eyes.

'Why your face wet, Dave?' she said.

'I just washed it, little guy.'

'Oh.' Then, 'Something ain't wrong?'

'Not "ain't." Don't say "ain't." '

She didn't answer. She just held me more tightly. I stroked her hair and kissed her, then picked her up and carried her back into her bedroom. I laid her down on the bed and pulled the sheet over her feet. Her stuffed animals were scattered on the floor. The yard and the trees were turning gray, and I could hear Tripod running up and down on his clothesline.

She looked up at me from the pillow. Her face was round, and I could see the spaces between her teeth.

'Dave, is bad people coming back?'

'No. They'll never be back. I promise.'

And I had to look away from her lest she see my eyes.

One week later I took Alafair for breakfast in New Iberia, and when I unfolded a discarded copy of the *Daily Iberian* I saw Dixie Lee's picture on the front page. It was a file photo, many years old, and it showed him onstage in boatlike suede shoes, pegged and pleated slacks, a sequined white sport coat, a sunburst guitar hanging from his neck.

He had been burned in a fire in a fish camp out in Henderson swamp. A twenty-two-year-old waitress, his 'female companion,' as the story called her, had died in the flames. Dixie Lee had been pulled from the water when the cabin, built on stilts, had exploded in a fireball and crashed into the bayou. He was listed in serious condition at Our Lady of Lourdes in Lafayette.

He was also under arrest. The St Martin Parish sheriff's department had found a dental floss container of cocaine under the front seat of his Cadillac convertible.

I am not going to get involved with his troubles, I told myself. When you use, you lose. A mean lesson, but when you become involved with an addict or a drunk, you simply become an actor in a script that they've written for you as well as themselves.

That afternoon Alafair and I made two bird feeders out of coffee cans and hung them in the mimosa tree in the backyard, then we restrung Tripod's clothesline out in the pecan trees so he wouldn't have access to Clarise's wash. We moved his doghouse to the base of a tree, put bricks under it to keep it dry and free of mud, and set his food bowl and water pans in front of the door. Alafair always beamed with fascination while Tripod washed his food before eating, then washed his muzzle and paws afterward.

I fixed *étoufée* for our supper, and we had just started to eat on the picnic table in the backyard when the phone rang in the kitchen. It was a nun who worked on Dixie Lee's floor at Lourdes. She said he wanted to see me.

'I can't come, Sister. I'm sorry,' I said.

She paused.

'Is that all you want me to tell him?' she asked.

'He needs a lawyer. I can give you a couple of names in Lafayette or St Martinville.'

She paused again. They must teach it in the convent, I thought. It's an electric silence that makes you feel you're sliding down the sides of the universe.

'I don't think he has many friends, Mr Robicheaux,' she said. 'No one has been to see him. And he asked for you, not an attorney.'

'I'm sorry.'

'To be frank, so am I,' she said, and hung up.

When Alafair and I were washing the dishes, and the

plowed and empty sugarcane fields darkened in the twilight outside the window, the telephone rang again.

His voice was thick, coated with phlegm, a whisper into the receiver.

'Son, I really need to see you. They got me gauzed up, doped up, you name it, an enema tube stuck up my ringus.' He stopped and let out his breath into the phone. 'I need you to listen to me.'

'You need legal help, Dixie. I won't be much help to you.'

'I got a lawyer. I can hire a bagful of his kind. It won't do no good. They're going to send me back to the joint, boy.'

I watched my hand open and close on top of the counter.

'I don't like to tell you this, podna, but you were holding,' I said. 'That fact's not going away. You're going to have to deal with it.'

'It's a lie, Dave.' I heard the saliva click in his throat. 'I don't do flake anymore. It already messed up my life way back there. Maybe sometimes a little reefer. But that's all.'

I pinched my fingers on my brow.

'Dixie, I just don't know what I can do for you.'

'Come over. Listen to me for five minutes. I ain't got anybody else.'

I stared out the screen at the shadows on the lawn, the sweep of night birds against the red sky.

It was windy the next morning and the sky was light blue and filled with tumbling white clouds that caused pools of shadow to move across the cane fields and cow pastures as I drove along the old highway through

Broussard into Lafayette. Dixie Lee's room was on the second floor at Lourdes, and a uniformed sheriff's deputy was playing checkers with him on the edge of the bed. Dixie Lee lay on his side, his head, chest, right shoulder, and right thigh wrapped in bandages. His face looked as though it were crimped inside a white helmet. There was mucus in his eyes, and a clear salve oozed from the edges of his bandages. An IV was hooked into his arm.

He looked at me and said something to the deputy, who set the checkerboard on the nightstand and walked past me, working his cigarette pack out of his shirt pocket.

'I'll be right in the hall. The door stays open, too,' he said.

I sat down next to the bed. There were oaks hung with moss outside the window. The pressure of Dixie's head against the pillow made him squint one eye at me.

'I knew you'd come. There's some guys that can't be any other way,' he said.

'You sound better,' I said.

'I'm on the edge of my high and about ready to slide down the other side of it. When the centipedes start crawling under these bandages, they'll be back with the morphine. Dave, I got to get some help. The cops don't believe me. My own lawyer don't believe me. They're going to send my butt to Angola. I can't do no more time, man. I ain't good at it. They tore me up over there in Texas. You get in thin cotton, you don't pick your quota, the boss stands you up on an oil barrel with three other guys. Hot and dirty and hungry, and you stand there all night.'

'They don't believe what?'

'This—' He tried to touch his fingers behind his head. 'Reach around back and feel on them bandages.'

'Dixie, what are—'

'Do it.'

I reached across him and touched my fingertips across the tape.

'It feels like a roll of pennies under there, don't it?' he said. 'That's because I woke up just before some guy with a tire iron or a jack handle came down on my head. He was going to bust me right across the lamps, but I twisted away from him just before he swung. The next thing I knew I was in the water. You ever wake up drowning and on fire at the same time? That's what it was like. There was a gas tank for the outboards under the cabin, and it must have blown and dumped the whole thing in the bayou. Burning boards was hanging off the stilts, the water was full of hot ash, steam hissing all over the fucking place. I thought I'd gone to hell, man.'

He stopped talking and his lips made a tight line. I saw water well up in his green eyes.

'Then I seen something awful. It was the girl, you remember, that redheaded waitress from the café in West Baton Rouge. She was on fire, like a big candle burning all over, hung in all them boards and burning against the sky.

'I can't clean it out of my head, not even when they hit me with the joy juice. Maybe they hit her in the head like they done me. Maybe she was already dead. God, I hope so. I can't stand thinking about it, man. She didn't do nothing to anybody.'

I wiped my palms on my slacks and blew out my breath. I wanted to walk back out into the sunshine, into the windy morning, into the oak trees that were hung with moss.

'Who was the guy with the tire iron?' I said.

'One of those fuckers I work with.'

'You saw his face?'

'I didn't have to. They knew I was going to drop the dime on them. For all the damn good it would do.'

'You told them that?'

'Sure. I got fed up with both of them. No, wait a minute. I got fed up being afraid. I was a little swacked when I stuck it in their face, but I done it just the same. Dalton Vidrine and Harry Mapes. One's a coonass and the other's a stump-jumper from East Texas.'

'I'm having one problem with all this. There's some people who think you're mixed up in dope. Up in Montana.'

His green eyes closed and opened like a bird's.

'They're wrong,' he said.

'—that maybe you're mixed up with a trafficker named Dio.'

His mouth smiled slightly.

'You been talking to the DEA,' he said. 'But they're sniffing up the wrong guy's leg.'

'You didn't lease land for him in Montana?'

'I leased and bought a bunch of land for him. But it don't have anything to do with dope. Sally Dee was my cell partner. Some guys were going to cut me up in the shower. Till Sally Dee told them they treat me just like they treat him. Which means they light my cigarettes, they pick in my sack when we get in thin cotton. The cat's half crazy, man, but he saved my butt.'

'What was the land deal about, Dixie?'

'I didn't ask. He's not the kind of guy you ask those

things to. He's got a lot of holdings. He hires people to act as his agents. He likes me for some reason. He paid me a lot of bread. What's the big deal?'

'As an old friend, Dixie, I'm going to ask you to save the Little Orphan Annie routine for the DEA.'

'You believe what you want.'

'What's your bond?'

'Fifteen thou.'

'That's not too bad.'

'They know I ain't going anywhere. Except maybe to Angola. Dave, I ain't giving you a shuck. I can't take another fall, and I don't see no way out of it.'

I looked out the window at the treetops, the way their leaves ruffled in the breeze, the whiteness of the clouds against the dome of blue sky.

'I'll come back and visit you later,' I said. 'I think maybe you have too much faith in one guy.'

'I'll tell you a story I heard Minnie Pearl tell about Hank. This was right after he brought the whole auditorium down singing "I Saw the Light" at the Opry. Backstage he turned to her and said, "But, Minnie, they ain't no light. They just ain't no light." That's when your soul is hanging on a spider's web right over the fire, son. That's right where I'm at now.'

That afternoon I stood on the levee and looked down at the collapsed and blackened remains of the fish camp that, according to Dixie Lee, had belonged to Star Drilling Company. Mattress springs, charred boards, a metal table, a scorched toilet seat, half the shingle roof lay in the shallows at the bottom of the stilt supports. A paste of gray ash floated among the cattails and lily pads.

I walked down to the water's edge. I found what was left of a Coleman stove and a pump twelve-gauge shotgun whose shells had exploded in the magazine. The gasoline drum that had been used to fuel outboard engines was ripped outward and twisted like a beer can.

The fire had made a large black circle from the water to halfway up the levee. Extending out from the circle were trails of ash through the buttercups and new grass like the legs of a spider. One of them led up to the road at the top of the levee.

I dug the soil loose from around the trail with my pocketknife and smelled it. It smelled like burnt grass and dirt.

I knew little about arson investigation, but I saw nothing on the levee that would help Dixie Lee's case.

I drove to St Martinville and parked across from the old church where Evangeline and her lover are buried under an enormous spreading oak. The wind blew the moss in the trees along Bayou Teche, and the four-o'clocks were opening in the shade along the banks. I was told by the dispatcher in the sheriff's department that the sheriff was out for a few minutes but that a detective would talk to me.

The detective was penciling in a form of some kind and smoking a cigarette when I walked into his office. He affected politeness but his eyes kept going to the clock on the wall while I talked. A side door opened on to the sheriff's office, and I could see his desk and empty chair inside. I told the detective the story that Dixie had told me. I told him about the leasemen, Dalton Vidrine and Harry Mapes.

'We know all about that,' he said. 'That's why the

sheriff been talking to them. But I tell you right now, podna, he don't believe that fella.'

'What do you mean he's been talking with them?'

He smiled at me.

'They in his office right now. He went down to the bat'room,' he said. Then he got up and closed the door to the sheriff's office.

I looked at him, stunned.

'They're sitting in there now?' My voice was incredulous.

'He called them up and ax them to come in and make a statement.'

I stood up, took a piece of paper off his desk, and wrote my name and telephone number on it.

'Ask the sheriff to call me,' I said. 'What's your name again?'

'Benoit.'

'Get into another line of work.'

I walked back outside to my pickup truck. The shadows were purple on the bayou and the church lawn. An elderly Negro was taking down the flag from the pole in front of the courthouse and a white man was closing and locking the side doors. Then two men came out the front entrance and walked hurriedly across the grass toward me, one slightly ahead of the other.

The first was a tall, angular man, dressed in brown slacks, shined loafers, a yellow sport shirt with a purple fleur-de-lis on the pocket, a thin western belt with a silver buckle and tongue. I could hear the change in his pocket when he walked. On his bottom lip was a triangular scar that looked like wet plastic.

The man behind him was shorter, dark, thick across the middle, the kind of man who wore his slacks below the navel to affect size and strength and disguise his advancing years. His eyebrows dipped down and met over his nose. Even though it was warm, he wore a long-sleeved white shirt, the pocket filled with a notebook and clip-on ballpoint pens.

Both men had the agitated look of people who might have seen their bus pass them by at their stop.

'Just a minute there, buddy,' the tall man said.

I turned and looked at him with my hand on the open truck door.

'You were using our names in there. Where the hell do you get off making those remarks?' he said. His eyes narrowed and he ran his tongue over the triangular scar on his lip.

'I was just passing on some information. It didn't originate with me, partner.'

'I don't give a goddamn where it came from. I won't put up with it. Particularly from some guy I never saw before,' he said.

'Then don't listen to it.'

'It's called libel.'

'It's called filing a police report,' I said.

'Who the fuck are you?' the other man said.

'My name's Dave Robicheaux.'

'You're an ex-cop or some kind of local bird dog?' he said.

'I'm going to ask you guys to disengage,' I said.

'You're asking us! You're unbelievable, man,' the tall man said.

I started to get in my truck. He put his hand around the window jamb and held it.

'You're not running out of this,' he said. The accent was East Texas, all right, piney woods, red hills, and sawmills. 'Pugh's a pathetic man. He melted his brains a long time ago. The company gave him a break when nobody else would. Obviously it didn't work out. He gets souped up with whiskey and dope and has delusions.' He took his hand from the window jamb and pointed his finger an inch from my chest. 'Now, if you want to spend your time talking to somebody like that, that's your damn business. But if you spread rumors about me and I hear about it, I'm going to look you up.'

I got in my truck and closed the door. I breathed through my nose, looked out at the shadows on the church, the stone statue of Evangeline under the spreading oak. Then I clicked my key ring on the steering wheel. The faces of the two men were framed through my truck window.

Then I yielded to the temptations of anger and pride, two serpentine heads of the Hydra of character defects that made up my alcoholism.

'It was the Coleman fuel for the stove, wasn't it?' I said. 'You spread it around the inside of the cabin, then strung it down the steps and up the levee. As an added feature maybe you opened the drain on the gas drum, too. You didn't expect the explosion to blow Dixie Lee out into the water, though, did you?'

It was a guess, but the mouth of the short man parted in disbelief. I started the engine, turned out into the traffic, and drove past the old storefronts and wood colonnades toward the edge of town and the back road to New Iberia.

In my dreams is a watery place where my wife and some of my friends live. I think it's below the Mekong River or perhaps deep under the Gulf. The people who live there undulate in the tidal currents and are covered with a green-gold light. I can't visit them there, but sometimes they call me up. In my mind's eye I can see them clearly. The men from my platoon still wear their pots and their rent and salt-caked fatigues. Smoke rises in bubbles from their wounds.

Annie hasn't changed much. Her eyes are electric blue, her hair gold and curly. Her shoulders are still covered with sun freckles. She wears red flowers on the front of her nightgown where they shot her with deer slugs. On the top of her left breast is a strawberry birthmark that always turned crimson with blood when we made love.

How you doing, baby love? she asks.

Hello, sweetheart.

Your father's here.

How is he?

He says to tell you not to get sucked in. What's he mean? You're not in trouble again, are you, baby love? We talked a long time about that before.

It's just the way I am, I guess.

It's still rah-rah for the penis, huh? I've got to go, Dave. There's a big line. Are you coming to see me?

Sure.

You promise?

You bet. I won't let you down, kiddo.

'You really want me to tell you what it means?' the psychologist in Lafayette said.

'Dreams are your province.'

'You're an intelligent man. You tell me.'

'I don't know.'

'Yes, you do.'

'Sometimes alcoholics go on dry drunks. Sometimes we have drunk dreams.'

'It's a death wish. I'd get a lot of distance between myself and those kinds of thoughts.'

I stared silently at the whorls of purple and red in his carpet.

The day after I visited the St Martin Parish courthouse I talked with the sheriff there on the phone. I had met him several times when I was a detective with the Iberia Parish sheriff's office, and I had always gotten along well with him. He said there was nothing in the coroner's report that would indicate the girl had been struck with a tire iron or a jack handle before the fish camp burned.

'So they did an autopsy?' I said.

'Dave, there wasn't hardly anything left of that poor girl to autopsy. From what Pugh says and what we found, she was right over the gas drum.'

'What are you going to do with those two clowns you had in your office yesterday?'

'Nothing. What can I do?'

'Pugh says they killed some people up in Montana.'

'I made some calls up there,' the sheriff said. 'Nobody has anything on these guys. Not even a traffic citation. Their office in Lafayette says they're good men. Look, it's Pugh that's got the record, that's been in trouble since they ran him out of that shithole he comes from.'

'I had an encounter with those two guys after I left your department yesterday. I think Pugh's telling the truth. I think they did it.'

'Then you ought to get a badge again, Dave. Is it about lunch-time over there?'

'What?'

'Because that's what time it is here. Come on by and have coffee sometime. We'll see you, podna.'

I drove into New Iberia to buy some chickens and sausage links from my wholesaler. It was raining when I got back home. I put 'La Jolie Blonde' by Iry LeJeune on the record player, changed into my gym shorts, and pumped iron in the kitchen for a half-hour. The wind was cool through the window and smelled of rain and damp earth and flowers and trees. My chest and arms were swollen with blood and exertion, and when the rain slacked off and the sun cracked through the mauve-colored sky, I ran three miles along the bayou, jumping across puddles, boxing with raindrops that dripped from the oak limbs overhead.

Back at the house I showered, changed into a fresh denim shirt and khakis, and called Dan Nygurski collect in Great Falls, Montana. He couldn't accept the collect call, but he took the number and called me back on his line.

'You know about Dixie Lee?' I said.

'Yep.'

'Do you know about the waitress who died in the fire?'

'Yes.'

'Did y'all have a tail on him that night?'

'Yeah, we did but he got off it. It's too bad. Our people might have saved the girl's life.'

'He lost them?'

'I don't think it was deliberate. He took the girl to a colored place in Breaux Bridge, I guess it was a zydeco place or something like that. What is that, anyway?'

'It's Negro-Cajun music. It means "vegetables" all mixed up.'

'Anyway, our people had some trouble with a big buck who thought it was all right for Pugh to come in the club but not other white folks. In the meantime Pugh, who was thoroughly juiced, wandered out the side door with the girl and took off.'

'Have you heard his story?'

'Yeah.'

'Do you believe it?'

'What difference does it make? It's between him and the locals now. I'll be square with you, Robicheaux. I don't give a damn about Pugh. I want that lunatic Sally Dio in a cage. I don't care how I get him there, either. You can tell Dixie Lee for me I'll always listen when he's on the subject of Sally Dee. Otherwise, he's not in a seller's market.'

'Why would he be buying leasing land for this character Dio? Is it related to the oil business?'

'Hey, that's good, Robicheaux. The mob hooking up with the oil business.' He was laughing out loud now. 'That's like Frankenstein making it with the wife of Dracula. I'm not kidding you, that's great. The guys in the office'll love this. You got any other theories?'

Then he started laughing again.

I quietly replaced the telephone receiver in the cradle, then walked down to the dock in the wet afternoon sunlight to help Batist close up the bait shop.

That evening Alafair and I drove down to Cypremort Point for boiled crabs at the pavilion. We sat at one of the checker-cloth tables on the screened porch by the bay, a big bib with a red crawfish on it tied around

Alafair's neck, and looked out at the sun setting across the miles of dead cypress, saw grass, the sandy inlets, the wetlands that stretched all the way to Texas. The tide was out, and the jetties were black and stark against the flat gray expanse of the bay and the strips of purple and crimson cloud that had flattened on the western horizon. Seagulls dipped and wheeled over the water's edge, and a solitary blue heron stood among the saw grass in an inlet pool, his long body and slender legs like a painting on the air.

Alafair always set about eating bluepoint crabs with a devastating clumsiness. She smashed them in the center with the wooden mallet, snapped off the claws, and cracked back the shell hinge with slippery hands and an earnest innocence that sent juice and pulp flying all over the table. When we finished eating I had to take her into the washroom and wipe off her hair, face, and arms with wet paper towels.

On the way back home I stopped in New Iberia and rented a Walt Disney movie, then I called up Batist and asked him and his wife to watch it with us. Batist was always fascinated by the VCR and never could quite understand how it worked.

'Them people that make the movie, they put it in that box, huh, Dave?' he said.

'That's right.'

'It just like at the show, huh?'

'That's right.'

'Then how it get up to the antenna and in the set?'

'It doesn't go up to—'

'And how come it don't go in nobody else's set?' he said.

'It don't go out the house,' Alafair said.

'Not "It don't." Say "It doesn't,"' I said.

'Why you telling her that? She talk English good as us,' Batist said.

I decided to heat up some *boudin* and make some Kool-Aid.

I rented a lot of Disney and other films for children because I didn't like Alafair to watch ordinary television in the evening or at least when I was not there. Maybe I was overly protective and cautious. But the celluloid facsimile of violence and the news footage of wars in the Middle East and Central America would sometimes cause the light to go out of her face and leave her mouth parted and her eyes wide, as though she had been slapped.

Disney films, Kool-Aid, *boudin*, bluepoint crabs on a breezy porch by the side of the bay were probably poor compensation for the losses she had known. But you offer what you have, perhaps even bless it with a prayer, and maybe somewhere down the line affection grows into faith and replaces memory. I can't say. I'm not good at the mysteries, and I have few solutions even for my own problems. But I was determined that Alafair would never again be hurt unnecessarily, not while she was in my care, not while she was in this country.

'This is our turf, right, Batist?' I said as I gave him a paper plate with slices of *boudin* on it.

'What?' His and Alafair's attention was focused on the image of Donald Duck on the television screen. Outside, the fireflies were lighting in the pecan trees.

'This is our Cajun land, right, podna?' I said. 'We make the rules, we've got our own flag.'

He gave me a quizzical look, then turned back to the

television screen. Alafair, who was sitting on the floor, slapped her thighs and squealed uproariously while Donald Duck raged at his nephews.

The next day I visited Dixie Lee again at Lourdes and took him a couple of magazines. The sunlight was bright in his room, and someone had placed a green vase of roses in the window. The deputy left us alone, and Dixie lay on his side and looked at me from his pillow. His eyes were clear, and his cheeks were shaved and pink.

'You're looking better,' I said.

'For the first time in years I'm not full of whiskey. It feels weird, I'm here to tell you. In fact, it feels so good I'd like to cut out the needle, too. But the centipedes start waking up for a snack.'

I nodded at the roses in the window and smiled.

'You have an admirer,' I said.

He didn't answer. He traced a design on the bed with his index finger, as though he were pushing a penny around on the sheet.

'You grew up Catholic, didn't you?' he said.

'Yes.'

'You still go to church?'

'Sure.'

'You think God punishes us right here, that it ain't just in the next world?'

'I think those are bad ideas.'

'My little boy died in a fire. A bare electric cord under a rug started it. If I hadn't been careless, it wouldn't have happened. Then I killed that man's little boy over in Fort Worth, and now I been in a fire myself and a young girl's dead.'

I looked at the confusion and pain in his face.

'I had preachers back home tell me where all that drinking and doping was going to lead me. I wouldn't pay them no mind,' he said.

'Come on, don't try to see God's hand in what's bad. Look outside. It's a beautiful day, you're alive, you're feeling better, maybe you've got alternatives now that you didn't have before. Think about what's right with your life, Dixie.'

'They're going to try and pop me.'

'Who?'

'Vidrine and Mapes. Or some other butthole the company hires.'

'These kinds of guys don't come up the middle.'

He looked back at me silently, as if I were someone on the other side of a wire fence.

'There're too many people looking at them now,' I said.

'You don't know how much money's involved. You couldn't guess. You don't have any idea what these bastards will do for money.'

'You're in custody.'

'Save the dog shit, Dave. Last night Willie out there said he was going for some smokes. It was eleven o'clock. He handcuffed my wrist to the bed rail and came back at one in the morning, chewing on a toothpick and smelling like hamburger and onions.'

'I'll talk to the sheriff.'

'The same guy that thinks I've got fried grits for brains? You think like a cop, Dave. You've probably locked a lot of guys up, but you don't know what it's like inside all that clanging iron. A couple of winging dicks want a kid brought to their cell, that's where he gets delivered. A guy wants you whacked out because you owe for a couple of decks of cigarettes, you get a shank in your spleen somewhere between the mess hall and lockup. Guys like Willie out there are a joke.'

'What do you want me to do?'

'Nothing. You tried. Don't worry about it.'

'I'm not going to leave you on your own. Give me a little credit.'

'I ain't on my own. I called Sally Dee.'

I looked again at the roses in the green vase.

'Floral telegram. He's a thoughtful guy, man,' Dixie Lee said.

'It's your butt.'

'Don't ever do time. You won't hack it inside.'

'What you're doing is not only stupid, you're starting to piss me off, Dixie.'

'I'm sorry.'

'You want to be on these guys' leash the rest of your life? What's the matter with you?'

'Everything. My whole fucking life. You want to pour yourself some iced tea? I got to use the bedpan.'

'I think I've been jerked around here, partner.'

'Maybe you been jerking yourself around.'

'What?'

'Ask yourself how much you're interested in me and how much you're interested in the drilling company that killed your old man.'

I watched him work the stainless steel bedpan out from the rack under the mattress.

'I guess you have dimensions I haven't quite probed,' I said.

'I flunked out my freshman year, remember? You're talking way above my league.'

'No, I don't think so. We'll see you around, Dixie.'

'I don't blame you for walking out mad. But you don't understand. You can't, man. It was big back then. The Paramount Theatre in Brooklyn with Allan Freed, on stage with guys like Berry and Eddie Cochran. I wasn't no drunk, either. I had a wife and a kid, people thought I was decent. Look at me today. I'm a fucking ex-convict, the stink on shit. I killed a child, for God's sake. You come in here talking an AA shuck about the beautiful weather outside when maybe I'm looking at a five-spot on Angola farm. Get real, son. It's the dirty boogie out there, and all the cats are humping to it in three-four time.'

I stood up from my chair.

'I'll speak with the sheriff about the deputy. He won't leave you alone again. I'll see you, Dixie,' I said.

I left him and walked outside into the sunlight. The breeze was cool and scented with flowers, and across the street in a grove of oak trees a Negro was selling rattlesnake watermelons off the back of a truck. He had lopped open one melon on the tailgate as an advertisement, and the meat was dark red in the shade. I looked back up at Dixie Lee's room on the corner of the second floor and saw a nun close the venetian blinds on the sunlight.

chapter three

I had never liked the Lafayette Oil Center. My attitude was probably romantic and unreasonable. As chambers of commerce everywhere are fond of saying, it provided jobs and an expanded economy, it meant progress. It was also ugly. It was low and squat and sprawling, treeless, utilitarian, built with glazed brick and flat roofs, tinted and mirrored windows that gave on to parking lots that in summer radiated the heat like a stove.

And to accommodate the Oil Center traffic the city had widened Pinhook Road, which ran down to the Vermilion River and became the highway to New Iberia. The oak and pecan trees along the road had been cut down, the rural acreage subdivided and filled with businesses and fast-food restaurants, the banks around the Vermilion Bridge paved with asphalt parking lots and dotted with more oil-related businesses whose cinder-block architecture had all the aesthetic design of a sewage-treatment works.

But there was still one café on Pinhook left over from my college days at Southwestern in the 1950s. The parking lot was oystershell, the now-defunct speakers from the jukebox were still ensconced in the forks of the spreading oak trees, the pink and blue and green neon tubing around the windows still looked like a wet kiss in the rain.

The owner served fried chicken and dirty rice that could break your heart. I finished eating lunch and drinking coffee and looked out at the rain blowing through the oaks, at the sheen it made on the bamboo that grew by the edge of the parking lot. The owner propped open the front door with a board, and the mist and cool air and the smell of the trees blew inside. Then a Honda stopped in a rain puddle out front, the windshield wipers slapping, and an Indian girl with olive skin and thick black hair jumped out and ran inside. She wore designer jeans, which people had stopped wearing, a yellow shirt tied across her middle, and yellow tennis shoes. She touched the raindrops out of her eyes with her fingers and glanced around the restaurant until she saw the sign over the women's room. She walked right past my table, her damp wrist almost brushing my shoulder, and I tried not to look at her back, her thighs, the way her hips creased and her posterior moved when she walked; but that kind of resolution and dignity seemed to be more and more wanting in my life.

I paid my check, put on my rain hat, draped my seersucker coat over my arm, and ran past the idling Honda to my truck. Just as I started the engine the girl ran from the restaurant and got into the Honda with a package of cigarettes in her hand. The driver backed around so that he was only ten feet from my cab and rolled his window down.

I felt my mouth drop open. I stared dumbfounded at the boiled pigskin face, the stitched scar that ran from the bridge of his nose up through one eyebrow, the sandy hair and intelligent green eyes, the big shoulders that made his shirt look as though it were about to rip.

Cletus Purcel.

He grinned and winked at me.

'What's happening, Streak?' he said into the rain, then rolled up the window, and splashed out on to Pinhook Road.

My old homicide partner from the First District in the French Quarter. Bust 'em or smoke 'em, he used to say. Bury your fist in their stomachs, leave them puking on their knees, click off their light switch with a slapjack if they still want to play.

He had hated the pimps, the Nicaraguan and Colombian dealers, the outlaw bikers, the dirty-movie operators, the contract killers the mob brought in from Miami, and if left alone with him, they would gladly cut any deal they could get from the prosecutor's office.

But with time he became everything that he despised. He took freebies from whores, borrowed money from shylocks, fought the shakes every morning with cigarettes, aspirin, and speed, and finally took ten thousand dollars to blow away a potential government witness in a hog lot.

Then he had cleaned out his and his wife's bank account, roared the wrong way down a one-way street into the New Orleans airport, bounced over a concrete island, and abandoned his car with both doors open in front of the main entrance. He just made the flight to Guatemala.

A month later I received a card from him that had been postmarked in Honduras.

Dear Streak,

Greetings from Bongo-Bongo Land. I'd like to tell you I'm off the sauce and working for the Maryknolls. I'm not. Guess what skill is in big demand down here? A guy that can run through the manual of arms is an automatic captain. They're all kids. Somebody with a case of Clearasil could take the whole country.

See you in the next incarnation,

C.

PS If you run into Lois, tell her I'm sorry for ripping her off. I left my toothbrush in the bathroom. I want her to have it.

I watched his taillights glimmer and fade in the rain. As far as I knew, there was still a warrant on him. What was Cletus doing back in the States? And in Lafayette?

But he was somebody else's charge now, not mine. So good luck, partner, I thought. Whatever you're operating on, I hope it's as pure and clean as white gas and bears you aloft over the places where the carrion birds clatter.

I drove across the street and parked in front of the Star Drilling Company's regional office. Confronting them probably seems a foolish thing to do, particularly in the capacity of a citizen rather than that of a law officer. But my experience as a policeman investigating white-collar criminals always led me to the same conclusion about them: they might envision a time when they'll have to deal with the law, but in their minds the problem will be handled by attorneys, in a court proceeding that becomes almost a gentlemen's abstraction. They tremble with both outrage and fear when a plainclothes cop, perhaps with an IQ of ninety-five, a

.357 showing under his coat, a braided blackjack in his pocket, steps into the middle of their lives as unexpectedly as an iron door slamming shut and indicates that he thinks habeas corpus is a Latin term for a disease.

I put on my coat and ran through the rain and into the building. The outer offices of Star Drilling, which was separated by half-glass partitions, were occupied by draftsmen and men who looked like geologists or lease people. The indirect lighting glowed on the pine paneling, and the air-conditioning was turned so high that I felt my skin constrict inside my damp seersucker. The geologists, or whatever they were, walked from desk to desk, rattling topography maps between their outstretched hands, their faces totally absorbed in their own frame of reference or a finger moving back and forth on the numbers of a township and range.

The only person who looked at me was the receptionist. I told her I wanted to see the supervisor about a mineral lease in Montana.

His desk was big, made of oak, his chair covered with maroon leather, the pine walls hung with deer heads, a marlin, two flintlock rifles. On a side table was a stuffed lynx, mounted on a platform, the teeth bared, the yellow glass eyes filled with anger.

His name was Hollister. He was a big man, his thick, graying hair cut military, his pale blue eyes unblinking. Like those of most managerial people in the Oil Center, his accent was Texas or Oklahoma and his dress eccentric. His gray Oshman coat hung on a rack, his cufflinks were the size of quarters and embossed with oil derricks. His bolo tie was fastened with a brown and silver brooch.

He listened to me talk a moment, his square hands

motionless on the desk, his face like that of a man staring into an ice storm.

'Wait a minute. You came to my office to question me about my employees? About a murder?'

I could see tiny stretched white lines in the skin around the corners of his eyes.

'It's more than one, Mr Hollister. The girl in the fire and maybe some people in Montana.'

'Tell me, who do you think you are?'

'I already did.'

'No, you didn't. You lied to my receptionist to get in here.'

'You've got a problem with your leasemen. It won't go away because I walk out the door.'

His pale eyes looked steadily at me. He lifted one finger off his desk and aimed it at me.

'You're not here about Dixie Pugh,' he said. 'You've got something else bugging you. I don't know what it is, but you're not a truthful man.'

I touched the ball of my thumb to the corner of my mouth, looked away from him a moment, and tapped my fingers on the leather arm of my chair.

'You evidently thought well enough of Dixie Lee to give him a job,' I said. 'Do you think he made all this up and then set himself on fire?'

'I think you're on your way out of here.'

'Let me tell you a couple of things about the law. Foreknowledge of a crime can make you a co-conspirator. Knowledge after the fact can put you into an area known as aiding and abetting. These guys aren't worth it, Mr Hollister.'

'This discussion is over. There's the door.'

'It looks like your company has made stonewalling an art form.'

'What?'

'Does the name Aldous Robicheaux mean anything to you?'

'No. Who is he?'

'He was my father. He was killed on one of your rigs.'

'When?'

'Twenty-two years ago. They didn't have a blowout preventer on. Your company tried to deny it, since almost everybody on the rig went down with it. A shrimper pulled a floorman out of the water two days later. He cost you guys a lot of money.'

'So you got a grudge that's twenty-two years old? I don't know what to tell you, Robicheaux, except I wasn't with the company then and I probably feel sorry for you.'

I took my rain hat off my knee and stood up.

'Tell Mapes and Vidrine to stay away from Dixie Lee,' I said.

'You come in here again, I'll have you arrested.'

I walked back outside into the rain, got in my truck, and drove out of the maze of flat, uniform brick buildings that composed the Oil Center. On Pinhook Road I passed the restaurant where I had seen Cletus an hour before. The spreading oak trees were dark green, the pink and blue neon like smoke in the blowing mist. The wind blew hard when I crossed the Vermilion River, ruffling the yellow current below and shuddering the sides of my truck.

*

'I don't buy that stuff about a death wish. I believe some guys in Vienna had too much time to think,' I said to the therapist.

'You don't have to be defensive about your feelings. Facile attitudes have their place in therapy, too. For example, I don't think there's anything complex about depression. It's often a matter of anger turned inward. What do you have to say about that, Dave?'

'I don't know.'

'Yes, you do. How did you feel in Vietnam when the man next to you was hit?'

'What do you think I felt?'

'At some point you were glad it was him and not you. And then you felt guilty. And that was very dangerous, wasn't it?'

'All alcoholics feel guilt. Go to an open meeting sometime. Learn something about it.'

'Cut loose from the past. She wouldn't want you to carry a burden like this.'

'I can't. I don't want to.'

'Say it again.'

'I don't want to.'

He was bald and his rimless glasses were full of light. He turned his palms up toward me and was silent.

I visited Dixie Lee one more time and found him distant, taciturn, perhaps even casually indifferent to my presence in the room. I wasn't pleased with his attitude. I didn't know whether to ascribe it to the morphine-laced IV hooked into his arm, or possibly his own morose awareness of what it meant to throw in his lot with his hold-cell partner.

'You want me to bring you anything else before I leave?' I asked.

'I'm all right.'

'I probably won't be back, Dixie. I'm pretty tied up at the dock these days.'

'Sure, I understand.'

'Do you think maybe you used me a little bit?' I grinned at him and held up my thumb and forefinger slightly apart in the air. 'Maybe just a little?'

His voice was languid, as though he were resting on the comfortable edge of sleep.

'Me use somebody else? Are you kidding?' he said. 'You're looking at the dildo of the planet.'

'See you around, Dixie.'

'Hell, yes. They're kicking me out of here soon, anyway. It's only second-degree stuff. I've had worse hangovers. We're in tall cotton, son.'

And so I left him to his own menagerie of snapping dogs and hungry snakes.

That Saturday I woke Alafair early, told her nothing about the purpose of our trip, and drove in the cool, rose-stippled dawn to the Texas side of Sabine Pass, where the Sabine River empties into the Gulf. A friend of mine from the army owned a small, sandy, salt-flecked farm not far from the hard-packed gray strip of sandbar that tried to be a beach. It was a strange, isolated place, filled with the mismatched flora of two states: stagnant lakes dotted with dead cypress, solitary oaks in the middle of flat pasture, tangles of black-jack along the edges of coulees, an alluvial fan of sand dunes that were crested with salt grass and from which protruded tall palm trees silhouetted blackly against the sun. Glinting through the pines on the back of my friend's farm were the long roll and pitch of the Gulf itself, and a cascade of waves that broke against the beach in an iridescent spray of foam.

It was a place of salt-poisoned grass, alligators, insects, magpies, turkey buzzards, drowned cows whose odor reached a half-mile into the sky, tropical storms that could sand the paint off a water tower, and people like my friend who had decided to slip through a hole in the dimension and live on their own terms. He had a bad-conduct discharge from the army, had been locked up in a mental asylum in Galveston, had failed totally at AA, and as a farmer couldn't grow thorns in a briar patch.

But he bred and raised some of the most beautiful Appaloosa horses I had ever seen. He and I had coffee in his kitchen while Alafair drank a Coke, then I picked up several sugar cubes in my palm and we walked out to his back lot.

'What we doing, Dave?' Alafair said. She looked up at me in the sunlight that shone through the pine trees. She wore a yellow T-shirt, baggy blue jeans, and pink tennis shoes. The wind off the water ruffled her bangs.

My friend winked and went inside the barn.

'You can't ride Tripod, can you, little guy?' I said.

'What? Ride Tripod?' she said, her face confused, then suddenly lighting, breaking into an enormous grin as she looked past me and saw my friend leading a three-year-old gelding out of the barn.

The Appaloosa was steel gray, with white stockings and a spray of black and white spots across his rump. He snorted and pitched his head against the bridle, and Alafair's brown eyes went back and forth between the horse and me, her face filled with delight.

'You think you can take care of him and Tripod and your rabbits, too?' I said.

'Me? He's for me, Dave?'

'You bet he is. He called me up yesterday and said he wanted to come live with us.'

'What? Horse call up?'

I picked her up and set her on top of the fence rail, then let the Appaloosa take the sugar cubes out of my palm.

'He's like you, he's got a sweet tooth,' I said. 'But when you feed him something, let him take it out of your palm so he doesn't bite your fingers by mistake.'

Then I climbed over the fence, slipped bareback on to the horse, and lifted Alafair up in front of me. My friend had trimmed the horse's mane, and Alafair ran her hand up and down it as though it were a giant shoe brush. I touched my right heel against the horse's flank, and we turned in a slow circle around the lot.

'What his name?' Alafair said.

'How about Tex?'

'How come that?'

'Because he's from Texas.'

'What?'

'This is Texas.'

'This where?'

'Never mind.'

I nodded for my friend to open the gate, and we rode out through the sandy stretch of pines on to the beach. The waves were slate green and full of kelp, and they made a loud smack against the sand and slid in a wet line up to a higher, dry area where the salt grass and the pine needles began. It was windy and cool and warm at the same time, and we rode a mile or so along the edge of the surf to a place where a sandbar and jetty had created a shallow lagoon, in the middle of which a wrecked shrimp boat lay gray and paintless on its side, a cacophony of seagulls thick in the air above it. Behind us the horse's solitary tracks were scalloped deep in the wet sand.

I gave my friend four hundred for the Appaloosa, and for another three hundred he threw in the tack and a homemade trailer. Almost all the way home Alafair stayed propped on her knees on the front seat, either looking backward through the cab glass or out the window at the horse trailer tracking behind us, her fine hair flattening in white lines against her scalp.

On Monday I walked up to the house for lunch, then stopped at the mailbox on the road before I went back to the dock. The sun was warm, the oak trees along the road were full of mockingbirds and blue jays, and the mist from my neighbor's water sprinkler drifted in a wet sheen over his hydrangea beds and rows of blooming azalea and myrtle bushes. In the back of the mailbox was a narrow package no more than ten inches long. It had been postmarked in New Orleans. I put my other mail in my back pocket, slipped the twine off the corners of the package, and cracked away the brown wrapping paper with my thumb.

I lifted off the cardboard top. Inside on a strip of cotton was a hypodermic needle with a photograph and a sheet of lined paper wrapped around it. The inside of the syringe was clouded with a dried brown-red residue. The photograph was cracked across the surface, yellowed around the edges, but the obscene nature of the details had the violent clarity of a sliver of glass in the eye. A pajama-clad Vietcong woman lay in a clearing by the tread of a tank, her severed head resting on her stomach. Someone had stuffed a C-ration box in her mouth.

The lined paper looked like the kind that comes in a Big Chief notebook. The words were printed large, in black ink.

Dear Sir,
The guy that took this picture is one fucked up dude. He liked it over there and didn't want to come back. He says he used this needle in a snuff flick out in Oakland. I don't know if I'd believe him or not. But your little pinto bean gets on the bus at 7:45. She arrives at school at 8:30. She's on the playground at 10 and back out there at noon. She waits on the south corner for the bus home at 3:05. Sometimes she gets off before her stop and walks down the road with a colored kid. It's hardball. Don't fuck with it. It's going to really mess up your day. Check the zipperhead in the pic. Now there's somebody who really had a hard time getting her C's down.

'For what your face like that? What it is, Dave?'

Batist was standing behind me, dressed in a pair of navy bell-bottoms and an unbuttoned sleeveless khaki shirt. There were drops of sweat on his bald head, and the backs of his hands and wrists were spotted with blood from cleaning fish.

I put the photograph, letter, and torn package back in the mailbox and walked hurriedly down to the dock. I called the elementary school, asked the principal to make sure that Alafair was in her classroom, then told her not to let Alafair board the school bus that afternoon, that I would be there to pick her up. When I walked back toward the house Batist was still at the mailbox. He was illiterate and so the letter inside meant nothing to him, but he had the photograph cupped in his big palm, an unlit cigar in the corner of his mouth, and there was an ugly glaze in his eyes.

'*Que ça veut dire*, Dave? What that needle mean, too?' he said.

'Somebody's threatening Alafair.'

'They say they gonna hurt that little girl?'

'Yes.' The word created a hollow feeling in my chest.

'Who they are? Where they at, them people that do something like this?'

'I believe it's a couple of guys in Lafayette. They're oil people. Have you seen any guys around here who look like they don't belong here?'

'I ain't paid it no mind, Dave. I didn't have no reason, me.'

'It's all right.'

'What we gonna do?'

'I'm going to pick up Alafair, then I'll talk to the sheriff.' I picked the photograph out of his palm by the edges and set it back inside the mailbox. 'I'm going to leave this stuff in there, then take it in later and see if we can find fingerprints on it. So we shouldn't handle it anymore.'

'No, I mean what we gonna *do*?' he said. His brown eyes looked intently into mine. There was no question about his meaning.

'I'm going to pick up Alafair now. Watch the store and I'll be back soon.'

Batist's mouth closed on his dry cigar. His eyes went away from me, stared into the shade of the pecan trees and moved back and forth in his head with a private thought. His voice was quiet when he spoke.

'Dave, in that picture, that's where you was at in the war?'

'Yes.'

'They done them kind of things?'

'Some did. Not many.'

'In that letter, it say that about Alafair?'

I swallowed and couldn't answer him. The hollow feeling in my chest would not go away. It was like fear but not of a kind that I had ever experienced before. It was an obscene feeling, as though a man's hand had slipped lewdly inside my shirt and now rested sweatily on my breastbone. The sunlight shimmered on the bayou, and the trees and blooming hyacinths on the far side seemed to go in and out of focus. I saw a cottonmouth coiled fatly on a barkless, sun-bleached log, its triangular head the color of tarnished copper in the hard yellow light. Sweat ran out of my hair, and I felt my heart beating against my rib cage. I snicked the mailbox door shut, got into my truck, and headed down the dirt road toward New Iberia. When I bounced across the drawbridge over Bayou Teche, my knuckles were white and as round as quarters on the steering wheel.

On the way back from the school the spotted patterns of light and shadow fell though the canopy of oaks overhead and raced over Alafair's tan face as she sat next to me in the truck. Her knees and white socks and patent leather shoes were dusty from play on the school ground. She kept looking curiously at the side of my face.

'Something wrong, Dave?' she said.

'No, not at all.'

'Something bad happen, ain't it?'

'Don't say "ain't." '

'Why you mad?'

'Listen, little guy, I'm going to run some errands this afternoon and I want you to stay down at the dock with Batist. You stay in the store and help him run things, okay?'

'What's going on, Dave?'

'There's nothing to worry about. But I want you to stay away from people you don't know. Keep close around Batist and Clarise and me, okay? You see, there're a couple of men I've had some trouble with. If they come around here, Batist and I will chase them off. But I don't want them bothering you or Clarise or Tripod or any of our friends, see.' I winked at her.

'These bad men?' Her face looked up at me. Her eyes were round and unblinking.

'Yes, they are.'

'What they do?'

I took a breath and let it out.

'I don't know for sure. But we just need to be a little careful. That's all, little guy. We don't worry about stuff like that. We're kind of like Tripod. What's he do when the dog chases him?'

She looked into space, then I saw her eyes smile.

'He gets up on the rabbit hutch,' she said.

'Then what's he do?'

'He stick his claw in the dog's nose.'

'That's right. Because he's smart. And because he's smart and careful, he doesn't have to worry about that dog. And we're the same way and we don't worry about things, do we?'

She smiled up at me, and I pulled her against my side and kissed the top of her head. I could smell the sun's heat in her hair.

I parked the truck in the shade of the pecan trees, and she took her lunch kit into the kitchen, washed out her thermos, and changed into her playclothes. We walked down to the dock, and I put her in charge of soda pop and worm sales. In the corner behind the beer cases I saw Batist's old automatic Winchester twelve-gauge propped against the wall.

'I put some number sixes in it for that cotton-mouth been eating fish off my stringer,' he said. 'Come see tonight. You gonna have to clean that snake off the tree.'

'I'll be back before dark. Take her up to the house for her supper,' I said. 'I'll close up when I get back.'

'You don't be worry, you,' he said, dragged a kitchen match on a wood post, lit his cigar, and let the smoke drift out through his teeth.

Alafair rang up a sale on the cash register and beamed when the drawer clanged open.

I put everything from the mailbox in a large paper bag and drove to the Iberia Parish sheriff's office. I had worked a short while for the sheriff as a plainclothes detective the previous year, and I knew him to be a decent and trustworthy man. But when he ran for the office his only qualification was the fact that he had been president of the Lions Club and owned a successful dry-cleaning business. He was slightly overweight, his face soft around the edges, and in his green uniform he looked like the manager of a garden-supply store. We talked in his office while a deputy processed the wrapping paper, box, note, and hypodermic needle for fingerprints in another room.

Finally the deputy rapped on the sheriff's door glass with one knuckle and opened the door.

'Two identifiable sets,' he said. 'One's Dave's, one's from that colored man, what's his name?'

'Batist,' I said.

'Yeah, we have his set on file from the other time—' His eyes flicked away from me and his face colored. 'We had his prints from when we were out to Dave's place before. Then there's some smeared stuff on the outside of the wrapping paper.'

'The mailman?' the sheriff said.

'That's what I figure,' the deputy said. 'I wish I could tell you something else, Dave.'

'It's all right.'

The deputy nodded and closed the door.

'You want to take it to the FBI in Lafayette?' the sheriff said.

'Maybe.'

'A threat in the mail is in a federal area. Why not make use of them?'

I looked back at him without answering.

'Why is it that I always feel you're not a man of great faith in our system?' he said.

'Probably because I worked for it too long.'

'We can question these two guys, what's their names again?'

'Vidrine and Mapes.'

'Vidrine and Mapes, we can let them know somebody's looking over their shoulder.'

'They're too far into it.'

'What do you want to do?'

'I don't know.'

'Dave, back off of this one. Let other people handle it.'

'Are you going to keep a deputy out at my house? Will one watch Alafair on the playground or while she waits for the bus?'

He let out his breath, then looked out the window at a clump of oak trees in a bright, empty pasture.

'Something else bothers me here,' he said. 'Wasn't your daddy killed on a Star rig?'

'Yes.'

'You think there's a chance you want to twist these guys, no matter what happens?'

'I don't know what I think. That box didn't mail itself to me, though, did it?'

I saw the injury in his eyes, but I was past the point of caring about his feelings. Maybe you've been there. You go into a police or sheriff's station after a gang of black kids forced you to stop your car while they smashed out your windows with garbage cans; a strung-out addict made you kneel at gunpoint on the floor of a grocery store, and before you knew it the begging words rose uncontrollably in your throat; some bikers pulled you from the back of a bar and sat on your arms while one of them unzippered his blue jeans. Your body is still hot with shame, your voice full of thumbtacks and strange to your own ears, your eyes full of guilt and self-loathing while uniformed people walk casually by you with Styrofoam cups of coffee in their hands. Then somebody types your words on a report and you realize that this is all you will get. Investigators will not be out at your house, you will probably not be called to pull somebody out of a lineup, a sympathetic female attorney from the prosecutor's office will not take a large interest in your life.

Then you will look around at the walls and cabinets and lockers in that police or sheriff's station, the gun belts worn by the officers with the Styrofoam coffee cups, perhaps the interior of the squad cars in the parking lot, and you will make an ironic realization. The racks of M-16 rifles, scoped Mausers, twelve-gauge pumps loaded with double-aught buckshot, .38 specials and .357 Magnums, stun guns, slapjacks, batons, tear gas canisters, the drawers that contain cattle prods, handcuffs, Mace, wrist and leg chains, hundreds of rounds of ammunition, all have nothing to do with your safety or the outrage against your person. You're an increase in somebody's work load.

'You've been on this side of the desk, Dave. We do what we can,' the sheriff said.

'But it's not enough most of the time. Is it?'

He stirred a paper clip on the desk blotter with his finger.

'Have you got an alternative?' he said.

'Thanks for your time, Sheriff. I'll think about the FBI.'

'I wish you'd do that.'

The sky had turned purple and red in the west and rain clouds were building on the southern horizon when I drove home. I bought some ice cream in town, then stopped at a fruit stand under an oak tree by the bayou and bought a lug of strawberries. The thunderheads off the gulf slid across the sun, and the cicadas were loud in the trees and the fireflies were lighting in the shadows along the road. A solitary raindrop splashed on my windshield as I turned into my dirt yard.

It rained hard that night. It clattered on the shingles and the tin roof of the gallery, sluiced out of the gutters and ran in streams down to the coulee. The pecan trees in the yard beat in the wind and trembled whitely when lightning leaped across the black sky. I had the attic fan on, and the house was cool, and I dreamed all night. Annie came to me about four A.M., as she often did, when the night was about to give way to the softness of the false dawn. In my dream I could look through my bedroom window into the rain, past the shining trunks of the pecan trees, deep into the marsh and the clouds of steam that eventually bleed into the saw grass and the Gulf of Mexico, and see her and her companions inside a wobbling green bubble of air. She smiled at me.

Hi, sailor, she said.

How you doing, sweetheart?

You know I don't like it when it rains. Bad memories and all that. So we found a dry place for a while. Your buddies from your platoon don't like the rain, either. They say it used to give them jungle sores. Can you hear me with all that thunder? It sounds like cannon.

Sure.

It's lightning up on top of the water. That night I couldn't tell the lightning from the gun flashes. I wish you hadn't left me alone. I tried to hide under the bed sheet. It was a silly thing to do.

Don't talk about it.

It was like electricity dancing off the walls. You're not drinking, are you?

No, not really.

Not really?

Only in my dreams.

But I bet you still get high on those dry drunks, don't you? You know, fantasies about kicking butt, 'fronting the lowlifes, all that stuff swinging dicks like to do.

A guy has to do something for kicks. Annie?

What is it, baby love?

I want—

Tell me.

I want to—

It's not your time. There's Alafair to take care of, too.

It wasn't your time, either.

She made a kiss against the air. Her mouth was red.

So long, sailor. Don't sleep on your stomach. It'll make you hard in the morning. I miss you.

Annie—

She winked at me through the rain, and in my dream I was sure I felt her fingers touch my lips.

It continued to rain most of the next day. At three o'clock I picked up Alafair at the school and kept her with me in the bait shop. The sky and the marsh were gray; my rental boats were half full of water, the dock shiny and empty in the weak light. Alafair was restless and hard to keep occupied in the shop, and I let Batist take her with him on an errand in town. At five-thirty they were back, the rain slacked off, and the sun broke through the clouds in the west. It was the time of day when the bream and bass should have been feeding around the lily pads, but the bayou was high and the water remained smooth and brown and undented along the banks and in the coves. A couple of fishermen came in and drank beer for a while, and I leaned on the window jamb and stared out at the mauve- and red-streaked sky, the trees dripping rain into the water, the wet moss trying to lift in the evening breeze.

'Them men ain't gonna do nothing. They just blowing they horn,' Batist said beside me. Alafair was watching a cartoon on the old black-and-white television set that I kept on the snack shelf. She held Tripod on her lap while she stared raptly up at the set.

'Maybe so. But they'll let us wonder where they are and when they're coming,' I said. 'That's the way it works.'

'You call them FBI in Lafayette?'

'No.'

'How come?'

'It's a waste of time.'

'Sometime you gotta try, yeah.'

'There weren't any identifiable prints on the package except yours and mine.'

I could see in his face that he didn't understand.

'There's nothing to tell the FBI,' I said. 'I would only create paperwork for them and irritate them. It wouldn't accomplish anything. There's nothing I can do.'

'So you want get mad at me?'

'I'm not mad at you. Listen—'

'What?'

'I want her to stay with you tonight. I'll pick her up in the morning and take her to school.'

'What you gonna do, you?'

'I don't know.'

'I been knowing you a long time, Dave. Don't tell me that.'

'I'll tell Clarise to pack her school clothes and her pajamas and toothbrush. There's still one boat out. Lock up as soon as it comes in.'

'Dave—'

But I was already walking up toward the house in the light, sun-spangled rain, in the purple shadows, in the breeze that smelled of wet moss and blooming four-o'clocks.

It was cool and still light when I stopped on the outskirts of Lafayette and called Dixie Lee at the hospital from a pay phone. I asked him where Vidrine and Mapes were staying.

'What for?' he said.

'It doesn't matter what for. Where are they?'

'It matters to me.'

'Listen, Dixie, you brought me into this. It's gotten real serious in the last two days. Don't start being clever with me.'

'All right, the Magnolia. It's off Pinhook, down toward the river. Look, Dave, don't mess with them. I'm about to go bond and get out of here. It's time to ease off.'

'You sound like you've found a new confidence.'

'So I got friends. So I got alternatives. Fuck Vidrine and Mapes.'

The sun was red and swollen on the western horizon. Far to the south I could see rain falling.

'How far out are these guys willing to go?' I said.

He was quiet a moment.

'What are you talking about?' he said.

'You heard me.'

'Yeah, I did. They burn a girl to death and you ask

me a question like that? These guys got no bottom, if that's what you mean. They'll go down where it's so dark the lizards don't have eyes.'

I drove down Pinhook Road towards the Vermilion River and parked under a spreading oak tree by the motel, a rambling white stucco building with a blue tile roof. Rainwater dripped from the tree on to my truck cab, and the bamboo and palm trees planted along the walks bent in the wind off the river and the flagstones in the courtyard were wet and red in the sun's last light. A white and blue neon sign in the shape of a flower glowed against the sky over the entrance of the motel, an electrical short in it buzzing as loud as the cicadas in the trees. I stared at the front of the motel a moment, clicking my keys on the steering wheel, then I opened the truck door and started inside.

Just as I did the glass door of a motel room slid open and two men and women in bathing suits with drinks in their hands walked out on the flagstones and sat at a table by the pool. Vidrine and Mapes were both laughing at something one of the women had said. I stepped back in the shadows and watched Mapes signal a Negro waiter. A moment later the waiter brought them big silver shrimp-cocktail bowls and a platter of fried crawfish. Mapes wore sandals and a bikini swimming suit, and his body was as lean and tan as a long-distance runner's. But Vidrine wasn't as confident of his physique; he wore a Hawaiian shirt with his trunks, the top button undone to show his chest hair, but he kept crossing and recrossing his legs as though he could reshape the protruding contour of his stomach. The two women looked like hookers. One had a braying laugh; the other wore her hair pulled back on her head like copper wire, and she squeezed Mapes's thigh under the table whenever she leaned forward to say something.

I got back in the truck, took my World War II Japanese field glasses out of the glove box, and watched them out of the shadows for an hour. The underwater lights in the swimming pool were smoky green, and a thin slick of suntan oil floated on the surface. The waiter took away their dishes, brought them more rounds of tropical drinks, and their gaiety seemed unrelenting. They left the table periodically and went back through the sliding glass door into the motel room, and at first I thought they were simply using the bathroom, but then one of the women came back out touching one nostril with her knuckle, sniffing as though a grain of sand were caught in her breathing passage. At ten o'clock the waiter began dipping leaves out of the pool with a long-handled screen, and I saw Mapes signal for more drinks and the waiter look at his watch and shake his head negatively. They sat outside for another half-hour, smoking cigarettes, laughing more quietly now, sucking on pieces of ice from the bottoms of their glasses, the women's faces pleasant with a nocturnal lassitude.

Then a sudden rain shower rattled across the motel's tile roof, clattered on the bamboo and palm fronds, and danced in the swimming pool's underwater lights. Vidrine, Mapes, and the women ran laughing for the sliding door of the room. I waited until midnight, and they still had not come back out.

I put on my rain hat and went into the motel bar. It was almost deserted, and raindrops ran down the windows. Outside, I could see the white and blue neon flower against the dark sky. The bartender smiled at me. He wore black trousers, a white shirt that glowed almost purple in the bar light, and a black string tie sprinkled with sequins. He was a strange-looking man. His eyes were close-set and small as dimes, and he smoked a Pall Mall with three fingers along the barrel of the cigarette. I sat at the corner of the bar, where I could see the front door of Vidrine and Mapes's rooms, and ordered a 7-Up.

'It's pretty empty tonight,' I said.

'It sure is. You by yourself tonight?' he said.

'Right now I am. I was sort of looking for some company.' I smiled at him.

He nodded good-naturedly and began rinsing glasses in a tin sink. Finally he said, 'You staying at the motel?'

'Yeah, for a couple of days. Boy, I tell you I got one.' I blew out my breath and touched my forehead with my fingertips. 'I met this lady last night, a schoolteacher, would you believe it, and she came up to my room and we started hitting the JD pretty hard. But I'm not kidding you, before we got serious about anything she drank me under the table and I woke up at noon like a ball of fire.' I laughed. 'And with another problem, too. You know what I mean?'

He ducked his head and grinned.

'Yeah, that can be a tough problem,' he said. 'You want another 7-Up?'

'Sure.'

He went back to his work in the sink, his small eyes masked, and a moment later he dried his hands absently on a towel, turned on a radio that was set among the liquor bottles on the counter, and walked into a back hallway, where he picked up a house phone. He spoke into the receiver with his back turned toward me so that I could not hear him above the music on the radio. Outside the window, the trees were black against the sky and the blue tile of the motel roof glistened in the rain.

The girl came through the side door ten minutes later and sat one stool down from me. She wore spiked heels, Levi's, a backless brown sweater, and hoop earrings. She shook her wet hair loose, lit a cigarette, ordered a drink, then had another, and didn't pay for either of them. She talked as though she and I and the bartender were somehow old friends. In the neon glow she was pretty in a rough way. I wondered where she came from, what kind of trade-off was worth her present situation.

I wasn't making it easy for her, either. I hadn't offered to pay for either of her drinks, and I had made no overture toward her. I saw her look at her watch, then glance directly into the bartender's eyes. He lit a cigarette and stepped out the door as though he were getting a breath of fresh air.

'I hate lounges, don't you? They're all dull,' she said.

'It's a pretty slow place, all right.'

'I'd rather have drinks with a friend in my room.'

'What if I buy a bottle?'

'I think that would be just wonderful,' she said, and smiled as much to herself as to me. Then she bit down on her lip, leaned toward me, and touched my thigh. 'I've got a little trouble with Don, though. Like a seventy-five-dollar bar tab. Could you lend it to me so they don't eighty-six me out of this place?'

'It's time to take off, kiddo.'

'What?'

I took my sheriff's deputy badge out of my back pocket and opened it in front of her. It was just an honorary one, and I kept it only because it got me free parking at Evangeline Downs and the Fairgrounds in New Orleans, but she didn't know that.

'Don's in deep shit. Go home and watch television,' I said.

'You bastard.'

'I told you you're not busted. You want to hang around and have some of his problems?'

Her eyes went from my face to the bartender, who was coming back through the side door. Her decision didn't take long. She took her car keys out of her purse, threw her cigarettes inside, snapped it shut, and walked quickly on her spiked heels out the opposite door into the rain. I held up the badge in front of the bartender's small, close-set eyes.

'It's Iberia Parish, but what do you care?' I said. 'You're going to do something for me, right? Because you don't want Lafayette vice down here, do you? You're a reasonable guy, Don.'

He bit down on the corner of his lip and looked away from my face.

'I got a number I can call,' he said.

'Not tonight you don't.'

I could see his lip discolor where his tooth continued to chew on it. He blew air out of his nose as though he had a cold.

'I don't want trouble.'

'You shouldn't pimp.'

'How about lightening up a bit?' He looked at the two remaining customers in the bar. They were young and they sat at a table in the far corner. Behind them, through the opened blinds, headlights passed on the wet street.

'Two of your girls are in room six. You need to get them out,' I said.

'Wait a minute . . .'

'Let's get it done, Don. No more messing around.'

'That's Mr Mapes. I can't do that.'

'Time's running out, partner.'

'Look, you got a beef here or something, that's your business. I can't get mixed up in this. Those broads don't listen to me, anyway.'

'Well, I guess you're a stand-up guy. Your boss won't mind you getting busted, will he? Or having heat all over the place? You think one of those girls might have some flake up her nose? Maybe it's just sinus trouble.'

'All right,' he said, and held his palms upward. 'I got to tell these people I'm closing. Then I'll call the room. Then I'm gone, out of it, right?'

I didn't answer.

'Hey, I'm out of it, right?' he said.

'I'm already having trouble remembering your face.'

Five minutes after the bartender phoned Mapes's room the two prostitutes came out the front door, a man's angry voice resounding out of the room behind them, and got into a convertible and drove away. I opened the wooden toolbox in the bed of my pickup truck and took out a five-foot length of chain that I sometimes used to pull stumps. I folded it in half and wrapped the two loose ends around my hand. The links were rusted and made an orange smear across my palm. I walked across the gravel under the dripping trees toward the door of room six. The chain clinked against my leg; the heat lightning jumped in white spiderwebs all over the black sky.

Vidrine must have thought the women had come back because he was smiling when he opened the door in his boxer undershorts. Behind him Mapes was eating a sandwich in his robe at a wet bar. The linen and covers on the king-sized bed were in disarray, and the hallway that led into another bedroom was littered with towels, wet bathing suits, and beer cups.

Vidrine's smile collapsed, and his face suddenly looked rigid and glazed. Mapes set his sandwich on his plate, wet the scar on his lower lip as though he were contemplating an abstract equation, and moved toward a suitcase that was opened on a folding luggage holder.

I heard the chain clink and sing through the air, felt it come back over my head again and again, felt their hands rake against the side of my face; my ears roared with sound – a rumble deep under the Gulf, the drilling-rig floor trembling and clattering violently, the drill pipe exploding out of the wellhead in a red-black fireball. My hand was bitten and streaked with rust; it was the color of dried blood inside a hypodermic needle used to threaten a six-year-old child; it was like the patterns that I streaked across the walls, the bedclothes, the sliding glass doors that gave on to the courtyard where azalea petals floated on the surface of a lighted turquoise pool.

chapter four

Alafair woke up with an upset stomach the next morning, and I kept her home from school. I fixed her soft-boiled eggs and weak tea, then took her down to work with me in the bait shop. The sun had come up in a clear sky that morning, and the trees along the dirt road were bright green from the rain. The myrtle bushes were filled with purple bloom in the sunlight.

'Why you keep looking down the road, Dave?' Alafair asked. She sat on one of the phone-cable spools on the dock, watching me unscrew a fouled spark plug from an outboard engine. The canvas umbrella in the center of the spool was folded, and her Indian-black hair was shiny in the bright light.

'I'm just admiring the day,' I said.

I felt her looking at the side of my face.

'You don't feel good?' she said.

'I'm fine, little guy. I tell you what, let's take a ride down to the store and see if they have any kites. You think you can put a kite up today?'

'There ain't no wind.'

'Don't say "ain't."'

'Okay.'

'Let's go get some apples for Tex. You want to feed him some apples?'

'Sure.' She looked at me curiously.

We walked up to the truck, which was parked under the pecan trees, got in, and drove down the road toward the old store at the four-corners. Alafair looked at the floor.

'What's that, Dave?'

'Don't mess with that.'

Her eyes blinked at my tone.

'It's just a chain. Kick it under the seat,' I said.

She leaned down toward the floor.

'Don't touch it,' I said. 'It's dirty.'

'What's wrong, Dave?'

'Nothing. I just don't want your hands dirty,'

I took a breath, stopped the truck, and went around to Alafair's side. I opened her door and lifted the loops of chain off the floor. They felt as though they were coated with paint that had not quite dried.

'I'll be right back,' I said.

I walked down on the bank of the bayou and sailed the chain out into the middle of the current. Then I stooped by the cattails in the shallows and scrubbed my palms with water and sand. Dragon-flies hovered over the cattails, and I saw a cotton-mouth slide off a log and swim into the lily pads. I pushed my hands into the sand, and water clouded around my wrists. I walked back up on to the bank with my hands dripping at my sides and wiped them on the grass, then I took a cloth out of the toolbox and wiped them again.

The ramshackle general store at the four-corners was dark and cool inside, the wood-bladed ceiling fan turning over the counter. I bought a sack of apples for

Alafair's horse, some sliced ham, cheese, and French bread for our lunch, and two soda pops to drink out on the gallery. The sun was brilliant on the white shale parking lot, and through the trees across the road I could see a Negro man cane fishing in a pirogue close into the cypress roots.

We went back to the house, and Alafair helped me weed my hydrangea and rose beds. Our knees were wet and dirty, our arms covered with fine grains of black dirt. My flower beds were thick with night crawlers, all of them close to the surface after the rain, and when we ripped weeds from the soil, they writhed pale and fat in the hard light. I knew almost nothing of Alafair's life before she came to Annie and me, but work must have been a natural part of it, because she treated almost any task that I gave her as a game and did it enthusiastically in a happy and innocent way. She worked her way through the rosebushes on all fours, pinging the weeds and Johnsongrass loudly in the bucket, a smear of dirt above one eyebrow. The smell of the hydrangeas and the wet earth was so strong and fecund it was almost like a drug. Then the breeze came up and blew through the pecan trees in the front yard; out on the edge of the trees' shade my neighbor's water sprinkler spun in the sunlight and floated across my fence in a rainbow mist.

They came just before noon. The two Lafayette plainclothes detectives were in an unmarked car, followed by the Iberia Parish sheriff, who drove a patrol car. They parked next to my truck and walked across the dead pecan leaves toward me. Both of the plainclothes were big men who left their coats in the car and wore their badges on their belts. Each carried a chrome-plated revolver in a clip-on holster. I rose to my feet, brushing the dirt off my knees. Alafair had stopped weeding and was staring at the men with her mouth parted.

'You've got a warrant?' I said.

One of the plainclothes had a matchstick in his mouth. He nodded without speaking.

'Okay, no problem. I'll need a few minutes, all right?'

'You got somebody to take care of the little girl?' his partner said. A Marine Corps emblem was tattooed on one of his forearms and a dagger with a bleeding heart impaled upon it on the other.

'Yes. That's why I need a minute or so,' I said. I took Alafair by the hand and turned toward the house. 'You want to come in with me?'

'Lean up against the porch rail,' the man with the matchstick said.

'Can't you guys show some discretion here?' I said. I looked at my friend the sheriff, who stood in the background, saying nothing.

'What the fuck are you talking about?' the tattooed man said.

'Watch your language,' I said.

I felt Alafair's hand close tightly in mine. The other detective took the matchstick out of his mouth.

'Put your hands on the porch rail, spread your feet,' he said, and took Alafair by her other hand and began to pull her away from me.

I pointed my finger at him.

'You're mishandling this. Back off,' I said.

Then I felt the other man shove me hard in the back, pushing me off-balance through the hydrangeas into the steps. I heard his pistol come out of his leather holster, felt his hand clamp down on my neck as he stuck the barrel of the revolver behind my ear.

'You're under arrest for murder. You think being an ex-cop lets you write the rules?' he said.

Out of the corner of my eye I saw Alafair staring at us with the stunned, empty expression of a person wakened from a nightmare.

They booked me into the parish jail on top of the old courthouse in the middle of Lafayette's original town square. The jail was an ancient one, the iron doors and bars and walls painted battleship gray. The words 'Negro Male' were still faintly visible on the door of one of the tanks. During the ride from New Iberia I had sat handcuffed in the back of the car, asking the detectives who it was I had killed. They responded with the silence and indifference with which almost all cops treat a suspect after he's in custody. Finally I gave up and sat back against the seat cushion, the cuffs biting into my wrists, and stared at the oak trees flicking past the window.

Now I had been fingerprinted and photographed, had turned over my wallet, pocket change, keys, belt, even my scapular chain, to a deputy who put them in a large manila envelope, realizing even then that something important was missing, something that would have a terrible bearing on my situation, yes, my Puma knife; and now the jailer and the detective who chewed on matchsticks were about to lock me in a six-cell area that was reserved for the violent and the insane. The jailer turned the key on the large, flat iron door that contained one narrow viewing slit, pulled it open wide, and pushed lightly on my back with his fingers.

'Who the hell was it?' I said to the detective.

'You must be a special kind of a guy, Robicheaux,' he said. 'You cut a guy from his scrot to sternum and don't bother to get his name. Dalton Vidrine.'

The jailer clanged the door behind me, turned the key, shot the steel lock bar, and I walked into my new home.

It was little different from any other jail that I had seen or even been locked in during my drinking years. The toilets stank, the air smelled of stale sweat and cigarette smoke and mattresses that had turned black with body grease. The walls were scratched with names, peace signs, and drawings of male and female genitalia. More enterprising people had climbed on top of the cells and burned their names across the ceiling with cigarette lighters. On the floor area around the main door was a 'deadline,' a white line painted in a rectangle, inside of which no one had better be standing when the door swung open or while the trusties were serving out of the food cart.

But the people in that six-cell area were not the ordinary residents of a city or parish prison. One was an enormous demented Negro by the name of Jerome who had smothered his infant child. He told me later that a cop had worked him over with a baton; although he had been in jail two weeks, there were still purple gashes on his lips and lumps the size of birds' eggs on his nappy head. I would come to know the others, too: a biker from New Orleans who had nailed a girl's hands to a tree; a serial rapist and sodomist who was wanted in Alabama; a Vietnamese thug who, with another man, had garroted his business partner with jump cables for a car battery; and a four-time loser, a fat, grinning, absolutely vacant-eyed man who had murdered a whole family after escaping from Sugarland Farm in Texas.

I was given one phone call and I telephoned the best firm in Lafayette. Like all people who get into serious trouble with the law, I became immediately aware of the incredible financial burden that had been dropped upon me. The lawyer's retainer was $2,000, his ongoing fee $125 an hour. I felt as though my head were full of spiders as it tried to think in terms of raising that kind of money, particularly in view of the fact that my bail hadn't been set and I had no idea how high it would be.

I found out at my arraignment the next morning: $150,000. I felt the blood drain out of my face. The lawyer asked for bail reduction and argued that I was a local businessman, an ex-police officer, a property owner, a war veteran, and the judge propped his chin on one knuckle and looked back at him as impassively as a man waiting for an old filmstrip to run itself out.

We all rose, the judge left the bench, and I sat dazed and light-headed in a chair next to the lawyer while a deputy prepared to cuff me for the trip back to jail. The lawyer motioned to the deputy with two fingers.

'Give us a minute, please,' he said. He was an older, heavyset man, with thinning cropped red hair, who wore seersucker suits and clip-on bow ties.

The deputy nodded and stepped back by the side door to the courtroom.

'It's the pictures,' he said. 'Vidrine's entrails are hanging out in the bathtub. It's mean stuff to look at, Mr Robicheaux. And they've got your knife with your prints on it.'

'It must have fallen out of my pocket. Both of those guys were all over me.'

'That's not what Mapes says. The bartender has some pretty bad things to say, too. What'd you do to him?'

'Told him he was going to be busted for procuring.'

'Well, I can discredit him on the stand. But Mapes—' He clicked his tongue against the roof of his mouth. 'There's the fellow we have to break down. A man with chain burns all over his face and back can make a hell of a witness. Tell me, what in God's name did you have in mind when you went through that door?'

My palms were damp. I swallowed and wiped them on my trousers.

'Mapes knew Vidrine was a weak sister,' I said. 'After I was gone, he picked up my knife and took him out. That's what happened, Mr Gautreaux.'

He drummed his fingers on the arm of the chair, made a pocket of air in his jaw, cleared his throat and started to speak, then was silent. Finally, he stood up, patted me on the shoulder, and walked out the side door of the courtroom into the sunlight, into the wind ruffling the leaves of the oak trees, the noise of black kids roaring by on skateboards. The deputy lifted my arm and crimped one cuff around my wrist.

Batist and his wife kept Alafair with them the day I was arrested, but the next day I arranged for her to stay with my cousin, a retired schoolteacher in New Iberia. She was taken care of temporarily, Batist was running the dock, and my main worry had become money. Besides needing a huge unknown sum for the lawyer, I had to raise $15,000 for the bondsman's fee in order to make bail. I had $8,000 in savings.

My half brother, Jimmie, who owned all or part of

several restaurants in New Orleans, would have written a check for the whole amount, but he had gone to Europe for three months, and the last his partners heard from him he was traveling through France with a group of Basque jai alai players. I then discovered the bankers whom I had known for years were not anxious to lend money to a man who was charged with first-degree murder and whose current address was the parish jail. I had been locked up nine days, and Batist was still visiting banks and delivering loan papers to me.

Our cells were unlocked at seven A.M. when a trusty and the night screw wheeled in the food cart, which every morning was stacked with aluminum containers of grits, coffee, and fried pork butts. Until lockup at five in the afternoon, we were free to move around in an area called the bull run, take showers, play cards with a deck whose missing members had been replaced with cards fashioned out of penciled cardboard, or stare listlessly out the window at the tops of the trees on the courthouse lawn. But most of the time I stayed in my cell, filling out loan applications or reading a stiffened, water-stained issue of *Reader's Digest*.

I was sitting on the side of my iron bunk, which hung from the wall on chains, printing across the top of an application, when a shadow moved across the page. Silhouetted in the open door of my cell was the biker who had nailed his girl's hands to a tree. He was thick-bodied and shirtless, his breasts covered with tattooed birds, and his uncut hair and wild beard made his head look as though it were surrounded by a mane. I could feel his eyes move across the side of my face, peel away tissue, probe for the soft organ, the character weakness, the severed nerve.

'You think you can cut it up there?' he said.

I wet my pencil tip and kept on writing without looking up.

'What place is that?' I said.

'Angola. You think you can hack it?'

'I'm not planning on being there.'

'That's what I said my first jolt. Next stop, three years up in the Block with the big stripes. They got some badass dudes there, man.'

I turned to the next page and tried to concentrate on the printed words.

'The night screw says you're an ex-cop,' he said.

I sat my pencil down and looked at the opposite wall.

'Does that make a problem for you?' I said.

'Not me, man. But there's some mean fuckers up on that farm. There's guys that'll run by your cell and throw a gasoline bomb in on you. Melt you into grease.'

'I don't want to be rude, but you're standing in my light.'

He grinned, and there was a malevolent light in his face. Then he stretched, yawned, laughed outright as though he were witnessing an absurdity of some kind, and walked away to the window that gave on to the courthouse lawn.

I did push-ups, I did curls by lifting the bunk with my fingertips, I took showers, and I slept as much as I could. At night I could hear the others breaking wind, talking to themselves, masturbating, snoring. The enormous Negro sometimes sang a song that began, 'My soul is in a paper bag at the bottom of your garbage can.' Then one night he went crazy in his cell, gripping the bars with both hands and bashing his head against them until blood and sweat were flying out into the bull run and we heard the screw shoot the steel lock bar on the door.

On the thirteenth day I received two visitors I wasn't prepared for. A deputy escorted me down the spiral metal stairs to a windowless room that was used as a visiting area for those of us who were charged with violent crimes. Sitting at a wood table scarred with cigarette burns were Dixie Lee Pugh, one arm in a sling, his yellow hair crisscrossed with bandages, and my old homicide partner, Cletus Purcel. As always, Clete looked too big for his shirt, his sport coat, the tie that was pulled loose from his throat, the trousers that climbed above his socks. His cigarette looked tiny in his hand, the stitched scar through his eyebrow a cosmetic distraction from the physical confidence and humor in his face.

Clete, old friend, why did you throw it in?

They were both smiling so broadly they might have been at a party. I smelled beer on Dixie's breath. I sat down at the table, and the deputy locked a barred door behind me and sat on a chair outside.

'You made your bail all right, huh, Dixie?' I said.

He wore a maroon shirt hanging outside his gray slacks, and one foot was bandaged and covered with two athletic socks. His stomach made a thick roll against the bottom of his shirt.

'Better than that, Dave. They cut me loose.'

'They did what?'

'I'm out of it. Free and clear. They dropped the

possessions charge.' He was looking at the expression on my face.

'They lost interest,' Clete said.

'Oh? How's that?'

'Come on, Dave. Lighten up. You know how it works,' Clete said.

'No, I think my education is ongoing here.'

'We already have a firm on retainer in New Orleans, and I hired the best in Lafayette. You know these local guys aren't going to get tied up in court for months over a chickenshit holding bust.'

'Who's this "we" you're talking about? What the hell are you doing with Dixie Lee?' I said.

'He's got a friend. I work for the friend. The friend doesn't like to see Dixie Lee suffering a lot of bullshit he doesn't deserve. You don't deserve it, either, Dave.'

'You work for this character Dio?'

'He's not such a bad guy. Look, there's not a lot of jobs around for a cop who had to blow the country, uh, with a few loose ends lying around.'

'How'd you get out of it? I thought there was still a warrant on you.'

'You've never learned, partner. First, they didn't have dog-doo to go on. Second, and this is what you don't understand, nobody cares about a guy like that. The best part of that guy ran down his daddy's leg. He met a bad fate. He should have met it earlier. The world goes on.'

'Do you know what he's talking about?' I said to Dixie Lee.

'It's his business,' he said quietly, and took a cigarette out of his pocket so that his eyes avoided mine.

'Forget the past, Dave. It's a decaying memory. That's

what you used to tell me, right? Great fucking line. Let's look at the problem we got now, namely, getting your butt out of here. I hear they've got you in a special place with the lovelies.'

I didn't answer. Both of them looked at my face, then Dixie's eyes wandered around the room.

'Come on, Streak, be my mellow man for a few minutes,' Clete said.

When Dixie Lee's eyes lighted on mine again, I said, 'To tell you the truth, Dixie, I feel like killing you.'

'So he feels bad. What the fuck's he supposed to do? Go to prison?' Clete said. 'Look, I was coming here on my own, anyway, but as soon as I got him kicked loose he told me we got to get your ass out, too. That's a fact.'

'You got the right to be mad,' Dixie Lee said to me. 'I got a way of pissing in the soup, and then everybody's got to drink out of it. I just didn't know you were going to—'

'What?' I said.

'Hell, I don't know. Whatever it was you did in that motel room. Lord, Dave, I heard a cop say they stuck Vidrine's guts back in his stomach with a trowel.'

'That was Mapes's work, not mine.'

I could see the amusement in Clete's face.

'Sorry,' he said. Then he laughed. 'But let's face it. I remember a couple of occasions when you really decorated the walls.'

'This wasn't one of them.'

'Whatever you say. Who cares anyway? The guy was a bucket of shit,' Clete said. 'Let's talk about getting you out of the zoo.'

'Wait a minute. You knew Vidrine?'

'Montana's a small community in a lot of ways. You'd like it there. I rent a place from Sally Dee right on Flathead Lake.'

'You used to hate those guys, Clete.'

'Yeah . . . well,' he said, and sucked his teeth. 'The CIA deals dope, guys in the White House run guns. You used to say it yourself – we keep the lowlifes around so we can have a dartboard we can hit.'

'Where'd you hook up with this guy?'

'Sal?' He scraped a piece of paint on the table with his fingernail. 'I've got a brother-in-law who's connected in Galveston. He got me a job dealing blackjack in one of Sal's places in Vegas. After a month they moved me up into house security. Most of the rent-a-cops in Vegas have chewing gum for brains. It's like running for president against Harpo Marx. In six months I was in charge of security for the whole casino. Now I do whatever needs doing – Vegas, Tahoe, Flathead.' He looked up at me. 'It beats cleaning up puke in a john, which is what I was doing in a dump over in Algiers. Look, you want out of here?'

'Hell, no, Clete. The ambience really grows on you.'

'I can do it in twenty minutes.'

'You're going to put up fifteen thousand?'

'I don't have to. There's a couple of bondsmen here who'd love to do a favor for Sally Dee. Why not? It doesn't cost them anything. Unless you jump the bond.'

'Let him do it for you, Dave,' Dixie Lee said.

'I think I'm going to have to sweat this one out.'

'Why? You got to prove you're an honest man?' Clete said.

'Thanks just the same, Cletus.'

'You're pissing me off. You think I'm trying to sign you up for the Mafia or something?'

'I don't know what you're trying to do. In fact, I don't understand anything you've done.'

'Maybe it's because you're not listening too well.'

'Maybe so.'

He lit a cigarette and flipped the burnt match against the wall. He blew smoke out his nose.

'There's no strings,' he said.

'Come on.'

'You got my word.'

'They'll boil you down to glue, Clete. Bartend in Algiers, sell debit insurance. Just get away from them.'

'I thought maybe I could make up for some bad things I did to you, partner.'

'I don't hold a grudge.'

'You never forget anything, Dave. You store it up in you and feed it and stoke it until it's a furnace.'

'I'm changing.'

'Yeah, that's why they got you locked up with the shitbags.'

'What can I say?'

'Nothing,' Clete said. 'Here's my cigarettes. Trade them to the geeks for their food.'

'Dave, I'd go your bond if I had the money,' Dixie Lee said. 'But if I stepped on a dime right now, I could tell you if it was heads or tails.'

'But the man's not hearing us,' Clete said. 'Right, Dave? You're up on the high road, and the rest of us sweaty bastards have to toil our way through the flies.'

He went to the door and banged the side of his fist against one of the bars.

'Open up,' he said.

'I'm sorry,' I said.

'Yeah, yeah, yeah. Write me a postcard. Polson, Montana, in fact, if you get out of this dog shit, come see me. The beer's cold, you got to knock the trout back in the lake with an oar. A reasonable person might even say it's better than taking showers with queers and child molesters. But what do I know?'

He mashed his cigarette out on the concrete floor while the deputy unlocked the door. The deputy took him and Dixie Lee downstairs in the elevator, and I sat alone in the room, waiting for the deputy to return, my back bent over, my forearms propped loosely on my thighs, my eyes staring at the tiny webbed cracks in the floor.

The next day two deputies brought Jerome back from the jail ward at the charity hospital. The stitches on his forehead looked like small black butterflies laced in his skin. He stared out the windows, talked to himself, urinated on the floor of his cell. The biker and the rapist from Alabama told him the jailer had left the key to the main door in the toilet. He knelt by the bowl, staring into the water, while the other two encouraged him.

'You can't see it. It's way down in the pipe,' the biker said, and grabbed himself and grinned at the other man.

Jerome's arm went into the bowl, and he worked his hand down deep in the drain, splashing water up on his shirt and face.

I put my hands on his shoulders. He looked up at me with his mouth open, his tongue pink and thick on his bottom teeth.

'Don't do that, Jerome. There's no key in there,' I said.

'What?' he said. He talked like a man who was drugged.

'Take off your shirt and wash yourself in the shower,' I said. 'Come on, walk over here with me.'

'We're just giving the cat a little hope,' the biker said.

'Your comedy act is over,' I said.

The biker wore black sunglasses. He looked at me silently and worked his tongue around his gums. The hair on his face and head looked like brown springs.

'Wrong place to be telling people shit,' he said.

I released Jerome's arm and turned back toward the biker.

'Go ahead,' I said.

'Go ahead, what?'

'Say something else clever.'

'What are you talking about, man?'

'I want you to get in my face one more time.'

I couldn't see his eyes behind the sunglasses, but his mouth was as still as though it had been painted on his skin.

Then he said, because the others were watching him, 'We're a family here, man. That's how you hack it inside. You don't know that, you ain't gonna make it.'

I turned on the shower for Jerome, helped him pull off his shirt, and gave him a bar of soap from my cell. Then I picked up my tin plate and banged it loudly on the main door. It didn't take long for the jailer to open up. I was standing inside the deadline when he did.

His lean face was electric with outrage.

'What the hell do you think you're doing, Robicheaux?' he said.

'You've got a retarded man here who's being abused

by other inmates. Either put him in isolation or send him to Mandeville.'

'Get your ass back across that line.'

'Fuck you.'

'That's it. You're going into lockdown,' he said, and slammed the iron door.

I turned around and stared into the grinning face of the four-time loser who had murdered a family after breaking out of Sugarland. He was completely naked, and the huge rolls of fat on his thighs and stomach hung off his frame almost like curtains. His eyes were pale, empty of all emotion, but his mouth was as red as a clown's. He took a puff of his cigarette and said, 'Sounds like you're getting pretty ripe, buddy.'

Then he laughed so hard, his eyes squinted shut with glee, that tears ran down his round cheeks.

Fifteen minutes later they moved me into a small room that contained a two-bunk cage, perforated with small squares and covered with thick layers of white paint that had been chipped and scratched with graffiti and prisoners' names. Years ago the cage had been used to hold men awaiting execution in the days when the electric chair, with two huge generators, traveled from parish to parish under tarpaulins on the back of a semi truck. Now it was used to house troublemakers and the uncontrollable. I was told that I would spend the next five days there, would have no visitors other than my lawyer, would take no showers, and would receive one meal a day at a time of my choosing.

That afternoon Batist tried to visit me and was turned away, but a Negro trusty brought me an envelope that contained a half-dozen crayon-filled pages from Alafair's coloring book, along with a note that she had printed out on lined paper. The colored-in pages showed palm trees and blue water, a lake full of fish, a brown horse by whose head she had written the word 'Tex.' Her note read: *I can spell. I can spell ant in the can. I can spell cat in the hat. I love Dave. I don't say ain't no more. Love. Alafair.*

I hung the coloring-book pages on the inside of the cage by pressing their edges under the iron seams at the tops of the walls. It started to rain, and mist blew through the window and glistened on the bars. I unrolled the thin striped mattress on the bottom bunk and tried to sleep. I was unbelievably tired, but I couldn't tell you from what. Maybe it was because you never really sleep in a jail. Iron doors slam all day and night; drunks shake doors against the jambs, and irritated street cops retaliate by raking their batons across the bars; people are gang-banged and sodomized in the shower, their cries lost in the clouds of steam dancing off the tiles; the crazies howl their apocalyptic insight from the windows like dogs baying under a yellow moon.

But it was an even deeper fatigue, one that went deep into the bone, that left the muscles as flaccid as if they had been traversed by worms. It was a mood that I knew well, and it always descended upon me immediately before I began a two-day bender. I felt a sense of failure, moral lassitude, defeat, and fear that craved only one release. In my troubled dream I tried to will myself into one of the pages from Alafair's coloring book – onto a stretch of beach dotted with palm trees, the sun hot on my bare shoulders while flecks of rain struck coldly on my skin. The water was blue and green, and red clouds of kelp were floating in the ground swell. Alafair rode her horse bareback along the edge of the surf, her mouth wide with a smile, her hair black and shiny in the sunlight.

But the pure lines of the dream wouldn't hold, and suddenly I was pouring rum into a cracked coconut shell and drinking from it with both hands. Like the sun and the rain, it was cool and warm at the same time, and it lighted my desires the way you touch a match to old newspaper stored in a dry box. I traveled to lowlife New Orleans and Saigon bars, felt a woman's breath on my neck, her mouth on my ear, her hand brush my sex. Topless girls in G-strings danced barefooted on a purple-lit runway, the cigarette smoke drifting across their breasts and braceleted arms. I knocked back double shots of Beam with draft chasers, held on to the edge of the bar like a man in a gale, and looked at their brown bodies, the watery undulations of their stomachs, their eyes that were as inviting as the sweet odor of burning opium.

Then I was back on the beach, alone, trembling with a hangover. The back of Alafair's horse was empty, and he was shaking the loose reins against his neck and snorting with his nose down by the edge of the surf.

Don't lose it all, I heard Annie say.

Where is she?

She'll be back. But you've got to get your shit together, sailor.

I'm afraid.

Of what?

They're serious. They're talking about life in Angola. That's ten and a half years with good time. They've got the knife and the witnesses to pull it off, too. I don't think I'm going to get out of this one.

Sure you will.

I'd be drunk now if I was out of jail.

Maybe. But you don't know that. Easy does it and one day at a time. Right? But no more boozing and whoring in your dreams.

Annie, I didn't do it, did I?

It's not your style, baby love. The rain's starting to slack and I have to go. Be good, darlin'.

I woke sweating in a bright shaft of sunlight through the window. I sat on the side of my bunk, my palms clenched on the iron edges, my mind a tangle of snakes. It was hot, the room was dripping with humidity, but I trembled all over as though a cold wind were blowing across my body. The water faucet in my rust-streaked sink ticked as loudly as a clock.

Two days later my loan was approved at a New Iberia bank, and fifteen minutes after I paid the bondsman's fee I was sprung. It was raining hard when I ran from the courthouse to the pickup truck with my paper sack of soiled clothes and toilet articles under my arm. Alafair hugged me in the snug, dry enclosure of the truck, and Batist lit a cigar and blew the smoke out his teeth as though we all had a lock on the future.

I should have been happy. But I remembered a scene I had witnessed years ago when I was a young patrolman in New Orleans. A bunch of Black Panthers had just been brought back to a holding cell on a wrist chain from morning arraignment, and their public defender was trying to assure them that they would be treated fairly.

'Believe it or not, our system works,' he said to them through the bars.

An unshaved black man in shades, beret, and black leather jacket rolled a matchstick across his tongue and said, 'You got it, motherfucker. And it *work* for somebody else.'

chapter five

Once out of jail I felt like the soldier who returns to the war and discovers that the battlefield is empty, that everyone else has tired of the war except him and gone home.

Dixie Lee had left a note at the house the day before:

Dave,
What I done to you grieves me. That's the honest to God truth, son. I got no excuse except everything I touch turns to shit. I'm leaving a box of milky ways for the little girl that lives with you. Big deal. Me and Clete and his lady friend are headed for the big sky today. Maybe later I might get a gig at one of Sals casinos. Like my daddy used to say, it don't matter if we're colored or not, we all got to pick the white mans cotton. You might as well pick it in the shade next to the water barrel.

Dave, dont do time.

Dixie Lee

And what about Harry Mapes, the man whose testimony could send me to Angola? (I could still smell his odor from the motel room – a mixture of rut, perfume from the whores, chlorine, bourbon and tobacco and breath mints.) I called Star Drilling Company in Lafayette.

'Mr Mapes is in Montana,' the receptionist said.

'Where in Montana?'

'Who is this, please?'

'An acquaintance who would like to talk with him.'

'You'll have to speak to Mr Hollister. Just a moment, please.'

Before I could stop her he was on the line.

'I need to know where Mapes is. Deposition time and all that,' I said.

'What?'

'You heard me.'

There was a pause.

'Is this Robicheaux?' he asked.

'If we don't get it from you, we'll get it from the prosecutor's office.'

'The only thing I'll tell you is that I think you're a sick and dangerous man. I don't know how they let you out of jail, but you stay away from my people.'

'You have Academy Award potential, Hollister,' I said. But he hung up.

I worked in the bait shop, shoed Alafair's horse, weeded the vegetable garden, cleaned the leaves out of the rain gutters and the coulee, tore down the old windmill and hauled it to the scrapyard. I tried to concentrate on getting through the day in an orderly fashion and not think about the sick feeling that hung like a vapor around my heart. But my trial was six weeks away and the clock was ticking.

Then one bright morning I was stacking cartons of red wrigglers on a shelf in the bait shop and one spilled out of my hand and burst open on the countertop. The worms were thin and bright red in the dark mixture of loam and coffee grounds, and I was picking them up individually with my fingertips and dropping them back in the carton when I felt that sickness around my heart again and heard the words in my head: *They're going to do it. In five and a half weeks.*

I had no defense except my own word, that of an alcoholic ex-cop with a history of violence who was currently undergoing psychotherapy. My trial wouldn't last more than three days, then I would be locked on a wrist chain in the back of a prison van and on my way to Angola.

'What's wrong your face, Dave?' Batist said.

I swallowed and looked at my palms. They were bright with a thin sheen of sweat.

I went up to the house, packed two suitcases, took my .45 automatic out of the dresser drawer, folded a towel around it, snapped it inside a suitcase pouch with two loaded clips and a box of hollow-points, and called the bondsman in Lafayette. I had known him for twenty-five years. His name was Butter Bean Verret; he wasn't much taller than a fire hydrant, wore tropical suits, neckties with palm trees painted on them, rings all over his fingers, and ate butter beans and ham hocks with a spoon in the same café every day of his life.

'What's happening, Butter Bean? I need to get off the leash,' I said.

'Where you going?'

'Montana.'

'What they got up there we ain't got here?'

'How about it, partner?'

He was quiet a moment.

'You're not going to let me get lonely down here, are

you? You're gonna call me, right? Every four, five days you gone, maybe.'

'You got it.'

'Dave?'

'What?'

'You done got yourself in a mess here in Lou'sana. Don't make no mo' mess up there, no.'

I told Batist that I was leaving him and Clarise in charge of the dock, my house and animals, that I would call him every few days.

'What you gonna do Alafair?' he said.

'My cousin will keep her in New Iberia.'

He made a pretense of wiping off the counter with a rag. His blue cotton work shirt was unbuttoned, and his stomach muscles ridged above his belt buckle. He put a gumdrop in the side of his mouth and looked out the window at the bayou as though I were not there.

'All right, what's wrong?' I said.

'You got to ask me that?'

'I have to do it, Batist. They're going to send me to prison. I'm looking at ten and a half years. That's with good time.'

'That don't make it right.'

'What am I supposed to do?'

'Her whole life people been leaving her, Dave. Her mama, Miz Annie, you in the jail. She don't need no mo' of it, no.'

I filled up the truck at the dock and waited on the gallery for the school bus. At four o'clock it stopped in the leafy shade by the mailbox, and Alafair walked through the pecan trees toward me, her tin lunch box clanging against her thigh. Her tan skin was dark in the shadows. As always, she could read a disturbed thought in my face no matter how well I concealed it.

I explained to her that I had to leave, that it wouldn't be for long, that sometimes we simply had to do things that we didn't like.

'Cousin Tutta is always nice to you, isn't she?' I said.

'Yes.'

'She takes you to the show and out to the park, just like I do, doesn't she?'

'Yes.'

'Batist will come get you to ride Tex, too. That'll be all right, won't it?'

This time she didn't answer. Instead she sat quietly beside me on the stoop and looked woodenly at the rabbit hutches and Tripod eating out of his bowl under the pecan tree. Then pale spots formed in her cheeks, and the skin around her bottom lip and chin began to pucker. I put my arm around her shoulders and looked away from her face.

'Little guy, we just have to be brave about some things,' I said. 'I've got some big problems to take care of. That's just the way it is.'

Then I felt incredibly presumptuous, vain, and stupid in talking to her about bravery and acceptance. She had experienced a degree of loss and violence in her short life that most people can only appreciate in their nightmares.

I stared across the road at a blue heron rising from the bayou into the sunlight.

'Have you ever seen snow?' I said.

'No.'

'I bet there's still snow on the ground in Montana. In the ponderosa and the spruce, high up on the mountain.

I went out there once with a friend from the army. I think you and I had better go check that out, little guy.'

'See snow?'

'You better believe it.'

Her teeth were white and her eyes were squinted almost shut with her smile.

By that evening we were highballing through the red-clay piney woods of East Texas, the warm wind blowing through the open truck windows, the engine humming under the hood, the inside of the cab aglow with the purple twilight.

We rode into the black, rain-swept night until the sky began to clear out in the Panhandle and the moon broke through the clouds in a spoked wheel of silver over the high plains. The next day, outside of Raton, New Mexico, I bought a bucket of fried chicken and we ate in a grove of cottonwoods by a stream and slept four hours on a blanket in the grass. Then we climbed out of the mesa country into Trinidad, Colorado, and the tumbling blue-green roll of the Rocky Mountains, through Pueblo, Denver, and finally southern Wyoming, where the evening air turned cold and smelled of sage, and the arroyo-cut land and buttes were etched with fire in the sunset. That night we stayed in a motel run by Indians; in the morning it rained and you could smell bacon curing in a smokehouse.

We crossed into Mountain south of Billings, and the land began to change. It was green and rolling, the rivers slow-moving and lined with cottonwood and willow trees, with sharp-toothed mountains in the distance. Then as we headed toward the Continental Divide the rivers became wider with the spring runoff, roiling in the center, flooding the trees along the banks, and the mountains in the distance tumbled higher and higher against the sky, their crests still packed with snow, the slopes covered with ponderosa pine and Douglas fir and blue spruce. Alafair slept on the seat beside me, her head on a comic book, while I topped the Divide outside of Butte and began the long grade down the western slope toward Missoula. White-tailed deer grazed near the road in the evening shadows, their heads flickering at me as I roared past them. Log ranch houses were set back against the base of the hills, their windows lighted, smoke flattening off their stone chimneys.

I followed the Clark Fork River through a cut in the mountains called Hellgate Canyon, and suddenly under a bowl of dark sky the city spilled out in a shower of light all the way across the valley floor. Missoula was a sawmill and university town, filled with trees and flowers, old brick homes, wooded parks, intersecting rivers glazed with neon light, the tinge of processed wood pulp, rows of bars where bikers hung in the doorways and the rock music thundered out into the street. My palms were thick and ringing with the pressure of the steering wheel, my ears almost deaf from the long hours of road wind. When I climbed the motel stairs with Alafair asleep on my shoulder, I looked out over the night sheen of the river, at the circle of mountains around the town and the way the timber climbed to the crests, and I wondered if I had any chance at all of having a normal life again, of being an ordinary person who lived in an ordered town like this and who did not wake up each morning with his fears sitting collectively on his chest like a grinning gargoyle.

*

All of my present troubles had begun with Dixie Lee Pugh, and I felt that their solution would have to begin with him, too. But first I had to make living arrangements for Alafair and me. One of the advantages of being Catholic is that you belong to the western world's largest private club. Not all of its members are the best or most likeable people, but many of them are. I rented a small yellow-brick house, with maple and birch trees in the yard, in a working-class neighborhood by the river, only two blocks away from a Catholic church and elementary school. The pastor called the principal at Alafair's school in New Iberia, asked to have her records sent to the rectory, then admitted her to the first-grade class. Then he recommended his housekeeper's widowed sister, who lived next door to the rectory, as a baby-sitter. She was a red-complected, bovine, and good-natured Finnish woman, and she said she could take care of Alafair almost any afternoon or evening, and in case I had to go out of town overnight, Alafair could stay at her house.

I bought Alafair a new lunch box, crayons, pencils, and a notebook, and on our third morning in town, I walked her down the tree-lined street to the schoolyard and watched her form in ranks with the other children while a lay teacher waited to lead them in the Pledge of Allegiance. Drinking a cup of coffee on the front steps of my home, I watched the high, brown current of the river froth around the concrete pilings of a railway bridge and the sun break above Hellgate Canyon and fall across the valley, lighting the maples as though their leaves were waxed. Then I chewed on a matchstick and studied the backs of my hands. Finally, when I could delay it no longer, in the way you finally accept major surgery or embark on a long journey that requires much more energy than you possess, I got in my truck and headed for the town of Polson and Flathead Lake and the home of Sally Dio.

The Jocko Valley was ranch and feed-grower country, covered with large areas of sun and shadow; the river ran along the side of the highway and was tea-colored with a pebbled bottom and bordered with willows and cottonwoods. In the distance the Mission Mountains rose up blue and snowcapped and thunderous against the sky. The rural towns were full of Indians in work denims, curled-brim straw hats, heel-worn cowboy boots, and pickup trucks, and when I stopped for gas they looked through me as though I were made of smoky glass. There were lakes surrounded by cattails set back against the mountain range, and high up on the cliffs long stretches of waterfall were frozen solid in the sunlight like enormous white teeth.

I passed a Job Corps camp and an old Jesuit mission, and followed the highway over a pine-covered hill. Suddenly I saw Flathead Lake open up before me, so blue and immense and dancing with sunlight that it looked like the Pacific Ocean. Young pines grew on the slopes of the hills above the beaches, and the eastern shore was covered with cherry orchards. Out in the lake were islands with gray cliffs and trees rooted among the rocks, and a red sailboat was tacking between two islands, clouds of spray bursting on its bow.

I stopped in Polson, which was at the south end of the lake, and asked a filling station operator for directions to Sal Dio's house. He took a cigar out of his mouth, looked at me, looked at my license plate, and nodded up the road.

'It's about two miles,' he said.

'Which side of the road?'

'Somebody up there can tell you.'

I drove up the road between the cherry orchards and the lake, then passed a blue inlet, a restaurant built out over the water, a strip of white beach enclosed by pine trees, until I saw a mailbox with the name Dio on it and a sign that said Private Road. I turned into the dirt lane and started up an incline toward a split-level redwood home that was built on a triangular piece of land jutting out above the lake. But up ahead was an electronically operated iron gate that was locked shut, and between the gate and the lake was a small redwood house whose veranda was extended on pilings over the edge of the cliff. It was obvious that the small and the large houses had been designed by the same architect.

I stopped the truck at the gate, turned off the engine, and got out. I saw a dark-skinned girl with black hair looking at me from the veranda of the small house; then she went inside through sliding glass doors and Clete walked out in a pair of Bermuda shorts, a T-shirt that exposed his bulging stomach, a crushed porkpie fishing hat, and a powder-blue windbreaker that didn't conceal his revolver and nylon shoulder holster.

He walked across the lawn and down the hill to the road.

'Man, I don't believe it. Did they cut you loose?' he said.

'I'm out on bond.'

'Out on bond and out of the state? That doesn't

sound right, Streak.' He was grinning at me in the sunlight.

'I know the bondsman.'

'You want to go fishing?'

'I need to talk to Dixie Lee.'

'You came to the right place. He's up there with Sally.'

'I need to talk to you, too.'

'Sounds like our First District days.'

'It becomes that way when you're about to do a jolt in Angola.'

'Come on, it's not going to happen. You had provocation to go after those guys. Then it was two against one, and finally it's your word against Mapes's about the shank. Besides, check out Mapes's record. He's a sick motherfucker if you ask me. Wait till your lawyer cross-examines him on the stand. The guy's as likeable as shit on melba toast.'

'That's another thing that bothers me, Cletus – how you know about these guys.'

'It's no mystery, partner,' he said, and took a package of Lucky Strikes out of his windbreaker pocket. The outline of his revolver was blue and hard against the nylon holster. 'Dixie Lee brought them around a couple times. They liked to cop a few free lines off Sal and hang around some of those rock people he's always flying in. Sal collects rock people. Vidrine was a fat dimwit, but Mapes should have been eased off the planet a long time ago.'

The skin of Clete's face was tight as he lit his cigarette and looked off at the lake.

'It sounds personal,' I said.

'He got coked to the eyes one night and started

talking about blowing up a VC nurse in a spider hole. Then he tried to take Darlene into the bedroom. Right there in the living room, like she was anybody's punch.'

'Who?'

'She's the girl who lives with me. Anyway, Sal told me to walk him down the road until he was sober. When I got him outside he tried to swing on me. I got him right on the mouth. With a roll of quarters in my hand. Dixie had to take him to the hospital in Polson.'

'I think you ought to have an early change of life.'

'Yeah, you were always big on advice, Dave. You see this .38 I have on? I have a permit to carry it in three states. That's because I work for Sally Dee. But I can't work as a cop anywhere. So the same people who won't let me work as a crossing guard license me to carry a piece for Sal. Does that tell you something? Anyway, I'm using the shortened version of your AA serenity prayer these days – "Fuck it." '

'Do I get through the gate?'

He blew cigarette smoke out into the wind. His green eyes were squinted, as though the sun hurt them, as though a rusted piece of wire were buried deeply in the soft tissue of his brain.

'Yeah, come on up to the house. I have to call up to Sal's,' he said. 'Meet Darlene. Eat lunch with us if you like. Believe it or not, I'm glad to see you.'

I didn't want to have lunch with them, and I surely didn't want to meet Sally Dio. I only wanted for Dixie Lee to walk down to Clete's and talk with me, and then I would be on my way. But it wasn't going to work out that way.

'They're just getting up. Sal said to bring you up in

about an hour,' Clete said, hanging up the phone in his living room. 'They had a big gig last night. Have you ever met the Tahoe crowd? For some reason they make me think of people cornholing each other.'

His girlfriend, whose full name was Darlene American Horse, was making sandwiches for us in the kitchen. Clete sat in a sway-backed canvas chair with a vodka Collins in his hand, one sandaled foot crossed on his knee, the other on a blond bearskin rug. Outside the sliding glass doors the lake was a deep blue, and the pines on an island of gray boulders were bending in the wind.

'The thing you won't forget,' he said, 'the guy who got whacked out back there in Louisiana – all right, the guy I whacked out – that psychotic sonofabitch Starweather, I *had* to kill him. They said they'd give me ten grand, and I said that's cool, but I was going to run him out of town, take their bread, and tell them to fuck off if they complained about it later. Except he was feeding his pigs out of a bucket with his back to me, telling me how he didn't rattle, how he wouldn't piss on a cop on the pad if he was on fire, then he put his hand down in his jeans and I saw something bright in the sun and heard a click, and when he turned around with it I put a big one in his forehead. It was his Zippo lighter, man. Can you dig that?'

Maybe the story was true, maybe not. I just wasn't interested in his explanation or his obvious obsession, one that left his eyes searching for that next sentence, hanging unformed out there in the air, which would finally set the whole matter straight.

'Why do they call him "the Duck"?' I said.

'What?'

'Why do they call Sally Dio "the Duck"?'

'He wears ducktails.' He took a long drink out of his Collins. His mouth looked red and hard. He shrugged as though dismissing a private, troubling thought. 'There's another story. About a card game and drawing a deuce or something. The deuce is the duck, right? But it's all guinea stuff. They like titles. Those stories are usually bullshit.'

'I tell you, Clete, I'd really appreciate it if you could just bring Dixie Lee down here. I really don't need to meet the whole crowd.'

'You're still the same guy, your meter always on overtime.' Then he smiled. 'Do you think I'm going to call up the man I work for and say, "Sorry, Sal, my old partner here doesn't want to be caught dead in the home of a greaseball"?' He laughed, chewing ice and candied cherries in his jaws. 'But it's a thought, though, isn't it? Dave, you're something else.' He kept smiling at me, the ice cracking between his molars. 'You remember when we cooled out Julio Segura and his bodyguard? We really made the avocado salad fly.'

'Last season's box score.'

'Yeah, it is.' He looked idly out the sliding doors at the lake a moment, then slapped his knee and said, 'Man, let's eat.'

He walked up behind his girlfriend in the kitchen, picked her up around the ribs, and buried his face in her hair. He half walked and carried her back into the living room with his arms still locked around her waist. She turned her face back toward him to hide her embarrassment.

'This is my mainline mama, her reg'lar daddy's sweet little papoose,' he said, and bit the back of her neck.

That's really cool, Cletus, I thought.

She wore a denim skirt with black stockings and a sleeveless tan sweater. There were three moles by the edge of her mouth, and her eyes were turquoise green, like a Creole's. Her hands were big, the backs nicked with gray scars, the nails cut back to the quick. The gold watch she wore on one wrist and the bracelet of tiny gold chains on the other looked like misplaced accidents above her work-worn hands.

'She's the best thing in my life, that's what she is,' he said, still pushing his mouth into her hair. 'I owe Dixie Lee for this one. She got his drunk butt off of a beer joint floor on the reservation and drove him all the way back to Flathead. If she hadn't, a few bucks there would have scrubbed out the toilet with his head. Dixie's got a special way about him. He can say good morning and sling the shit through the fan.'

She eased Clete's arms from around her waist.

'Do you want to eat out on the porch?' she said.

'No, it's still cool. Spring has a hard time catching on here,' he said. 'What's it in New Orleans now, ninety or so?'

'Yeah, I guess.'

'Hotter than hell. I don't miss it,' he said.

His girlfriend set the table for us by the sliding doors, then went back into the kitchen for the food. A wind was blowing across the lake, and each time it gusted, the dark blue surface rippled with light.

'I don't know why she hooked up with me, but why question the fates?' he said.

'She looks like a nice girl.'

'You better believe she is. Her husband got killed felling trees over by Lincoln. A Caterpillar backed over him, ground him all over a rock. She spent five years opening oysters in a restaurant in Portland. Did you see her hands?'

I nodded.

'Then she was waiting tables in that Indian beer joint. You ought to check out a reservation bar. Those guys would make great pilots in the Japanese air force.'

'They're going to send me up the road unless I nail Mapes.'

He pushed at the thick scar on his eyebrow with his finger.

'You're really sweating this, aren't you?' he said.

'What do you think?'

'I can't blame you. An ex-cop doing time. Bad scene, mon. But I got off the hook, zipped right out of it, and if anybody should have gone up the road, it was me. Tell your lawyer to get a couple of continuances. Witnesses go off somewhere, people forget what they saw, the prosecutor loses interest. There's always a way out, Streak.'

His girl brought out a tray filled with ham sandwiches, glasses of iced tea, a beet and onion salad, and a fresh apple pie. She sat down with us and ate without talking. The three moles by the corner of her mouth were the size of BBs.

'You actually think Dixie can help you?' Clete said.

'He has to.'

'Good luck. He told me once his life's goal is to live to a hundred and get lynched for rape. He's an all-right guy, but I think he has a wet cork for a brain.'

'He said Mapes and Vidrine killed a couple of guys and buried them back in a woods. Can you connect that to anything?'

His big face looked vague. 'No, not really,' he said.

I saw his girl, Darlene, look directly into the plate, her head turned down, as though she wanted to hide her expression. But I noticed the color of her eyes darken in the corners.

'I'm sorry for the way I talk,' I said. 'I think Clete and I were cops too long. Sometimes we don't think about what we say in front of other people.' I tried to smile at her.

'I don't mind,' she said.

'I appreciate you having me for lunch, it's very good.'

'Thank you.'

'I came out here fishing with a friend of mine years ago,' I said. 'Montana's a beautiful place to live, isn't it?'

'Some of it is. When you have a job. It's a hard place to find work in,' she said.

'Everything's down here,' Clete said. 'Oil, farming, cattle, mining. Even lumber. It's cheaper to grow trees down south. These dumb bastards voted for Reagan, then got their butts reamed.'

'Then why is your buddy up here? And these lease people?'

His green eyes moved over my face, then he grinned.

'You never could resist mashing on a guy's oysters,' he said. 'He's not my buddy. I work for him. I get along with him. It's a professional relationship.'

'All right, what's he doing here?'

'It's a free country. Maybe he likes the trout.'

'I met a DEA man who had some other theories.'

'When it comes to Sal's business dealings, I turn into a potted plant. I'm also good at taking a smoke in the yard.'

'Tell it to somebody else. You were the best investigative cop I ever knew.'

'At one time,' he said, and winked. Then he looked out at the lake and the inland seagulls that were wheeling over the shoreline. He pushed a piece of food out from behind his teeth with his tongue. 'You've read a lot more books than I have. You remember that guy Rhett Butler in *Gone With the Wind?* He's a blockade runner for the Confederates or something. He tells Scarlett that fortunes are made during a county's beginning and during its collapse. Pretty good line. I think Sal read that book in the Huntsville library. He wheels and deals, mon.'

I didn't say anything. I finished the rest of my sandwich and glanced casually at my watch.

'All right, for God's sake,' Clete said. 'I'll take you up there. But do me a favor. That's my meal ticket up there. Don't look at these people like they're zoo creatures. Particularly Sal's father. He's a bloated old degenerate, but he's also a vicious sonofabitch who never liked me to begin with. I mean it, Dave. Your face doesn't hide your feelings too well. It gets that glaze on it like an elephant broke wind in the room. Okay? We got a deal, right, partner?'

'Sure,' I said.

'Oh boy.'

Sally Dio had brought Galveston, Texas, with him. His glassed-in sun porch, which gave on to the lake, was filled with potted banana, umbrella, orange, and Hong Kong orchid trees, and in the center of the house was a heavily chlorinated, lime-green swimming pool with steam rising off the water. A half-dozen tanned people sat on the edge of the tiles or drifted about lazily on inflated rubber rafts. The living room was paneled with white pine, the carpet was a deep red, and the waxed black piano, with the top propped open, gleamed in the indirect lighting. Dixie Lee, dressed only in a pair of Hawaiian beach shorts and an open bathrobe, sat at the piano bench and ran his fingers back and forth over the keys, his shoulders hunched, then suddenly his arms outspread, his florid face confident with his own sound. He sang,

'I was standing on the corner
Corner of Beale and Main,
When a big policeman said,
"Big boy, you'll have to tell me your name."
I said, "You'll find my name
On the tail of my shirt.
I'm a Tennessee hustler
And I don't have to work."'

Sally Dio sat behind a set of drums and cymbals in a pair of pleated gray slacks, bare-chested, his red suspenders hooked over his shoulders. He was a lean, hard-bodied man, his face filled with flat and sharp surfaces like a person whose bone is too close to the skin so that the eyes look overly large for the face. Under his right eye was a looped scar that made his stare even more pronounced, and when he turned his head toward Dixie Lee and fluttered the wire brushes across the snare drum, the ridge of his ducktails glistened against the refracted sunlight off the lake.

Out on the redwood veranda I could see the back of a

wheelchair and a man sitting in it. Sally Dio and Dixie finished their song. No one asked me to sit down.

'Dixie says you used to be a police officer. In New Orleans,' Sally Dio said. His voice was flat, his eyes casually interested in my face.

'That's right.'

'What do you do now?'

'I'm a small-business man.'

'Probably pays better, doesn't it?'

'Sometimes.'

He made a circular pattern on the drumhead with the wire brushes.

'You like Louisiana?' he asked.

'Yes.'

'Why are you up here, then?'

Clete walked to the wet bar by the pool's edge and started fixing a drink.

'I have some things to take care of. I wanted a few words with Dixie,' I said.

'He says you're in a lot of trouble down there. What's he got to do with your trouble?'

'A lot.'

He looked me evenly in the eyes. Then he fluttered and ticked the brushes lightly on the drum skin.

'Dixie never hurt anybody. Not intentionally, anyway,' he said.

'I mean him no harm, Mr Dio.'

'I'm glad of that.'

A dripping blond girl in a silver swimsuit that was as tight as tin on her body, with a terry cloth robe over her shoulder, walked toward us, drying her hair with a towel.

'You want me to take Papa Frank in, Sal?' she said.

'Ask Papa Frank.'

'He gets cold if he stays out there too long.'

'Then go ask him, hon.'

She walked to the glass doors, then stopped and hooked up the strap on her sandal, pausing motionlessly against the light as though she were caught in a photographer's lens. Sally Dio winked at her.

I looked at Dixie Lee. I had to talk to him alone, outside. He refused to see any meaning in my face. A moment later the blond girl pushed the man in the wheelchair into the living room.

He wore a checkered golf cap, a knitted sweater over his protruding stomach, a muffler that almost hid the purple goiter that was the size of an egg in his neck. His skin was gray, his eyes black and fierce, his face unevenly shaved. Even from several feet away his clothes smelled of cigar smoke and Vick's VapoRub. With his wasted legs and swollen stomach, he reminded me of a distended frog strapped to a chair.

But there was nothing comical about him. His name had been an infamous one back in the forties and fifties. He had run all the gambling on Galveston Island and all the prostitution and white slavery on Post Office and Church Streets. And I remembered another story, too, about a snitch on Sugarland Farm who tried to cut a deal by dropping the dime on Frank Dio. Somebody caught him alone in the shower and poured a can of liquid Drāno down his mouth.

He fixed one watery black eye on me.

'Who's he?' he said to his son.

'Somebody Clete used to know,' Sally Dio said.

'What's he want?'

'He thinks Dixie Lee can get him out of some trouble,' Sally Dio said.

'Yeah? What kind of trouble you in?' the father said to me.

'He's up on a murder charge, Pop. Mr Robicheaux used to be a police officer,' Sally Dio said. He smiled.

'Yeah?' His voice raised a level. 'Why you bring this to our house?'

'I didn't bring anything to your house,' I said. 'I was invited here. By Clete over there. Because the man I wanted to talk with couldn't simply walk down the hill and spend five minutes with me.'

'I invite. Sal invites. You don't get invited by somebody that works for me,' the father said. 'Where you used to be a cop?'

'New Orleans.'

'You know—?' He used the name of an old-time Mafia don in Jefferson parish.

'Yes, I helped give him a six-year jolt in Angola. I heard he complained a lot about the room service.'

'You a wiseguy, huh?'

'You want me to fix you a drink, Mr Frank?' Clete said.

The old man flipped his hand at Clete, his eyes still fixed on me, as though he were brushing away bad air.

'That's my cousin you're talking about,' he said.

I didn't reply. I looked again at Dixie Lee, who sat hunched forward on the piano bench, his hands in his lap, his gaze averted from us.

'Tell him to get the fuck out of here,' the father said. 'Tell that other one he don't bring smartass guys up to our house, either.' Again, he didn't bother to look in Clete's direction.

Then he motioned with his hand again, and the girl in the silver bathing suit wheeled him through a far door into a bedroom. The bed was piled with pink pillows that had purple ruffles around them. I watched the girl close the door.

'Got to do what Pop says. See you around, Mr Robicheaux,' Sally Dio said. He tapped one wire brush across the drumhead.

'Dixie, I want you to walk down to my car with me,' I said.

'Conversation time's over, Mr Robicheaux.'

'The man can speak for himself, can't he?' I said.

But before all my words were out, Sally Dio did a rat-a-tat-tat on the drum with the brushes.

'Are you coming, Dixie?'

Again he slapped the brushes rapidly on the drum, looking me steadily in the eyes with a grin at the corner of his mouth.

'A footnote about your relative in Angola,' I said. 'I not only helped put him away, I maced him in the face after he spit on a bailiff.'

'Clete, help our man find his car,' he said.

Clete took his drink away from his mouth. His face reddened. Behind him, the people in the pool were in various attitudes of embrace among the rubber cushions and wisps of steam.

'Sal, he's a good guy. We got off to a bad start this morning,' he said.

'Mr Robicheaux's late for somewhere else, Clete.'

Clete looked as though he had swallowed a thumbtack.

'No problem. I'm on my way. Take it easy, Clete,' I said.

'Sal, no kidding, he's a solid guy. Sometimes things just go wrong. It's nobody's fault,' Clete said.

'Hey, Robicheaux – something to take with you,' Sally Dio said. 'You came in here on somebody's shirt-tail. Then you talked rude to an old man. But you're in my house and you get to leave on a free pass. You been treated generous. Don't have any confusion about that.'

I walked outside into the sunlight, the wind riffling the lake, the hazy blue-green roll of the hills in the distance. The flagstone steps that led down the hill to Clete's place and my truck were lined with rosebushes and purple clematis.

'Wait a minute, Dave,' I heard Clete say behind me.

He had on his crushed porkpie hat, and as he descended the flagstone steps in his Bermuda shorts his legs looked awkward, the scars on his knees stretched and whitened across the bone.

'Hey, I'm sorry,' he said.

'Forget it.'

'No, that was bad in there. I'm sorry about it.'

'You weren't a part of it. Don't worry about it.'

'Everybody was saying the wrong things, that's all.'

'Maybe so.'

'I didn't want it to go like that. You know that.'

'I believe you, Cletus.'

'But why do you have to scratch a match on their scrots, man?'

'I thought I was pretty well behaved.'

'Oh fuck yeah. Absolutely. Dave, a half-dozen like you could have this whole state in flames.'

'What's Dio's gig here?'

He snuffed inside his nose.

'I take his money. I don't care what he does. End of subject,' he said.

'See you around. Thanks again for the lunch. Say good-bye to Darlene for me.'

'Yeah, anytime. It's always a kick. Like having a car drive through your house.'

I smiled and started toward my pickup.

'Stay in your truck a few minutes. Dixie'll be down,' he said, walking up a gravel path toward his house.

'How do you know?'

'Because even though he acts like a drunk butthole, he wants to help. Also because I told him I'd beat the shit out of him if he didn't.'

I sat in my pickup for ten minutes and was about to give it up when I saw Dixie Lee walk down from Sally Dio's. He had put on a yellow windbreaker and a pair of brown slacks, and the wind blew strands of his blond hair on his forehead. He opened the door on the passenger's side and got in.

'How about we go down to the restaurant on the water for a brew?' he said. 'I'm so dry right now I'm a fire hazard.'

'All right, but I want you to understand something first, Dixie. I don't want you to talk to me because of something Clete said to you.'

'Clete didn't say anything.'

'He didn't?'

'Well, he's a little emotional sometimes. I don't pay him any mind. He don't like to see you in trouble.'

'But this is what's going to happen if I don't hear what I need from you. I'm going to take down Mapes one way or another. If that means getting you locked up as a material witness, that's what's going to happen. I can't promise I'll pull it off, but I'll use all the juice I can to turn the key on you, Dixie.'

'Oh man, don't tell me stuff like that. Not this morning, anyway. My nerve endings are fried as it is.'

'That's another item. I don't want to hear any more about your drinking problems, your theological concerns, or any of the other bullshit you spoon out to people when you're in a corner. Are we clear on this?'

'You come down with both feet, son.'

'You dealt me into this mess. You'd better be aware of that, partner.'

'All right. Are we going for a brew or are you going to sit here and saw me apart?'

I started the truck and drove up the dirt lane through the spines to the main road, which was bordered on the far side by a short span of cherry orchards and then the steep rock face of the mountain. We drove along the lake toward the restaurant that was built on pilings out over the water. Dixie Lee had his face turned into the breeze and was looking wistfully at the sandy beaches, the dense stands of pine, the sailboats that tacked against the deep blue brilliance of the lake.

'Why don't you let me get you some real estate here?' he said.

'To tell you the truth, Dixie, I mortgaged my house and business to make bail.'

'Oh.'

'Why is the Dio family buying up land around here?'

'The state is recessed. Property values are way down. The Dios are going to make a lot of money later on.'

I pulled into the parking lot of the restaurant. A narrow dock protruded out from behind the building, and skiffs and sailboats were moored to it. There was a glaze of gasoline and oil on the water, and seagulls dipped and turned over an open bait well in one of the boats. I turned off the ignition.

'I don't think you've been hearing me very well, Dixie,' I said.

'What?'

'I'm really tired of you trying to pull strings on me. We're operating on the outer edges of my patience here.'

'What'd I say?'

'The mob doesn't make money out of real estate speculation. You stop lying to me.'

'You hurt me, man. Maybe I'm a lush, but that don't mean I'm a liar.'

'Then tell me why they're buying up property.'

'Dave, if you go to prison, and, Lord, I hope you don't, you'll learn two things in there. You stay out of the boss man's eye, and you *never* try to find out the other side of a cat like Sal. You go along and you get along. When you were a cop, did you want to know everything that was going on in your department? How many guys were on a pad? How many of them copped some skag or flake at a bust and sold it off later? Look, in another three or four weeks I'm going to start playing a gig at one of Sal's places in Tahoe. It's not a big deal – a piano bar, a stand-up bass, maybe a guitar. But it's Tahoe, man. It's rhythm and blues and back in the lights. I just got to ease up on the fluids, get it under control.'

'Why not get it the hell out of your life?'

'Everybody don't chop cotton the same way. I'm going inside for a brew. You want to come?'

I watched him walk across a board ramp into the bar

side of the restaurant. I had wasted most of the morning, part of the afternoon, had accomplished nothing, and I felt a great weariness both with Dixie Lee and my situation. I followed him inside. He sat at the far end of the bar, by the windows, silhouetted against the sunlight on the lake. The walls of the bar were decorated with life preservers and nautical ropes and fishnets. Dixie was drinking from a bottle of Great Falls with a shot of whiskey on the side.

The bartender walked toward me, but I motioned him away.

'You don't want anything?' Dixie said.

'Who would Mapes and Vidrine have reason to kill?' I said.

'Not Vidrine. Mapes.'

'All right.'

He looked out the window.

'I don't know,' he said.

'It was somebody who was in his way, somebody who would cost him money.'

'Yeah, I guess so.'

'So who would cause Mapes trouble?'

'Maybe the crazoids. The tree spikers. Star Drilling wants to get into a wilderness area on the eastern slope. The tree spikers want everybody out.'

'But they don't represent anybody. You said they were cultists or something.'

'I don't know what they are. They're fucking wild men.'

'What could they do to keep Star out of a wilderness area?'

'Nothing, really. People up here don't like them.

Them gyppo loggers will rip their ass if they get the chance.'

'Who's that leave?'

He sipped off his whiskey, chased it with beer, and looked out at the lake. His face was composed and his green eyes were distant with either thought or perhaps no thought at all.

'Come on, partner, who could really mess up Mapes's plans?'

'The Indians,' he said finally. 'Star wants to drill on the Blackfeet Reservation. It shouldn't be a problem, because in 1896 the Indians sold all their mineral rights to the government. But there're some young guys, AIM guys, that are smart, that are talking about a suit.'

'The American Indian Movement?'

'Yeah, that's them. They can tie everything up in court, say the treaty was a rip-off or the reservation is a religious area or some other bullshit. It can cost everybody a lot of money.'

'You know some of these guys?'

'No, I always stayed away from them. Some of them been in federal pens. You ever know a con with a political message up his butt? I celled with a black guy like that. Sonofabitch couldn't read and was always talking about Karl Marx.'

'Give me one name, Dixie.'

'I don't know any. I'm telling you the truth. They don't like white people, at least white oil people. Who needs the grief?'

I left him at the bar and drove back toward Missoula. In the Jocko Valley I watched a rain shower move out from between two tall white peaks in the Mission Mountains, then spread across the sky, darken the sun, and march across the meadows, the clumped herds of Angus, the red barns and log ranch houses and clapboard cottages, the poplar windbreaks, the willow-lined river itself, and finally the smooth green hills that rose into another mountain range on the opposite side of the valley. Splinters of lightning danced on the ridges, and the sky above the timberline roiled with torn black clouds. Then I drove over the tip of the valley and out of the rain and into the sunshine on the Clark Fork as though I had slipped from one piece of geographical climate into another.

I picked up Alafair at the baby-sitter's, next door to the rectory, then took her to an ice-cream parlor by the river for a cone. There was a big white *M* on the mountain behind the university, and we could see figures climbing up to it on a zigzag trail. The side of the mountain was green with new grass, and above the *M* ponderosa pine grew through the saddle of the mountain and over the crest into the next valley. Alafair looked small at the marble-topped table, licking her cone, her feet not touching the floor. Her red tennis shoes and the knees of her jeans were spotted with grass stains.

'Were they nice to you at school?' I said.

'Sure.' Then she thought for a moment. 'Dave?'

'Yes.'

'The teacher says I talk like a Cajun. How come she say that?'

'I can't imagine,' I said.

We drove back to the house, and I used my new phone to call Dan Nygurski at the DEA in Great Falls. At first he didn't know where I was calling from, then I heard his interest sharpen when I told him I was in Montana.

'What do you think you're doing here?' he said.

'I'm in some trouble.'

'I know about your trouble. I don't think you're going to make it any better by messing around up here in Montana.'

'What do you mean, you know about it?'

'I got feedback from our office in Lafayette. Vidrine and Mapes worked with Dixie Pugh, and Pugh lives with Sally Dio. It's like keeping track of a daisy chain of moral imbeciles. You shouldn't have gotten involved, Robicheaux.'

I couldn't resist it.

'I was at Sally Dio's today,' I said.

'I think that's dumb, if you're asking my opinion.'

'You know who Cletus Purcel is?'

'Yeah, he was your old homicide partner. I heard he blew away a witness. It looks like he found his own level.'

'He told me Dio is called the Duck because he wears ducktails, but I think he left something out of the story.'

'I bet he did. Dio was playing poker with one of the Mexico City crowd on a yacht out in the Gulf. They were playing deuces wild, and the greaseball had taken six or seven grand off our friend. Except Dio caught him with a deuce hidden under his thigh. Sal's old man used to be known as Frankie "Pliers." I won't tell you why. But I guess Sal wanted to keep up the tradition. He had another guy hold the greaseball down on the deck and he cut off most of his ear with a pair of tin snips. Then he told him, "Tell everybody a duck ate your ear." That's the guy you were visiting today. That's the guy who takes care of your buddy Dixie Lee.'

'Why does he care about Dixie Lee?'

'He gets something out of it. Sal doesn't do anything unless there's a blow job in it for him somewhere.'

'Leasing or buying land for him?'

'Maybe. But don't concern yourself. Go back to Louisiana.'

'You know anything about some AIM members who might have disappeared from the Blackfeet Reservation?'

'I'm really wondering about the soundness of your mind at this point.'

'It's a simple question.'

'If you really want to step into a pile of shit, you've found a good way to do it.'

'Look, Mr Nygurski, I'm all on my own. Maybe I'm going to Angola pen. That's not hyperbole, I'm just about wiped out financially, my own testimony is my only defense, and my personal history is one that'll probably make a jury shudder. Tell me what you'd do in my circumstances. I'd really appreciate that.'

He paused, and I heard him take a breath.

'I never heard anything about any AIM guys disappearing,' he said. 'You'll have to talk with the tribal council or the sheriff's department. Maybe the FBI, although they don't have any love lost for those guys. Look, the reservation is a world unto itself. It's like a big rural slum. Kids cook their heads huffing glue, women cut each other up in bars. The Browning jail is a horror show on Saturday night. They're a deeply fucked-up people.'

'I may be over to see you in Great Falls.'

'Why?'

'Because I think Dio is mixed up in this. Harry Mapes has been around his place, and I don't think it's simply because he knows Dixie Lee.'

'Dio is mixed up with narcotics, whores, and gambling. Let me set you straight about this guy. He's not Bugsy Siegel. Comparatively speaking, he's a small-time player in Vegas and Tahoe. Anything he owns, he's *allowed* to own. But he's an ambitious guy who wants to be a winging dick. So he's come up here to Lum 'n' Abner land to make the big score. Now, that's all you get, Robicheaux. Stay away from him. You won't help your case, and in the meantime you might get hurt. If I hear anything about missing Indians, I'll let you know.'

'Is it possible you feel you have the franchise on Sally Dio?'

'That could be, my friend. I grew up in West Virginia. I don't like what shitheads can do to good country. But I'm also a federal agent. I get paid for doing certain things, which doesn't include acting as an information center. I think I'm already overextended in this conversation. So long, Mr Robicheaux.'

That evening I walked Alafair downtown in the twilight, and we ate fried chicken in a restaurant by the river. Then we walked over the Higgins Street Bridge, where old men fished off the railing in the dark swirls of current far below. The mountains in the west were purple and softly outlined against the red sun, and the wind was cold blowing across the bridge. I could smell chimney smoke and wood pulp in the air, diesel and oil from a passing Burlington Northern. We walked all the way to the park, where a group of boys was trying to hurry summer with a night baseball game. But in the hard glare of the lights the wind grew colder and the dust swirled in the air and finally drops of rain clicked across the tin roof of the dugout. The sky over the valley was absolutely black when we made it home.

Firewood was stacked on the back porch of our house, and I broke up kindling from an orange crate in the fireplace, placed it and balls of newspaper under three pine logs on the andirons, and watched the bright red cone of flame rise up into the brick chimney. It was raining hard outside now, clattering against the roof and windows, and I could see a sawmill lighted across the river in the rain.

During the night lightning flickered whitely on the far wall of my bedroom. It created a window in the soft green plaster, and through it I saw Annie sitting on a rock by a stream's edge. Cylindrical stone formations rose against the cobalt sky behind her. Her hair and denim shirt were wet, and I could see her breasts through the cloth.

I'm worried, Dave, she said.

Why's that?

You haven't been going to AA meetings. You think maybe you're setting yourself up for a slip?

I haven't had time.

She pulled her wet shirtfront loose from her skin with her fingers.

Will you promise me to look in the yellow pages today and find a meeting? she said.

I promise.

Because I think you're flying on the outer edges now. Maybe looking at something worse than a slip.

I wouldn't do that.

What?

I'm Catholic.

I'm talking about something else, baby love. You blow out your doors and they put you in a place like Mandeville.

I've still got it between the ditches. I'm sober.

But you keep calling on me. I'm tired, sweetheart. I have to come a long way so we can talk.

I'm sorry.

She put a finger to her lips.

I'll come again. For a while. But you have to keep your promise.

Annie.

When I woke I was sleepwalking, and my palms were pressed against the cold green plaster of the bedroom wall.

chapter six

It was still raining and cold in the morning. The logs in the fireplace had crumbled into dead ash, and the sky outside was gray. The trees in the yard looked wet and black in the weak light. I turned on the furnace, put fresh logs in the fireplace, lit the kindling and balls of wadded newspaper, and tried to fix French toast for me and Alafair while she dressed for school. I thought I could hear the drone of mosquitoes in my brain, I had on a long-sleeved flannel shirt, and I kept wiping the perspiration out of my eyes on my forearm.

'Why you shaking, Dave?' Alafair said.

'I have malaria. It comes back sometimes. It's not bad, though.'

'What?'

'I got it in the army. In the Philippines. It comes from mosquito bites. It goes away soon.'

'You ain't suppose to be up when you sick. I can fix my own breakfast. I can cook yours, too.'

'Don't say "ain't." '

She took the spatula and the handle of the frying pan out of my hands and began turning the toast. She wore fresh denims with an elastic waistband, and a purple sweater over her white shirt. Her black hair was shiny under the kitchen light.

I felt weak all over. I sat down at the kitchen table and wiped my face with a dry dish towel. I had to swallow before I could speak.

'Can you put on your raincoat and walk yourself to school this morning?' I said.

'Sure.'

'Then if I don't pick you up this afternoon you go to the baby-sitter's. Okay?'

'Okay.'

I watched her pack her lunch box and put on her yellow raincoat and hood.

'Wait a minute. I'll drive you,' I said.

'I can take myself. You sick, you.'

'Alafair, try not to talk like Batist. He's a good man, but he never went to school.'

'You still sick, Dave.'

I rubbed the top of her head and hugged her briefly around the shoulders, then put on my raincoat and hat. The wind outside was cold and smelled of the pulp mill down the river. In the wet air the smell was almost like sewage. I drove Alafair to the school and let her off by the entrance to the playground. When I got back home I was trembling all over, and the heat from the fireplace and the furnace vents wouldn't penetrate my skin. Instead, the house seemed filled with a dry cold that made static electricity jump off my hand when I touched a metal doorknob. I boiled a big pot of water on the kitchen stove to humidify the air, then sat in front of the fireplace with a blanket around my shoulders, my teeth clicking, and watched the resin boil and snap in the pine logs and the flames twist up the chimney.

As the logs softened and sank on the andirons, I felt as though I had been sent to a dark and airless space on the earth where memory became selective and flayed the skin an inch at a time. I can't tell you why. I could never explain these moments, and neither could a psychologist. It happened first when I was ten years old, after my father had been locked up a second time in the parish jail for fighting in Provost's Pool Room. I was at home by myself, looking at a religious book that contained a plate depicting the souls in hell. Suddenly I felt myself drawn into the illustration, caught forever in their lake of remorse and despair. I was filled with terror and guilt, and no amount of assurance from the parish priest could relieve me of it.

When these moments occurred in my adult life, I drank. I did it full tilt, too, the way you stand back from a smoldering fire of wet leaves and fling a glass full of gasoline on to the flames. I did it with Beam and Jack Daniel's straight up, with a frosted Jax on the side; vodka in the morning to sweep the spiders into their nest; four inches of Wild Turkey at noon to lock Frankenstein in his closet until the afternoon world of sunlight on oak and palm trees and the salt wind blowing across Lake Pontchartrain reestablished itself in a predictable fashion.

But this morning was worse than any of those other moments that I could remember. Maybe it *was* malaria, or maybe my childlike psychological metabolism still screamed for a drink and was writing a script that would make the old alternative viable once again. But in truth I think it was something else. Perhaps, as Annie had said, I had found the edge.

The place where you unstrap all your fastenings to the earth, to what you are and what you have been, where you flame out on the edge of the spheres, and the sun and moon become eclipsed and the world below is as dead and remote and without interest as if it were glazed with ice.

Is this the way it comes? I thought. With nothing dramatic, no three-day bender, no delirium tremens in a drunk tank, no cloth straps and Thorazine or a concerned psychiatrist to look anxiously into your face. You simply stare at the yellow handkerchief of flame in a fireplace and fear your own thoughts, as a disturbed child would. I shut my eyes and folded the blanket across my face. I could feel my whiskers against the wool, the sweat running down inside my shirt; I could smell my own odor. The wind blew against the house, and a wet maple branch raked against the window.

Later, I heard a car stop outside in the rain and someone run up the walk on to the porch. I heard the knock on the door and saw a woman's face through the steamed glass, but I didn't get up from my chair. She wore a flat-brim black cowboy hat with a domed crown, and her hair and face were spotted with rain. She knocked more loudly, straining to see me through the glass, then she opened the door and put her head inside.

'Is something wrong?' she asked.

'Everything's copacetic. Excuse me for not getting up.'

'Something's burning.'

'I've got a fire. I built one this morning. Is Clete out there?'

'No. Something's burning in your house.'

'That's what I was saying. Somebody left some firewood on the back porch. The furnace doesn't work right or something.'

Her turquoise eyes looked at me strangely. She walked past me into the kitchen, and I heard metal rattle on the stove and then ring in the sink. She turned on the faucet, and steam hissed off something hot. She walked back into the living room, her eyes still fixed on me in a strange way. She wore rubber boots, a man's wide belt through the loops of her Levi's, and an army field jacket with a First Cav patch over her red flannel shirt.

'The pot was burned through the center,' she said. 'I put it in the sink so it wouldn't smell up the place.'

'Thank you.'

She took off her hat and sat down across from me. The three moles at the corner of her mouth looked dark in the firelight.

'Are you all right?' she said.

'Yes. I have malaria. It comes and goes. They just buzz around in the bloodstream for a little while. It's not so bad. Not anymore, anyway.'

'I think you shouldn't be here alone.'

'I'm not. A little girl lives with me. Where'd you get the First Cav jacket?'

'It was my brother's.' She leaned out of her chair and put her hand on my forehead. Then she picked up one of my hands and held it momentarily. 'I can't tell. You're sitting too close to the fire. But you should be in bed. Get up.'

'I appreciate what you're doing, but this is going to pass.'

'Yeah, I can tell you're really on top of it. Do you know a pot holder was burning on your stove, too?'

She helped me up by one arm and walked me into the bedroom. I sat on the edge of the bed and looked numbly out the window at the wet trees and the rain on the river. When I closed my eyes my head spun and I could see gray worms swimming behind my lids. She took the blanket off my shoulders and pulled off my shirt, pushed my head down on the pillow and covered me with the sheet and bedspread. I heard her run water in the bathroom and open my dresser drawers, then she sat on the side of the mattress and wiped my face and chest and shoulders with a warm, damp towel and pulled a clean T-shirt over my head.

She felt my forehead again and looked down in my face.

'I don't think you take very good care of yourself,' she said. 'I don't think you're a wise man, either.'

'Why have you come here?'

'Leave Sally Dee and his father alone. It's bad for you, it's bad for Clete.'

'Clete got in bed with that bunch on his own.' I blew out my breath and opened my eyes. I could feel the room spinning, the same way it used to spin when I would try to go to sleep drunk and I'd have to hang my head off the side of the mattress or couch to put the blood back in my brain.

'He's done some bad things, but he's not a bad man,' she said. 'He looks up to you. He still wants you to be his friend.'

'He betrayed me when I needed him.'

'Maybe he's paid for it, too. You sleep. I'll stay here and fix lunch for you when you wake up.'

She spread the blanket on top of me and pulled it up to my chin. Her hand touched mine, and involuntarily I cupped her palm in my fingers. Her hand was wide across the back and callused on the edges, and her knuckles were as hard as dimes under the skin. I could not remember when I had last touched a woman's hand. I closed her fingers in my palm, felt the grainy coarseness of her skin with my thumb, let both our hands rest on my chest as though the moment had given me a right that was in reality not mine. But she didn't take her hand away. Her face was kind, and she wiped the wetness out of my hair with the towel and remained on the edge of the bed while the rain swept across the yard and the roof and I felt myself slipping down to the bottom of my own vertigo, down inside a cool, clean, and safe place where no fires burned, where the gray morning was as harmless as the touch of my forehead against her thigh.

It was early afternoon when I woke again, and the sun was out, the sky blue, the yard a deeper green. I felt weak all over, but whatever had invaded my metabolism had gone away like a bored visitor. I opened the front door in my bare feet, and the air was cool and full of sunlight, and in the south the ragged peaks of the Bitterroot Mountains were white with new snow. Out on the river the rooted end of an enormous tree bounced wet and shining through the current. I heard her in the kitchen behind me, then remembered my earlier behaviour the way a shard of memory comes back from a drunken dream.

She saw it in my face, too.

'I called Clete. He knows where I am. He doesn't mind,' she said.

'I want to thank you for your kindness.'

Her eyes softened and moved over my face. I felt uncomfortable.

'I have strange moments in my life. I can't explain them,' I said. 'So I tell people it's malaria. Maybe it's true, but I don't know that. Maybe it's something else, too. Sometimes people at AA call it a dry drunk. It's nothing to wear on your chest.'

I took a bottle of milk out of the icebox and sat down at the kitchen table. Through the back screen I could see an elderly woman hoeing in her vegetable garden. Next door somebody was cutting his grass with a hand mower. Darlene's eyes had never left my face.

'Clete said you lost your wife,' she said.

'Yes.'

'He said two men murdered her.'

'That's right.'

'How did it happen?' Her hand turned off the burner under a soup pot.

'I messed with some people I should have let alone.'

'I see.' She took two soup bowls out of the cabinet and set them on the table with spoons. 'It bothers you a lot?'

'Sometimes.'

'I blamed myself when my husband got killed. I'd locked him out of the house the night before. I'd found out he was cheating with a white girl who worked in the truck stop. He had to stay all night in the car in zero weather. He went to work like that in the morning and a bulldozer backed over him. He was like a little boy.

Always in the wrong place. He always got caught. He spent a year in Deer Lodge for stealing game meat out of some rental lockers at a grocery. He used to lie about it and tell people he went to jail for armed robbery.'

'Why do you tell me this?'

'You shouldn't hurt yourself because of what happened to your wife. You don't realize what you did yesterday. Sally Dee's crazy.'

'No, he's not. He just likes people to think he is. His kind come by the boxcarload.'

She filled our bowls and sat down across from me.

'You don't know Sal. Clete said you made Sal look bad in front of his friends. He came down to the house after you left and they went out on the veranda. I could hear Sal yelling through the glass. I didn't think Clete would let anyone talk to him like that.'

'It's expensive to work for a guy like Sally Dio.'

'He degraded him.'

'Listen, there's an expression in the oil field – "I was looking for a job when I found this one." You tell Clete that.'

'Sal said something else, too. About you.'

'What?'

' "Don't bring him around here again, don't let him be talking to Dixie Lee, either. He does, I'm gonna cut off his dick." '

I looked to the door again at the woman hoeing in her garden across the alley. Her face was pink, her hair white, and her arms were as thick as a man's.

'That's what our man had to say?'

'Clete and Dixie Lee pretend he's all right because they have to. But he's cruel. He frightens me.'

'You should get away from him.'

She put her spoon in her soup and lowered her eyes.

'You're an intelligent woman,' I said. 'You're a good person, too. You don't belong among those people.'

'I'm with Clete.'

'Clete's going to take a big fall with that guy. Or he'll take a fall *for* him, one or the other. Down inside, he knows it, too. Until he started screwing up his life, he was the best partner I ever had. He carried me down a fire escape once while a kid put two .22 rounds in his back. He used to put the fear of God in the wiseguys. They'd cross the street when they saw him on the sidewalk.'

'He's been good to me. Inside he's a good man. One day, he'll see that.'

Her attitude toward him struck me as strange. It seemed more protective than affectionate. But maybe she was that kind of woman. Or maybe it was what I wanted to believe.

'I wonder if you can help me with something,' I said.

'What?'

'Did Clete tell you about some trouble I've had in Louisiana?'

'Yes.'

'Harry Mapes is my way out of it. I think he killed two people up here. Maybe they were Indians, members of AIM.'

She looked down at her food again, but I saw her eyes narrow, the light in them sharpen.

'Why do you think that? About the Indians?' she said.

'Mapes killed these people because they were in the way of his oil deals. Dixie Lee said these AIM guys can tie the oil companies up in court over a nineteenth-century treaty.'

'It's a big fight over on the Rocky Mountain Front.'

'The what?'

'It's the eastern face of the Continental Divide. The Blackfeet called it the backbone of the world. The oil companies want into the roadless areas by Glacier Park. That was Blackfeet land. The government took it or got it for nothing.'

'Did you ever hear about any AIM people disappearing?'

'Why don't you ask up at the reservation?'

'I plan to. Why are you angry?'

'It has nothing to do with you.'

'It seems to.'

'You don't understand the reservation.'

She stopped, and it was obvious that she regretted her abruptness. She wet her lips and began again, but her voice had the quiet, tense quality of someone who had bought seriously into a private piece of discontent.

'Whites have always taken from the Blackfeet. They massacred them on the Marias River, then they starved them and gave them a rural slum to live in. Now they've given us their missile sites. The government admits that in a war everybody on the eastern slope will be killed. But what whites don't understand is that Indians believe spirits live in the earth. That all the treaties and deeds that took our land don't mean anything. Sometimes people hear the crying of children and women in the wind on the Marias. An Indian woman in a white doeskin dress appears at missile silos. Air Force people have seen her. You can talk to them.'

'You believe in these spirits?'

'I've been on the Marias at night. I've heard them. The sound comes right off the edge of the water, where the camp was. It happened in the winter of 1870. An army officer named Baker attacked an innocent band of Blackfeet under Heavy Runner. They killed a hundred and thirty people, then burned their robes and wickiups and left the survivors to freeze in the snow. You can hear people weeping.'

'I guess I don't know about those things. Or the history of your people.'

She ate without answering.

'I think maybe it's not a good idea to keep things like that alive in yourself, though,' I said.

She remained silent, her face pointed downward, and I gave it up.

'Look, will you give Clete a message for me?' I said.

'What is it?'

'That he doesn't owe me, that he doesn't need to feel bad about anything, that I don't sweat a character like Sally Dio. You also tell him to take himself and a nice girl to New Orleans. That's the place where good people go when they die.'

She smiled. I looked at her eyes and her mouth, then caught myself and glanced away.

'I have to go now,' she said. 'I hope you're feeling better.'

'I am. You were a real friend, Darlene. Clete's a lucky guy.'

'Thank you, but he's not a lucky guy. Not at all.'

I didn't want to talk about Clete's problems anymore or carry any more of his load. I walked outside with her to her Toyota jeep and opened the door for her. The sidewalks were still drying in the sunlight, and the pines on the mountains were sharp and green against the sky.

'Maybe you all would like to come into town and

have dinner one evening, or walk up one of those canyons in the Bitterroots and try for some cutthroat,' I said.

'Maybe. I'll ask him,' she said, and smiled again.

I watched her drive past the school yard and turn toward the interstate. It was one of those moments when I did not care to reflect upon my own honesty or to know in reality what I was thinking about.

I washed the dishes, put on my running shoes, shorts, and a sweatshirt, and did two miles along the river, then circled back through a turn-of-the-century neighborhood of yellow- and orange-brick homes whose yards were dotted with blue spruce, fir, maple, birch, and willow trees. I was sweating heavily in the cool air, and I had to push hard to increase my speed across an intersection; but my wind was good, the muscles tight in my thighs and back, my mind clear, the rest of the day a bright expectation rather than an envelope of grayness and gloom and disembodied voices.

Ah, voices, I thought. She believes in them. Which any student of psychology will tell you is a mainline symptom of a schizophrenic personality. But I had never bought very heavily into the psychiatric definitions of singularity and eccentricity in people. In fact, as I reviewed the friendships I had had over the years, I had to conclude that the most interesting ones involved the seriously impaired – the Moe Howard account, the drunken, the mind-smoked, those who began each day with a nervous breakdown, people who hung on to the sides of the planet with suction cups.

When I rounded the corner on my block by the river, I heard the bell ring at the elementary school and saw the children burst out of the doors on to the sidewalks. Alafair walked with her lunch box among three other children. I ran backward when I passed her.

'Meet you at the house, little guy,' I said.

I shaved and showered and took Alafair with me to an AA meeting three blocks from our house. She drank a can of pop and did her homework in the coffee room while I sat in the nonsmokers' section of the meeting and listened. The members of the group were mostly mill workers, gyppo loggers, Indians, waitresses, tough blue-collar kids who talked as much about dope as they did about alcohol, and skid-row old-timers who had etched the lines in their face a shot glass at a time. When it was my turn to talk, I gave my name and passed. I should have talked about my nightmares, the irrational depression that could leave me staring eviscerated and numb at a dying fire; but for most of them their most immediate problem was not psychological or in the nature of their addiction – they were unemployed and on food stamps – and my own basket of snakes seemed an unworthy subject for discussion.

Alafair and I ate an early supper, then we walked up on a switchback trail to the big white concrete *M* on the mountain overlooking the university. We could see out over the whole valley: the Clark Fort winding high and yellow through town, the white froth over the breakers, the tree-filled neighborhoods, the shafts of sunlight in the canyons west of town, the plume from the pulp mill flattening out on the river's surface, the bicyclists and joggers like miniature figures on the campus far below. Then as the sun dimmed behind a peak and the air became more chill and the valley filled with a purple haze, house and street and neon lights came on all over town, and in the south we could see the sun's afterglow on the dark strands of ponderosa high up in the Bitterroots.

Alafair sat beside me on the concrete *M*. She brushed dirt off her knees; I saw her frown.

'Dave, whose hat that is?' she said.

'What?'

'In the chair. By the fireplace. That black hat.'

'Oh,' I said. 'I think a lady must have left that there.'

'I sat on it. I forgot to tell you.'

'Don't worry about it.'

'She won't be mad?'

'No, of course not. Don't worry about things like that, little guy.'

The next day I made arrangements for Alafair to stay with the baby-sitter if I had to remain out of town that night, and I headed for the Blackfeet Reservation, on the other side of the Divide, east of Glacier Park. In the early morning light I drove up the Blackfoot River through the trees from the cabins set back in the meadows. The runoff from the snowpack up in the mountains was still high, and the current boiled over the boulders in the center of the river. Then the country opened up into wider valleys and ranch-land with low green hills and more mountains in the distance. I started to climb into more heavily wooded country, with sheer rock cliffs and steep-sided mountains that ran right down to the edge of the road; the canyons and trees were dark with shadow, and by the time I hit the logging town of Lincoln the air had turned cold and my windows were wet with mist. I drove into clouds on the Divide at Rogers Pass, my ears popping now, and rivulets of melted snow ran out of the pines on the mountainside, bled across the highway, and washed off the dirt shoulder into a white stream far below. The pine trees looked almost black and glistened with a wet sheen.

Then I was out into sunlight again, out on the eastern slope, into rolling wheat and cattle country with no horizon except the Rocky Mountain Front in my rear-view mirror. I made good time into Choteau and Dupuyer, and a short while later I was on the Blackfeet Indian Reservation.

I had been on or through several Indian reservations, and none of them was a good place. This one was not an exception. Ernest Hemingway once wrote that there was no worse fate for a people than to lose a war. If any of his readers wanted to disagree with him, they would only have to visit one of the places in which the United States government placed its original inhabitants. We took everything they had and in turn gave them smallpox, whiskey, welfare, federal boarding schools, and penitentiaries.

At a run-down filling station I got directions to the tribal chairman's office, then drove through several small settlements of clapboard shacks, the dirt yards littered with the rusted parts of junker cars, old washing machines on the porches, chicken yards, privies, and vegetable patches in back, with seed packages stuck up on sticks in the rows.

The tribal chairman was a nice man who wore braids, jewelry, a western vest, green-striped trousers, and yellow cowboy boots. On his office wall was an associate of arts degree from a community college. He was polite and listened well, his eyes staying focused attentively on my face while I spoke; but it was also obvious that he did not want to talk about AIM or the oil business with a white man whom he didn't know.

'Do you know Harry Mapes?' I said.

This time his gaze broke. He looked out the window on to the street, where three Indian men were talking in front of a poolroom. The neon sign above the door said only Pool.

'He's a leaseman. He's around here sometimes,' he said. 'Most of the time he works on the edge of the reservation.'

'What else do you know about him?'

He unwrapped the cellophane from an inexpensive cherry-blend cigar.

'I don't have any dealings with him. You'll have to ask somebody else.'

'You think he's bad news?'

'I don't know what he is.' He smiled to be pleasant and lit his cigar.

'He killed his partner, Dalton Vidrine, down in Louisiana.'

'I don't know about that, Mr Robicheaux.'

'I think he killed two of your people, too.'

'I don't know what to tell you, sir.'

'Do you know of two guys from AIM who disappeared?'

'Not on the reservation. And that's what I'm elected to take care of – the reservation.'

'What do you mean, "not on the reservation"?'

'I'm not in AIM. I don't mix in their business.'

'But you've heard about somebody disappearing?'

He gazed out the window against the men in front of

the poolroom and breathed cigar smoke out his nose and mouth.

'Just south of here, down in Teton County. Clayton Desmarteau and his cousin,' he said. 'I don't remember the cousin's name.'

'What happened?'

'I heard they didn't come home one night. But maybe they just went off somewhere. It happens. Talk to the sheriff's office in Teton. Talk to Clayton's mother. She lives just off the reservation. Here, I'll draw you directions.'

A half hour later I was back off the reservation and driving down a narrow gray dirt road by the edge of a stream. Cottonwoods grew along the banks, then the ground sloped upward into thick stands of lodgepole pine. Ahead I could see the plains literally dead-end into the mountains. They rose abruptly, like an enormous fault, sheer-faced and jagged against the sky. The cliff walls were pink and streaked with shadow, and the ponderosa was so thick through the saddles that I doubted a bear could work his way through the trunks.

I found the home the tribal chairman had directed me to. It was built of logs and odd-sized pieces of lumber, up on a knoll, with a shingled roof and sagging gallery. Plastic sheets were nailed over the windows for insulation, and coffee cans filled with petunias were set along the gallery railing and the edges of the steps. The woman who lived there looked very old. Her hair was white, with dark streaks in it, and her leathery skin was deeply lined and webbed around the eyes and mouth.

I sat with her in her living room and tried to explain who I was, that I wanted to find out what happened to her son, Clayton Desmarteau, and his cousin. But her face was remote, uncertain, her eyes averted whenever I looked directly at them. On a table by the tiny fireplace was a framed photograph of a young Indian soldier. In front of the picture were two open felt boxes containing a Purple Heart and a Silver Star.

'The tribal chairman said maybe your son simply left the area for a while,' I said. 'Maybe he went looking for other work.'

This time she looked at me.

'Clayton didn't go off nowhere,' she said. 'He had a job in the filling station in town. He came home every night. They found his car in the ditch, two miles from here. He wouldn't go off and leave his car in the ditch. They did something to him.'

'Who?'

'People that want to hurt his organization.'

'AIM?'

'He was beat up one time. They were always trying to hurt him.'

'Who beat him up?'

'People that's no good.'

'Mrs Desmarteau, I want to help you find out what happened to Clayton. Did he ever mention someone's name, somebody who gave him trouble?'

'The FBI. They came around the filling station and called up people on the phone about him.'

'How about Harry Mapes or Dalton Vidrine? Do you remember his using those names?'

She didn't answer. She simply looked out into space, took a pinch of snuff out of a Copenhagen can, and put it between her lip and gum. Motes of dust spun in the light through the windows. I thanked her for her time and drove back down the road toward the county seat, the shadows of the cottonwoods clicking across my windshield.

The sheriff was out of town, and the deputy I spoke to at the courthouse soon made me feel that I was a well-meaning, obtuse outsider who had as much understanding of rural Montana and reservation life as a seasonal tourist.

'We investigated that case about four months ago,' he said. He was a big, lean man in his khaki uniform, and he seemed to concentrate more on the smoking of his cigarette than on his conversation with me. His desk was littered with papers and manila folders. 'His mother and sister filed a missing-persons report. We found his car with a broken axle in the ditch. The keys were gone, the spare tire was gone, the radio was gone, somebody even tore the clock out of the dashboard. What's that tell you?'

'Somebody stripped it.'

'Yeah, Clayton Desmarteau did. It was going to be repossessed. Him and his cousin were in the bar three miles up the road, they got juiced, they ran off the road. That's the way we see it.'

'And he just didn't bother to come home after that?'

'Where are you from again?'

'New Iberia, Louisiana.'

He blew smoke out into a shaft of sunlight shining through the window. His hair was thin across his pate.

'Believe it or not, that's not uncommon here,' he said. Then his voice changed and assumed a resigned and tired note. 'We're talking about two guys in AIM. One of them, Clayton's cousin, was in the pen in South Dakota. There's also a warrant out on him for nonsupport. Clayton's had his share of trouble, too.'

'What kind?'

'Fights, carrying a concealed weapon, bullshit like that.'

'Has he ever just disappeared from his home and job before?'

'Look, here's the situation. There's one bar on that road. They were in there till midnight. It's five miles from that bar up to Clayton's house. Three miles up the road they wrecked the car. Maybe they walked up to Clayton's house without waking the old lady and took off before she got up. Maybe she doesn't remember what they did. Maybe they hitched a ride with somebody after they stripped the car. I don't know what they did. You think a bear ate them?'

'No, I think you're telling me Desmarteau was an irresponsible man. His mother says otherwise. The guy had the Silver Star. What do you make of that?'

'I don't guess I'm communicating with you very well. What you don't understand is the way some people live around here. Come back on a Saturday night and take your own tour. Look, when a white person hires Indians to work for him, he hires six so maybe three will show up in the morning. They cut up their own relatives at wedding parties, they hang themselves in jail cells, they get souped up and drive into the sides of trains. Last winter three kids climbed in a boxcar with a gallon of dago red and a tube of airplane glue. The train went on up into Canada and stopped on a siding in a blizzard. I went up with the families to bring their bodies back. The RCMP said they were frozen so hard you could break their parts off with a hammer.'

I asked him to show me where Clayton Desmarteau's

car had gone off the road. He was irritated, but he consented and drove me down the same dirt road I had been on earlier. We passed the bar where Desmarteau and his cousin had been last seen, a wide, flat log building with neon Grain Belt and Great Falls beer signs in the windows; then we curved up the road through bare, hardpan fields and finally picked up the creek, the cottonwoods, and the sloping stands of lodgepole pine that began on the far bank. The deputy stopped his car on the shoulder and pointed.

'Right over there in the ditch,' he said. 'He hooked one wheel over the side and went in. Snapped the axle like a stick. No mystery, my friend. It's a way of life.'

I got back to Missoula late but in time to pick up Alafair at the baby-sitter's before she went to sleep. The baby-sitter had run an errand, and a friend of hers, a third-grade teacher and assistant principal at the school named Miss Regan, had come over to stay with Alafair. The two of them were watching television and eating from a bowl of popcorn in the enclosed side porch. Miss Regan was a pretty girl in her late twenties, with auburn hair and green eyes, and although her skin was still pale from the winter months, I could see sun freckles on her shoulders and the bottom of her neck.

'Come see, Dave,' Alafair said. 'Miss Regan drew a picture of Tex and she ain't ever seen him.'

'Don't say "ain't," little guy,' I said.

'Look,' Alafair said, and held up a piece of art paper with a pastel drawing of an Appaloosa on it.

'That's very nice of Miss Regan,' I said.

'My name's Tess,' she said, and smiled.

'Well, thank you for watching Alafair. It was good meeting you.'

'She's a sweet little girl. We had a lot of fun together,' she said.

'Do you live in the neighborhood?'

'Yes, only two blocks from the school.'

'Well, I hope to see you again. Thanks for your help. Good night.'

'Good night,' she said.

We walked home in the dark. The air was warm, and the maple trees looked black and full under the moon. The lights of the bridge reflected off the swirling brown surface of the river.

'Everybody says she's the best teacher in the school,' Alafair said.

'I bet she is.'

'I told her to come down to New Iberia and visit us.'

'That's good.'

'Because she don't have a husband.'

'Say "doesn't." '

'She doesn't have a husband. How come that, Dave?'

'I don't know. Some people just don't like to get married.'

'How come?'

'You got me.'

We ate a piece of pie before we turned out the lights and went to bed. Our bedrooms adjoined, and the door was opened between them. Across the river I could hear the whistle of a Burlington Northern Freight.

'Dave?'

'What?'

'Why don't you marry Miss Regan?'

'I'll give it some thought. See you tomorrow, little guy.'

'Okay, big guy.'

'Good night, little guy.'

'Good night, big guy.'

The next morning I made long-distance calls to Batist, the bondsman, and my lawyer. Batist was managing fine at the bait shop and the bondsman was tranquil about my returning to Louisiana by trial date, but the lawyer had not been able to get a continuance and he was worried.

'What have you come up with in Montana?' he said.

'Nothing definite. But I think Dixie Lee was telling the truth about Mapes, that he killed a couple of people here, maybe Indians.'

'I tell you, Dave, that might be our only out. If you can get him locked up in Montana, he won't be a witness against us in Louisiana.'

'It's not the ninth race yet.'

'Maybe not, but so far we don't have a defense. It's that simple. I hired a PI to do a background on Mapes. He beat the shit out of another kid with a golf club in Marshall, Texas, when he was seventeen, but that's the only trouble he's been in. He graduated from the University of Texas and flew an army helicopter in Vietnam. The rest of the guy's life is a blank. It's hard to make him out as Jack the Ripper.'

'We'll see,' I said. I didn't want to concede the truth in his words, but I could feel my heart tripping.

'The prosecutor's talking a deal,' he said.

I remained silent and listened to the wire of long-distance sound in the earpiece. Through the window I could see the maple tree in my front yard ruffling with the breeze.

'Dave, we're reaching the point where we might have to listen to him.'

'What deal?'

'Second-degree homicide. We'll show provocation, he won't contend with us, you'll get five years. With good time, you can be out in three or less.'

'No deal.'

'It may turn out to be the only crap game in town.'

'It's bullshit.'

'Maybe so, but there's something else I'm honor-bound to tell you. We're going up against Judge Mouton. He's sent six men I know of to the electric chair. I don't think he'd do that in this case. But he's a cranky old sonofabitch, and you never know.'

After I hung up the phone I tried to read the paper on the front porch with a cup of coffee, but my eyes couldn't concentrate on the words.

I washed the dishes, cleaned the kitchen, and started to change the oil in my truck. I didn't want to think about my conversation with my lawyer. One day at a time, easy does it, I told myself. Don't live in tomorrow's problems. Tomorrow has no more existence than yesterday, but you can always control *now*. We live in a series of nows. Think about now.

But that sick feeling around the heart would not go away. I worked my way under my truck, fitted a crescent wrench around the nut on the oil pan, and applied pressure with both hands while flakes of dried mud fell in my eyes. Then the wrench slipped and I raked my knuckles across the pan. I heard the telephone ring inside.

I crawled out from under the truck, went in the house, and picked up the receiver. The skin was gone on the tops of two of my knuckles.

'What's happening, Dave?'

'Dixie?'

'Yeah. What's happening?'

'Nothing important. What is it?'

'Are you always this happy in the morning?'

'What do you want, Dixie?'

'Nothing. I'm in the lounge over in that shopping center on Brooks. Come on over.'

'What for?'

'Talk. Relax. Listen to a few sounds. They got a piano in here.'

'You sound like your boat already left the dock.'

'So?'

'It's nine o'clock in the morning.'

'Big deal. It's twelve o'clock somewhere else. Come on over.'

'No thanks.'

'Darlene dumped me in here while she went running around town. I don't want to sit in here by myself. It's a drag, man. Get your butt over here.'

'I've got a few other things on my mind.'

'That's what I want to talk with you about. Dave, you think you're the only guy who understands your problem. Look, man, I pick cotton every day in the same patch.'

'What are you talking about?'

'Some people are born different. That's just the way we are. You go against what you are, you're gonna have a mess of grief. Like Hank Junior says, some people are born to boogie, son. They just got to be willing to pay the price.'

'I appreciate all this, but I'm going to sign off now.'

'Oh no you don't. You listen to me, 'cause I been there in spades, right where you're at now. When I got to Huntsville from the county jail, I hadn't had a drink in six weeks. I felt like I had fire ants crawling on my brain. Except I learned you can get almost anything in the joint you can get outside. There was a Mexican cat who sold short-dogs of black cherry wine for five bucks a bottle. We'd mix it with syrup, water, and rubbing alcohol, and it'd fix you up just about like you stuck your head in a blast furnace.

'So one time we had a whole crock of this beautiful black cherry brew stashed in a tool shack, and one time while the boss man was working some guys farther on down the road, we set one guy out as a jigger and the rest of us crapped out in the shack and decided to coolerate our minds a little bit. Except about an hour later, when we're juiced to the eyes, the guy outside comes running through the door, yelling, "Jigger, jigger."

'The boss man was a big redneck character from Lufkin named Buster Higgins. He could pick up a bale of hay and fling it from behind the truck all the way to the cab. When he took a leak he made sure everybody saw the size of his dick. That's no shit, man. The next thing I know, he's standing there in the door of the toolshed, sweat running out of his hat, his face big as a pumpkin. Except this guy was not funny. He thought rock 'n' roll was for niggers and Satan worshipers. He looks down at me and says, "Pugh, didn't your parents have enough money?"

'I said, "What d'you mean, Mr Higgins?"

'He says, "For a better quality rubber," then he took his hat off and whipped the shit out of me with it. Next stop – one month in isolation, son. I'm talking about down there with the crazoids, the screamers, the guys who stink so bad the hacks have to wash them down with hoses. And I had delirium tremens for two fucking days. Weird sounds snapping in my head, rockets going off when I closed my eyes, a big hard-on and all kinds of real sick sexual thoughts. You know what I'm talking about, man. It must have been ninety degrees in the hole, and I was shaking so bad I couldn't get a cup of water to my mouth.

'I got through two days and thought I was home free. But after a week I started to have all kinds of guilt feelings again. About the little boy in the accident in Forth Worth, about my own little boy dying in the fire. I couldn't stand it, man. Just that small isolation cell and the light through the food slit and all them memories. I would have drunk gasoline if somebody would have given it to me. So you know what I done? I didn't try to get the guilt out of my mind. I got high on it. I made myself so fucking miserable that I was drunk again. When I closed my eyes and swallowed, I could even taste that black cherry wine. I knew then it wasn't never gonna be any different. I was always gonna be drunk, whether I was dry or out there juicing.

'So in my head I wrote a song about it. I could hear all the notes, the riffs, a stand-up bass backing me up. I worked out the lyrics for it, too—

You can toke, you can drop,
Drink or use.
It don't matter, daddy,
'Cause you never gonna lose
Them mean old jailhouse
Black cherry blues.'

I rubbed my forehead with my hand. I didn't know what to say to him.

'You still there?' he said.

'Yes.'

'You gonna come over?'

'Maybe I'll see you another time. Thanks for the invitation.'

'Fuck, yeah, I'm always around. Sorry I wasted your time.'

'You didn't. We were good friends in college. Remember?'

'Everybody was good friends in college. It all died with Cochran and Holly. I got to motivate on over to another bar. This place bugs me. Dangle easy, Dave.'

He hung up. I stared listlessly out into the sunlight a moment, then walked outside and finished changing the oil in my truck.

She drove up in her red Toyota jeep a half-hour later. I guess I knew that she was coming, and I knew that she would come when Alafair was at school. It was like the feeling you have when you look into the eyes of another and see a secret and shared knowledge there that makes you ashamed of your own thoughts. She wore a yellow sundress, and she had put on lipstick and eye shadow and hoop earrings. The sacks of groceries in the back of the jeep looked as though they were there only by accident.

Her lipstick was dark, and when she smiled her teeth were white.

'Your hat,' I said.

'Yes. You found it?'

'It's in the living room. Come in. I have some South Louisiana coffee on the stove.'

She walked ahead of me, and I looked at the way her black hair sat thickly on her neck, the way the hem of her dress swung across her calves. When I opened the screen for her I could smell the perfume behind her ears and on her shoulders.

I went into the kitchen while she found her hat in the living room. I fooled with cups and saucers, spoons, a bowl of sugar, milk from the icebox, but my thoughts were as organized as a puzzle box that someone had shaken violently between his hands.

'I try to shop in Missoula. It's cheaper than Polson,' she said.

'Yeah, food's real cheap here.'

'Dixie Lee came along with me. He's in a bar right now.'

'He called me. You might have to drag him out of the place on a chain.'

'He'll be all right. He's only bad when Sal lets him take cocaine.' She paused a moment. 'I thought maybe you wouldn't be home.'

'I got a late start today. A bunch of phone calls, stuff like that.'

She reached for the cups and saucers on the drainboard and her arm brushed against mine. She looked at my eyes and raised her mouth, and I slipped my arms around her shoulders and kissed her. She stepped close against me, so that her stomach touched lightly against my loins, and moved her palms over my back. She opened and closed her mouth while she held and kissed me, and then she put her tongue in my mouth and felt her body flatten against me. I ran my hands over her bottom and her thighs and gently bit her shoulder as she wrapped one calf inside my leg and rubbed her hair on the side of my face.

We pulled the shades in the bedroom and undressed without speaking, as if words would lead both of us to an awareness about morality and betrayal that we did not care to examine in the heated touch of our skin, the dry swallow in the throat, the silent parting of our mouths.

There had been one woman in my life since my wife's death, and I had lived celibate almost a year. She reached down and took me inside her and stretched out her legs along me and ran her hands along the small of my back and down my thighs. The breeze clattered the shades on the windows, the room was dark and cool, but my body was rigid and hot and my neck filmed with perspiration, and I felt like an inept and simian creature laboring above her. She stopped her motion, kissed me on the cheek and smiled, and I stared down at her, out of breath and with the surprise of a man whose education with women always proved inadequate.

'There's no hurry,' she said quietly, almost in a whisper. 'There's nothing to worry about.'

Then she said, 'Here,' and pressed on my arm for me to move off her. She brushed her hair out of her eyes, sat on top of me, kissed me on the mouth, then raised herself on her knees and put me inside her again. Her eyes closed and opened, she tightened her thighs against me, and propped herself up on her hands and looked quietly and lovingly into my face.

She came before I did, her face growing intense and small, her mouth suddenly opening like a flower. Then I felt all my nocturnal erotic dreams, my fear, my aching celibacy, rise and swell in my loins, and burst away outside of me like a wave receding without sound in a cave by the sea.

She lay close to me under the sheet, her fingers in the back of my hair. A willow tree in the backyard made shadows on the shade.

'You feel bad, don't you?' she said.

'No.'

'You think what you've done is wrong, don't you?'

I didn't answer.

'Clete's impotent, Dave,' she said.

'What?'

'He goes to a doctor, but it doesn't do any good.'

'When did he become impotent?'

'I don't know. Before I met him. He says a fever did it to him in Guatemala. He says he'll be all right eventually. He pretends it's not a problem.'

I raised up on my elbow and looked into her face.

'I don't understand,' I said. 'You moved in with an impotent man?'

'He can't help what he is. He's good to me in other ways. He's generous, and he respects me. He takes me places where Indians don't go. Why do you have that look on your face?'

'I'm sorry. I don't mean to,' I said.

'What are you thinking?'

'Nothing. I just don't quite understand.'

'Understand what?'

'Your relationship. It doesn't make sense.'

'Maybe it isn't your business.'

'He was my partner, I'm in bed with his girl. You don't think I have some involvement here?'

'I don't like the way you're talking to me.'

I knew that anything else I said would be wrong. I sat on the edge of the bed with my back toward her. The wind fluttered the shade in the window, casting a brilliant crack of sunlight across the room. Finally I looked over my shoulder at her. She had pulled the sheet up over her breasts.

'I try not to be judgmental about other people. I apologize,' I said. 'But he and I used to be good friends. You said he was impotent. You were suggesting I didn't have anything to feel bad about. There's something wrong in the equation here. Don't pretend there isn't.'

'Look the other way, please,' she said, gathered the sheet around her, picked up her clothes from the chair, and walked into the bathroom. A few minutes later she came back out in her yellow dress, pushing the top back on her lipstick, pressing her lips together.

'I like you just the same,' I said.

'You don't know anything,' she said.

And she left me there, with a wet spot in the center of my bed and a big question mark as to whether I had acquired any degrees of caution or wisdom in the fiftieth year of my life.

chapter seven

I needed to go back to the Divide and talk to more people about the disappearance of Clayton Desmarteau and his cousin. But I had gotten too late a start that day, and instead I drove up to Flathead Lake and spent two hours searching through property records in the county clerk's office. I was still convinced that there was some tie between Sally Dio, Dixie Lee, Harry Mapes, and Star Drilling Company. I didn't buy the story that Sally Dio kept Dixie Lee around to effect innocuous real estate deals or because he simply liked over-the-hill rockabilly musicians. I had known too many like him in New Orleans. They liked women but didn't consider them important; they liked power but would share it out of necessity; they were cruel or violent upon occasion but usually in a pragmatic way. However, they loved money. It was the ultimate measure of success in their lives, the only subject of interest in their conversations. They paid with cash in restaurants, not with credit cards, and their elaborate tipping was as much a part of their predictable grandiosity as their lavender Cadillacs and eight-hundred-dollar tropical suits.

But all I found in the courthouse with Dixie Lee's or Dio's name on them were deeds or leases to house lots, corner business property, and a couple of marinas, nothing that surprised me, nothing that suggested anything more than investments in local real estate.

I drove up the east shore of the lake, through the orchards of cherry trees, past the restaurant built out over the water and the blue lagoon with the rim of white beach and the pines growing thickly up the incline back toward the road, and finally to the entrance of Sally Dio's split-level redwood home built up on a cliff that overlooked the dazzling silklike sheen of the lake. I drove around the next curve, parked my truck off the shoulder, and walked back through a stand of pine trees that ended abruptly at the lip of a cliff that fell away to the lake's edge. Green, moss-covered rocks showed dully in the sunlight just below the water's surface.

Across the lagoon I could see Dio's house and the cottage below where Clete and Darlene lived. I knelt on one knee among the pine needles and steadied my World War II Japanese field glasses against a tree trunk. An American flag popped in the breeze on Dio's veranda, his flower boxes were brilliant with pink and blue and crimson petunias, and a cream-colored Mercury and black Porsche with Nevada plates were parked in the gravel at the edge of his lawn. I wrote the tag numbers down in a notebook, buttoned it in my shirt pocket, then watched a big van with bubble side windows, followed by a Toyota jeep, drive out on the beach. The side door, which was painted with a tropical sunset, slid open and a group of swimmers jumped out on the sand and began inflating a huge yellow raft with a foot-operated air pump.

I refocused the glasses on their faces. It was Dio and

what Clete called the Tahoe crowd. Dio wore an open shirt, flop sandals, and a luminescent purple bikini that fitted tightly against his loins and outlined his phallus. He was in a good mood, directing the outing of his entourage, pointed at a milk-white two-engine amphibian plane that came in low over the hills of the far side of the lake, unlocking his father's wheelchair from the mechanical platform that extended from the van's open door and lowered to the sand. Clete walked from the Toyota, wheeled Dio's father by a barbecue pit, lighted a bag of charcoal, and began forking a box of steaks on to the grill. He wore his crushed porkpie fishing hat, and I could see his nylon shoulder holster and revolver under his sweater.

The amphibian made one pass over the beach, gunned its engines and banked into the cloudless sky over my head, then made a wide turn and came in over the top of a cherry orchard and a sailboat dock, flattening out and touching its belly and wing pontoons down on the water in a spray of white foam and mist from the back draft of the propellers.

While Clete cooked and attended to the elder Dio, who sat sullen and wrapped in a shawl with a glass of red wine in his hand, the others took rides on the plane. I was amazed at the carelessness of the pilot and the faith of those who flew with him. They lifted off the water and into the wind and cleared the pines by no more than thirty feet, then climbed high into the sun, banked at a sharp angle, and came back between a cut in the hills, dipping down over beachfront houses in a roar of noise that made fishermen in outboards pull their anchors and turn in to shore.

I watched them for two hours. They smoked dope in

the lee of the van, drank wine and canned beer out of a washtub filled with crushed ice, ate bleeding steaks and tossed salads off paper plates, swam out breathlessly into the lake and climbed laughing into their yellow raft, their bodies hard and pickled with cold. The girls were pretty and tan and good to look at. Everyone was happy, except maybe Clete and the elder Dio. The Tahoe crowd were the kind of people who knew that they would never die.

The sun had moved into the western sky, which was absolutely blue above the green hills, and the light must have glinted on my field glasses because I saw Sally Dio look up suddenly and squint at the pine trees in which I knelt. I stepped back into the shadows and refocused through the branches. Dio stood by Clete and his father and was pointing in my direction. Clete stopped cleaning up paper plates from a picnic table, glanced up briefly at the cliff, then resumed his work. But Sally Dio and his father looked as if they were staring at an angry dog that was running against its chain. The elder Dio's mouth was wide when he spoke to Clete again, and Clete flung a handful of picnic trash into a garbage can, walked down to the water's edge where the swimmers had left the raft, dragged it up on the sand, and began pulling out the air plugs. Then he loaded the hampers, the washtub of beer and wine coolers, and the elder Dio back into the van.

I could have gotten out of there, I suppose, without being seen. But sometimes self-respect requires that you float one down the middle, letter high, big as a balloon, and let the batter have his way. I walked through the trees back to the road. The air was cool in the shade and heavy with the smell of pine needles on the ground.

Bluebirds with yellow wings flew in and out of the smoky light at the tops of the trees. I walked up the shoulder of the road, got in my truck, put my field glasses inside their case, put the case inside the glove box, and started the engine just as Dio's van and Clete's jeep turned out of the entrance to the public beach and headed toward me.

I saw Sally Dio's face through the wide front window of the van, saw the recognition and anger grow in it as he looked back at me and took his foot off the accelerator. Clete was slowing behind him at the same time.

Dio stopped opposite my cab and stared at me.

'What the fuck you think you're doing, man?' he said.

Through the bubble side window of the van I could see people sitting in leather swivel chairs. Their faces gathered at the window as though they were looking out of a fishbowl.

'Wonderful day,' I said.

'What the fuck you doing up in that woods?'

'What do you care? You're not shy. Come on, Dio. That air show was first-rate.'

I saw his nostrils whiten around the edges.

'We told you the other day you don't come around,' he said. 'You're not a cop. You seem to have confusion about that.'

I turned off my engine and clicked my nails on the window jamb. He turned off his engine, too. It was silent on the road, except for the wind blowing through the pines. The western sun over the lake made his waxed black van almost glow with an aura.

'I heard you like to take off parts of people,' I said.

'You heard what?'

'The Sal the Duck story. It's the kind of stuff they enjoy at the DEA. It brightens up a guy's file.'

He opened the door and started to step out on the road. I saw his father lean forward from the back and try to hold his shoulder. The father's lips looked purple against his gray skin; his goiter worked in this throat and his eyes were intense and black when he spoke. But Sally Dio was not listening to his father's caution, and he slid off the seat and stepped out on the road.

I set my sunglasses on the dashboard and got out of the truck. Out of the corner of my eye I could see Clete standing by his jeep. Dio had put on a pair of Levi's over his bathing suit. His denim shirt was open, and his stomach was flat and ridged with muscle. I heard the van door slide open on the far side, and a sun-bleached boy and girl walked around the back and stared at me, but it was obvious they intended to remain spectators. Through the trees I could see the sun click on the deep blue rippling sheen of the lake.

'You've got a serious problem,' Sally Dio said.

'How's that?' I said, and I smiled.

'You hear an Italian name, you think you can piss on it. A guy's been up the road, you think he's anybody's fuck.'

'You're not a convincing victim, Dio.'

'So you keep coming around, provoking a guy, bothering his family, bothering his friends.' He touched me lightly on the chest with three stiff fingers. There were small saliva bubbles in the corner of his mouth. His ducktailed hair was the color of burnt copper in the slanting light.

'It's time to back off, partner,' I said, and smiled again.

'And it don't matter you been warned. You get in people's faces, you got no respect for an old man, you got no respect for people's privacy. You're a jitterbird, man.' His three stiffened fingers tapped against my chest again, this time harder. 'You get off hanging around swinging dicks, 'cause you got nothing going on your own.'

His face came closer to mine and he poked me in the chest again. The looped scar under his right eye looked like a flattened piece of string on his skin. I slipped my hands into the back pockets of my khakis, as a third-base coach might, and looked off at the sunlight winking through the pine trees.

'Let me run something by you, Sal,' I said. 'Did you ever ask yourself why you have a certain kind of people hanging around you? Hired help, rummy musicians, beachboys with rut for brains. Do you think it's just an accident that everybody around you is a gumball? When's the last time somebody told you you were full of shit?'

I could hear his breathing.

'You got a death wish, man. You got something wrong with you,' he said.

'Let's face it, Sal. I'm not the guy with the electronic gate on my driveway. You think the Fuller Brush man is going to whack you out?'

He wet his lips to speak again, the suddenly one side of his face tightened and he swung at my head. I ducked sideways and felt a ring graze across my ear and scalp. Then I hooked him, hard, between the mouth and the nose. His head snapped back, and his long hair collapsed over his ears. Then he came at me, swinging wildly with both fists, the way an enraged child would.

Before I could hit him squarely again, he locked both arms around me, grunting, wheezing in my ear; I could smell his hair tonic and deodorant and the reefer smoke in his clothes. Then he released one of his arms, bent his knees, and swung at my phallus.

But his aim was not as good as his design. He hit me inside the thigh, and I brought my elbow into his nose, felt it break like a chicken bone, saw the shock and pain in his eyes just before I hit him again, this time in the mouth. He bounced off the van's side panel, and I hit him hard in the face again. He was trying to raise his hands in front of him, but it did him no good. I heard the back of his head bounce off the metal again, saw the genuine terror in his eyes, saw his blood whipped across the glass bubble in the panel, felt my fists hit him so hard that his face went out of round.

Then Clete was between us, his revolver drawn, one arm held out stiffly toward me, his eyes big and glaring.

'Back away, Dave! I'll shoot you in the foot! I swear to God I will!' he said.

On the edge of my vision I could see cars stopped on the road in each direction. Clete was breathing through his mouth, his eyes riveted on mine. Sally Dio had both hands pressed to his face. His fingers were red in the sunlight through the trees. In the distance I heard a police siren. I felt the heat go out of my chest the way a hot-eyed, hook-beaked raven would fly out of a cage.

'Sure,' I said.

'I mean it, all the way across the road,' he said.

I held up my palms.

'No problem,' I said. 'Don't you want me to move my truck, though? We're blocking a lot of traffic.'

I saw the sun-bleached boy and the girl walk Sally

Dio around to the other side of the van. A sheriff's car was driving around the traffic jam on the edge of the road. Cletus put his revolver back in his nylon shoulder holster.

'You crazy sonofabitch,' he said.

The holding cell in the county jail was white and small, and the barred door gave on to a small office area where two khaki-uniformed deputies did their paperwork. The cell contained nothing to sit or sleep on but a narrow wood bench that was bolted into the back wall, and no plumbing except a yellow-streaked drain in the center of the cement floor. I had already used the phone to call the baby-sitter in Missoula to tell her that I would probably not be home that night.

One of the deputies was a big Indian with a plug of chewing tobacco buttoned down tightly in his shirt pocket. He bent over a cuspidor by the side of his desk and spit in it. He had come into the office only a few minutes earlier.

'They already told you Dio's not pressing charges?' he asked.

'Yes.'

'So it's just a disorderly conduct charge. Your bond's a hundred bucks.'

'I don't have it.'

'Write a check.'

'I don't have one.'

'You want to use the phone again?'

'I don't know anyone I can call.'

'Look, guilty court's not for two days.'

'There's nothing I can do about it, podna.'

'The judge's already gone home or the sheriff could

ask him to let you out on your own recognizance. We'll see what we can do tomorrow.'

'I appreciate it.'

'You came all the way up here from Louisiana to stomp Sally Dio's ass?'

'It sort of worked out that way.'

'You sure picked on one bad motherfucker. I think you'd be better off if you'd blown out his light altogether.'

For supper I ate a plate of watery lima beans and a cold Spam sandwich and drank a can of Coca-Cola. It was dark outside the window now, and the other deputy went home. I sat in the gloom on the wood bench and opened and closed my hands. They felt thick and stiff and sore on the knuckles. Finally the Indian looked at his watch.

'I left a message for the judge at his house. He didn't call back,' he said. 'I got to take you upstairs.'

'It's all right.'

As he took the keys to the cell out of his desk drawer his phone rang. He nodded while he listened, then hung up.

'You got the right kind of lady friend,' he said.

'What?'

'You're cut loose. Your bail's your fine, too. You ain't got to come back unless you want to plead not guilty.'

He turned the key in the iron lock, and I walked down the wood-floored corridor toward the lighted entrance that gave on to the parking lot. She stood under the light outside, dressed in blue jeans and a maroon shirt with silver flowers stitched on it. Her black hair was shiny in the light, and she wore a deerskin bag on a string over her shoulder.

'I'll drive you back to your truck,' she said.

'Where's Clete?'

'Up at Sal's.'

'Does he know where you are?'

'I guess he does. I don't hide anything from him.'

'Nothing?' I said.

She looked at me and didn't answer. We walked toward her jeep in the parking lot. The sheen on her hair was like the purple and black colors in a crow's wing. We got in and she started the engine.

'What's China pearl?' she asked.

'High-grade Oriental skag. Why?'

'You knocked out one of Sal's teeth. They gave him a shot of China pearl for the pain. You must have been trying to kill him.'

'No.'

'Oh? I saw his face. There're bloody towels all over his living room rug.'

'He dealt it, Darlene. He's a violent man and one day somebody's going to take him out.'

'*He's* a violent man? That's too much.'

'Listen, you're into some kind of strange balancing act with these people. I don't know what it is, but I think it's crazy. Clete said he met you when you drove Dixie Lee all the way back to Flathead from a reservation beer joint. Why would you do that for Dixie Lee?'

'He's a human being, isn't he?'

'He's also barroom furniture that usually doesn't get hauled across the mountains by pretty Indian girls.'

She drove up the east short of the lake without answering. The trunks of the aspens and birch trees were silver in the moonlight, the rim of the mountains around the lake black against the sky. I tried one more time.

'What does it take to make you understand you don't belong there?' I said.

'Where do I belong?'

'I don't know. Maybe with another guy.' I swallowed when I said it.

The scars on the backs of her hands were thin and white in the glow of moon- and starlight through the window.

'Do you want to take a chance on living with me and my little girl?' I said.

She was silent a moment. Her mouth looked purple and soft when she turned her face toward me.

'I won't always be in this trouble. I've had worse times. They always passed,' I said.

'How long will you want me to stay?'

'Until you want to leave.'

Her hands opened and then tightened on the steering wheel.

'You're lonely now,' she said. 'After we were together, maybe you'd feel different.'

'You don't know that.'

'I know the way people are when they're lonely. It's like the way you feel at night about somebody. Then in the daylight it's not the same.'

'What would you lose by trying?'

She slowed the jeep on the gravel shoulder a few feet behind my parked pickup truck and cut the engine. It was dark in the heavy shadow of the pines. Out over the lake the sky was bursting with constellations.

'You're a nice man. One day you'll find the right woman,' she said.

'That's not the way you felt this morning. Don't put me off, Darlene.'

I put my arm around her shoulders and turned her face with my hand. Her eyes looked up quietly at me in the dark. I kissed her on the mouth. Her eyes were still open when I took my mouth away from hers. Then I kissed her again, and this time her mouth parted and I felt her lips become wet against mine and her fingers go into my hair. I kissed her eyes and the moles at the corner of her mouth, then I placed my hand on her breast and kissed her throat and tried to pull aside her shirt with my clumsy hand and kiss the tops of her breasts.

Then I felt her catch her breath, tear it out of the air, stiffen, push against me and turn her face out into the dark.

'No more,' she said.

'What—'

'It was a mistake. It ends here, Dave.'

'People's feelings don't work like that.'

'We're from different worlds. You knew that this morning. I led you into it. It's my fault. But it's over.'

'Are you going to tell me Clete's from your world?'

'It doesn't matter. It's not going anywhere. Maybe at another time—'

'I'm just not going to listen to that stuff, Darlene.'

'You have to accept what I tell you. I'm sorry about all of it. I'm sorry I'm hurting you. I'm sorry about Clete. But you go back home or you're going to be killed.'

'Not by the likes of Sally Dee, I'm not.'

I put my arm around her shoulders again and tried to brush back her hair with my hand.

'I'm sorry,' she said, but this time calmly, with her eyes straight ahead. Then she got out of the jeep and stood in the dark with her arms folded and her face turned toward the lake. The water's surface was black and flecked with foam in the wind. I walked up next to her and put my fingers lightly on her neck.

'It's not good,' she said softly.

I could not see her face in the shadows. I walked away from her toward my truck. The gravel crunched loudly under my feet, and the wind was cold through the pines.

The next morning was Friday. I was headed back to the other side of the Divide when my water pump went out at Bonner, on the Blackfoot River, ten miles east of Missoula. I had my truck towed to a garage in town and was told by the mechanic that he would not have the repairs done until Monday at noon. So I had to mark off two days that I could sorely afford to lose.

The air was cool and smelled of woodsmoke when I woke Monday morning, and the sun was bright on the lip of Hellgate Canyon and the valley was filled with blue shadows. I made *cush-cush* for Alafair and me, walked her to school in the spreading sunlight, then sat on the front porch in a long-sleeved flannel shirt and drank another cup of coffee and read the paper. A few minutes later a Landrover with a fly rod case in the gun rack pulled to a stop in front. Dan Nygurski got out, dressed in a pair of beltless jeans, an army sweater, and a floppy hat covered with trout flies.

'I've got a day off. Take a drive with me up the Blackfoot,' he said.

'I have to pick up my truck in the shop later.'

'I'll take you there. Come on. You got a fishing rod?'

His seamed, coarse face smiled at me. He looked like he could bench three hundred pounds or break a baseball bat across his knee. I invited him in and gave him a cup of coffee in the kitchen while I got my Fenwick rod out of the closet and tied on my tennis shoes.

'What have you got in the way of flies?' he asked.

'Nothing really, popping bugs.'

'I've got what you need, brother. A number-fourteen renegade. It drives them crazy.'

'What's this about?'

His mouth twitched, and the muscles in the side of his face and throat jumped.

'I thought I'd pick up some tips from you on how to handle Sally Dee,' he said. 'I think you've got a first there. I don't believe anybody's ever cleaned Sal's clock before.'

'How'd you hear about it?'

'The sheriff's office reports to us whenever Sal comes to their attention. A deputy told me you tried to use Sal's face to repaint the side of his van. I always knew he had some worthwhile potential.'

'He's got skag and coke in that house.'

'How do you know?'

'A friend told me.'

'Purcel?'

'No.'

'Ah, the Indian girl.'

'What do you know about her?'

'Nothing. She's just some gal Purcel picked up. They

come and go at Sally Dee's. What's your point about the coke and the skag?'

'Get a warrant and bust the place.'

'When I put Sal away, it's going to be for the rest of his worthless life, not on a chickenshit possessions charge. He'd have one of those lamebrain beachboys doing his time, anyway.'

'I spent some time up at the Flathead courthouse. Why's he buying and leasing up property around the lake?'

Nygurski set his cup in the saucer and looked out the window at the backyard. The grass was wet and green in the shade, and the sunlight was bright on the tops of the trees across the alley.

'He thinks casino gambling's going through the legislature,' he said. 'The time's right for it. People are out of work, they've used up all their compo, agriculture's in the toilet. Casino gambling could turn Flathead Lake into another Tahoe. Sal would be in on the ground floor.'

'It's that simple?'

'Yeah, more or less. I don't think it's going to happen, though. People here don't like outsiders, anyway. Particularly greasers and Californians.'

'What did you come over here to tell me?'

'Don't worry about it. Come on, I've got an appointment with an eighteen-inch rainbow.'

We drove up through the Blackfoot River canyon, which was still dark and cool with shadows and smelled of woodsmoke blowing up from the mill at Bonner. Then we broke out into meadowland and ranch country and sunshine again, turned off the highway and crossed the river on a planked log bridge, and began climbing on a dirt road through hills and lodgepole pine and scrub brush, where white-tailed deer sprang in a flick of the eye back into the dense cover of the woods. Then we came back into the canyon again, into the most beautiful stretch of river that I had ever seen. The rock cliffs were red and sheer and rose straight up three hundred feet. The crests were thick with ponderosa, and the water, blue and green, turned in deep pools where the current had eaten under the cliffs. The rocks along the shore were bone white and etched with dried insects, and out beyond the canyon's shadows, the great boulders in the middle of the river were steaming in the sun and flies were hatching out in a gray mist above the riffle.

I tied a renegade fly on the tippet of my nylon leader and followed Nygurski into the shallows. The water was so cold inside my tennis shoes and khakis that my bones felt as though they had been beaten with an ice mallet. I false-cast in a figure eight above my head, laid out the line upstream on the riffle, and watched the fly swirl through the eddies and around the boulders toward me. I picked it up, false-cast again, drying it in the air with a whistling sound inches from my ear, and dropped it just beyond a barkless, sun-bleached cottonwood that beavers had toppled into the stream. The riffle made a lip of dirty foam around the end of the log, and just as my leader swung around it and coursed across the top of a deep pool, I saw a rainbow rise from the bottom like an iridescent bubble released from the pebble-and-silt bed and snap my renegade down in a spray of silvery light.

I raised my rod high and stripped off-line with my left hand and let him run. He headed out into the current, into deep water, and my Fenwick arched and vibrated in my palm, drops of water glistening and trembling on the line. Then he broke the surface, and the sun struck the red and pink and green band on his side. I had to go deeper into the current with him, up to my chest now, and strip off my line to keep from breaking the tippet. I kept walking with him downstream while he pumped against the rod and tried to wrap the line around a submerged boulder, until I was back in the deep shade of the canyon, with the wind cold on my neck and the air heavy with the smell of ferns and wet stone.

Then I was around a bend, up into shallow water again, the gravel firm under my tennis shoes. It was all over for him. I worked him up into a small lagoon, watched him gin impotently over the clouded bottom with his dorsal fin out of the water; then I wet my hand and knelt in the shallows and picked him up under the stomach. He felt cold and thick in my hand, and his mouth and gills pumped hard for oxygen. I slipped the fly loose from the corner of his mouth and placed him back in the water. He hovered momentarily over the gravel, his tail moving for balance in the light current, before he dropped away over a ledge and was gone in the current.

While Nygurski fished farther upstream, I kicked together a pile of driftwood out in the sunlight, started a fire on the stones, and fixed a pot of cowboy coffee from his rucksack. It was warm in the sun. I sat on a dead cottonwood and drank the coffee black from one of his tin cups and watched him fish. There was a ranch farther upstream, and a curious Angus wandered out of the unfenced pasture and rode through the willows and clattered across the stones on the beach into the shallows. I saw Nygurski break his leader on a snag, then look back at me in frustration. I pointed to my watch.

He walked up the beach with his fly rod over his shoulder. His jeans were wet up to his thighs. He slipped his straw creel off his shoulder, slit open the stomachs of three rainbow, scooped out the guts and threw them back into the willows. Then he stooped by the edge of the stream and dug the blood and membrane out of the vertebrae with his thumbnail.

'I saw you turn that big one loose,' he said.

'I don't keep them much anymore. I don't have a Montana license, anyway.'

'You hunt?'

'I used to. I don't much anymore.'

'You give it up in the army?'

'Something like that.'

He poured himself a cup of coffee, took two wax-paper-wrapped pork chop sandwiches out of his rucksack and gave me one, then sat down on the log next to me. The veins in his thick neck stuck out like webs of cord when he chewed.

'What kind of gun do you have?' he said.

'An army .45 automatic.'

'You have a permit for it?'

'In Louisiana I do. Not here.'

'They're not real big on gun permits in Montana, but let's get you one, anyway.'

'What are we talking about?'

'We have a tap on Sally Dio's telephone. He knows it.'

'So?'

'He doesn't know that we have a tap on a pay phone

down the shore from his house. The one that he uses for some of his long-distance calls.'

I picked up a small, flat, gray stone and skipped it out on the water.

'He called a bar in Vegas,' Nygurski said. 'He said to the guy who answered, "Tell Charlie I've got a yard job for him up here." You know what that is?'

'No, that's a new one.'

'I've heard a couple of Quentin graduates use it. It's when they do somebody out on the yard. The last time we heard Sal say something like that on a tap, a witness against him got a .22 Magnum round behind the ear. But we don't know who Charlie is.'

I tossed another small stone in a gentle arc out on the water. It made a circle like a trout rising, then the circle floated on down the riffle into white water.

'Maybe it doesn't have anything to do with you,' he said. 'The Dios have lots of enemies.'

I brushed the gravel off my palms and I didn't say anything for a while. The sun was hot now, and flies were hatching out of the cattails, rainbows popping at them in a shaded pool under the cliff.

'What do you think I ought to do?' I said finally.

'Maybe it's time to go back to New Iberia.'

'You think he'd bring in a mechanic, risk his whole operation, because of pride?'

'Look, he's got a little clout in the mob because he's Frank Dio's son. But basically Sal's a loser. He's a lousy musician, he did time for stolen credit cards, his wife dumped him after he broke her nose, his friends are bought-and-paid-for rummies and cokeheads. Then you come along and remodel his face while everybody gets to watch. What do you think a guy like that is feeling for you right now?'

'It won't matter, then, if I go back to Louisiana or not.'

'Maybe not.'

I looked at my watch. Across the stream I saw a hawk drop suddenly into a meadow and hook a field mouse in its talons.

'Thanks for the fishing trip. I need to pick up my truck now,' I said.

'I'm sorry to be the one to drop this on you.'

'Don't worry about it.'

'Why in God's name did you do it, Robicheaux?'

I didn't sleep that night. As we say in AA, the executive committee held a session in my head. I thought about sending Alafair back to Louisiana, to stay with my cousin or Batist and his wife, but then I would lose all control over her situation. I doubted that Harry Mapes would make a move against either of us as long as my trial was pending and it looked like I was going to take the fall for Dalton Vidrine's murder; but then again you can't second-guess a psychopath, and I believed that's what he was.

I still wasn't convinced by Dan Nygurski about Sally Dio's calling Vegas to bring in a contract killer. The mob, or at least its members I had known in New Orleans, did not operate like that. They whacked out witnesses, Colombian competitors, and each other, but they didn't hit ordinary people because of a personal grudge. Their own leadership didn't allow it; it brought down too much heat on their operation and compromised their hard-bought relationships with politicians, police officials, and judges.

Sally Dee was a vicious punk, but his father was smart and cautious, a survivor of gang wars and Mafia power struggles. I just didn't believe they would be willing to blow it all over a broken tooth.

So the executive committee stayed in session until the false dawn and then adjourned with little resolved. As always when I was weak and drained and absolutely burnt-out with my own failed attempts at reasoning through a problem, I turned it over to my Higher Power; then I cooked sausage and eggs for our breakfast, walked Alafair to school, made arrangements for her to stay with the baby-sitter, put my .45 and an extra clip under the truck seat, and headed over the Divide for the Blackfeet Reservation.

My fan belt broke ten miles south of the reservation, and I hitched a ride with an Indian feed grower to a filling station at a four-corners four miles up the road. I bought a new fan belt, then started walking on the shoulder of the road back toward my truck. It was a mistake. Rain clouds drifted down over the low green hills to the east, shadowing the fields and sloughs and clumps of willows and cottonwoods; suddenly the sky burst open and a hard, driving rain stung my skin and drenched my clothes in minutes. I took cover against the rock face of a small hill that the road cut through, and watched the storm shower work its way across the land. Then a paintless and battered school bus, with adhesive tape plastered on its cracked windows, with bicycles, collapsed tents, shovels, and two canoes roped to its sides and roof, came highballing around the corner like a highway-borne ghost of the 1960s.

When the driver stopped for me I could hear screws

scouring into brake shoes, the twisted exhaust pipe hammering against the frame, the engine firing as if all the spark-plug leads had been deliberately crossed. The driver threw open the folding door with a long lever, and I stepped inside of what could have been a time capsule. The seats had all been torn out and replaced with hammocks, bunks, sleeping bags, a butane stove, a bathtub, cardboard boxes bursting with clothes. A woman nursed a child at her breast; a white man with Indian braids sat on the floor, carving an animal out of a soap bar; another woman was changing an infant's diapers on the backseat; a bearded man in a ponytail slept facedown in a hammock, so that his body looked like a netted fish's suspended from the ceiling. I could smell sour milk, reefer, and burnt food.

The driver had dilated blue eyes and a wild red beard, and he wore leather wristbands and a fatigue jacket open on his bare chest, which was deeply tanned and scrolled with dark blue jailhouse tattoos. He told me to sit down in a wood chair that was located next to him at the head of the aisle. Then he slammed the door shut with the lever, crunched the transmission into gear, and we careened down the road in the blowing rain. I told him where I was going, and held on to a metal rail to keep from bouncing out of the chair.

'That's a bad place to stand, man,' he said. 'There's fuckers come around that curve seventy miles an hour, crazy sonsobitches in log trucks think they own the fucking road. What one of them needs is somebody to wind up a brick on a string and put it through his window. You live around here?'

'No. I'm just a visitor.'

'That's a weird accent. I thought maybe you was a Canuck.'

'No, I'm from Louisiana.'

His eyes were curious, and they moved over my face. The bus drifted toward the shoulder.

'Say, there's a café up on the right. I think I'll get off and get something to eat,' I said.

'I said we'd take you to your truck. You'll get there, man. Don't worry about it.'

The woman who was breast-feeding the child wiped his chin with her shirt, then put his mouth on the nipple again and looked impassively out the window. Her face was without makeup, her hair dull brown, long, and stuck together on the tips.

'You keep looking in the back of the bus. Something bothering you?' the driver said.

'Not at all.'

'You think we're spikers or something?'

'What?'

'Spikers. You think we go around driving railroad spikes in trees?'

'No, I don't think that.'

''Cause we don't, man. A tree is a living thing, and we don't wound living things. Does that make sense to you?'

'Sure.'

'We live up on the reservation. We're a family. We lead a natural way of life. We don't get in nobody's face. All we ask is nobody fuck with us. That ain't a lot to ask, is it?'

I looked out the streaked windowpanes of the folding door. The countryside was green and wet and covered with a gray mist.

'Is it?' he said.

'No, it's not.'

''Cause a lot of people won't let you alone. They're at war with the earth, man. That's their fucking problem. You don't do it their way, they try to kick a two-by-four up your ass.'

The ride was becoming increasingly more uncomfortable. I figured it was three more miles to my truck.

'Do you know a girl named Darlene American Horse on the reservation?' I said.

'I don't know her.'

'She's from there.'

'That might be, man, but I don't know her. Check with my old lady.' He nodded backward toward the woman with the child at her breast.

I asked her about Darlene. She wore large wire-rimmed glasses, and she looked at me quietly with no expression in her face.

'I don't know her,' she said.

'You've lived there long?'

'A year.'

'I see.'

'It's a Blackfeet reservation,' she said. Her speech had that flat quality of quasi-omniscience that you hear in women who have reached a certain gray plateau in their lives from which they know they'll never escape.

'Yes?' I said.

'They're all Blackfeet. The Sioux live over in South Dakota.'

'I don't understand what you mean.'

'American Horse is a Sioux name,' she said. 'He fought with Sitting Bull and Crazy Horse against the whites.'

It's her married name, I thought.

'You know how they bought it, too?' the driver said. 'Dealing with the Man under a flag of truce. They went into the fort and got their asses shot. That's what happens when you trust those fuckers.'

My God, why didn't I see it, I thought.

'Hey, you're looking a little gray,' the driver said.

'What?'

'You want some food? We got extra,' he said.

'No. Thank you. D' y'all know a guy by the name of Clayton Desmarteau?'

'You better believe it. Same outfit as me. First Cav.'

'Did he have a sister?'

'What d'you mean "did"?'

'You haven't seen him around in a while, have you?'

He thought for a moment.

'I guess not,' he said.

'Do you know if he had a sister?'

'I don't know nothing about his family. He don't live on the reservation. He used to come on it to organize for AIM against them oil and gas companies. They're gonna mess up the East Front, try to build pipelines and refineries and all kinds of shit.'

'What color were his eyes?'

'His eyes?' He turned and grinned at me through his red beard. His teeth were missing in back. 'I look like I go around looking at guys' eyes?'

'Come on, were they turquoise?'

'What the fuck I know about a guy's eyes? What kind of stuff are you into, man?'

'He's a policeman,' the woman with the child said.

'Is that for real?' the driver said.

'No.'

'Then why you asking all these questions? You trying to give some shit to Clayton's people?' The hair on his forearms grew like red metal wires on the edges of his leather wristbands.

'No.'

''Cause the Indians don't need no more hassle. These are native people, man, I mean it was their *place*, and whites been taking a dump on them for two hundred years.'

'I'll get off here,' I said.

'You bothered by something I said?'

'Not in the least, partner. The rain's stopping now, and I need to walk. My truck's just over the rise.'

''Cause we got no beef with nobody. We thought we were helping you out. You gotta watch out for a lot of people in this state. I ain't blowing gas, Jack. It's the times,' he said.

I stood on the side of the road in the damp, sunlit air, a green pasture behind me, and watched the bus disappear over the rise. My truck was still a mile down the road.

The old woman was hoeing in a rocky vegetable patch behind her house. She wore laced boots, a man's oversized wool trousers, and a khaki shirt, and a shawl was wrapped around her head. In the distance the wet land sloped toward the Divide, where the mountains thrust up violently against the sky, their sheer cliffs now purple with shadow. Up high it had snowed, and the ponderosa was white on the crests and through the saddles. The old woman glanced sideways at me when I opened her wood gate and walked into the yard, then continued chopping weeds in the rows as though I were not there.

'Darlene American Horse is your daughter, isn't she?' I asked.

She didn't answer. Her white hair bunched out under her shawl, and the corners of her eyes were creased with concentration on her work.

'Mrs Desmarteau, believe me, I'm a friend,' I said. 'I want to find out what happened to your son. I want to help Darlene, if I can.'

She thudded and raked the hoe in the dirt and stones and notched out weeds between the cabbages without ever touching a leaf.

'I think Darlene lives among some bad people. I want to get her away from them,' I said.

She pulled back the door of an abandoned, dilapidated privy, put away the hoe and took out a shovel. In the back of the privy a calico cat was nursing her litter on top of a pile of gunnysacks. Mrs Desmarteau laid the shovel across a wheelbarrow loaded with manure and began pushing it toward the edge of the vegetable patch. I took the handles out of her hands and wheeled it across the dirt yard, then began spreading the manure at the end of each row. The clouds were purple on top of the mountains, and snow was blowing off the edges of the canyons. Behind me I heard the plastic sheets of insulation rattling on her windows.

'She's your daughter, isn't she?' I said again.

'Are you one of the FBI?' she said.

'No, I'm not. But I used to be a policeman. I'm not any longer. I'm just a man who's in some trouble.'

For the first time her eyes looked directly at mine.

'If you know Darlene, why are you asking me if she's

my daughter?' she said. 'Why are you here and asking that question? You don't make sense.'

Then I realized that perhaps I had underestimated this elderly lady. And like most people who consider themselves educated, I had perhaps presumed that an elderly person – like someone who is foreign-speaking or unschooled – could not understand the complexities of my life and intellect.

'I didn't relate the name to yours,' I said. 'But I should have. She wears her brother's First Cav army jacket, doesn't she? She also has turquoise eyes. Your family name is French-Canadian, not Indian. Darlene and Clayton's father was part white, wasn't he?'

'Why do you say she lives among bad people?'

'The man she stays with isn't bad, but the people he works for are. I believe she should come back home and not stay with these people on the lake.'

'You've been there?'

'Yes.'

'Are they criminals?'

'Some of them are.'

Her hand slipped down over mine and took the shovel. Her palm was rough and edged with callus. She was motionless, the shovel propped against her wool trousers, her eyes fixed on the jagged outline of the mountains against the sky. The clouds on the high peaks looked full of snow.

'Are they the ones that killed my boy?' she said.

'Maybe they were involved in some way. I don't know.'

'Why is she with them?'

'She thinks she can find out what happened to

Clayton and his cousin. She worked in a bar. Where is it?'

'Five miles down the road. You passed it when you came here.'

'Do you know a man named Dixie Lee Pugh?'

'No.'

'Do you see Darlene?'

'She comes one day a week and brings groceries.'

'Talk to her, Mrs Desmarteau. She's a good girl. Between the two of us we'll get her back home.'

I saw her breathe through the mouth. Her lips moved without sound.

'What?' I said.

'Clayton never did no harm to anybody. They said he carried a gun. If he did, they made him. They wouldn't let him alone. They were afraid of him because he was brave.'

It was turning cold, I helped her finish spreading manure in her vegetable patch, then said good-bye and latched the wooden gate behind me. The sky was overcast and gray now. She looked small and alone with her hoe, in her dirt yard, in the wind that blew down off the backbone of the world.

I drove back down the dirt road and stopped at the place where Clayton Desmarteau and his cousin had put their car in the ditch. Did Mapes and Vidrine kidnap and drive them someplace, or did it all happen here? I asked myself. I jumped across the stream that bordered the far side of the road and walked up the slope into the lodgepole pine. The ground was thick with pine needles. Chipmunks played in the rocks, and red squirrels chased each other around the tree trunks. I walked about a quarter of a mile through the pines, then intersected a trace of a road that somebody had used at one time to dump garbage. The road dead-ended in a pile of rusted box springs, tin cans, mattresses, beer and wine bottles, and plastic soap containers. I went on another four hundred yards or so through the pines, then the trunks thinned and I came out on a tea-colored stream coursing over gray rocks. The stream cut along the edge of a low, rock-faced hill that rose abruptly into box elder, wild rosebushes, and thick scrub brush. I walked up and down the stream bank, crossed the sculpted tracks of deer, the delicate impressions of turkey and grouse in the wet sand, found the rotted, soft logs of an old cabin, tripped over the half-buried remains of a wood stove, and flushed a white-tailed buck that must have had ten points on his rack; but I saw nothing that was out of the ordinary or that could be helpful in discovering the fate of Clayton Desmarteau and his cousin.

Finally I came to a spring that flowed out of the hillside on the far bank of the stream. The spring dripped over rocks, and had eroded away the dirt and exposed the gnarled roots of small pines on the hillside. The water drained over a wide area of wet pine needles and black leaves, and the ground there was spongy and bursting with mushrooms and dark fern. I could smell the water, the coolness of the stone, the dank humus, the exposed tree roots that trailed like brown cobweb in the current. It smelled like the coulee on my property back in Louisiana. I wondered when I would be going back there, or if in fact I would be able to. Because I had decided that if I did not develop a better defense than the one I presently had, I was not going to deliver myself up for trial and a sure jolt in Angola pen.

I was tired. After hiking back to my truck, I drove up the road in the gray light between the wet fields, then I glanced in the side mirror at a black Willys Jeepster, a remake of the classic model manufactured right after World War II. Because the road was wet and there was no dust, I could see the driver's tall outline behind the steering wheel. Then he accelerated and closed on my rear bumper, as though he wanted to see my reflection in the side mirror or some detail of my pickup – the dealer's name, a bumper sticker that read Mulate's, Breaux Bridge, Louisiana.

Up ahead was the wide, squat log tavern where Clayton Desmarteau and his cousin had probably spent the last night of their lives, where Darlene had waited tables, and where she had probably met Dixie Lee Pugh while he was in a drunken stupor, saved him from getting his head kicked in, and driven him over the mountains to Sally Dio's on Flathead Lake. It was starting to mist, and a purple and orange neon war bonnet was lighted on the roof against the gray sky.

I pulled on to the gravel parking lot and waited to see what the driver in the Jeepster would do. He slowed abreast of me, his long hands on the top of the steering wheel, and stared intently out the passenger's window. His face, forehead, and neck were streaked with thin scabs, as though he had walked through a nest of rust-colored spiderweb.

I wanted him to stop, to open his door, to confront me with his injury and his anger. I wanted to see a weapon in his hand and feel that adrenaline surge, that violent sanction, that lights and clarifies the mind and resolves all the complexities.

But Harry Mapes was holding all the good cards.

Harry Mapes had been a helicopter pilot in Vietnam, and he knew that you don't change the terms of your situation when your Gatling guns are locked in on a solitary pajama-clad target in the middle of a grassy rice field.

He turned into the parking lot and parked by the front door, where three Indians in work clothes were drinking canned beer next to a truck. He lit a cigarette with a gold lighter before he got out of his Jeepster, then went inside without looking back at me.

By the time I got back to Missoula that night Alafair had already had her supper at the baby-sitter's, but I took her for a late snack at a pizza place called Red Pies Over Montana. She wore her soft denim jeans with the elastic waistband, patent leather shoes with white socks that were now gray with dust from the playground, and her yellow T-shirt printed with a smiling purple whale and the words 'Baby Orca' on it. Her cheeks were spotted with red pizza sauce. Through the restaurant window I could see the stars over the mountains.

'Dave?' she said.

'What is it, little guy?'

'When we going back home?'

'Don't you like it here?'

'I want to see Tex. Maybe Batist needs us at the shop. He can't read.'

'You don't have to read to sell worms and shiners.'

'Nothing here is like it is at home.'

'It has a lot of good things, though, doesn't it?'

'I miss Tripod. I miss Clarise. It's cold at night.'

I brushed her shiny black hair with my hand.

'It won't be long. You'll see,' I said.

But my assurance was an emotional lie. I didn't know when we could go back. I wasn't sure if I ever could. That night in the dark, with the door open between our bedrooms, I heard her saying her prayers by the side of the bed, then climbing in under the covers.

'Dave?'

'What?'

'Are people trying to hurt us? Is that why we had to move?'

I got up and walked barefoot into her room and sat on the edge of the bed. Her face looked round and tan in the moonlight through the window. Her blanket was pulled up to her chin.

'Don't think like that, Alf. Nobody wants to hurt guys like us. We're good guys,' I said. 'Think of all the people who love you. Batist and Clarise and your friends and teachers at school. They all love you, Alfie. And I love you most of all.'

I could see her wide-spaced teeth and the brightness of her eyes when she smiled up from the pillow.

But her thoughts were not far from my own. That night I dreamed of South Louisiana, of blue herons standing among flooded cypress trees, fields of sugarcane beaten with purple and gold light in the fall, the smell of smoldering hickory and pork dripping into the ash in our smokehouse, the way billows of fog rolled out of the swamp in the morning, so thick and white that sound – a bass flopping, a bullfrog falling off a log into the water – came to you inside a wet bubble, pelicans sailing out of the sun over the breaks out on the Gulf, the palm trees ragged and green and clacking in the salt breeze, and the crab and crawfish boils and fish fries that went on year-round, as though there were no end to a season and death had no sway in our lives, and finally the song that always broke my heart, 'La Jolie Blonde,' which in a moment made the year 1945. Our yard was abloom with hibiscus and blue and pink hydrangeas and the neighbors came on horseback to the *fais-dodo* under our oaks.

The next morning I got a call from Tess Regan, the third-grade teacher and assistant principal at Alafair's school. She said she had a one-hour break at eleven o'clock, and she asked if she could walk down to the house and talk with me.

'Is there something wrong?' I said.

'Maybe it's nothing. I'd rather talk to you about it at your house.'

'Sure. Come on down.'

A few minutes later she knocked on the screen door. She wore a pale green cotton dress, and her auburn hair was tied back with a green kerchief. I could see baby powder on her freckled shoulders.

'I hope I'm not bothering you,' she said.

'No, not at all. I have some iced tea made. It's a beautiful day. Let's have some on the porch.'

'All right,' she said. The corners of her eyes wrinkled good-naturedly at the deference to her situation as a lay person in a Catholic elementary school.

I brought the tea out on the porch, and we sat on two old metal chairs. The light was bright on the lawn and the trees, and bumblebees hummed over the clover in the grass.

'A man called earlier,' she said. 'He said he was a friend of yours from Louisiana. He wanted to know where you and Alafair lived.'

'What was his name?'

'He wouldn't give it.'

'Did you tell him?'

'No, of course not. We don't give out people's addresses. I told him to call information. He said he tried, but your number was unlisted.'

'It isn't, but my address isn't in the phone book, and information usually won't give out addresses. Why did the call bother you?' I leaned slightly forward.

'He was rude. No, it was more than that. His voice was ugly.'

'What else did he say?'

'He kept saying he was an old friend, that it was important he talk with you, that I should understand that.'

'I see.'

'Alafair said you used to be a police officer. Does this have something to do with that?'

'Maybe. Could you tell if it was long-distance?'

'It didn't sound like it.'

I tried to think. Who knew that Alafair went to a parochial school in Missoula? Darlene, perhaps. Or maybe I said something to Clete. Or maybe the person called New Iberia and got something out of Batist or Clarise. Then he could have phoned every Catholic elementary school in town until he hit the right combination.

'What was the first thing this guy said?' I asked.

Her mouth was wet and red when it came away from her glass. Her green eyes looked thoughtfully out into the sunlight.

'He said, "I'm calling for Dave Robicheaux,"' she said. 'I told him I didn't understand. Then he said it again, "I'm calling for Dave." So I said, "You mean you're delivering a message for him?"'

'Then he knew he'd found the right school.'

'What?'

'He's a slick guy.'

'I'm sorry if I handled it wrong,' she said.

'Don't worry about it. He's probably a bill collector. They follow me around the country.' I smiled at her, but she didn't buy it.

She set her iced tea on the porch railing and sat with her knees close together and her hands folded in her lap. She dropped her eyes, then looked up at me again.

'I'm probably being intrusive, but you're in some trouble, aren't you?'

'Yes.'

'Who is this man?'

'I'm not sure. If he called again, though, I'd appreciate your letting me know.'

'Is he a criminal?'

I looked at her face and eyes. I wondered how much of the truth she was able to take. I decided not to find out.

'Maybe,' I said.

She pinched her fingers together in her lap.

'Mr Robicheaux, if he's a threat to Alafair, we need to know that,' she said. 'You have an obligation to tell us that, I think.'

'This guy didn't have a Texas accent, did he?'

'No. He didn't have an accent.'

'A couple of guys have a beef with me. Maybe he works for one of them. But their beef is with me. It's not going to affect anything at your school.'

'I see,' she said, and her eyes went away into the sunlight on the yard.

'I'm sorry. I didn't mean to sound sharp,' I said.

'You weren't. I'm sorry you're having this trouble.' She stood up to go. 'I think you should consider calling the police. Your daughter is a beautiful little girl.'

'There's no law against a guy asking for somebody's address.'

'You probably understand these things better than I, then. Thank you for the tea.'

'Wait a minute. I appreciate your help. I really do. And Alafair thinks the world of you. But I could start explaining my situation to you now and we'd still be talking tomorrow morning. It's a mess, and it involves a bunch of bad people. I don't have any answers for it, either. Sometimes cops can't do any good. That's why as I get older I believe more and more in prayer. At least I feel like I'm dealing with somebody who's got some real authority.' I smiled again, and this time it took.

'I'll bet you handle it all right,' she said, and her eyes crinkled. She squeezed my hand and walked down the steps on to the sidewalk, out of the porch's shadow, into the sunshine, her calves clicking with light in the bright air.

I went into the kitchen and fixed a bowl of Grape-Nuts for lunch. While I ate I stared out the window at the neighbor's orange cat climbing up the roof of the garage out by the alley. Overhead, two doves sat on the telephone wires. Who had been the man on the telephone? I thought. Sally Dio's mechanic out of Vegas? Or maybe somebody who worked with Harry Mapes. Why not? It would be a safe way for Mapes to keep me agitated and off-balance. He was a mailer of hypodermic needles and threats against a child. A telephone call to the school would be consistent with his past behavior. At least that's what a police department psychologist would say.

Except for the fact that I was the defendant in an upcoming murder trial and Mapes was the prosecution witness. The apparatus of the law was on his side; he was the friend of the court, the chain-whipped victim of an alcoholic, burnt-out cop. Mapes didn't need to shave the dice.

Which brought me back to my original speculation and Dan Nygurski's warning, one I truly did not want to confront. A faceless button man whose only name was Charlie.

Call the police, she had said. Suffering God, I thought, why is it that in problematic situations almost everyone resorts to axioms and societal remedies that in actuality nobody believes in? Tess Regan was a good girl, and obviously I was being too hard on her in my frustration, but ask yourself, have you ever known anyone whose marriage was saved by a marriage counselor, whose drinking was cured by a psychiatrist, whose son was kept out of reform school by a social worker? In a badass, beer-glass brawl, would you rather have an academic liberal covering your back or a hobnailed redneck?

I drove to Bob Ward's Sporting Goods, a mountaineering and tackle-and-gun store I had heard about even in Louisiana, and used my MasterCard to buy a .38 revolver, a box of rounds and a cutaway holster for it, a secondhand twelve-gauge shotgun, and a box of double-aught buckshot. Back home I carried the tool chest from my truck into the kitchen, slipped the top shelf out of the cupboard, and tacked the .38 holster to its bottom. I replaced the shelf, loaded five rounds into the revolver, set the hammer on the empty chamber, slipped the revolver into the holster, and snapped the leather strap across the base of the hammer.

Then I took a hacksaw from the tool chest, lay the shotgun on the back porch step, placed my knee hard against the stock, and sawed through the ventilated rib sight and both barrels ten inches above the chambers. I broke open the breech, looked through the barrels at the clean, oily whorls of light, plopped two double-aughts in the chambers, snapped the breech shut, set the safety, and put the shotgun on the top shelf of the closet in the front hallway.

With the .45 in the bedroom, there would now be no place in the house where I would not have almost immediate access to a weapon. It wasn't a panacea, but it was all I had. I could have spent time regretting that I had bounced Sally Dio's head off his van in front of his friends, but if he was involved with Harry Mapes or Star Drilling Company, and I believed he was, it would have been only a matter of time before I had trouble with the Dio family, anyway.

I was still tired from yesterday's drive over the Divide. No, it went deeper than that. I was tired of pursuing a course that seemed to have no resolution, of walking about in what seemed to be a waking nightmare, of feeling that I deserved all this, that somehow I had asked for it, that it was inevitable that I ride in a wood cart like a condemned seventeenth-century criminal, creaking over the cobbled street through the mob toward the elevated platform where a hooded man waited with wheel and iron bar.

I put on my gym shorts, running shoes, and a cutoff sweatshirt, and ran four miles along the river. It was a cloudless day, the sky hard and blue, and the pines high up on the mountains seemed to tremble with light. In the south the Bitterroots were as sharp and etched against the sky as if they had been cut out with a razor blade. The spring runoff of melted snow was starting to abate in the river, and great round boulders that had been covered by the current only two days ago were now exposed and hot-looking in the sun, the skeletal remains of hellgrammites welded to their sides. I ran all the way to the university district, thumped across the river on an abandoned railroad bridge, and looked down below at a fisherman horsing a rainbow out of the current on to the gravel. The riverbank was lined with cottonwoods and willows, and the wind blew out of Hellgate Canyon and flattened the new leaves so that the trees looked like they had changed, in a flick of the eye, to a pale green against the brown rush of water.

When I turned into my block my body was running with sweat, and I could feel the sun's heat deep in my skin. I did fifty push-ups off the back steps, fifty stomach crunches, one hundred leg lifts, and twenty-five chin-ups on the iron stanchion that supported the clothesline, while my neighbor's orange cat watched me from the garage roof. Then I sat quietly in the grass, my forearms on my knees, breathing the sweet smell of the clover, my heartbeat as regular and strong and temporarily as confident as it had been twenty years before.

The moon was down that night, somewhere beyond the black outline of the Bitterroots, and dry lightning leaped whitely between the clouds over the mountains. I could smell electricity and impending rain through the screen door, and the trees along the street were dark and shaking in the wind. At nine o'clock the phone rang.

'Hello,' I said.

'Can you come up here, Dave?' The line was heavy with static.

'Clete?'

'I need you up here, man. Real bad.'

'What is it?'

'Darlene . . . Fuck, man. She's dead.'

chapter eight

The regular baby-sitter wasn't home. I found Tess Regan's number in the telephone book, called her, then took Alafair over to her house.

An hour and a half later I drove up the dirt lane to Clete's small redwood house on Flathead Lake. All the lights were on. It was raining, and the lake was black in the background, and I could see the rain blowing in the light from the windows. Farther up the dirt lane, past the electronic gate, the Dio house was dark. I knocked on Clete's front door; when no one answered, I went inside.

I heard a toilet flush somewhere in back, then he walked out of the bedroom with a wet towel held to his mouth. His face looked bloodless, the skin as tight as a lampshade. His tie was pulled loose, and his white shirt was wet down the front. He sat down at the table by the sliding glass doors and drank noisily out of a coffee cup, his whole hand wrapped around the cup to keep it from shaking. On the table were a carton of milk and a fifth of Cutty Sark. He drew in deeply on a Camel and held the smoke down as though he were taking a hit off a reefer. His breath jerked in his chest when he let the smoke out. Out on the lake a lighted, anchored sailboat pitched in the troughs.

He rubbed the towel on his mouth again, then on the back of his thick neck.

'I can't keep anything down. I think I got a peptic ulcer,' he said.

'Where is she?'

'In the main bathroom.' He looked up at me with his poached face and swallowed.

'Get yourself together.'

'I came back from Missoula, she was like that. I can't take this shit.'

But I wasn't listening to him. I walked down the hall to the bathroom. When I looked inside I had to clasp one hand on the doorjamb. The safety razor lay on the tile floor, glued thickly to the surface with her blood. She was nude and had slipped down in the tub on her side so that only half her face floated above the soapy red water. There was a deep incision across the inside of both forearms.

Oh, Lord God, I thought, and had to take a deep breath and look away.

She had bled until she was almost white. I sat on the edge of the tub and touched her soft, wet hair with my fingertips. It felt like wet feathers.

Written in lipstick on the bathroom mirror were the words:

C,
Checking out,
Bye-bye, love,
D

I ran my hand through my hair and stared numbly at her. Then I saw the tiny scratches and the red discolorations, like pale strawberry bruises, like love bites, on her neck and shoulder. I took a sheet out of the bedroom and draped it over her, then went back into the living room.

Clete was pouring another scotch and milk at the table. The smoke from his Camel curled up over the nicotine stains on his fingers. The skin around his eyes flexed abruptly when he saw my expression.

'Hey, you get that look out of your face, man,' he said.

'What were you doing in Missoula?' I said.

'I pick up cigars for Sal's old man. There's only one store in Missoula that carries his brand.'

'Why tonight?'

'He told me to.'

'Why haven't you called the locals?'

'They're going to bust me for it.'

'For a suicide?' I watched his face carefully.

'It's no suicide. You know it's not.'

'Clete, if you did this—'

'Are you crazy? I was going to ask her to marry me. I'm seeing a therapist now because I'm fucked up, but when I'm straightened out I was going to see about taking us back to New Orleans, living a regular life, opening up a bar maybe, getting away from the greaseballs.'

I looked steadily into his eyes. They stared back at me, hard as green marbles, as though they had no lids. The stitched scar that ran from the bridge of his nose through one eyebrow looked as red as a bicycle patch.

Then his eyes broke, and he took a hit of the scotch and milk.

'I don't care what you believe,' he said. 'If you think I got jealous over you and her, you're right. But I didn't blame her for it. I got a condition I can't do anything about right now. The therapist says it's because of all that stuff back in New Orleans and because I'm working for greaseballs and pretending I like it when actually I wouldn't spit on these guys. But I didn't blame her. You got that?'

'She told you?'

'What's to tell? There's ways a guy knows. Butt out of my personal affairs, Streak.'

'I put a sheet over her. Don't go back in there till the cops get here.' I picked up the telephone. The moon had broken through a crack in the clouds over the mountains on the far side of the lake, and I could see the froth on the waves blowing in the wind.

'You saw the bruises?' Clete said.

'Yes.'

'Most of the locals aren't real bright. But when the coroner does the autopsy, they're going to pick them up.'

'Maybe. What's the point?'

He drank out of the cup again, then drew in on the cigarette. His breath was ragged coming out.

'You're not big on sympathy tonight, are you?' he said.

'To be honest, I don't know what I feel toward you, Clete.'

'It's Sal. It's gotta be. I'm going to be on ice, he's going to be playing rock 'n' roll with Dixie Lee and the Tahoe cornholers. I'm going to nail that fucker, man.

I'm going to blow up his shit. I'm going to do it in pieces, too.'

'What's his motive?' I set the receiver back down.

'He doesn't need one. He's psychotic.'

'I don't buy that.'

'She was on to something. It's got to do with oil, with Dixie Lee, maybe with dope. I don't know. She believed in spirits. She thought they told her things. Then yesterday she saw Sal chopping up lines for Dixie Lee and a couple of the Tahoe broads, and she told him he was a fucking cancer, that one day his kind were going to be driven into holes in the earth. Can you dig that? Holes in the earth.'

'Where are the Dios now?'

'They said they were going to play up in Bigfork.'

'Have you heard Sally Dio say anything about a guy named Charlie?'

'Charlie? No. Who is he?'

'A hit man out of Vegas.'

'Wait a minute, they picked up a guy at the airport in Missoula last night. I thought he was just another one of Sal's buttwipes. I offered to drive in and get him, but Sal said I needed a night off.'

'What did he look like?'

'I don't know, I didn't see him.'

The clouds over the lake were silver where the moon had broken through, and the water below was black and glazed with light.

'I'm going to call the cops now, then I'm taking off,' I said. 'I don't want my name in it, all right?'

'Whatever you say.' Then he said, 'You're pretty cool. A cool operator. You always were. Nobody shakes ole

Streak's cookie bag. They could strike matches on your soul and not make you flinch.'

I didn't answer him. I walked out into the misting rain and the broken moonlight and drove my pickup truck back down the lakefront road toward Polson. The cherry trees in the orchards were dripping with rain-water in my headlights. The wooded hills were dark, and down on the beach I could see a white line of foam sliding up on the sand. With the windows up I was sweating inside the cab. I passed a neon-lit bar, a boat dock strung with light bulbs, a wind-sheltered cove where the pines grew right down to the water's edge, a clapboard cottage where people were having a party and somebody was still barbecuing in the darkness of the porch. Then I turned east of Polson, at the foot of the lake, and headed for the Jocko Valley, and I knew that I would be all right. But suddenly the clouds closed over the moon again, the sky became as black as scorched metal, and a hard wind blew out of the ice-capped Missions. A curtain of driving rain swept across meadow, irrigation canal, slough, poplar windbreak, and willow-lined stream. Lightning leaped from the crest of the Missions to the black vault of sky overhead, thunder rolled out of the canyons, and hailstones the size of dimes clattered on my truck like tack hammers.

I pulled to the side of the road, sweat boiling off my face, my windows thick with steam. The truck shook violently in the wind. My knuckles were round and white on the steering wheel. I felt my teeth grinding, felt the truck's metal joints creak and strain, the tailgate tremble and reverberate against the hooked chain; then a shudder went through me that made my mouth drop open, as though someone had clapped me on both ears with the flats of his hands. When I closed my eyes I thought I saw a copper-colored stream beaten with raindrops, and in it a brown trout with a torn mouth and blood roaring in clouds from its gills.

The next morning I walked down to the old brick church next to Alafair's school. The sun was brilliant in the bowl of blue sky above the valley. High up on one of the mountains above Hellgate Canyon, I could see horses grazing in the new grass and lupine below the timber, and the trees along the river were dark green from the rain. The current looked deep and cold between the sunbaked boulders that protruded from the water's surface. Someone had planted a garden by the side door of the church, and yellow roses and spearmint bloomed against the red-brick wall. I went inside, crossed myself at the holy water fount, and knelt in a pew close to the altar. Like almost all Catholic churches, this one smelled like stone and water, incense, and burning wax. I think that fact is no accident inside a Catholic church. I think perhaps the catacombs, where the early Christians celebrated mass, smelled the same way.

I prayed for Darlene, for Alafair, my father and brother, and finally for myself. A muscular, blond-headed priest in black trousers, scuffed cowboy boots, and a T-shirt came out of the sacristy and began removing the flower vases from the altar. I walked to the communion rail, introduced myself, and asked if he would hear my confession.

'Let's go out into the garden,' he said.

Between the church and the rectory was a sunny enclosure of lawn and flower beds, stone benches, bird feeders, and a small greenhouse. The priest and I sat next to one another on a bench, and I told him about my relationship with Darlene and finally about her death. While I talked he flipped small pieces of dirt at the leaves of a potted caladium. When I finished he was silent a moment; then he said, 'I'm not quite sure what you're confessing to. Do you feel that you used this woman?'

'I don't know.'

'Do you think you contributed to her death?'

'I don't think so. But I'm not sure.'

'I think that something else is troubling you, something that we're not quite talking about.'

I told him about Annie, the shotgun blasts that leaped in the darkness of our bedroom, the sheet drenched with her blood, the coldness of her fingers when I put them in my mouth. I could hear him breathing next to me. When I looked up at him I saw him swallow.

'I'm sorry,' he said.

'It won't go away, Father. I don't believe it ever will.'

He picked up another piece of hard dirt off the grass and started to flip it at the plant, then dropped it from his hand.

'I feel inadequate in trying to advise you,' he said. 'But I think you're a good man and you're doing yourself an unnecessary injury. You were lonely when you met the Indian lady. You obviously cared for her. Sometimes maybe it's a vanity to judge ourselves. Did you ever think of it that way? You make your statement in front of God, then you let Him be the measure of right and wrong in your life. And I don't believe you caused your wife's death. Sometimes when that kind of evil comes into our lives, we can't explain it, so we blame it on God or ourselves. In both cases we're wrong. Maybe it's time you let yourself out of prison.'

I didn't answer him.

'Do you want absolution?'

'Yes.'

'What for?'

'I don't know. For my inadequacies. My failures. For any grief or injury I've brought an innocent person. That's the best I can say. I can't describe it.'

His forearms were folded on his thighs. He looked down at his boots, but I could see a sad light in his eyes. He took a deep breath.

'I wish I could be of more help to you,' he said. 'We're not always up to the situation. Our experience is limited.'

'You've been more than kind.'

'Give it time, Mr Robicheaux.' Then he smiled and said, 'Not everybody gets to see a blinding light on the way to Damascus.'

When I left that sunny, green enclosure between the buildings, he was kneeling down in a flower bed, troweling out a hole for the pink-and-gray-striped caladium, his eyes already intent with his work, his day obviously ordered and serene and predictable in a way that I could not remember mine being since I walked off the plane into a diesel-laced layer of heat at Tan Son Nhut air base in 1964.

I wanted to go into yesterday. And I don't think that's always bad. Sometimes you simply have to walk through a door in your mind and lose thirty or forty years in order to remember who you are. Maybe it's a self-deception, a mental opiate that I use to escape my problems, but I don't care. We are the sum total of what we have done and where we have been, and I sincerely believe that in many ways the world in which I grew up was better than the one in which we live today. I stuck a paperback copy of Ernest Gaines's *Of Love and Dust* in my pocket, and walked down to Bonner Park and sat on a bench under a maple tree and read. The fountain and concrete wading pool looked dry and white in the sun, and in the distance the mountains were a sharp blue against the clouds. The wind was cool blowing out of the shade, but I was already inside the novel, back on a hot sugarcane and sweet potato plantation in South Louisiana in the 1940s. No, that's not really true. I was back in New Iberia the summer after my second year in college, when my brother, Jimmie, and I worked on an offshore seismograph rig and bought a 'forty-six Ford convertible that we put dual Hollywood mufflers on, lowering blocks and fender skirts, painted canary yellow and lacquered and waxed until the metal seemed to have the soft, deep gleam of butter. It was the best summer of my life. I fell in love seriously for the first time, with a girl who lived on Spanish Lake, outside of town, and as is always the case with your first love, I remembered every detail of the season, as though I had never experienced summer before, sometimes with a poignancy that would almost break my heart. She was a Cajun like myself, and her hair was brown and bleached in streaks by the sun so that it looked like dark honey when the wind blew it. We danced at Voorhies Roof Garden in Lafayette and Slick's in St Martinville, drank twenty-cent long-necked Jax beer under the oaks at Deer's Drive-In in New Iberia; we fished for white trout out on the salt, went to crab boils and fish fries at Cypremort Point and drove home in the lilac evening, down that long two-lane black-top parish road between the cypress and the oaks, with the wind warm off the gulf, the new cane green in the fields, the western sky streaked with fire, the cicadas deafening in the trees.

She was one of those girls who love everything about the man they choose to be theirs. She never argued or contended, she was happy in any place or situation where we were together, and I only had to touch her cheek with my fingers to make her come close to me, to press herself against me, to kiss my throat and put her hand inside my shirt. It rained every afternoon, and sometimes after it cleared and clouds were pink and maroon on the horizon, we'd drive down the levee to the dock where my father kept his boat, the cypress dripping into the dead water, and in the soft light her face would have the color and loveliness of a newly opened flower.

Jimmy Clanton's 'Just a Dream' was on every jukebox in southern Louisiana that summer, and car radios at the drive-in were always tuned to 'Randy's Record Shop' in Memphis at midnight, when Randy kicked it off with 'Sewannee River Boogie.' Each morning was one of expectation, of smoky light in the pecan trees outside my bedroom window, of innocent desire and the confidence that within a few hours I would be with her again, and that absolutely nothing would ever come between us. But it ended over an unreasonable and youthful concern. I hurt her without meaning to, in a way that I could not explain to myself, much less to her, and my silence caused her an even greater injury that these many years later still troubles me on occasion.

I'll never forget that summer, though. It's the cathedral I sometimes visit when everything else fails, when the heart seems poisoned, the earth stricken, and dead leaves blow across the soul's windows like bits of dried parchment.

My experience has been that grief and loss do not necessarily become more acceptable with time, and commitment to them is of no value to either the living or the dead. The next morning I was back in the Lake County courthouse.

The sheriff looked as hard and round as a wooden barrel. His dark blue suit was spotted with cigarette ash that he had tried to clean off with a wet paper towel; he wore his gray hair in a crew cut, his white shirt lapels ironed flat so that his chest hair stuck out like a tangle of wire. He was one of those elected law officers who have probably been diesel mechanics or log-truck drivers before someone had talked them into running for office. He sat at the corner of his desk when he talked, rather than behind it, and smoked a cigarette and looked out the window at the lake with such private concentration that I had the feeling that he already knew the outcome of our conversation, and that he was talking to me now only because of a public relations obligation that the office imposed upon him.

'You were a homicide detective in New Orleans?' he said.

'That's right.'

'Then a detective in the sheriff's department in . . . what's the name of that place?'

'New Iberia. Where they make Tabasco sauce.' I

smiled at him, but his eyes were looking through his cigarette smoke at the blue wink off the lake.

'You know a DEA agent named Dan Nygurski?'

'Yep.'

'He was here yesterday. He said I could count on you coming to see me.'

'I see.'

'He said I should tell you to go back to Louisiana. What do you think about that?'

'Advice is cheap.'

'You wondering about the coroner's report?'

I let out my breath. 'Yes, sir, I am,' I said.

'Because you think she was murdered?'

'That's right.'

'What for? Who had reason to kill her?'

'Check out Sally Dee's record. Check on a guy named Harry Mapes, too.' I felt the heat start to rise in my voice, and I paused. 'I'd give some thought to Purcel, too.'

'From what I've been told, these are all people you've had trouble with at one time or another. You think you're being entirely objective here?'

'The Dios are animals. So is Mapes. Purcel killed a guy for some paramilitary crazies in New Orleans. I wouldn't underestimate the potential of any of them.'

'Why would Purcel kill her?'

He looked at me with interest for the first time. I dropped my eyes to my shoes. Then I looked back at him.

'I was involved with Darlene,' I said. 'He knew about it.'

The sheriff nodded and didn't reply. He opened his desk drawer and took out a clipboard on which were attached Xeroxed copies of the kinds of forms that county medical examiners use in autopsies.

'You were right about the bruises,' he said. 'She had them on her neck and her shoulders.'

I waited for him to continue.

'She also had a bump on the back of her head,' he said.

'Yes?'

'But it's going down as a suicide.'

'What?'

'You got it the first time.'

'What's the matter with you? You're discounting your own autopsy report?'

'Listen, Robicheaux, I don't have any evidence that she didn't kill herself. On the other hand, I have every indication that she did. She could have hit her head on the tub. She could have gotten the bruises anywhere. Maybe you don't like to hear this, but Indians around here get into trouble. They get drunk, they fight in bars, families beat the shit out of each other. I'm not knocking them. I've got nothing against them. I think they get a lousy break. But that's the way it is. Look, if I suspected anybody, it'd have to be Purcel. But I don't believe he did it. The guy's really strung out on this.'

'What about Sally Dee?'

'You give me the motive, you put him in the house, I'll cut the warrant.'

'You're making a big mistake, Sheriff.'

'Tell me how. Fill me in on that, please.'

'You're taking the easy choice, you're letting them slide. The Dios sense weakness in you, they'll eat you alive.'

He opened a deep drawer in the bottom of his desk

and took out a baton. The layers of black paint were chipped, and the grip had been grooved in a leather and drilled to hold a leather wrist loop. He dropped it loudly on the desktop.

'The guy I replaced gave me this the day I took office,' he said. 'He told me, "Everybody doesn't have to go to jail." And there's days when maybe I got that kind of temptation. I see Dio in the supermarket and I shudder. This is good country. He doesn't belong here. But I don't bust heads, I don't let my deputies do it, either. If that don't sit right with somebody, that's their problem.' He mashed out his cigarette without looking at me.

'I guess I'll be on my way,' I said, and stood up. Then, as an afterthought, I said, 'Did the autopsy show anything else unusual?'

'Not to me or the medical examiner.'

'What else?'

'I think we've ended this discussion.'

'Come on, Sheriff, I'm almost out of your day.'

He glanced again at his clipboard.

'What she had for supper, traces of semen in the vagina.'

I took a breath and looked out the window at the electric blueness of the lake in the sunlight and the low green hills and pine trees in the distance. Then I pinched my eyes and the bridge of my nose with my fingers and put on my sunglasses.

'You were on the money about Cletus,' I said.

'What are you talking about?'

'He didn't do it. He's impotent. She was raped before she was murdered.'

He sucked his teeth, smiled to himself, shook his

head slightly, and opened his newspaper to the sports page.

'You'll have to excuse me,' he said. 'It's the only chance I get to read it.'

I found out from the medical examiner's office that Darlene's family had picked up the body that morning and that the funeral was the next afternoon on the Blackfeet Reservation. The next day was Saturday, so Alafair drove across the mountains with me to Dupuyer, on the south end of the reservation. I found out from the local newspaper that the service was to be held at a Baptist church up on the Marias River at two o'clock. We had lunch in a clapboard café that was built on to the side of a grease-stained, cinder-block filling station. I had little appetite and couldn't finish my plate, and I stared out the window at the dusty street while Alafair ate her hamburger. The bars were doing a good business. Rusted pickup trucks and oversized jalopy gas burners were parked at an angle to the curb, and sometimes whole families sat listlessly in them while the old man was inside the juke joint. People who looked both devastated and broke from the night before sat on the curb, their attention fixed on nothing, their mouths open like those of silent, newly hatched birds.

Then I saw Alafair watching them, her eyes squinting, as though a camera lens were opening momentarily in her mind.

'What do you see, little guy?' I said.

'Are those Indians?'

'Sure.'

'They're like me?'

'Well, not exactly, but maybe you're part Indian. An Indian Cajun from Bayou Teche,' I said.

'What language they talk, Dave?'

'English, just like you and me.'

'They don't know no Spanish words?'

'No, I'm afraid not.'

I saw a question mark, then a troubled look slip into her face.

'What's on your mind, little guy?' I asked.

'The people in my village. They sat in front of the clinic. Like those people there.' Her eyes were looking at an elderly man and woman on the curb. The woman was fat and wore army shoes and dirty athletic socks, and her knees were splayed open so that you could see up her dress. 'Dave, they ain't got soldiers here, have they?'

'You get those thoughts out of your head,' I said. 'This is a good country, a safe place. You have to believe what I tell you, Alf. What happened in your village doesn't happen here.'

She put her hamburger on her plate and lowered her eyes. The corners of her mouth were turned downward. Her bangs hung in a straight line across her tan forehead.

'It did to Annie,' she said.

I looked away from her face and felt myself swallow. The sky had clouded, the wind had come up and was blowing the dust in the street, and the sun looked like a thin yellow wafer in the south.

The funeral was in a wood-frame church whose white paint had blistered and peeled into scales. All the people inside the church were Indians, people with braided hair, work-seamed faces, hands that handled lumber without gloves in zero weather, except for Clete and Dixie Lee, who sat in a front pew to the side of the casket. It was made of black metal, lined and cushioned with white silk, fitted with gleaming brass handles. Her hair was black against the silk, her face rouged, her mouth red as though she had just had a drink of cold water. She had been dressed in a doeskin shirt, and a beaded necklace with a purple glass bird on it, wings outstretched in flight, rested on her breast. Only the top portion of the casket was opened, so that her forearms were not visible.

The skin of Clete's face was shiny and stretched tight on the bone. He looked like a boiled ham inside his blue suit. I could see his cigarettes tight against his shirt pocket; his big wrists stuck out of his coat sleeves; his collar had popped loose under the knot of his tie; the strap of his nylon shoulder holster made a hard line across his back. His eyes had the glare of a man staring at a match flame.

I didn't hear, or rather listen to, much of what the preacher said. He was a gaunt and nervous man who read from the Old Testament and made consoling remarks in the best fashion he was probably capable of, but the rain that began clicking against the roof and windows, sweeping in a lighted sheet across the hardpan fields and river basin, was a more accurate statement of the feelings that were inside me.

I made a peculiar prayer. It's a prayer that sometimes I say, one that is perhaps self-serving, but because I believe that God is not limited by time and space as we are, I believe perhaps that He can influence the past even though it has already happened. So sometimes when I'm alone, especially at night, in the dark, and I begin to dwell on the unbearable suffering that people probably experienced before their deaths, I ask God to retroactively relieve their pain, to be with them in mind and body, to numb their senses, to cool whatever flame licked at their eyes in their final moments. I said that prayer now for Darlene. Then I said it again for my wife, Annie.

The cemetery, a windswept and weed-grown square of land enclosed by wire strung between concrete posts, was located a short distance from the edge of the river bottoms. The Marias basin was strange country; the bluffs and the gradated channelings of the river looked as if they had been formed with a putty knife, the clay and silt layered and smoothed in ascending plateaus. Even the colors were strange. The eroded bluffs on the far side of the basin were gray and yellow and streaked with a burnt orange that looked like rust. The water in the main channel was high and brown, and leafless cottonwood limbs floated in it. The sky was sealed with gray clouds from horizon to horizon; in the thin rain the countryside looked as if it were poisoned by the infusion of toxic waste. This was the place Darlene had told me about, the site of what was called the Baker massacre of 1870. On this afternoon, except for a solitary purple dogwood blooming by the cemetery fence, it looked as though the spring had never touched the land here, as though this place had been predestined as a moonscape, a geographical monument to what was worst in us.

I watched the pallbearers lower Darlene's casket into the freshly dug hole in the cemetery. The piled orange-and-gray dirt next to the grave was slick with rainwater. The graves around hers were littered with jelly glasses and dime-store vases filled with dead wildflowers. A small American flag lay sideways on a soldier's grave, spotted with mud. A picture of a little girl, not more than five or six, was wrapped in plastic and tied to a small stone marker with baling wire. On the incline to one side of the cemetery a long length of black plastic pipe ran from a house trailer down to the lip of the river basin. The pipe had cracked at a joint, and a stream of yellow-black effluent had leaked its way in rivulets into one side of the cemetery.

I walked over to the pickup truck, where Alafair slept on the seat with the door open; I stared out over the wet land. In the distance I could see rain falling heavily on some low gray-green hills dotted with a few pine trees. After a while I heard cars and pickups driving away over the dirt road, rocks knocking up under their fenders; then it became quiet again, except for the sound of the two gravediggers spading the mound of dirt on Darlene's casket. Then a strange thing happened: the wind began to blow across the fields, flattening the grass, wrinkling the pools of rainwater in the road. It blew stronger and stronger, so unexpectedly hard, in fact, that I opened my mouth to clear my ears and looked at the sky for the presence of new storm clouds or even a funnel. A cloud shifted temporarily away from the sun and a curtain of light moved suddenly across the bluffs and the gradated layers of the river basin. As it did, the wind stripped away the purple flowers of the dogwood blooming by the cemetery fence and blew them in a pocket of air out over the river's surface like a fragmented bird.

Then it was all over. The sky was gray again, the wind dropped, the weeds stood up stiffly in the fields.

I heard someone standing behind me.

'It looks like the end of the earth, don't it?' Dixie Lee said. He wore a gray western suit and a maroon shirt that had pearl snap buttons on it. 'Or what the earth'll look like the day Jesus ends it.'

I saw Clete behind the wheel of Dixie's pink Cadillac convertible, waiting for him.

'Who paid for the casket?' I said.

'Clete.'

'Who did it, Dixie?'

'I don't know.'

'Sally Dio?'

'I can't believe something like that.'

'Don't tell me that.'

'Fuck, I don't know.' He looked at Alafair, who was sleeping with her rump in the air. 'I'm sorry . . . but I don't know. I ain't sure about anything anymore.'

I continued to look out over the river flats, the swirl of dark current in the middle of the river, and the orange-streaked bluffs beyond.

'It ain't any good to stand out here studying on things,' he said. 'Convoy on back with us and we'll stop in Lincoln for something to eat.'

'I'll be along after a while.'

I heard him light a cigarette, click his lighter shut and put it in his pocket. I could smell his cigarette smoke drifting from behind me.

'Walk over here with me. I don't want to wake up that little girl,' he said.

'What is it, Dixie?' I said irritably.

'Some people say life's a bitch and you die. I don't

know if that's right or not. But it's what you're starting to think right now, and it ain't your way. You get yourself a lot of distance between you and them kind of thoughts, son. Look, you got involved with her. Everything ain't lost on me. I know what you're feeling.'

'You're sober.'

'So I eased up a couple of days. I got my own program. You guys stay sober a day at a time. I get drunk a day at a time. Convoy on back with us. Give me a break from Clete. Sonofabitch is driving me crazy. It's like being next to a balloon that's fixing to float down on a hot cigarette. I tell you, he catches the guy that did this, it ain't ever getting to the jailhouse.'

I followed them back toward the Divide, across the greening plains and into the mountains, up the glistening black highway into thick stands of ponderosa pine, blue shadow in the canyons, white water breaking over the boulders in the streambeds far below, long strips of cloud hanging wetly in the trees. It was misting heavily in the town of Lincoln; the air was cool and purple in the twilight and smelled of cut logs and woodsmoke and food cooking and the diesel exhaust from the eighteen-wheel log trucks idling in café parking lots. I saw Clete and Dixie pull off the road next to a café and look back at me. I shifted into second, accelerated through the traffic light, and kept going through town. Alafair looked at me in the light from the dashboard. Her window was half down, and there were drops of water in her hair and on her face.

'We ain't going to stop?' she said.

'How about I buy you a buffalo burger on the other side of the mountain?'

'They wanted you to stop with them, didn't they?'

'Those guys want lots of things. But like somebody once told me, I just don't want to be there when they find it.'

'Sometimes you don't make no sense, Dave.'

'I've got to have a talk with your teacher,' I said.

On Monday morning I started to call my lawyer, then decided I didn't need higher phone bills or more depressing news. If he had gotten a continuance, he would have called me, and anything else he might have to say would be largely irrelevant. I walked Alafair to school, then ate a bowl of Grape-Nuts at the kitchen table and tried to think, as I had all day Sunday, of a reasonable plan to push Harry Mapes and Sally Dio to the wall. But I was quickly running out of options. I would never be able to find the bodies of the dead Indians, much less prove that they were killed by Harry Mapes and Dalton Vidrine. I wondered how I had ever thought I could solve my legal problems by myself, anyway. I wasn't a cop; I had no authority, access to police information, power of warrant, arrest, or interrogation. Most motion pictures portray private investigators as chivalric outsiders who solve crimes that mystify the bumbling flatfeet of officialdom. The reality is that most PIs are former jocks, barroom bouncers, and fired or resigned cops who would cut off their fingers to still have their civil service ratings. Their licenses give them about as much legal authority as a postman.

I could go back on the eastern slope of the Divide and start checking oil leases in county courthouses. Maybe somehow I would tie Dio into Harry Mapes and Star

Drilling Company and the Indians, but even if the connection existed, how would they help my defense on the murder charge in Louisiana? And who had killed Darlene and why? My thoughts became like dogs snapping at each other.

I was distracted by the sound of somebody walking between my house and the neighbor's. I got up from the table and looked through thc bedroom door and out the screen window. In the leafy shade I saw a thick-bodied blond man in a yellow hard hat and denim shirt with cutoff sleeves disappear through some bushes into the backyard. A tool belt clinked on his side. I walked quickly to the back door and saw him standing in the sunlight, in the middle of the lawn, staring up at the telephone pole with his hands on his hips. His biceps were big and red with sunburn.

'Could I help you?' I said.

'Telephone company. There's trouble on the line.'

I nodded and didn't reply. He continued to stare up the pole, then he glanced back at me again.

'Did you use your phone this morning?' he asked.

'No.'

'Did it ring and just stop?'

'No.'

'Well, it's no big thing. I got to get up on your pole, and then maybe I'll have to use your phone in a little bit. We'll get it fixed, though.' He grinned at me, then walked out into the alley and behind the garage where I couldn't see him.

I went into the hallway, picked up the telephone, and listened to the dial tone. Then I dialed the operator. When she answered, I hung up. I looked out the back door again and couldn't see the repairman. I sat back down at the kitchen table and continued eating from my cereal bowl.

Something bothered me about the man, but I couldn't think what it was. Maybe I'm just wired, I thought. Or maybe I wanted the dragons to come finally into my own yard. No, that wasn't it. There was something wrong in the picture, something that was missing or that didn't fit. I went to the front of the house and stepped out on the porch. There was no telephone truck parked on the street. Four houses down a short man in a cloth cap with two canvas sacks cross-strung on his chest was putting handbills with rubber bands on people's doors. The bags were full and heavy, and there were sweat marks on his T-shirt.

I returned to the kitchen and thought I heard somebody between the houses again. I looked out the screen door, but the backyard was empty and the repairman was nowhere in sight. Then two doves settled on the telephone wire, and I glanced at the pole for the first time. The lowest iron climbing spikes were set in the wood some fifteen feet above the ground so children could not get up on the pole.

That's it, I thought. He didn't have climbing spurs strapped on to his boots and ankles, and he didn't wear a safety belt. I went back into the hallway and picked up the telephone receiver. It was dead.

I took the .45 out of the drawer of the nightstand next to my bed. It felt cold and heavy in my hand. I pulled back the receiver, eased a hollow-point round into the chamber, and reset the hammer. It was quiet outside, and the bushes next to the bedroom windows made deep shadows on the screens. I went to the front door just as the handbill carrier was stepping up on the porch. I stuck the .45 inside the back of my trousers and went outside.

'Listen, go to the little grocery on the corner, dial the operator, ask for the police,' I said. 'All you have to say is "Assault in progress at 778 Front Street." Can you do that for me, podna?'

'What?' He was middle-aged, but his stiff, straw-colored hair sticking out from under his cap and his clear blue eyes gave him a childlike appearance.

'I've got some trouble here. I need some help. I'll give you five dollars after the cops get here. Look, just tell the operator you need the cops out here and give them this number—' I pointed to the tin numerals on the screen door. Then I took out my pocketknife, pried the set of attached numbers loose from the wood, and handed it to him. 'Just read the numbers into the phone. Seven-seventy-eight Front Street. Then say "Emergency." Okay, podna?'

'What's going on?' His face looked confused and frightened.

'I'll fill you in later.'

'Just dial?' A drop of sweat ran out of his cloth cap.

'You got it.'

He started off the porch, the heavy canvas sacks swinging from his sides.

'Leave your sacks here. Okay?' I said.

'Yeah, sure. I'll be right back with the cops.'

He headed down the street, the metal house numbers in his hand. I watched him go inside the little yellow-brick grocery store on the corner, then I headed around the side of the house, through the shrubs and shadows toward the backyard. I could see my telephone box, partly obscured by hedge under the bathroom window, and I was sure that the wires on it had been cut; but before I could look I saw the repairman walk across the sunny lawn toward my back door.

I moved quickly up to the edge of the house, the .45 in my right hand. I could feel the moisture in my palm against the thin slick of oil on the metal. The wind was cool between the houses and smelled of damp earth and old brick. The repairman pushed his yellow hard hat up on his forehead, rested his hand on the leather pouch of his tool bag, and started to knock on the screen door. Surprise time, motherfucker, I thought, cocked the .45, stepped out into the yard, and pointed it at him with both hands.

'Right there! Hands behind your head, down on your knees!' I shouted.

'What?' His face went white with shock. He stared incredulously at the automatic.

'Do it! Now!'

I saw his right hand flutter on his tool pouch.

'You're an inch from the next world, bubba,' I said.

'All right, man! What the hell is this? All right! All right! I'm not arguing.' He knelt on the wood steps and laced his fingers behind his neck. His hard hat slipped down over his eyes. His arms looked thick and red in the sunlight, and I could see the taut whiteness of his chest where the sleeves of his denim shirt were cut off. He was breathing loudly.

'You got me mixed up with somebody else,' he said.

'Where's your truck?'

'Down the street. In the fucking alley.'

'Because you're shy about parking it on the street. With your left hand unstrap your tool belt, let it drop, then put your hand behind your head again.'

'Look, call my company. You got the wrong guy.'

'Take off the belt.'

His hand worked the buckle loose, and the heavy pouch clattered to the step. I rattled the tools loose out on the concrete pad – pliers, blade and Phillips screwdrivers, wire cutters, an ice pick with a small cork on the tip. I held the ice pick up to the corner of his vision.

'You want to explain this?' I asked.

'Wasps build nests inside the boxes sometimes. I use it to clean out the corners.'

'Drop your wallet behind you.'

His fingers went into his back pocket, jerked the wallet loose, and let it fall. I squatted down, the .45 pointed at the center of his back, picked up the wallet, moved back on the grass, and shook everything out. The back of his neck was red and hot-looking in the bright air, and his shirt was peppered with sweat marks. I fingered through the dollar bills, ID cards, photographs, and scraps of paper at my feet, and gradually became more and more uncomfortable. He had a Montana driver's license with his picture on it, a social security card with the same name on it, a local Elks membership card, and two tickets to a US West Communications employees' dance.

I let out my breath.

'Where did you say your truck was?' I asked.

'Down the alley.'

'Let's take a look,' I said, getting to my feet. 'No, you walk ahead of me.'

He stayed in front of me, as I had told him, but by this time I had eased down the hammer on the .45 and had let it hang loose at my side. We walked past the garage into the alley. Parked at the end of the alley, hard against somebody's toolshed in the shade of a maple tree, was his company truck. I stuck the pistol in my back pocket. His face was livid with anger, and he closed and unclosed his fists at his sides.

'I'm sorry,' I said.

'You're sorry? You sonofabitch, I ought to knock your fucking teeth down your throat.'

'You got a right to. You probably won't understand this, but somebody is trying to do me and maybe a little girl a lot of harm. I thought you were that guy.'

'Yeah? Well, you ought to call the cops, then. I tell you, buddy, I feel like ripping your ass.'

'I don't blame you.'

'That's all you got to say? You don't blame me?'

'You want a free shot?'

There was an intense, measured look in his eye. Then the moment passed. He pointed his finger at me.

'You can tell the cops about it. They'll be out to see you. I guarantee it,' he said. Then he walked to the back steps, put his tools back in his leather pouch, and replaced all the articles in his wallet. He didn't bother to look at me as he recrossed the lawn toward the alley and his parked truck. My face felt round and tight in the wind.

Two uniformed cops were there ten minutes later. I didn't try to explain my troubles with Sal Dio; instead, I simply told them that I was an ex-police officer, that the DEA had warned me that an attempt might be made on my life, that they could call Dan Nygurski in Great Falls to confirm my story, and that I had made a serious mistake for which I wanted to apologize. They were irritated and even vaguely contemptuous, but the telephone man had not filed charges against me, he had only phoned in a report, and I knew that it wasn't going anywhere and that all I had to do was avoid provoking them.

'I just didn't act very smart, I'm sorry,' I said.

'Where is the gun?' the older of the two cops said. He was big and bareheaded and wore pilot's sunglasses.

'In the house.'

'I suggest you leave it there. I also suggest you call us the next time you think somebody's trying to hurt you.'

'Yes, sir, I'll do that. Actually I tried. Didn't the handbill man call you all?'

'The what?'

'A guy who puts handbills on front doors. I sent him to the grocery to call you when I thought my line was cut.' I realized that I was getting back into the story again when I should let it drop.

'I don't know anything about it. Believe me, I hope I don't hear any more reports from this address. Are we fairly straight on that?'

'Yes, sir, you're quite clear.'

They left, and I tried to reorder my morning. When the squad car had pulled up out front, some of the neighbors had come out on the porches. I determined that I was not going to be a curiosity who would hide in his house, so I put on my running shorts and an old pair of boat shoes and began pulling weeds in the front flower bed. The sun was warm on my back, and the clover among the rye grass in the yard was full of small bees. The willow trees out on the river were bent in the breeze. After a few minutes a man's shadow fell across my face and shoulders.

'The phone was broke. I had to go up on Broadway,'

the man said. His clear blue eyes looked down at me from under his cap.

'Oh, yeah, how you doing?' I said. 'Look, I'm sorry to send you running off like that. It was sort of a misfire.'

'I saw the cops leave from the corner. So I had me a soda. Everything worked out all right, huh?'

'Yeah, and I owe you five bucks. Right?'

'Well, that's what you said. But you don't have to, though. It was three blocks before I found a phone.'

'A deal's a deal, partner. Come inside. I'll get my wallet.'

I opened the screen and walked ahead of him. He caught the screen with his elbow rather than his hand when he came in.

'Could I have a glass of water?' he asked.

'Sure.'

We went into the kitchen, and as I took a jelly glass out of the cabinet I saw him slip both hands into his back pockets and smile. I filled the glass from the tap and thought how his smile reminded me of lips painted on an Easter egg. He was still smiling when I turned around and he raised the slapjack and came across my forehead with it. It was black and flat and weighted at the end with lead, and I felt it knock into bone and rake across my eye and nose, then I was falling free into a red-black place deep under the basement floor, with a jelly glass that tumbled in slow motion beside me.

I woke as though I were rising from a dark, wet bubble into light, except my arms were locked behind my head, I couldn't breathe or cry out, and I was drowning. Water cascaded over my face and ran down my nostrils and over the adhesive tape clamped across my mouth. I gagged and choked down in my throat and fought to get air into my lungs and felt the handcuffs bite into my wrists and the chain clank against the drainpipe under the sink. Then I saw the handbill man squatting on his haunches next to me, an empty iced-tea pitcher in his hand, a curious expression on his face as though he were watching an animal at the zoo. His eyes were sky blue and laced with tiny threads of white light. He wadded up a ball of paper towels in his hand and blotted my face dry, then widened my eyes with his fingers as an ophthalmologist might. By his foot was one of his handbill sacks.

'You're doing all right. Rest easy and I'll explain the gig to you,' he said. He took an Instamatic camera from his bag, focused on my face and the upper half of my body, his mouth askew with concentration, and flashed it twice in my eyes. My head throbbed. He dropped the camera back in his bag.

'I got to take a piss. I'll be right back,' he said.

I heard him urinate loudly in the toilet. He flushed it, then walked back into the kitchen and knelt beside me.

'The guy wants before-after shots,' he said. 'So I give him before-after shots. He's paying for it, right? But that don't mean I have to do everything else he wants. It's still my gig. Hell, it's both our gig. I don't think you're a bad dude, you just got in the wrong guy's face. So I'm going to cut you all the slack I can.'

He looked steadily into my face. His eyes were vacuous, as clear and devoid of meaning as light itself.

'You don't understand, do you?' he asked. 'Look, you piss a guy off bad, you make him look like shit in front of people, you keep turning dials on him, you show him up a punk in front of his gash so they ain't interested in his Dreamsicle anymore, he's going to stay up nights thinking about you.'

His eyes were serene, almost kind, as though it had all been explained in a way that should be acceptable to even the most obtuse.

'You're a little thick, aren't you?' he said. 'Look, you're supposed to go in pieces, left lung, then cock in the mouth. But I say fuck that. At least not while the guy knows it. Nobody tells me how to do my work, man. Hey, this maybe isn't much comfort to you, but it could be a lot worse. Believe me.'

He put his left palm flat on my chest, almost as if he were reassuring or comforting me or feeling for my heartbeat as a lover might, and reached behind him into the canvas sack with his right hand. The knife was a foreign imitation of the Marine Corps K-Bar, with a stainless steel blade, sawteeth on the top, a black aluminum handle with a bubble compass inserted in the butt. I remembered seeing them advertised for six dollars in the *Times-Picayune* Sunday magazine.

The back door was shut, the yellow linoleum floor glistened with sunlight from the window, water ran from my hair and drenched shirt like ants on my skin, my own breathing sounded like air being forced through sand. His hand moved down my sternum over my stomach, toward my loins, and he shifted his weight on his knees, cupped the knife palm up in his right hand, and moved his eyes slowly over my face. I clanged the handcuff chain against the drainpipe, tried to twist away from him, then jerked my knees up in front of my stomach as a child might, my voice strangling in my throat.

He took his hand away from my body and looked at me patiently.

'Come on, man. Trust me on this one,' he said.

A shadow went across the glass window in the back door, then the handle turned and Clete came through the door as though he were bursting through barrel slats, flinging the door back against the wall, knocking a chair across the linoleum, his .38 revolver aimed straight out at the handbill man's face. He looked ridiculous in his old red and white Budweiser shorts, T-shirt, blue windbreaker, crushed porkpie hat, loafers without socks, and nylon shoulder holster twisted across one nipple.

'What's happening, Charlie?' he said, his face electric with anticipation. 'Throw away the shank or I blow your shit all over Streak's wallpaper.'

The handbill man's vacuous blue eyes never changed expression. The white threads of light in them were as bright as if some wonderful promise were at hand. He set the knife on the floor and grinned at nothing, resting comfortably on one knee, his right forearm draped across his thigh.

'Charlie almost got away from me,' Clete said. 'Sal told me he took his rental back to Missoula and caught a flight last night. Except Charlie's been getting some nook up on the lake and his punch told me she's supposed to meet him at the airport tonight. I thought you were a pro, Charlie. You ought to keep your hammer in your pants when you're working. Roll over on your stomach and put your hands behind your neck.'

Clete knelt behind him and shook him down, patting his pockets, feeling inside his thighs.

'Where's the key to the cuffs?' Clete said.

The handbill man's face was flat against the floor, pointed at me. His eyes were bright with light.

'Hey, you got problems with your hearing?' Clete said, and kicked him with the point of his loafer in the rib cage.

Still, the handbill man didn't say anything. His breath went out of his lungs, and he breathed with his mouth open like a fish out of water. Clete started to kick him again, then his eyes went to the top of the kitchen table. He slid the knife across the linoleum with his foot and picked up the handcuff key from the table. He knelt beside me and unlocked one of my wrists. I started to raise up, but before I could he snapped the loose cuff around the drainpipe.

'Sorry, Streak, not just yet,' he said. 'Get the tape off your mouth and dangle loose a minute while we talk to Charlie here.' He picked up the canvas sack by the bottom and shook it out on the floor. The Instamatic, a roll of pipe tape, and a .22 revolver clattered on the linoleum among the scatter of handbills. 'Sal wanted some pictures for his scrapbook, huh? And it looks like we got a Ruger with a magnum cylinder. Streak, we're looking at your genuine, all-American psychopath here. I got a friend at Vegas PD to pull Charlie's sheet for me.'

I had the tape worked loose from my mouth now. I sat up as best I could under the lip of the sink and pinched the skin around my mouth. It was stiff and dead to the touch. I could feel a swollen ridge through my hairline and down my forehead.

'What are you doing, Clete?' I said. My words sounded strange and outside of myself.

'Meet Charlie Dodds. Vegas says he's been tied to

five syndicate hits they know about, and maybe he iced a guy on the yard at Quentin. His finest hour was whacking out a federal witness, though. The guy's fourteen-year-old daughter walked in on it, so Charlie took her out, too.'

'Give me the key,' I said.

'Be mellow, Dave.' He had put the .22 in one of the big pockets of his Budweiser shorts. He started to lean over the man on the floor.

'Call the locals, Clete.'

He straightened up and looked at me as he would at a lunatic.

'You think you or I can keep this guy in jail? What's the matter with you?' he said. 'He'd be out on bond in three hours, even if these hicks would file charges. No matter how you cut it, he'd be back doing lines with the cornholers before the five o'clock news. I'll tell you something else, too, Dave. The mortician told me a tear was sealed inside Darlene's eye, he couldn't clean it out. You know what she must have gone through before she died?'

His jaw flexed, the skin of his face tightened, the scar that ran through his eyebrow and across his nose reddened, and he kicked the man on the floor hard in the rectum. He kicked him in the same place again, then leaned over him and whipped the barrel of the .38 across the back of his head. Then he said 'Fuck' as though an insatiable rage had released itself in him, put his revolver in his other deep pocket, hoisted the man to his feet by his belt, as if he were made of rags and sticks, threw him against the wall and drove his huge fist into his face.

Then Clete held him erect by the throat, hit him

again and again, until his knuckles were shiny and red and the man's eyes were crossed and a bloody string of saliva hung from his mouth.

'For God's sakes, cut it out, Clete!' I said. 'The guy's all we've got. Use your head, man.'

'Bullshit. Charlie's no sissy. Our man here is a stand-up con.' And with that, he wrapped his hand around the back of the man's neck, ran him across the room, and smashed his head down on the side of the stove. I saw the skin split above the eye; then Clete threw him to the floor. The man's eyes had rolled, and his straw-colored hair was matted with sweat.

Clete stuck his wrist down at my face.

'Feel my pulse,' he said. 'I'm calm, I'm copacetic, I'm fucking in control of my emotions. I don't have a hard-on. I'm extremely tranquil. I saved your fucking ass this morning. How about a little gratitude for a change?'

'You unlock me, Clete, or I'm going to square this. I swear it.'

'You'll never change, Streak. You're unteachable.'

Clete picked up the roll of pipe tape and the survival knife from the floor and knelt next to the unconscious man. He ripped off a ten-inch length of tape, sliced through it with the knife, and wrapped the man's mouth. Then he pulled his arms behind him, wrapped each wrist individually, made a thick figure eight between both wrists, and sliced the tape again. The knife was honed as sharp as a barber's razor. He wrapped the man's ankles just as he had done the wrists.

'I don't know what your plan is, but I think it's a bad one,' I said.

'I'm not the one up on a murder charge in Louisiana. I'm not the guy cuffed to a drainpipe. I don't have a knot on my head. Maybe I do something right once in a while. Try some humility along with the gratitude.'

He went into the front of the house, and I heard him pushing furniture around, tumbling a chair or a table to the floor. A moment later he came back into the kitchen, dragging my living room rug behind him. His face was flushed, and sweat ran out of the band of his porkpie hat. He ripped off his windbreaker and used it to wipe the sweat out of his eyes. The powder-blue sleeves were flecked with blood.

'Sorry to fuck up your house. See if you can write it off on the IRS as part of Neighborhood Watch,' he said.

He kicked the rug out flat on the floor and began rolling the man up in it.

'Clete, we can bring Dio down with this guy.'

But he wasn't listening. He breathed hard while he worked, and there was a mean bead in his eye.

'You got out of that murder beef in New Orleans. You want them to stick you with another one?' I said.

Again he didn't answer. He went out the back door, then I heard his jeep grinding in reverse across the lawn to the steps. Clete came back into the kitchen, unhooked the spring from the screen door, lifted up the man inside the rolled rug, and dragged him outside to the jeep. When he came back inside his face was dusty from the rug and running with sweat and his big chest heaved up and down for air. He put a cigarette in his mouth, lit it from a book of matches, and flipped the burnt match out through the open screen into the sunlight.

'You got a hacksaw?' he said.

'In my toolbox. Behind the driver's seat.'

He went back outside, and I heard him clattering around in my truck. Then he walked back up the wood steps with the saw hanging from his hand.

'You can cut through the chain in about fifteen minutes,' he said. 'If you want to call the locals then, ask yourself how much of this they'll believe. Also ask yourself how much trouble you want over a shitbag like that guy out there.'

'What are you going to do with him?'

'It's up to him. Are you really worried about a guy who'd kill a fourteen-year-old girl? The guy's a genetic accident.' He pulled up a chair, sat down, and leaned toward me while he puffed on his cigarette and tried to get his breath back at the same time. 'Did you ever think about it this way, Streak? You know how the real world works, just like I do. But half the time you act like you don't. But it lets you feel good around guys like me. What do your AA pals call it – "drinking down"?'

'That's not the way it is, Cletus.'

'Why'd you keep partnering with me at the First District after you saw me bend a couple of guys out of shape?' He grinned at me. 'Maybe because I'd do the things you really wanted to. Just maybe. Think about it.'

'Don't kill this guy.'

'Hey, I got to be on the road. You want anything before I split? A glass of water or something?' He put the hacksaw in my hand.

'It's never too late to turn it around.'

'That's solid gold, Dave. I wonder if ole Charlie out there thinks of something like that while he's doing a job on somebody. Man, that's fucking noble. I got to remember that.'

He hooked the spring on the screen door again, worked it back and forth a couple of times, then looked at me and said, 'After you cut through the chain, the cuff key's there on the table. You want to take down Sal and that other fart that framed you in Louisiana, get real or buy yourself some Mouseketeer ears. In an hour I'll have Charlie's life story. You want in on it, call me at the Eastgate Lounge at six o'clock.'

Then he was gone.

chapter nine

I filled a clean dish towel with ice cubes and cracked them into a fine, wet paste with a rolling pin on the edge of the sink, then lay down on the living room couch and held the towel to my head. What a sharp ex-cop I proved myself this morning, I thought. I had managed to roust, terrify, and infuriate an innocent telephone man, then invite a contract killer into my house, right after the cops had left, turn my back on him unarmed, when I had access to a .45, a double-barreled twelve-gauge, and a .38 revolver nailed in a holster under a cabinet shelf, and get sapped and manacled to a drainpipe. I didn't want to think about the rest of it: the moist touch of his hand sliding across the quivering muscles of my stomach, the total absence of moral light in his eyes, the transfixed, almost opiated shine in his face while he let the knife hover over my heart cavity.

I had seen the work of his kind before, in New Orleans. They created object lessons that no one in the criminal community ever forgot: a grand-jury witness garroted with wire, a hooker drenched with gasoline and turned into a cone of flame, a mob member who had cuckolded a friend emasculated and his phallus stuffed in his mouth. The men who did the work made you shudder. I've heard all kinds of explanations for their behavior and their perverse nature. My personal feeling is that they're simply evil. The hooker, the street dips, the check writers, the fences and hot-money passers at the track, that bumbling urban army of brain-fried misfits, are often people with families and other jobs who eventually disappear into the normalcy of American life without ever leaving more than a forgettable scratch on it. Charlie Dodds's kind are a special bunch, however. I don't think there are many of them around, but enough perhaps to remind us that not every human being can be fixed or explained and that the jailer who keeps them in maximum-security lock-down, chained ankle, waist, and wrist when they're moved only a short distance in the prison, knows and appreciates something about them that the rest of us do not.

I had decided not to call the heat about Charlie Dodds's visit. As Clete had said, how much of it would they be willing to believe, particularly after I had rousted the telephone man? Also, I was tired of having to prove myself to cops. Sometimes it's not good to interfere with the fates. Maybe Clete and Dodds had found each other.

The ice melted in the towel. I got up from the couch, my forehead numb and tight from the cold and swelling, and cleaned up the kitchen. I wiped Dodds's blood off the wall, stove, and linoleum with wet paper towels, cleaned the same areas again with detergent and rubbing alcohol, then put the towels, his survival knife, his cloth cap, and the sawed handcuffs into his canvas handbill bag, wadded it up, and threw the whole mess down the basement stairs.

Then I showered and took a nap in the bedroom. The breeze ruffled the bushes outside the window and blew coolly across the sheets. In my dream I saw Annie sitting on the rail of my father's houseboat in the misty early morning light down in the Atchafalaya marsh. The houseboat was weathered and paintless, streaked with moisture, and clouds of vapor billowed out of the islands of willow and cypress trees and hung low on the motionless water. Her hair was gold, her skin tan, her mouth red in the mist, but she wouldn't speak to me. She smiled and looked toward my father, who waited for me in the outboard, and I realized that I was only fifteen and that I had to help him run the crab line, dripping with catfish heads, that we had strung across the bay the night before. As the sun burned the mist off the water and back into the trees, we filled the bait well with bluepoint crabs, then began picking up the conical fishnets that we had weighted with bricks, marked with sealed, plastic Clorox containers, and dropped into deep current yesterday morning. We worked through lunch, shaking huge mud cat and *gaspagoo*, what Texans called buffalofish and Negroes goo-fish, into the bottom of the boat, our backs hot and striped with sweat under the white sun. My father's hair was curly and wild, like black wire, his hands big as skillets, his teeth strong and white, his laugh genuine and full of fun, his shoulders and arms so powerful and corded with muscle that he could fight three men at one time in the middle of a dance floor and take blows from every direction without going down. On the pipeline and in the oil field they called him Big Al Robicheaux with the kind of respect and affection that working people have for a man who possesses their best qualities. I leaned over the gunnel, grabbed a floating Clorox container, and got the lip of the net almost to the surface. But it was as heavy as concrete, the wooden hoops fouled, the netting torn, and no matter how I strained I couldn't lift the first hoop clear of the water.

My father cut the engine, climbed to the bow so he wouldn't capsize the boat, and jerked the net up with his massive arms, until he could see the outline of the trapped gar just below the yellow surface.

'*Fils p'tain*,' he said. He hadn't shaved in three days, and his hair and beard were dripping with sweat.

The gar must have been five feet long. Its fins and tail and armorlike scales and long, teeth-filled snout were mired in the netting, and there was no way to get it back out through the series of hoops. My father pulled up the bricks that we used to anchor the net, cut them loose, and dropped them into the bottom of the boat; then we towed the net slowly behind us back to the willow island where the houseboat was moored in the shade.

We shook the gar out of the ruined net on the bank and watched it flop and gasp for air and coat its gills with sand. Its teeth could cut a bass in half like a razor slicing through it. My father got behind it, hit it once on the head with a brick, then drove his skinning knife through a soft place between the head and the armored shell, pushing down with both hands until the knife point went through the throat into the sand and blood roared from the gar's mouth and gills. But the gar continued to flop, to twist against the knife and flip sand into the air, until my father crushed its head and its eyes became as suddenly lifeless and cold as black glass. Then he brought the knife straight back along the dorsal fin, and the black-green armor cracked away from the rows of pink meat as cleanly as pecan shell breaking.

It wasn't a good day. The gar wasn't a commercial fish, and we couldn't afford the loss of a net, but my father always put the best light on a situation.

'We can't sell him, no,' he said. 'But he gonna be some good garfish balls. You mess with Aldous and Dave, you gonna get fry, you gonna get eat, you better believe, podna.'

We cleaned the filleted fish in pans of bloody water until evening, when the mosquitoes started to boil out of the shadows and purple rain clouds gathered on the horizon and lightning flashed far out on the Gulf. We packed the fish in the ice bin, so tomorrow we could take them downriver to sell in Morgan City. I went to sleep in my bunk bed with the wind blowing cool through the window from across the bay, then I woke to a smell that shouldn't have been there. It was thick and gray, as fetid as excrement and sweet at the same time. But we had thrown all the fish guts and heads and piles of stripped mud-cat skins into the current and had washed the deck and all the pans clean. I kept the pillow over my head and tried to push myself deeper into sleep, but I could feel the stench against my face like a rat's breath.

In the first blue light of dawn I went out on the deck, and Annie was leaning against the rail in the mist, dressed like a Cajun fisher girl in sun-faded jeans, tennis shoes without socks, a khaki shirt with the arms cut off. The smell was everywhere. She pointed toward my father, who waited for me on the sandbar, a shovel over his shoulder.

Don't be afraid, she said. *Go with Al.*

I don't want to this time.

You mustn't worry about those things. We both love you.

You're about to go away from me, aren't you?

Her face was kind, and her eyes moved over my face as though she were an older sister looking at her younger brother.

I followed my father into the marsh, our tennis shoes splashing through the sloughs, the wet willow branches winging back into our faces. The early sun was big and hot on the edge of the flooded woods, and the cypress trees looked black against the red light. The water was dead and covered with green algae; cotton-mouth moccasins were coiled on the low branches of the trees. The smell became stronger, so that I had to hold my hand to my face and breathe through my mouth. We came up out of a slough on to a hard-packed sandbar, and lying stretched on the sand, huge divots cut out of its back by a boat propeller, was the rotting carcass of the biggest bull alligator I had ever seen. His tail drag and the sharp imprints of his feet trailed off the sandbar back through the trees. I could see the open water where he had probably been hit by a commercial boat of some kind, or the screw on a seismograph drill barge, and had beached himself and begun his crawl to this spot, where he had died on high ground and turkey buzzards and snakes had begun feeding on his wounds.

'*Mais*, that stink,' my father said, and waved at the air in front of his face. 'You start dig a hole.' He handed me the shovel, then he grinned as he sometimes did when he was about to play a joke on me. 'Where you gonna dig a hole, you?'

I didn't understand him. I started to scrape in the dry sand with the shovel's tip.

'*Que t'as près faire, cher? Tu veux travailler comme un neg?*' he said, and laughed. ('What are you doing, dear one? You want to work like a Negro?')

I pressed down again into the hard sand, felt it grate and slide over the blade. He took the shovel out of my hand, walked to a dip in the sandbar where the water from two sloughs had washed a small channel, and dug deeply and easily into the wet sand and flung it out into the sunlight, his face grinning at me.

'You do it where it soft,' he said. 'Ain't you learned nothing from your old man?'

I woke to a clatter of birds in the trees outside the window, my head thick with afternoon sleep. I rinsed my face in the bathroom sink and looked at the tight purple lump that ran down through my hairline. The dream made no sense to me, other than the facts that I missed my father and Annie, that I feared death, and that I conducted a foolish quarrel with the irrevocable nature of time.

Al, what are you trying to tell me? I thought, as the water streamed off my face in the mirror's silent reflection.

Shortly before three o'clock I walked down to the school and waited for Alafair by the side of the playground. A few minutes later the doors of the building were flung open, and she came running across the small softball diamond with a group of other children, her Donald Duck lunch box clanging against her thigh. Her elastic-waisted jeans were grimed at the knees, and there were dirt and sweat rings around her neck.

'What did you guys do today at recess? Mud-wrestling?' I said.

'Miss Regan let us play dodgeball. It's fun. I got hit in the seat. You ever play it, Dave?'

'Sure.'

'What happened to your head?'

'I hit it when I was working on the truck. Not too smart, huh?'

Her eyes looked at me curiously, then she put her hand in mine and swung her weight on my arm.

'I forgot,' she said. 'Miss Regan said to give you this note. She said she'd call you anyway.'

'About what?'

'About the man.'

'What man?'

'The one at the school yard.'

I unfolded the piece of paper she had taken from her lunch box. It read: *Mr Robicheaux, I want to have a serious talk with you. Call me at my home this afternoon – Tess Regan.* Under her name she had written her phone number.

'Who's this man you're talking about, Alafair?' I said.

A bunch of children ran past us on the sidewalk. The sunlight through the maple trees made patterns on their bodies.

'The other kids said he was in a car on the corner. I didn't see him. They said he was looking through, what you call those things, Dave? You got some in the truck.'

'Field glasses?'

'They called them something else.'

'Binoculars?'

'Yeah.' She grinned up at me when she recognized the word.

'Who was he looking at, Alafair?'

'I don't know.'

'Why does Miss Regan want to talk to me about it?'

'I don't know.'

'What time was this guy out there?'

'At recess.'

'What time is recess?'

'First- through third-graders go at ten-thirty.'

'Is that when he was out there?'

'I don't know, Dave. Why you look so worried?'

I took a breath, released her hand, and brushed my palm on the top of her head.

'Sometimes strange men, men who are not good people, try to bother little children around schools or at playgrounds. There're not many people like this, but you have to be careful about them. Don't talk with them, don't let them give you anything, don't let them buy you anything. And no matter what they say, never go anywhere with them, never get in a car with them. Do you understand that, little guy?'

'Sure, Dave.'

'That kind of man will tell you that he's a friend of your father's. That your father sent him to pick you up, maybe. But if he was a friend, you'd recognize him, right?'

'They hurt children?'

'Some of them do. Some of them are very bad people.'

I saw doubt and fear working into her face like a shadow. Her throat swallowed. I picked up her hand in mine again.

'Don't be scared, little guy,' I said. 'It's the same thing I've told you before. We just have to be cautious sometimes. Miss Regan tells all the children that, doesn't she? It's no big deal.'

But it wasn't working. Her eyes were locked on images in her memory that I could not touch or eradicate.

'Look, when I tell you not to stick your hand in the window fan, that doesn't mean you should be afraid of the fan, does it?' I said.

'No.'

'If I tell you not to put your finger in Tripod's mouth, that doesn't mean you should be afraid of Tripod, does it?'

'No.' Her eyes crinkled slightly at the corners.

'If Clarise won't let Tex eat at the breakfast table, that doesn't mean she's afraid of horses, does it?'

She grinned up at me, her face squinting in the sunlight. I swung her on my arm under the maple trees, but there was a feeling in my chest like a chunk of angle iron.

At the house she poured a glass of milk and cut a piece of pie at the kitchen table for her afternoon snack, then washed out her lunch box and thermos and began straightening her room. I took the telephone into the bathroom so she could not hear me talking to Tess Regan.

'What's the deal with this guy at the school ground?' I said.

'I beg your pardon?'

'You sent a note home. Then Alafair told me about the guy with binoculars.'

'I was referring to your tone. Are you always this cross with people over the telephone?'

'It's been an unusual day. Look, Miss Regan – Tess – what's the deal?'

'At recess we use some of the eighth-graders as monitors for the lower grades. Jason, one of the monitors, said a man was parked in his car under the trees across the street. He said the man walked over to the fence and asked where Alafair Robicheaux was. He said he was a friend of her father's, and he had a message for her. We teach all the children not to talk to people off the street, to direct all visitors to the principal's office. Jason told him he should see Sister Louise inside the building. Then the man pointed to where the little ones were playing dodgeball and said, "Oh, there she is." Jason said, "Yeah, but you have to see Sister Louise." The man said he didn't have time but he'd be back later. When he got back in the car, the children said, he looked at the school ground through a pair of binoculars.'

'What time was he there?'

'It must have been about eleven o'clock.'

Then it wasn't Charlie Dodds, I thought. He was already inside my house by then.

'What kind of car?'

'The kids said it was yellow.'

'What did the guy look like? Did he have an accent?'

'Jason just said he was tall. I didn't ask about an accent.'

'That's all right. Was there anything unusual about him? A scar on his lip?'

'Children usually don't remember those kinds of details

about adults. In their world adults are simply "big people" whom they either trust or dislike.'

'I'd like to talk to Jason.'

'Then you'll need to make an appointment with Sister Louise, and maybe she'll ask the parents to bring Jason in. But I doubt it. Not unless you want to tell us what this is about and also call the police. Because that's what we're going to do.'

'That's good. But you need to listen to me now and not be afraid of what I'm going to tell you. This guy is not a child molester. He wanted to get at me through Alafair. He may work for the mob out of Vegas or Reno. I had one like that in my house this morning. That's why it's been an unusual day. Or he may be somebody connected with an oil company, a guy named Mapes or somebody who works for him. Either way, the local cops don't have much experience with this kind of guy.'

'The mob?' she said.

'That's right.'

'You mean like in *The Godfather*? The honest-to-God Mafia?'

'The real article.'

'And you didn't tell me this before?'

'It wouldn't have changed anything. Except maybe to alarm you.'

'I think I'm very angry right now.'

'Look, I don't want to be the guy to mess up your day. You asked for the truth, I gave it to you. There's no big revelation in what I told you, either. There's some Reno transplants right up there at Flathead Lake. The mob's any place there's money to be made in gambling or dope or any kind of vice.'

She didn't answer.

'Listen,' I said, 'if that guy comes back, you try to get his license number, then you call the heat, then you call me. Okay?'

'What do you plan to do?' she said. Her voice was dry, the way heat is when it lifts off a metal surface.

'I'm going to seriously impair his interest in children on school yards.'

'I'll give your words some thought. In the meantime you might reflect a bit on the need for a little more candor in your relationships with other people. Maybe they don't like to feel that they're not to be trusted with this great body of private information that you have.'

The line went dead in my hand.

I couldn't blame her. How would any ordinary person deal with the knowledge that an emissary of the mob could stroll into a world as innocent and predictable as a children's playground? But was the man indeed one of Dio's people, a partner of or a backup for Charlie Dodds? Why would Dodds need a backup? It was a simple hit, probably a five-thou whack that a guy like Dodds considered a cakewalk. Unless Dio's outraged pride was so great that he wanted a child's death as well as my own.

It didn't compute, though. If Dodds had been paid to hurt Alafair also, he would have waited until after three o'clock, when we were both home, or he would have come on the weekend.

So that left Harry Mapes. He had been driving a black Jeepster when I had seen him just south of the Blackfeet Reservation, but maybe the man in the yellow car with the binoculars worked with Mapes or had been hired by him. Why would he want to turn the screws on me now? Did he think I was close to finding something or turning it around on him? If he did, he had a lot more confidence in me than I did in myself.

I called Sister Louise, the principal, at the school and caught her just before she left the office. She had already talked with Tess Regan, and she was no more happy with me than Tess Regan had been. She sounded like some of the nuns I had known as a child, the ones who wore black habits that were probably like portable stoves and who whacked your knuckles with tricorner rules and who could hit you on the run with their fifteen-decade rosaries. She told me that she had just made a police report, that I should do the same, and that a patrol car would be parked by the school tomorrow morning.

'I'd still like to talk with the little boy, what's his name, Jason,' I said.

'He's told me everything he knows. He's a shy boy. He's not one to study detail in adults.'

'Does he remember if the man had an accent?'

'He's fourteen years old, he's not a linguist.'

'Sister, it's good that you'll have a patrol car out there tomorrow. But our man won't be back while the cops are around.'

'That's the point, isn't it?'

'But he may well be when they're gone. That's when we can nail him.'

'There's no "we" involved in this, Mr Robicheaux.'

'I see.'

'I'm glad you do. Good-bye.'

For the second time in ten minutes someone had hung up on me.

*

I took Alafair to the park to play, then we went back home and fixed supper. Clete had told me I could call him at the Eastgate Lounge at six o'clock. I wasn't sure that I should. Whatever he had done with Charlie Dodds, it wasn't good. But at that point my legal problems as well as the threat to Alafair's and my safety were so involved and seemingly without solution that I wondered why I should be troubled over some marginal involvement with the fate of a depraved and psychotic character like Dodds, whom nobody cared about except perhaps Sally Dio because he had probably paid him half the hit money up front. It was five-thirty, and we were five minutes into our meal when I heard a car park in front and somebody walk up on the porch.

Even before I could make out his silhouette against the screen door, I saw Dixie Lee's battered pink Cadillac convertible parked with two wheels on the edge of my grass. The top was up, but I could see that the backseat was loaded with suitcases, boxes of clothing and cowboy boots, hangered western suits racked on a wire.

His sudden change of fortune, his plans for himself, his rehearsed entreaty, were altogether too obvious and predictable. I didn't open the door. I was even a bit ashamed at my lack of sympathy. But it had been a bad day, and I really didn't need Dixie Lee in it. He was eloquent in his desperation, though. He had marshaled all the raw energies of a drunk who knew that he was operating on the last fuel in his tank.

'Things are coming apart up there at the lake,' he said. 'You were right, Sal's a shit. No, that ain't right. He's a crazy person. He wants your ass cooked in a pot. I couldn't abide it. I had to get out.'

'Watch your language. My daughter's here.'

'I'm sorry. But you don't know what Sal's like when lights start going off in his head. He's got this twisted-up look on his face. Nobody can say anything around him unless you want your head snapped off. One of the broads is eating her dessert at the dinner table, and Sal keeps smoking his cigarette and looking at her like she crawled up out of a drain hole. Her eyes are blinking and she's trying to smile and be pretty and cute and get off the hook, then he says, "You eat too much," and puts out his cigarette in her food.

'He hates you, Dave. You really got to him. You bend up the wheels inside a guy like Sally Dee, and smoke starts to come out of the box. I don't want to be around it. That's where it stands. You tell me to get out of your life, I can relate to it. But I picked myself into some thin cotton, son, and I got nowhere to turn. I'll be straight with you on something else, too. I'm in to Sal for fifteen thou. That's how much flake I put up my nose on the tab. So I got that old Caddy out there, thirty-seven dollars in my pocket, and a quarter tank of gas. I'm trying to keep it all in E major, but I blew out my amps on this one.'

'Save the rock 'n' roll corn pone for somebody else,' I said. 'I had Charlie Dodds in my house this morning.'

'Dodds? I thought he went back to Vegas last night. What was he doing here?'

'You don't know?'

'You mean he's a mechanic? I didn't know. I swear in front of God I didn't. I thought he was one of Sal's mules. Is that how you got that purple knot on your head?'

'Something like that.'

'Man, I'm sorry. I didn't have any idea. The guy didn't say three words when he was around me. I thought he was retarded. All those mules got that meltdown look in their eyes. They swallow balloons full of skag, fly in and out of canyons, land on dirt roads at night. We're talking about the dumbest white people you ever met.'

'I think he might have a backup man still after me. Is there some other new guy hanging around Sal's place?'

'No.'

'You're sure?'

'Yeah.'

'Anyway, I can't help you, Dixie.'

He looked at me blankly through the screen. He swallowed, glanced up the street as though something of significance were waiting for him there, then started to speak again.

'I've got too many problems of my own. That's about it, partner,' I said.

'No way, huh?'

'I'm afraid not.'

He blew his breath up into his face.

'I can't blame you,' he said. 'I just ain't got many selections right now.'

'Start over.'

'Yeah, why not. It ain't my first time washing dishes or living in a hallelujah mission. Hey, I want you to remember one thing, though, Dave. I ain't all bad. I never set out to harm anybody. It just worked out that way.'

'Whatever you do, good luck with it, Dixie,' I said, and closed the inside door on him and went back to the kitchen table, where Alafair had already started in on her dessert.

I looked at my watch – it was a quarter to six now – and tried to finish supper. The food seemed tasteless, and I couldn't concentrate on something Alafair was telling me about the neighbor's cat chasing grasshoppers in the flower bed.

'What's wrong?' she said.

'Nothing. It's just a little headache. It'll pass.'

'That man made you mad or something?'

'No, he's just one of those guys who'll always have his elevator stuck between floors.'

'What?'

'Nothing, little guy. Don't worry about it.'

I chewed my food and looked silently out the window at the shadows and the cool gold light on the backyard. I heard Alafair wash her dishes in the sink, then walk toward the front of the house. A moment later she was back in the kitchen.

'That man's still out there. Just sitting in his car. What's he doing, Dave?' she said.

'Probably figuring out ways to sell the Rocky Mountains to Arab strip miners.'

'What?'

'Just ignore him.'

But I couldn't. Or at least I couldn't ignore the twelfth-step AA principle that requires us to help those who are afflicted in the same way we are. Or maybe I knew that I had asked for all my own troubles, and it wasn't right any longer to blame it on Dixie Lee. I set my knife and fork down on my plate and walked outside to his car. He was deep in thought, a cigarette burned almost down to his fingers, which rested on top of the steering wheel. His face jerked around with surprise when he heard me behind him.

'Lord God, you liked to give me a heart attack,' he said.

'You can't drink while you stay with us,' I said. 'If you do or if you come home with it on your breath, you're eighty-sixed. No discussion, no second chance. I don't want any profanity in front of my daughter, and you go outside if you want to smoke. You share the cooking and the cleaning, you go to bed when we do. The AA group down the street has a job service. If they find you some work, you take it, whatever it is, and you pay one third of the groceries and the rent. That's the deal, Dixie. If there are any rules here you can't live with, now's the time to tell me.'

'Son, you say "Frog" and I'll say "How high?" '

He began unloading the backseat of his car. His face wore the expression of a man who might have been plucked unexpectedly from the roof of a burning building. As he piled his boxes and suitcases and clothes on the sidewalk, he talked without stop about the 1950s, Tommy Sands, Ruth Brown, the Big Bopper, the mob, cons in Huntsville, the actress wife who paid goons to beat him up behind Cook's Hoe Down in Houston. I looked at my watch. It was five minutes to six.

He was still talking while I looked up the number of the Eastgate Lounge.

'—called him "the hippy-dippy from Mississippi, yes indeed, Mister Jimmy Reed," ' he said. 'When that cat went into "Big Boss Man," you knew he'd been on Parchman Farm, son. You don't fake them kind of feelings. You don't grow it in New York City, either.

You don't put no mojo in your sounds unless you picked cotton four cents a pound and ate a mess of them good ole butter beans. My daddy said he give up on me, that somebody snuck me into the crib, that I must have been a nigra turned inside out.'

Alafair sat delighted and amazed as she listened to Dixie Lee's marathon storytelling. I dialed the Eastgate Lounge, then listened to the hum and clatter of noise in the background while a woman called Clete to the phone. I heard him scrape the receiver off a hard surface and place it to his ear.

'Streak?'

'Yep.'

'Did I surprise you? Did you think maybe your old partner had headed for Taco Greaso Land again?'

'I wasn't sure.'

'I don't rattle, mon. At least not over the shitbags.'

'Maybe you should be careful what you tell me.'

'Do I sound like I'm sweating it? When are you going to stop pretending you still got your cherry?'

'You're starting to get to me, Clete.'

'What else is new? All I did was save your life today.'

'Is there something you want me to say?'

'Yeah. Get your butt over here. You know where the Eastgate is?'

'Yeah, but I'm bringing Alafair with me. I'll meet you in the park across the river from the shopping center. You walk across an old railway trestle that's been made into a footbridge.'

'And you'll be eating ice-cream cones at a picnic table. Man, how do I get in on the good life?' he said, and hung up.

I told Dixie Lee there was a cold roast, bread, and

mayonnaise in the icebox, and he could fix himself sandwiches if he hadn't eaten yet. Then Alafair and I drove across town to the ice-cream place on the north bank of the Clark Fork, bought cones, and walked across the river on the footbridge to the park on the opposite side. In the past, there had been a bad fire up the sides of Hellgate Canyon, and the pines that grew down from the crest had been scorched black and then the ash and the burnt needles had been washed away by rain and the spring snowmelt so that the steep gray-pink cliffs of the canyon were exposed high above the river. The wind was up, and the leaves of the cottonwoods along the river's edge clicked and flickered in the soft light; because the spring runoff had ended and the water was dropping each day, more and more white, moss-scaled stones were exposed in the riverbed and the main channel was turning from copper-colored to a dark green. The white water had formed into long, narrow trout riffles that fanned out behind big rocks into deep pools.

The park was full of blue spruce and Russian olive trees, and kids from the university, which was only a block away, sailed Frisbees overhead and played rag football. We sat on the mowed grass, high up on the riverbank, so we could look out over the tops of the willows and watch two men who were fishing with worms and spinning rods, throwing lead weights far out into the channel. I saw Clete walk across the bridge with a paper sack hefted in one arm. I got Alafair started on one of the swing sets and then sat back down on the bank. His knees cracked, his stomach hung over his Budweiser shorts, and he grunted hard in his chest when he sat down beside me.

'You look undressed,' I said.

'Oh.' He touched his chest and smiled. 'I don't work for Sal anymore. I don't have to walk around with a piece all the time. Feels good, mon.'

He twisted the cap off a bottle of Great Falls.

'Dixie Lee says he didn't know Dodds was a hit man.'

'He probably didn't. Where'd you see Dixie Lee?'

'He's living at my house.'

'I'll be damned. He cut the umbilical cord? I didn't think he had the guts. Sal doesn't handle rejection well.'

'Dodds may have had a partner, a backup guy. Does Dio have another guy in town?'

'If he does, I don't know about it. I know a lot of them, too. At least the ones Sal hangs with. They're New York transplants who think the essence of big time is playing bridge by the pool with a lot of gash lying around. Hey, dig this. Sal had a bunch of them staying at his motel, and the motel manager is this little Jewish guy who used to run a book for the mob out of a pizza joint in Fort Lauderdale. Of course, the Jew can't do enough for the dagos because they scare the shit out of him. But he's got this kid who's a wiseass college student at Berkeley, and the kid works for his old man as the poolside waiter during the summer. So four of the dagos are playing cards at one of the umbrella tables. And these are big, mean-looking cocksuckers, shades, wet black hair all over their stomachs, big floppers tucked in their bikinis, and they're giving the kid a terrible time – sending food back to the kitchen, complaining the drinks taste like there's bathroom antiseptic in them, running the kid back and forth for cigarettes and candied cherries and sun cream for the gash and anything else they think of.

'Then one guy spills ice and vodka all over the table and tells the kid to mop it up and bring him another deck of cards. The kid says, "Hey, I've been studying Italian at school this year. What does *Eatta my shitta* mean?"

'The old man hears it and slaps his kid's face in front of everybody. Then he starts swallowing and sweating and apologizing to the dagos while they stare at him from behind those black shades. Finally one of them stands up, hooks his finger in the old man's mouth, and throws him down in an iron chair. He said, "He don't have manners 'cause you didn't teach him none. So you shut up your face and don't be talking to impress nobody. You clean this up, and bring everybody what they want, you sit over there and you don't go nowhere till we say."

'They made him sit out there in the sun like an organ-grinder's monkey for four hours. Till the kid finally begged them to let the old man go back inside.

'It's good to say *Ciao, ciao, bambino* to the grease-balls. The next time the United States drops an A-bomb on anyone, I think it should be Palermo.'

'Where's Dodds?'

'You really want to know?'

'I want to know if he's going to be back after me.'

'First you tell me why you didn't drop the dime on me.' There was a half grin on his face as he raised the beer bottle to his mouth.

'No games, Clete.'

'Because a guy out on bond for murder doesn't like to introduce cops to his blood-splattered kitchen. Because maybe he knows they might just take the easy route and haul his butt down to the bag. Sounds like your faith might be waning, Streak.'

'Is that guy going to be back?'

'That's one you don't have to worry about.'

'Where is he?' I asked.

'Get serious. You don't need to know anymore, Streak. Except the fact that our man didn't like heights.'

'What?'

'Did you ever meet a psychopath yet that wasn't scared of something? It's what makes them cruel. Charlie didn't like high places. At least not the one I showed him.'

I looked out silent at the river. A Frisbee sailed by overhead.

'Too grim for you?' Clete said.

'Did he kill Darlene?'

'No, I'm convinced that's one he didn't do.'

'Dio, then?'

'He didn't know. Put it in the bank, too.'

I stood up and began brushing the grass off my pants.

'You're going to turn to stone on me, huh?' he said.

'It's a school night. Alafair has to get home.'

'Why is it you always make me feel like anthrax, Streak?'

'You're right about one thing today. I didn't call the heat because I didn't want to be part of another criminal investigation. Particularly when I was left with the problem of explaining how somebody's blood got smeared all over my walls and stove and floor. Right now I'm going to believe that Charlie Dodds is on a flight to new opportunities in Mexico City. Beyond that, I wouldn't count on anything, Clete.'

'I'm going to get the guy that did her. You want to sit around and bite your nails, that's cool with me.'

I walked off toward a group of children with whom Alafair was playing tag. Then Clete called after me, in a voice that made people turn and stare. 'I love you anyway, motherfucker.'

I needed some help. I had accomplished virtually nothing on my own; I had been locked up for punching out Sally Dio, had persuaded nobody of my theories, and instead had managed to convince a couple of local cops that I was a gun-wielding paranoid. That night I called Dan Nygurski at his home in Great Falls. A baby-sitter answered and said that he was at a movie with his wife, that she would take down my name and number. He returned my call just after ten, when I was drifting off to sleep with a damp towel folded across the lump on my forehead. I took the phone into the kitchen and closed the hallway door so as not to wake Alafair or Dixie Lee, who was sleeping on the living room couch.

I told him about Charlie Dodds in my house. About the slapjack across the head, the handcuffs, the Instamatic camera, the survival knife that he had been about to shove into my heart. Then I told him about Clete, the working over that Dodds had taken, the rolled rug, and the trip in the jeep probably up a log road in either the Bitterroot Valley or the Blackfoot Canyon.

'You realize what you're telling me?' Nygurski said.

'I don't give a damn about Dodds. That's not why I called.'

'You didn't tell the cops any of this?'

'I'm telling you. Do with it what you want. I'll bet

nobody ever finds Dodds, though. Clete's done this kind of thing before and gotten away with it.'

'You should have called the cops.'

'Bullshit. I'd be trying to arrange bond right now.'

'I'll have to report this to them.'

'Go ahead. I think their interest level on a scale of one to ten will be minus eight. Look, Nygurski, there's somebody else after me or my daughter. He was hanging around her school this morning. Maybe it's Mapes, maybe it's another one of Dio's people. I need some help.'

'I think it takes a hell of a lot of nerve to ask a federal agent for help after you run around two states with a baseball bat.'

'We both want the same thing – Sally Dee doing some serious time.'

'No, you've got it wrong. I want to do my job. You want to write your own rules on a day-to-day basis.'

'Then you give me a solution. You pledge the safety of my daughter, you assure me that I won't be headed for Angola Farm in about three weeks, and I won't be a problem to you.'

'What kind of help do you want?'

'Can you find out if Dio might have another hit man in town?'

'If he does, we don't know about it. Maybe he put out the contract and let Dodds hire a backup guy. I tell you, though, if this new guy is working with Dodds, he's not going to try for any "before-and-after" stuff, not after Dodds blew it. He'll go for a clean hit, one that you'll never see coming. I don't want to be graphic, but you know how they usually do it – one behind the head, one in the ear, and three under the chin.'

'Run Mapes for me.'

'What do you expect to find?'

'I don't know. My lawyer says he was in trouble only once, for beating up a kid with a golf club when he was seventeen. But I've seen this guy in action, and I can't believe he hasn't bumped into the furniture more than once.'

'Where's he from?'

'He beat up the kid in Marshall, Texas.'

'I'll see what I can do.'

'There's one other thing. Dixie Lee moved out of Dio's place. He says he's through with him. You might talk to him.'

'About what?'

'That's your province. How about grand-jury testimony? It took guts to walk out on Dio, particularly when he owes him fifteen thou.'

'When did you decide to start sharing Pugh's secrets?'

'He's probably going to need federal protection sometime. He might be a drunk, but his head sops up information and people's conversations like a blotter.'

'Where is he?'

'He's staying with me.'

'What did you do for kicks as a kid? Swallow thumbtacks?'

'The guy's up against the wall,' I said.

'No, I take that crack back. You're a slick operator, Robicheaux. Pugh becomes a federal witness, Pugh lives at your house, your house and the people in it go under our umbrella. Right?'

'Not really.'

'I hope not. Because we choose the accommodations.'

'Clever people don't end up in the mess I'm in, Nygurski.'

'I think maybe there's solid truth in that statement. I'll get back to you. In the meantime you watch your butt.'

'When can I hear from you about Mapes?'

'I'm going the extra mile for you. Ease up on the batter, okay? Have a little trust. If you ever get out of this, get your badge back. I think everybody would rather have you inside the tent pissing out the flap than the other way around. I'm sure of it.'

Dixie Lee was up early the next morning and had breakfast with me and Alafair at the kitchen table. He was one of those drunks whose eyes clear and whose skin becomes pink and unlined with only a twenty-four-hour respite from alcohol. This morning his face was shaved and bright, and he wore a pair of pleated, white summer shorts and a white sport shirt with green parrots on it. I walked Alafair to school, then made him go to an AA meeting with me down the street and put his name in with the job-placement service. His mood was not as cheerful on the way home as it had been earlier.

'Them people make me nervous, son,' he said. 'I feel like a turd floating around in somebody's soup bowl.'

'It's the one place where maybe people can understand guys like us, Dixie.'

'Yeah, well, I've been to them meets before, and it didn't take. I think that's just the way it is with some guys. Jesus pointed his finger at the people he wanted. I ain't seen nobody point his finger at me. Hey, you remember those jokes we used to tell in the fifties? Like, what'd the bathtub say to the toilet? "I get the same amount of ass you do, but I don't have to take all that shit." '

'Come on, partner, what's really bothering you?'

'I don't relate to that fourth- and fifth-step stuff. Where you got to go over all you done wrong and confess everything to somebody. I really don't dig that at all. I got enough damn guilt without poking at it all with a stick.'

'Take it a step at a time. You don't have to do that now. Besides, haven't you owned up to a lot of things already? You told me some pretty honest stuff when you were in the hospital in Lafayette.'

'I got all kinds of things that make me ashamed. Hell, I knew Sal was no good when I met him in the pen. He was a geek. But he had bread, a lot of dope, and he liked me. So I didn't have to sweat the wolves and the swinging dicks and the guys who'd blow out your candle if they ever thought you snitched for the boss man. So I pretended not to see what went on in our cell. I wrote it off. A lot of guys turn homosexual inside the joint. I didn't go for it myself, but I didn't knock the guys who did. So Sal had a punk. Big deal, I thought. The fucking system does it to guys. That's what I said to myself. So I'd take a walk when this Mexican kid would come to our cell. It wasn't my business, right? Except something very weird started happening.'

We sat down on the front steps of my porch. Birds flew in and out of the shade. There was no wind, and the maple trees looked green and bright and stiff against the sky.

'You see, in that kind of relationship, in the pen, I mean, the punk is disposable,' Dixie Lee said. 'A pair of pork chops. All right, it's sickening stuff, but that's the way it is. But this kid was a real lover for Sal. He'd bring lipstick and women's underwear to the cell, and he'd wash and comb Sal's hair and then they'd hang a blanket down off the top bunk and really go at it. Except the kid turned out to be a lot more than Sal's punk. Sal really fell for him. The kid always had cigarettes, candy bars, ludes, magazines, an easy job in the infirmary, safe-conduct pass with the badasses. Then the kid started acting like a celebrity, walking around with a little pout on his face, making cow eyes at some very dangerous guys in the shower. A couple of guys told Sal he'd better straighten out his punk, but it wasn't too long before everybody knew that his kid could jerk Sal around any way he wanted to.

'The problem was some black guys wanted to take over Sal's drug action. But he had too many mean guys working for him, and they knew he was connected on the outside, too, so they always walked around him. Then the kid started making him look like a douche bag, and they decided it was time for them to get into some serious pharmaceutical sales. Sal had been bringing in about four or five hundred bucks a week, which is a lot of money in the joint, and in three weeks' time the blacks cut that in half. His mules came around the cell like scared mice and asked him what he was going to do about it, since the blacks were telling them they were in the business for good, and Sal tried to blow it off and tell them everything was cool and that he was bringing in a load of Afghan skunk that would cook brains all over the joint.

'But everybody was laughing at him behind his back. The kid treated Sal like he was the punk instead of the other way around, and in the meantime he was hanging with a couple of other yard bitches who were anybody's punch, and the three of them would go swishing around the place while the kid talked in a loud voice about Sal like he was some Dagwood Bumstead the kid put up with.

'But somebody called up Sal's old man in Galveston, and the shit hit the fan. The old man came up to Huntsville, and I don't know what he said to Sal in the visiting room, but whatever it was it put the fear of God in him. His face was white when he came back to our cell. He sat up all night smoking cigarettes on the side of his bunk, and in the morning he puked his breakfast out on the work detail. I asked him what was wrong, and he said, "I got to do something." I said, "What?" He said, "Something I don't want to do."

'So I said, "Don't do it." Then he said, "I'm a made guy. When you're a made guy, you do what they tell you."

'See, that's that dago stuff. They got some kind of ritual with knives and blood and magical bullshit, and they get to be made guys, which means they can smoke cigars at front tables in Vegas and pretend they're not a bunch of ignorant fish peddlers anymore.

'Two days later, right before lockup, Sal went to the kid's cell, where the kid was reading a comic book on his bunk with another fairy. He told the other kid to take off, then he took a piece of pipe out of his pants and beat that Mexican boy almost to death. He broke his nose, busted out his teeth, cauliflowered his ears, hurt that boy so bad his mother wouldn't know him.

'When he come back to the cell he had his shirt wadded up in his hand to hide the blood. After lights-out he tore it up in strips and flushed it down the toilet.

In the morning he was all smiles, like he'd just made his first jump in the airborne or something. That kid was in the hospital three weeks. They shaved his head bald and put a hundred stitches in it. He looked like a lumpy white basketball with barbed wire wrapped all over it.

'Then Sal put out the word the kid was anybody's bar of soap. You know what that means in the joint for a kid like that? There're some cruel, sick sonsobitches in there, son. That kid had an awful time of it. I don't like remembering it.'

'Why are you telling me this, Dixie?'

'Because most of them people at the meet are just drunks. Liquor's only part of my problem. I lived off a guy like Sal. The reason I done it was because it was easy. You can't beat lobster and steak every day, plus the sweet young things were always ready to kick off their panties. If I didn't cut it with the oil business, life was still a pure pleasure around Sal's swimming pool. It didn't have nothing to do with liquor or dope. It has to do with a lack of character.'

'It's part of the illness. You'll learn that if you keep going to meetings,' I said.

He pulled a long-bladed weed from the edge of the step and bounced it up and down between his feet.

'You'll see,' I said.

'You want me to talk to the DEA, don't you?'

'Why do you think that?'

'I heard you on the phone last night.'

'You want to?'

'No.'

He bounced the weed on the toe of his loafer, then picked up a small red bug with the weed's tip and watched it climb toward his hand.

'You wouldn't use me, would you, Dave?' he said.

'No, I wouldn't do that.'

'Because I'd be sorely hurt. I mean it, son. I don't need it. I surely don't.'

I stood up and brushed off the seat of my pants.

'I don't know how you do it,' I said.

'What's that?' He squinted up at me in the sunlight. His hair was gold and wavy and shiny with oil.

'No matter what I talk to you about, somehow I always lose.'

'It's your imagination. They don't come much more simple than me.'

I remember one of the last times I saw my mother. It was 1945, just before the war ended, and she came to our house on the bayou with the gambler she had run away with. I was out front on the dirt road, trying to catch my dog, who was chasing chickens in the ditch, when he stopped his coupe, one with a rumble seat and hand-cranked front window with gas-ration stamps on it, thirty yards down from the house. She walked fast up the lane into the shade of our oaks and around to the side yard, where my father was nailing together a chicken coop. She worked in a drive-in and beer garden in Morgan City. Her pink waitress uniform had a white trim on the collar and sleeves, and because her body was thick and muscular it looked too small on her when she walked. Her back was turned to me while she talked to my father, but his face was dark as he listened and his eyes went up the road to where the coupe was parked.

The gambler had his car door open to let in the breeze. He was thin and wore sideburns and brown zoot pants with suspenders and a striped shirt and a green necktie with purple dots on it. A brown fedora sat in the back window.

He asked me in French if the dog was mine. When I didn't answer, he said, 'You don't talk French, boy?'

'Yes, sir.'

'That your dog?'

'Yes, sir.'

'You know how to make him stop running them chicken? Break a stick on him. You ain't got to do it but once.'

I walked away in the dust toward the house and the trees, and I didn't look at my dog. I heard my father say to my mother, 'In five minutes I'm coming there. That little gun won't do him no good, neither.'

She took me by the hand and walked me quickly to the front steps and sat me in her lap. She brushed my face and hair with her hands and kissed me and patted my thighs. There were drops of perspiration behind her neck, and I could smell her perfume, like four-o'clocks, and the powder on her breasts.

'You been good at school, huh?' she said. 'You been going to mass, too, you? You been making confess and go to communion? Aldous been taking you? You got to do good in school. The brothers gonna teach you lots of t'ings.'

'Why you stay with him?'

She pressed my face against her breasts. I could feel the hard shape of her stomach and her thighs.

'He shot somebody. In a card game,' I said.

'He ain't bad. He's good to me. We brung you a present. You gonna see.'

She picked me up and carried me to the road. I could

see my father watching from the side yard, the hammer in his hand. She set me down by the open door of the coupe. The air was humid and hot in the sun, and the cattails in the ditch were coated with dust.

'Come see,' she said. 'Show it him, Mack. Behind the seat.'

His face had no expression. He reached behind the seat, his eyes looking out down the yellow road, and pulled out a paper bag. It was folded across the top and tied with string.

'Here,' she said, and unwrapped it for me. Her dress was tight across her thighs and there were dimples in her knees. The man got out of the car and walked out on the road and lit a cigarette. He didn't look in my father's direction, but they could see each other well.

'You like a top, huh?' my mother said. 'See, it got a crank. You push it up and down and it spin around and whistle.'

There was perspiration in her black hair. She put the top in my hands. The metal felt hot against my palms.

'Is he coming out?' the man said.

'No. He promised.'

'The last time was for free. You told him that?'

'He don't want no more trouble, Mack. He ain't gonna bother us.'

'I give a damn, me.'

'Don't be talking that way. We gotta go. Don't be looking over there. You hear me, Mack?'

'They gonna keep him in jail next time.'

'We going right now. Get in the car. I gotta be at work. Dave don't need be standing out in the hot road. Ain't that right, Davy? Mack, you promised.'

He flipped his cigarette away in the ditch and got

behind the steering wheel. He wore two-tone brown and white shoes, and he wiped the dust off the shine with a rag from under the seat. I saw my father toss his hammer up on the workbench, then pick up the chicken coop and look at the angles of its side.

My mother leaned over me and pressed me against her body. Her voice was low, as though the two of us were under a glass bell.

'I ain't bad, Davy,' she said. 'If somebody tell you that, it ain't true. I'll come see you again. We'll go somewheres together, just us two. Eat fried chicken, maybe. You gonna see, you.'

But a long time would pass before I would see her again. The Victory gardens, the picket-fenced donation centers of worn tires and bundled coat hangers, the small tasseled silk flags with blue and gold service stars that hung in house windows to signify the number of family members who were in uniform or killed in action, would all disappear within the year, an era would end, and the oil companies would arrive from Texas. I would hear that my mother worked in the back of a laundry with colored women in Baton Rouge, that Mack died of tuberculosis, that she married a man who operated carnival rides. Then when I was sixteen years old and I went for the first time to the Boundary Club on the Breaux Bridge highway, a rough, ramshackle roadhouse where they fought with knives and bottles in the shale parking lot, I saw her drawing draft beer behind the bar. Her body was thicker now, her hair blacker than it should have been, and she wore a black skirt that showed a thick scar above one knee. She brought a beer tray to a table full of oil-field workers, then sat down with them. They all knew her and lit her cigarettes, and when she danced with one of them she pressed her stomach against his loins. I stood by the jukebox and waved at her, and she smiled back at me over the man's shoulder, but there was no recognition in her face.

I waited out in the car for my friends to come out of the club. I saw a drunk man pushed out the side door on to the shale. I saw some teenagers throw a Coke bottle at a car full of Negroes. I saw a man in a yellow cowboy shirt and tight blue jeans without a belt slap a woman against the side of a car. He hit her hard and made her cry and shoved her in the backseat and made her stay there by herself while he went back inside. It was hot and still in the parking lot, except for the sounds of the woman. The willow trees were motionless on the banks of the Vermilion River, and the moonlight looked like oil on the water's surface. Dust drifted through the car window, and I could smell the stench of dead garfish out on the mudbank and hear the woman weeping quietly in the dark.

The opinion of certain people has always been important to me. Most of those people have been nuns, priests, Catholic brothers, and teachers. When I was a child the good ones among them told me I was all right. Some in that group were inept and unhappy with themselves and were cruel and enjoyed inculcating guilt in children. But the good ones told me that I was all right. As an adult, I still believe that we become the reflection we see in the eyes of others, so it's important that someone tell us we're all right. That may seem childish, but only to those who have paid no dues and hence have no question mark about who they are, because their own experience or lack of it has never required them to define themselves. You can meet some of these at university cocktail parties; or sometimes they are journalists who fear and envy power and celebrity but who love to live in its ambience. There is always a sneer buried inside their laughter. They have never heard a shot fired in anger, done time, walked through a mortared ville, seen a nineteen-year-old door gunner go apeshit in a free-fire zone. They sleep without dreaming. They yawn at the disquietude of those whom they can't understand. No one will ever need to tell them that they are all right.

I think for some the soul has the same protean shape as fire, or a collection of burning sticks that melts and hisses through the snow until only an ill-defined and soot-streaked hollow remains to indicate the nature of flame and its passage through ice.

Then somebody tells you that you are all right.

I had to go back on the other side of the Divide. It was a good time to take Alafair out of Missoula, too. I walked down to the school and found Tess Regan in her office. A vase of mock orange sat on her desk, and her cork-board was a litter of thumbtacked crayon drawings. Through a sunny window I could see the children on the playground, a solitary basketball hoop, and the brick wall of the church next door. She wore a cotton knit yellow dress, a gold neck chain, and gold earrings that were almost hidden by her auburn hair. Her nails were cut short and painted with clear polish, and her fingers were spread on her desk blotter while she listened to me talk. I liked her and respected her feelings, and I didn't want her to be angry with me any longer or to be uncomfortable because of our conversation yesterday.

'People hang up on me all the time. I expect it,' I said. 'A Treasury agent once told me I had the telephone charm of Quasimodo.'

'That purple lump on your head, that happened at your house yesterday?'

'I was careless. It'll be gone soon.'

'You want to take Alafair out of school today and tomorrow?'

'That's right. She'll be back Thursday.'

'Where are you going, if you don't mind my asking?'

'I have to take care of some business across the mountains.'

'I'm very concerned about all this. You give me bad feelings. These men you talk about are evil, aren't they? But you seem almost cavalier.'

'You're wrong about that, kiddo.'

'I wish you wouldn't call me that.'

'All right.'

'Alafair is a wonderful little girl. I worry about her. I worry about your attitudes.'

'She thinks the world of you, too. I don't want to be unpleasant or to upset you in any way, but I want you to understand something. Somebody sent me a used hypodermic needle and a letter and a photograph. I won't tell you what was in the photograph, but the person who wrote the letter said the needle had been used in a snuff film. His threat was not aimed at me. It was directed at Alafair. I believe he was serious, too.

'Now, in the movies potential murder or assault victims are given twenty-four-hour protection by the cops. But it doesn't happen that way. You're on your own. If you don't believe me, ask anybody who has been hunted down by a guy who they had locked up and who made bail by the next morning. They tell a great story. A lot of them tend to become NRA members.'

Her green eyes were steady and intelligent. She was a good soldier and obviously was trying to look beyond the abrasive quality of my words; but I had gone over a line, almost like an emotional bully, and she wasn't up to handling it.

'I'll gct Alafair for you,' she said.

'Miss Regan . . . Tess, I'm at a real bad place in my life. I apologize for the way that I talk, but I'm really up against it. Don't make me walk out of here feeling like a shit.'

But it was no use. She brushed past me, her hips creasing inside her knit dress, her eyes welling with tears.

Later that day Alafair and I drove into the clouds on the Divide. It rained hard and the trees looked thick and black in the wet light, and water sluiced off the road into the canyons far below. It was too late to get anything done at the Teton County courthouse, so we stayed the night at a motel in Choteau, the county seat.

The next day I found the connection between Sally Dee and the oil business. I found it all over the East Front, in Teton, Pondera, and Glacier counties. And I found out the service that Dixie Lee had been performing for him.

chapter ten

That evening I called Dan Nygurski at his house in Great Falls.

'Where've you been? I called you three times today,' he said.

'Over here, east of the Divide.'

'Now? Where?'

'Right outside of Great Falls.'

'What are you doing right now?'

'Nothing. Going to a motel. I don't feel like driving back tonight.'

'We're fixing to cook out in the backyard in a few minutes. You want to come over?'

'My little girl's with me.'

'Bring her. We've got three kids she can play with. I've got some heavy stuff on Mapes that you ought to know about.'

'The DEA had a file on him?'

'FBI. He was part of a kidnap investigation. You better come over.'

He gave me his address and directions, and Alafair and I drove in the twilight to a 1950s suburb of split-level ranch homes, maple-lined streets, sprinklers twirling on the lawns, flower beds full of blue clematis, yellow and red roses, with tree bark packed on the dirt to prevent the growth of weeds. We sat on the redwood deck built out back, behind sliding glass doors, while Alafair played on a small seesaw with two of his little girls. The coals in his hibachi had already turned gray and hot before we arrived, and his wife brought out a tossed salad and a pitcher of iced tea on a tray, then laid a row of venison and elk steaks on the grill. The grease hissed and steamed off the coals and the smell was wonderful.

His wife was attractive and polite and had the same accent as he.

She wore makeup and a dress, and her eyes were shy when you looked too closely at them. She went back into the kitchen and began slicing a loaf of French bread on a cutting board.

'You're wondering why a woman who looks like that married a guy who looks like me,' he said.

'Not at all.'

'Come on, Robicheaux.'

'Women have kind hearts.'

'Yeah, they do,' he said, and got up from his chair and closed the sliding glass door. 'So let's walk around the side of the house so nobody else has to hear what I have to tell you. In fact, maybe we ought to wait until after you've eaten.'

'Let's do it.'

We walked into his side yard, which was planted with apple trees and climbing red roses on trellises set in small circular beds. There were small, hard green apples in the leaves of the trees. A picket fence separated his yard from his neighbor's swimming pool. It was dusk now, and the reflection of the neighbor's porch light looked like a yellow balloon under the pool's surface. He picked up two metal chairs that were leaned against the side of his house and shook them open. His mouth twitched when he started to speak, and I saw the web of vein and sinew flex and pulse in his throat.

'Where'd your lawyer get his information on Mapes?'

'He hired a PI.'

'Tell him to get your money back. The PI blew it. I suspect he checked the sheriff's and city police's office in Mapes's hometown, came up with the assault arrest, the golf club deal, when Mapes was seventeen, then sent your lawyer a bill for two days' services, which is usually about six hundred dollars. In the meantime he didn't check anything else.'

'What's the story?'

'Look, you were a cop a long time. You know that once in a while you run across a guy, a guy who everybody thinks is normal, maybe a guy with an education, a good job, service record, a guy who doesn't focus much attention on himself. At least he doesn't give cops reason to think about him. But there's something wrong with him. The conscience isn't there, or maybe the feelings aren't. But he's out there, in suburbs just like this, and he's the one who commits the murders that we never solve. I think that's your man Harry Mapes.

'In 1965 an eighteen-year-old soldier on leave from Fort Polk picked up his girlfriend in Tyler, Texas, and took her to a drive-in movie. Then it looks like they went on a back road and parked behind an old greenhouse where somebody used to grow roses. At least that's where the sheriff's department found that girl's dress and underwear. They found the car five miles away in a creek bed. Somebody had torn the gas line loose and set it on fire. Both those kids were in the trunk. The pathologist said they were alive when it burned.'

I leaned forward on the folding metal chair and picked a leaf from a rosebush. My throat felt tight. I could hear the children playing on the seesaw in the backyard.

'Mapes was involved?' I said.

'That's the big question. The fingerprints of another kid from Marshall were on the victims' car, but not Mapes's. But that would figure, if Mapes drove one car and the other kid drove the victims' car to the place where they burned it. Both of them were seen together earlier that night, and it took two people to pull it off, unless the kid they had dead-bang was on foot, which is improbable, since he owned a car and was driving around in it with Mapes earlier.'

'The other kid didn't implicate Mapes?'

'He denied everything. Evidently he had a reputation around Marshall as a lunatic. Acid, speed, all that bull-shit. In his cell he wrapped himself in toilet paper, soaked it in lighter fluid, and set himself on fire. It looked like good theater. But later on he showed every-body he was sincere. He unwrapped some wire from a broom and hanged himself.

'In the meantime, Mapes's old man, who owned a sawmill there, hired a law firm, and they got a Mexican prostitute to swear Mapes and another friend of his were trying out their magic twangers that night. The other kid backed her up. But later on it looks like he might have had problems with his conscience.'

'And he was the one Mapes worked over with the golf club.'

'You got it, brother. Case closed. On top of it, that other kid got zapped in Vietnam two years later.'

I rubbed my hands up and down on my trousers.

'I've got to nail him, Dan. I'm all out of leads, and I keep coming up with a handful of air.'

'Let's eat some dinner.'

'I don't think I'm up to it. I'm sorry. I've got less than one and a half weeks to trial. I'm being straight with you. I'm just not going to do time.'

'You're a good man, and you're going to be all right,' he said, and put his big hand on the corner of my shoulder. It felt hard and cupped, like a starfish that had dried on hot sand.

It was time to turn things around on Sally Dee, to plant some dark thoughts in his head about his own vulnerability, so I could concentrate on Harry Mapes. I knew that Charlie Dodds had probably become bear food at the bottom of a canyon, but Sally Dee didn't. However, he was well aware of Charlie Dodds's potential, and I doubted if he would enjoy being in an adversarial relationship with him. Snapping dogs don't like having their collars chained together.

After Alafair and I got back to Missoula, I rented an hour's typewriter time at the University of Montana library and composed the following letter. I worked hard on it. Chaucer and Dickens created wonderful rogues. I wondered what they would have thought of my attempt. But the more I read over my final draft, the more I was certain that they just might have winked at me with approval.

Dear Sal,

The flowers that go with this you can stick up your butt. When you called Vegas, you said it was a simple yard job. You didn't say anything about pictures and this before-and-after bullshit. That little stunt almost got me killed. In fact, maybe I think you set me up. You go around telling everybody you're a made guy but made guys don't get their nose bent out of joint by some ex-cop that nobody cares about. I think you're not only a dago shitbag and a welsher but a yellow cunt, too. I heard about you from some guys that were in Huntsville. They say your punk had the whole joint laughing at you behind your back. The only reason you got straight is because you were more afraid of your old man than you were of your punk. But you're not getting out of this one. You owe me the rest of the money, and you know where to deliver it. I don't get it, and I mean right away, I'm coming after you. Nobody back in Vegas is going to make a beef about it, either. They all think you're a prick that should have been clipped a long time ago.

C.D.

I drove up to Polson, found a florist's, then called them from a pay phone across the street and got the price of a small floral delivery to Sally Dio's house. Then I found the state employment office, parked by the curb, and watched the men who went in and out of the entrance or who sat against the wall in the shade and smoked cigarettes and passed a bottle back and forth in a paper sack. Finally a middle-aged man in work clothes with uncut dull blond hair came out the door and sat down on the curb with his friends.

I got out of my truck and walked up to him.

'Say, I'll pay you five bucks to go into a florist's and put in an order for me,' I said. 'I'm playing a joke on a guy, and I don't want him to know where the flowers came from. How about it?'

He took a hand-rolled cigarette out of his mouth and looked at me quizzically. He shrugged his shoulders.

'I don't give a shit,' he said.

I drove him back over to the street where the florist's was located, parked three stores down, and gave him the money for the order and a sealed envelope with the letter inside. I didn't know Dio's address, but I had printed his name on the envelope and drawn the approximate location of his house on Flathead Lake.

'Don't tell them you're doing this for anybody else,' I said. 'Just give them the money and the order and the envelope. Okay?'

'Can you make it ten? If I don't buy them other guys a can of beer or something, they might cut me out of a job they get.'

He went into the store and was back out in five minutes. I drove him back to the state employment office.

'You didn't tell them anything, did you?' I asked.

'What's to talk about in a flower place? I give them the money, I give them the envelope. You got any more jobs like this one you want done?'

That night Dixie Lee and I took Alafair to a movie. Before I went to bed I got Dixie to give me Sally Dee's unlisted telephone number.

'What for? You don't want no more truck with that man,' he said. He sat in his undershirt, candy-striped undershorts, and black shoes at the kitchen table, eating a piece of pie.

'Don't worry about it.'

'Are you kidding? He's got mental diseases they haven't named yet. I ain't putting you on, son. He's got a hard-on for you you couldn't knock down with a hammer.'

'Don't use that language in the house.'

'Sorry, it's a speech defect or something. His head reminds me of a flowerpot somebody dropped on the concrete. It's full of cracks and the dirt's starting to leak out, but he don't know it yet. Dig this. Sal built an elevator platform for the piano at his club, one of these deals that rises up into the spotlight while the guy's playing. Except after the club closed this two-hundred-and-eighty-pound bouncer got on top of the piano with this topless dancer for some serious rumba boogie, and somehow the machinery got cranked up and the elevator went right up to the ceiling and mashed them both against a beam. It broke the guy's neck, and the broad was trapped up there with him all night. So Sal says it's a real big tragedy, and he holds the funeral on a Sunday afternoon at the club, with the casket covered with flowers out in the middle of the dance floor. But the undertaker messed up the job, and the guy's neck was bent and his head was out of round, like a car tire had run over it, and the dagos were slobbering and wailing all over the place while Sal's singing on the mike in a white suit like he's Tony Bennett. It was so disgusting the waiters went back to the union and threatened to quit. Later Sal says to me, "It was a class send-off, don't you think? Jo-Jo would have liked it." Except I found out he only rented the casket, and he had Jo-Jo planted in a cloth-covered box in a desert cemetery outside of town that lizards wouldn't crawl across.'

'Good night, Dixie.'

He shook his head and forked another piece of pie in his mouth.

'You worry about my bad language, and you're fixing to squeeze Sal in the peaches. You're a wonder to behold, son.'

I set the alarm on my Seiko watch for two A.M. and went to sleep. It was raining lightly when I was awakened by the tiny dinging sound on my wrist. I dialed Sal's number, then hung up when a man with sleep in his voice answered. I waited fifteen minutes, then hung up again as soon as the same man said 'Hello' irritably into the receiver. I drank a glass of milk and watched the rain fall in the yard and run down the window, then at two-thirty I called again. I put a pencil crossways in my teeth and covered the mouthpiece with my handkerchief.

'Who the fuck is this?' the same man said.

'Where's Sal?' I kept my voice in the back of my throat and let it come out in a measured rasp.

'Asleep. Who is this?'

'Go wake him up.'

'Are you crazy? It's two-thirty in the morning. What's with you, man?'

'Listen, you get that dago welsher out of bed.'

'I think you're loaded, man, and you'd better stop playing on the phone and forget you ever called here.'

'You don't recognize my voice, huh? Maybe it's because a guy put a wrench across my windpipe, a guy that gutless kooze sent me to see. I didn't catch a plane back to Vegas, either. I'm one hour away. I better not find out you're hitting on my broad, either.'

He was quiet a moment, then he said, 'Charlie?'

I didn't answer.

'Charlie?' he said. 'Hey, man . . .'

'What?'

'I didn't know. Hey, man, I'm sorry. You should have told me. It's late, and I been asleep, and I didn't know it was you.'

'Get him on the phone.'

'Man, he's out. I mean, like him and Sandy must have smoked a whole shoe box of shit before they crashed. How about he calls you in the morning?'

'You got some kind of skin growth over your ears?'

'Look, man, I go in there, he'll tear my dick off. He's been crawling the walls all day, anyway. Look, I don't know what's going on between you guys, but I don't want to get caught in it. Okay? I'm not putting you on, man, he can't talk to you. He really smoked his brains tonight.'

I waited five seconds and listened to him breathe.

'Tell him I'm coming,' I said, and hung up.

I overslept the next morning and was awakened by the sound of Alafair fixing breakfast in the kitchen. She was too short to function well around the stove, and she clattered the pan loudly on the burners.

'I can walk myself today, Dave,' she said.

'No, that's out. We do everything together, little guy. We're a team, right?'

She stood in front of the stove, her face quiet, her head even with the top of the stove, looking at the skillet full of French toast.

‘It makes me feel funny in front of the other kids,’ she said.

‘I’ll drive you, then. It’ll be like I’m dropping you off on the way to work. That’ll be okay, won’t it?’

‘Clarise don’t know how to take care of Tripod. She’s always mad at him.’

I turned off the stove, picked up the skillet with a dish towel, and set it in the sink to cool. The French toast was burned around the edges.

‘We’re just going to have to accept some things now. That’s the way it is, Alf,’ I said.

She packed her lunch box silently, then ate only half of her French toast, and went outside and waited for me on the front step. The wind was blowing off the river, and the sunlight through the maple tree made shifting patterns of leaves on her face.

Later, Dixie and I went to an early AA meeting. Afterward, one of the members who worked in the job-placement service told Dixie that he had found him a part-time job operating a forklift at the pulp mill out on the river. We walked home, and it was obvious that Dixie was not happy at the news. He sulked around the house, then took his sunburst guitar out on the back steps and began playing with a thumb pick and singing a song that I had heard only once before, many years ago. The words went to the tune of ‘Just a Closer Walk with Thee.’

‘Now, bread and gravy is all right,
And a turnip sandwich is a delight,
But my kids always scream
For more of them ole butter beans.

Well, just a little piece of country ham,
Just pass the butter and the jam,
Just pass the biscuits if you please,
And some more of them good ole butter beans.

Just see that woman over there,
The one with both her hands in the air.
She's not pregnant as she seems
She's just full of good ole butter beans.'

I opened the screen and sat down on the steps beside him. It was warm, and the clover in the grass was alive with bees.

'You're supposed to report to the plant at noon, aren't you?' I said.

'That's what he said.'

'You going out there in slacks and a Hawaiian shirt?'

'Look, that job ain't exactly what I had in mind.'

'Oh?'

'Ain't that place a toilet-paper factory or something? Besides, I don't have experience running heavy equipment.'

'A forklift isn't heavy equipment. And I thought you told me you operated one in Huntsville.'

'For about two days, till I dropped the prongs on a guy's foot.'

'We had a deal, podna. We don't renegotiate the terms.'

He made a sliding blues chord high up on the guitar's neck, then ran it all the way down to the nut.

'I learned that from Sam Hopkins,' he said. 'I went out to his house in the Fifth Ward in Houston. People said them nigras'll leave you bleeding in the street for the garbageman to find. They treated me like royalty, man.'

'I spent some time Wednesday in some courthouses east of the Divide.'

His face went blank.

'I found some of the deals you made over there.'

He continued to look out at the lawn and the bees lifting off the clover.

'I'm not an expert on the oil business, but I saw some peculiar stuff in those lease files,' I said.

'They're public records. A person can look all they want to.' He began fishing in his shirt pocket for a cigarette.

'Every time you leased up a big block of land for Star Drilling, there was a hole or two left in it.'

He lit his cigarette and smoked it with his elbow propped on the belly of his guitar.

'Those holes were leased or bought up by one of Sal's businesses in Vegas,' I said. 'The same company name is on some of the deals you made for him around Flathead Lake.'

'I'm not proud of it.'

'So he does want into the oil and gas business.'

'He wants to cover his action every way he can. He's shooting for the big score in gambling and lake property development, he wants in on the gas domes on the East Front. In the drilling business, it don't matter if they tap in on top of your property or not. As long as you're in the pool, part of the dome, you're going to get royalties. That ain't all he's got on his mind, either. They make a big strike over there, it could be like that pipeline deal up in Alaska. All them sonsobitches are horny, and they got plenty of money for dope, too.

Them conservation people are hollering because the gas is full of hydrogen sulfide, it stinks like rotten eggs, but they ought to hear what Sal's got planned for the place.'

'So you took Star over the hurdles?'

'That's about it.'

'And you helped Sal start out in a brand-new enterprise.'

'You want me on the cross? I told you I done it. I ain't lied about it.'

'But that's not all of it.'

'What?'

'Dalton Vidrine and Harry Mapes had to know what you were doing.'

'At first they didn't but Vidrine heard about it from another guy who was working the same township and range as me. He told Mapes, and they stuck it to me at the motel one night. I thought they were going to drop the dime on me with the home office, but they just wanted me to piece off the action. Sal said no problem. It cost him a little coke. Everybody was happy.'

'You've got to give me something I can use against Mapes.'

'I got nothing to offer. I told you all of it. They're like piranha in a goldfish bowl. You stick your finger in it, you take back a polished bone.'

I left him thumbing the bass string on his guitar and staring out at the lawn, as though the blue and green shades in the grass held a secret for him. A few minutes later he came into the house and changed into an old shirt and a pair of ripped and faded pink slacks and drove off toward the smoking stacks of the pulp mill west of town.

*

After he was gone, I sat alone in the silence of the house with the realization that there was nothing I could do today to help my case. I knew of nothing I could do tomorrow or the next day either. I had run out of options. The time has come, I thought, to think not in terms of what to do but instead of where to go. Any jail or prison is a bad place. The person who thinks otherwise has never been in one. Angola is worse than most. The man who would willingly submit to do time unjustly in a place like that would take pleasure in his own crucifixion, I thought. It was a big country, and there were lots of places to get lost in it.

But the idea of being a permanent fugitive from the law was so strange and removed from any concept I had ever had about my fate in this world that thinking about it left me numb and staring at phantasms in the air.

Annie, I thought.

But she came to me only in the darkness, and her visits had become less frequent and her voice had grown weaker across the water and in the din of the rain. I had only myself to depend on now, and my Higher Power and the AA program that I followed. Maybe, as I had told Dixie Lee in the hospital, it was time to look at the things that I had rather than at the problems that seemed to beset me without a solution. I was sober, even though I had set myself up for a fall by not attending meetings. When I had wanted to join Annie in that watery place more than anything in the world, I had gone into therapy rather than let that morning arrive when I would awaken in the blue-gray light, sit quietly on the side of my bed in my underwear, and fit the iron sight of my .45 against the roof of my mouth.

And, last, I had Alafair, who was given to me inside a green bubble of air from below the Gulf's surface.

Maybe it's like the seventh-inning stretch, I thought, when they've shelled your fastball past your ears and blown your hanging curve through the boards. Afternoon shadows are growing on the field, your arm aches, the movement and sound of the fans are like an indistinct hum in the stands. Then a breeze springs up and dries the sweat on your face and neck, you wipe your eyes clear on your sleeve, scrub the ball against your thigh, fork your fingers tightly into the stitches, and realize that the score is irrelevant now, that your failure is complete, that it wasn't so bad after all because now you're free and alone in a peculiar way that has put you beyond the obligations of victory and defeat. The batter expects you to float another balloon past his letters, and instead you take a full windup, your face dry and cool in the breeze, your arm now weightless, and you swing your leg and whole butt into the delivery, your arm snaps like a snake, and the ball whizzes past him in a white blur. And that's the way you pitch the rest of the game, in the lengthening shadows, in the dust blowing off the base paths, in the sound of a flag popping on a metal pole against the blue sky; you do it without numbers in your head, right into the third out in the bottom of the ninth.

And I wasn't going to let Tess Regan have the final statement, either. You don't walk out of a room on someone, with tears in your eyes, as though he's an ogre, unless you want to inflict a certain amount of damage. I ate lunch, then told her that over the phone. Then I asked her to have dinner with me and Alafair at a restaurant that evening.

'I don't know what to say. I don't want to be unkind to you. I just don't understand you,' she said.

'Stop hiding behind that elementary-school-teacher stuff.'

'You stop talking to me like that.'

'Don't treat me like I fell through a hole in the dimension, either.'

'You're an incredible person. You can't say everything that's on your mind to somebody, then ask them out to dinner.'

'I've been straight with you, Tess. I'm indebted to you for the care you've given Alafair. I respect and like you. I don't want you to be unaware of that fact. That's all I had to say. We'll leave it at that.'

She paused a moment, then away from the receiver, cleared her throat.

'I have a PTA buffet at five-thirty,' she said. 'We could go out for dessert later, if you'd like to.'

That evening I shined my loafers, put on a pair of seersucker slacks, a long-sleeved blue shirt with a red-and-black-striped tie, and Alafair and I picked her up in the truck at seven-thirty. She lived on the bottom floor of an old orange-brick apartment building, with a wood porch and thick wood columns and an enormous white-trunked birch tree in the front yard. She wore beige sandals and a print dress covered with small blue and pink flowers. We went to an outdoor café by the river and had ice cream and Black Forest chocolate cake, and I paid for it with my MasterCard, hoping that it hadn't been canceled yet. It rained briefly; now the sky looked like an ink wash above the mountains and I could see lightning striking hard on a distant ridge.

Alafair was overjoyed at the thought of Tess Regan

and me being together. But it wasn't a romantic overture on my part. Or at least that was what I told myself, although she was surely good to look at. I think she reminded me of one of those girls whom Catholic boys were always told, when I was growing up, that they should marry. I doubt that a girl of that kind ever existed, but we believed she did, anyway. Before I met Darlene, I was involved seriously with only three women in my adult life. My first wife was from Martinique, a descendant of French Huguenots, or probably iconoclasts who liked to smash statues in cathedrals. She tired quickly of living with a drunk, for which I couldn't blame her, but she also tired of living on a policeman's salary and became fond of wealth and clubhouse society. She married a Houston geologist, and the last I heard they lived in River Oaks and raced quarter horses at Rio Dosa.

Annie was not only the best woman I ever knew; she was also the best human being. I called her my Mennonite girl, sewn together from cornflowers and bluebonnets. Her faults were those of excess – in love, forgiveness, worry over others, faith that goodness would always prevail over evil. She was seldom if ever critical of others, and when their views didn't coincide with her eccentric Kansas vision of the world, she saw them as victims of what she called weirdness, a condition that she saw virtually everywhere.

I became involved with Robin Gaddis after Annie's death. She was a stripper and sometime hooker on Bourbon Street, but she was brave in her way and kind and gave much more than she received. What some will not understand is that it takes courage to grow up in a place like the welfare project by the old St Louis

Cemetery in New Orleans. Ask a tourist who has visited that cemetery in anything less than a large group, even in broad daylight. Or if one is suicidal and would like to have a truly existential experience, he might try walking through Louis Armstrong Park, right next to the welfare project, at night. Robin's body was outraged in many ways long before she began taking off her clothes for men simply for money. I don't know where she is today. I wish I did. I have two Purple Hearts. I believe they belong much more to Annie, Robin, and Darlene than they do to me.

The wind began to blow, and in the fading twilight I could see the smoke from the pulp mill flatten in the valley west of town and smell its odor like a tinge of sewage in the wet air. We drove Tess Regan back to her apartment house, and I walked her to her door. The porch light was on, and there was a sheen in her auburn hair, and her shoulders looked pale against her pink-and-blue-flowered dress.

'Thank you for this evening,' she said, and she touched me lightly on the arm with her fingers and let them rest there for perhaps three seconds. Her green eyes were warm and genuine, and I wondered if she had been rehearsing for a long time to be that Catholic girl the nuns and the brothers had told us about.

We drove under the dark shadows of the trees toward our house, and the glow from the street lamps looked like long slicks of yellow light ironed into the street's wet surface. I turned the corner on to our block while Alafair kept looking out the passenger window at a pair of headlights behind us.

'That same car stopped down from Miss Regan's,' she said.

'What?'

'That car stopped behind us while you were talking to Miss Regan on the porch.'

I parked in front of our house. The street was dark, and the strings of lights on the sawmill across the river shone on the water's surface.

'Don't get out of the truck,' I said, and I reached under the seat for my .45. The vehicle behind me pulled to the curb, and the driver cut the headlights just as I stepped out of the cab with the automatic held behind my leg.

Clete stuck his head out of the window of his Toyota jeep, his mouth grinning, a white billed cap cocked over his eye.

'Hey, can you tell me where I can catch the St Charles streetcar?' he said. 'What have you got hidden behind you, noble mon? Are we into heavy shit here?'

'What are you doing following me?'

'I was on my way over and just happened to see you on the other street. Slow your pulse down, Streak.' He got out of the Toyota and stretched and yawned. He wore a purple and gold LSU football jersey with a big tiger's head on the front. His love handles stuck out from the sides of his blue jeans. He reached back through the car window and took out a pint of whiskey in a paper bag, unscrewed the cap, and took a neat drink.

'Who was the broad?' he said.

I didn't answer him. I walked Alafair into the house, turned on all the lights, looked in each of the rooms, and came back outside. He sat on the steps, smoking a cigarette, the pink bottle by his knee.

'Who's the new broad?' he said.

'Wrong word.'

'All right, who's the *lady*?'

'Just a friend, one of the teachers at the school. She looks after Alafair sometimes.'

'I wonder why she isn't homely. Probably just a coincidence.'

'What are you up to, Clete?'

'Nothing. Maybe I just want to talk a minute. You got a minute, don't you?'

I sat down next to him on the steps. Against the lights on the sawmill, I could see the outline of suitcases and a couple of rolled sleeping bags in the back of his jeep. He took his billfold out of his back pocket and began counting through a thick sheaf of twenties in the bill holder.

'How you doing on money?' he said.

'Not bad.'

'I bet.'

'I've still got my credit cards.'

'You remember that time I dropped a deuce at Jefferson Downs? You lent it to me so Lois wouldn't find out.'

'You paid it back. When we took that charter fishing trip out of Gulfport.'

'Not quite. I didn't pay the guy.'

I looked at him.

'He was a lousy guy. He ran us up on the sandbar, he didn't bring enough bait, his mate was a smartass. You think I'm going to give a guy like that four hundred dollars?' he said.

'Thanks, Clete. I don't need it right now.'

He folded a stack of bills between his fingers and shoved them into my shirt pocket.

'Take it and stop irritating me.'

'It looks like you're packed up.'

'You can't ever tell.'

'What are you doing, partner?'

'I think my greatest potential lies in population control and travel. Who'd you tell about Charlie Dodds?'

'The DEA.'

'I knew it.'

'The agent said he was going to the locals with it, too.'

'Big deal. But I knew you'd do it, Streak. You'll always be a straight cop.'

'There's worse things.'

'What's that mean?'

'Nothing. I'm just talking about myself. I've got to go inside now. You want to come in?'

'No, thanks. I think I'll just take a drive somewhere, maybe eat a steak.'

'You've been lucky so far, Clete. Walk away from it.'

'You ought to come up to the Nine Mile House at Alberton with me. They've got steaks you can cut with a spoon. Watch out for that schoolteacher. Those kind will marry you.'

I watched him drive away in the darkness. I went into the kitchen and put the folded sheaf of bills from my pocket on the table. Then I looked at the bills again and counted them. Some of the bills were fifties, not twenties. He had given me over six hundred dollars.

Later that night, Dixie came home with a black-and-white television set that he had bought for ten dollars, and was watching the late show on the couch in his underwear when the phone rang. I sat up sleepily on the edge of the bed and looked out at him in the lighted hallway as he answered the phone. His hairy stomach protruded over the elastic of his candy-striped shorts. He put his hand over the mouthpiece of the receiver.

'It's that DEA Polack in Great Falls,' he said. 'You want me to tell him you're bombed out?'

'That's all right,' I said, took the phone from him, went into the bathroom, and closed the door.

'What's up, Dan?' I said.

'I'm just glad to find you home.'

'I'm glad to be home, too. My watch says it's one in the morning.'

'An hour ago, somebody took a shot at Sally Dee. They damn near got him, too. The sheriff over there is going to have you high up on his list.'

'Give him a call in the morning, will you, and tell him what time you got ahold of me. I don't want anymore dealings with that guy.'

'Sure. Hey, the deputy who called me said Sal's real shook up. The shooter got up on the knoll above the house and parked a big one right through the kitchen window while Sal was drinking a glass of milk and eating cookies at the table. It blew glass and parts of a flowerpot all over him. Guess who wants police protection now?'

'What do they have so far?'

'Not much. They know about where the shot came from. That's about it.'

'No witnesses?'

'Not so far. You got some ideas?'

'Put it this way. How many people *wouldn't* like to see him cooled out?'

'No, no, let's be a little more candid here.'

'My speculations aren't of much value these days.'

'We're talking about Purcel.'

'He was here earlier tonight.'

'How much earlier?'

'Three hours.'

'That'd give him time to get up there, wouldn't it?'

'Yeah, it would.'

'You think he did it, don't you?'

'Maybe.'

'Well, ole Sal's on the other end of the stick now. I wonder how he's going to handle it.'

'He'll bring in some more of his hired shitheads. I'm real tired, Dan. Is there anything else?'

'Stay clear of Purcel.'

'You better tell that to the Dio family. I wouldn't want Clete hunting me.'

'I don't think these guys want advice from the DEA. It's not a federal situation, anyway. Sometimes you get to sit back and watch the show.'

I went back to bed and slept until the sun came up bright in my eyes and I heard the Saturday-morning sound of children rollerskating out on the sidewalk.

For one morning I didn't want to think about my troubles, so when the lady next door gave me a venison roast, Alafair and I packed my rucksack for a picnic, took Dixie Lee with us, and drove down into the Bitterroot Valley to Kootenai Creek Canyon. The sky was cloudless, a hard ceramic blue from the Sapphire Mountains all the way across the valley to the jagged, snow-tipped ridges of the Bitterroots. We walked two miles up a US Forest Service trail by the streambed, the water white and boiling over the rocks, the floor of the canyon thick with cottonwoods and ponderosa pine, the layered rock walls rising straight up into saddles of more pine and peaks that were as sharp as ragged tin. The air was cool and so heavy with the smell of mist from the rocks, wet fern, pine needles, layers of dead cottonwood leaves, logs that had rotted into humus, that it was almost like breathing opium.

We climbed down the incline of the streambed and started a fire in a circle of rocks. The stream flattened out here, and the current flowed smoothly over some large boulders and spread into a quiet pool by the bank, where we set out cans of pop in the gravel to cool. I had brought along an old refrigerator grill, and I set it on the rocks over the fire, cut the venison into strips, put them on the grill with potatoes wrapped in tinfoil, then sliced up a loaf of French bread. The grease from the venison dripped into the fire, hissed and smoked in the wind, and because the meat was so lean it curled and browned quickly in the heat and I had to push it to the edge of the grill.

After we ate, Dixie Lee and Alafair found a pile of rocks that was full of chipmunks, and while they threw bread crumbs down into the crevices I walked farther down the stream and sat by a pool whose surface was covered by a white, swirling eddy of froth and leaves and spangled sunlight. Through the cottonwoods on the other side of the stream I could see the steep, moss-streaked cliff walls rise up straight into the sky.

Then a strange thing happened, because she had never appeared to me during the waking day. But I saw her face in the water, saw the sunlight spinning in her hair.

Don't give up, sailor, she said.

What?

You've had it worse. You always got out of it before.

When?

How about Vietnam?

I had the US Army on my side.

Listen to the voices in the water and you'll be all right. I promise. Bye-bye, baby love.

Can you stay a little longer?

But the wind blew the cottonwoods and the light went out of the water, and the pool turned to shadow and an empty pebble-and-sand bottom.

'Don't be down here talking to yourself, son,' Dixie Lee said behind me. 'You'll give me cause to worry.'

I didn't have to wait long to learn how Sally Dio would try to handle his new situation. He called me that evening at the house.

'I want a meet,' he said.

'What for?'

'We talk some stuff out.'

'I don't have anything to say to you.'

'Look, man, this is going to get straightened out. One way or another. Right now.'

'What have I got that you're interested in?'

'I ain't interested in anything you got. What's the matter with you? You got impacted shit in your head or something?'

'I'm busy tonight. Plus, I don't think I want to see you again, Sal.'

I could almost hear his exasperation and anger in the silence.

'Look, I'm making an effort,' he said. 'I'm going the extra mile. I don't have to do that. I can handle it other ways. But I'm treating you like a reasonable man.'

I deliberately waited a good five seconds.

'Where?' I said.

'There's a bar and restaurant in Missoula, the Pink Zebra, right off Higgins by the river. It's in an alley, but it's a classy place. Nine o'clock.'

'I'll think it over.'

'Listen, man—'

I hung up on him.

Later, I put the .45 back under the seat of the truck, dropped Alafair off at the baby-sitter's, then drove to the Pink Zebra downtown. It was located in a brick-paved alley that had been refurbished into a pedestrian walkway of small cafés and shops and bars that offered philodendron and brass elegance more than alcohol.

I went inside and walked past the espresso machines and a row of booths that had copper champagne buckets affixed to the outside. The brick walls and the ceiling were hung with gleaming kettles and pots of ivy and fern, and in the back was a small private dining room, where I saw Sally Dio at a table with two men whom I hadn't seen before. But they came out of the same cookie cutter as some I had known in New Orleans. They were both around thirty, heavier than they should have been for their age, their tropical shirts worn outside their gray slacks, their necks hung with gold chains and religious medals, their pointed black shoes shined to the gloss of patent leather, their eyes as dead and level and devoid of emotion as someone staring into an empty closet.

I stopped at the door, and one of them stood up and approached me.

'If you'll step inside, Mr Robicheaux, I need to make sure you're not carrying nothing that nobody wants here,' he said.

'I don't think we'll do that,' I said.

'It's a courtesy we ask of people. It's not meant to insult nobody,' he said.

'Not tonight, podna.'

'Because everybody's supposed to feel comfortable,' he said. 'That way you have your drink, you talk, you're a guest, there ain't any tensions.'

'What's it going to be, Sal?' I said.

He shook his head negatively at the man next to me, and the man stepped back as though his body were attached to a string.

Sal wore a cream-colored suit, black suspenders, and an open-necked purple sport shirt with white polka dots. His ducktails were combed back on the nape of his neck, and he smoked a cigarette without taking his hand from his mouth. He looked at me steadily out of his blade-face, his stare so intense that the bottom rim of his right eye twitched.

'Get the waiter,' he said to the man who was standing.

'What are you having, Mr Robicheaux?' the man said.

'Nothing.'

He motioned the waiter to the door anyway.

'Bring a bottle of something nice for Mr Dio's guest,' he said.

'Bring Mr Dio another Manhattan, too. You want anything else, Sal?'

Sal shook his head again, then motioned the two men out of the room. I sat down across the table from him. A half dozen cigarette butts were in the ashtray, and ashes were smeared on the linen tablecloth. I could smell the heavy odor of nicotine on his breath. The looped scar under his right eye was tight against his skin.

'What the fuck's going on?' he said.

'What do you mean?'

'With Charlie Dodds.'

'I don't know anything about him.'

'Cut the shit. He tried to clip me last night.'

'What has that got to do with me?'

He breathed through his nose and wet his lips.

'I want to know what's going on,' he said.

'You got me, Sal. I don't know what you're talking about.'

'You and Dodds cut some kind of deal.'

'I think maybe you've burned out some cells in your brain.'

'Listen, you stop trying to fuck with my head. You and him got something going. You paid him or something, you turned him around. I don't know what kind of deal you're working, but believe me, man, it ain't worth it.'

'This is why you wanted to meet? Big waste of time.'

'What do you want?'

'Nothing.'

'I mean it, you quit jerking me around. We're talking business. We straighten all this out right now. We don't, my old man will. You understand that? You and

Charlie Dodds aren't going to fuck up millions of dollars in deals people got around here.'

'You're hitting on the wrong guy, Sal.'

The waiter brought in a Manhattan and a green bottle of wine in a silver ice bucket. He uncorked the wine and started to pour it into a glass for me to taste.

'Get out of here,' Sal said.

After the waiter was gone, Sal lit a fresh cigarette and drew the smoke deep into his lungs.

'Listen,' he said, 'there's nothing between us.'

'Then you shouldn't send bad guys around my house.'

'It was a personal beef. It's over. Nobody got hurt. It ends now. There's a lot of money going to be made here. You can have in on it.'

I looked at my watch.

'I have to be somewhere else,' I said.

'What the fuck is with you? I'm talking a score you couldn't dream about. I'm talking three, four large a week. Broads, a condo in Tahoe, any fucking thing you want. You going to turn that down because you got a personal beef to square?'

'I'll see you, Sal. Don't send anybody else around my house. It won't help your troubles with Charlie Dodds.'

I started to get up. He put his hand on my forearm.

'I know something you want, you need, man. And I'm the cat can give it to you,' he said.

'What's that?'

'That guy Mapes. Dixie said he can send you up the road. How'd you like it if Mapes wasn't around to worry you anymore?' He took a drink from his Manhattan. His eyes were level and intent over the glass.

'I don't even know where he is,' I said.

'You say the word, you end this bullshit between you and me, you deliver up that cocksucker Charlie Dodds, Mapes is dead meat. You'll get Polaroids, then you burn them. You don't have any connection with it. Nobody'll ever see the guy again. It'll be like he never existed.'

'I'll think about it.'

'You'll think about it?'

'That's what I said, Sal. Call me tomorrow afternoon.'

I walked out of the restaurant into the coolness of the night. The streets were full of college kids, and I could smell pine woodsmoke from people's chimneys and the heavy, cold smell of the river in the air.

When I got home Dixie showed me the business card a Missoula city detective had left in the mailbox. The detective had penciled a note on the back to the effect that he wanted me to call him, since he had missed me twice at the house. I suspected this had to do with Dan Nygurski's calling the local police about Charlie Dodds's visit to my house. I dropped the card on top of the icebox, put Alafair to bed, and watched the late show with Dixie Lee.

I slept through until morning without dreaming or once getting up in the night. When I woke and stepped out on the porch with a cup of coffee, the river was green and running fast in the shadows of the bridge, riffling over the boulders in the deepest part of the current, and the sunlight through the maples in the yard looked like spun glass.

chapter eleven

It was Sunday morning. I took Alafair to nine o'clock mass, then we fixed *cush-cush* and ate breakfast with Dixie Lee. He had shaved, pressed his slacks, and put on a white shirt.

'Where are you going?' I said.

'Some Holy Rollers asked me to play piano at their church. I hope the plaster don't fall out of the ceiling when I walk in.'

'That's good.'

He looked down at his coffee cup, then played with the big synthetic diamond ring on his finger.

'I got something bothering me,' he said.

'What is it?'

He looked at Alafair.

'Alafair, why don't you start on the dishes while Dixie helps me with something outside?' I said.

We went out to the truck, and I took the small whisk broom from behind the seat and began sweeping out the floor.

'I'm afraid I'm going to drink. I woke up scared about it this morning,' he said.

'Just do it a day at a time. Do it five minutes at a time if you have to.'

'Why the fuck am I scared, man?'

'Because it's fear that makes us drink.'

'I don't understand. It don't make sense. I felt real good yesterday. Today I'm shaking inside. Look at my hands. I feel like I just got off a jag.'

'Dixie, I'm not a psychologist, but you're going into a church today that's like the one you grew up in. Maybe you're dealing with some memories that bring back some bad moments. Who knows? Just let it go, partner. You're sober this morning. That's all that counts.'

'Maybe some people ain't supposed to make it.'

'You're not one of them.'

'You'd really throw me out if I went back on the juice?'

'Yep.'

'Somehow that just made a cold wind blow through my soul.'

'You work the steps, and I promise all that fear, all those weird mechanisms in your head, will go away.'

'What mechanisms?'

'Strange thoughts and images, things that don't make any sense, stuff that you won't talk about with anybody. If you work the program, all those things will gradually disappear.'

The morning was cool, and there was a breeze off the river, but there were drops of perspiration on his forehead and in his eyebrows.

'Dave, I just feel downright sick inside. I can't explain it.'

'It's going to pass,' I said. 'Just don't drink today.'

But his eyes were forlorn, and I well understood the peculiar chemical misery he was experiencing at the moment; I also knew that my words would mean more to him later than they did now.

'While we're out here, let me tell you about something else,' I said 'I'm going to receive a phone call this afternoon. I don't want you to answer it.'

'All right.'

'It'll be from Sally Dee. I don't want him to know you're living here.'

'You're putting me on?'

I continued sweeping the floor mat with the whisk broom.

'Dave, that ain't true?'

'It's complicated.'

'So is shit. This is some kind of nightmare. What are you doing, man?'

'Just don't answer the phone.'

'I wouldn't touch the sonofabitch at gunpoint.'

An hour later the phone rang. But it was Tess Regan, not Sally Dio.

'Jason, the eighth-grader I told you about, the one who talked with the man in the yellow car, he just came over on his bicycle,' she said. 'Last night he went to the Heidelhaus for dinner with some of his relatives. He saw the yellow car behind the restaurant. He's sure it's the same one. He remembered that the back window was cracked and there was a University of Wyoming sticker on it.'

'What kind of car?'

'A Mercury.'

'Did he get the license number?'

'No, I asked him. He said he didn't have a piece of paper or a pencil. Kids don't quite pull it all off sometimes, Dave.'

'He did just fine,' I said. 'It was at dinnertime, you say?'

'Yes. He said the Mercury was there when he went into the restaurant, and it was still there when he left. He tried to tell his uncle about it, but it was a birthday party and adults tend not to hear children sometimes.'

'Thanks very much, Tess. Tell Jason I appreciate what he's done.'

Alafair and I drove over to the Heidelhaus, a large Bavarian-style restaurant on the south side of town. The lunch crowd had started to come in, and the parking lot was half filled with cars, but none of them was a yellow Mercury. I drove behind the building and around the sides but had no luck there, either. I took Alafair for an ice-cream cone, returned in a half-hour, and still came up empty.

When we got home Dixie Lee was reading the newspaper on the front steps.

'It ain't rung. At least not while I was here,' he said.

'How was church?'

'It went okay. They asked me to play again Wednesday night. They ain't a bad bunch for people that probably left their toast in the oven too long.'

Alafair went inside just as the phone rang.

'Damn, there it is,' Dixie Lee said. 'Go easy, boy. Let's stay on the sunny side for a while.'

Alafair had picked up the receiver, but I eased it out of her hand before she could speak. I stepped into the bathroom and closed the door on the cord.

'You had time to think, Robicheaux?' Sally Dee said.

'I still believe you have things mixed up.'

'I'm not interested in opinions. You want to do some business, or you want to keep fucking around?'

'You've got it backwards, Sal. You hired Charlie Dodds to take me out.'

'That's past history. You come up to the lake uninvited, you provoked my father, you started that beef out on the road. I mark it off even. That's the way I see it.'

'What's the offer?'

'What d'you mean, what's the offer? I spelled it out to you yesterday.'

'No, you didn't. You said three or four grand a week. Are you going to pay that kind of money for house security?'

'We'll set you up with your own action. You manage a club in Vegas. All you got to do is count the receipts. You know what the skim is on a half-dozen lobby slots?'

'I'm about to go on trial.'

'You're breaking my knob off.'

'No, I think you're trying to do a number on me, Sal. You'll talk a lot of shit about the big score out in Vegas, let me think I got no worries about Harry Mapes, then a little time passes and I'm back in Louisiana in handcuffs.'

'You think I'm playing games while that crazy fucker is shooting at me?'

'That's your problem. My big worry is prison. That and your shitheads coming around my house.'

'I told you, there ain't anybody after you now. What is it I can't get through to you? This is a simple deal. You make money, I make money, Mapes gets whacked. You're home free. I guarantee it. People don't get out from under us. You were a cop. You know that.'

'I don't think I want to do business with you, Sal.'

'What?'

'I think you're about to take another fall.'

'What is this? What the fuck are you up to, man?'

'Don't call here again. I'm out of your life. Don't even have thoughts about me.'

'You shit-eating motherfucker, you're setting me up . . . It won't work, cocksucker . . . it's entrapment . . . you tell that to Nygurski . . . I've got lawyers that'll shove it up his ass.'

I placed the receiver quietly in the cradle and went outside and sat down on the steps beside Dixie Lee, who was reading the comics in the newspaper. He turned the page and popped the paper straight between his hands.

'Don't start telling me about it. My system's puny as it is. I just as soon drink razor blades,' he said.

I called Nygurski at his house a few minutes later. He wasn't home, so I put Alafair in the truck and we drove back to the Heidelhaus. This time the yellow Mercury with the cracked back window and the University of Wyoming sticker was parked in the shade of the building behind the dumpster.

I parked in the main lot, away from the Mercury, took Alafair inside and bought her a Coke by a stone fireplace that was now filled with a huge tropical aquarium.

I went up to the male cashier at the bar.

'I backed into a yellow Mercury by the side of the building,' I said. 'I think it might belong to somebody who works here. I think I just scratched it, but I'd like to make it right.'

'Next to the building? Right out there?' he asked,

gesturing toward the side of the restaurant where the dumpster was located.

'Yeah, that's it.'

'It sounds like Betty's. That's her down the bar.'

She was around thirty, blond, thick across the stomach, overly rouged, too old for the Bavarian waitress costume that she wore.

'Is that your Mercury by the side of the building, the one with the Wyoming sticker?' I said.

'Sure.' She stopped washing glasses and smiled at me. There were tiny lines in the corners of her eyes.

'I'm afraid I backed into it. I don't think I really hurt it, but you might take a look at it to be sure.'

'You couldn't hurt that thing. It's twelve years old and has eighty-five thousand miles on it.'

'Well, I just didn't want to drive off and not say anything.'

'Just a minute.' She took several glass steins out of the tin sink, set them top down on a folded dish towel, then said something to the cashier. 'I have to hurry. We're real busy right now.'

I told Alafair I would be right back, and the waitress and I went outside to her car. I ran my hand over some scratches by the Mercury's taillight.

'That's about where I hit it,' I said. 'I couldn't tell if that was old stuff or not. Maybe I just hit the bumper.'

'Forget it. It's not worth worrying about. I'm getting rid of it, anyway.'

'Aren't you a friend of Harry's?' I said.

'Which Harry?'

'Mapes.'

'Sure. How'd you know that?'

'I guess I saw y'all together.'

'How do you know Harry?'

'Through the oil business. I thought he was doing lease work east of the Divide.'

'He is. He's just visiting right now.'

'Well, I'm sorry to have taken you away from your work.'

'It's all right. It's nice of you to be concerned. Not many people would bother.'

She was a nice lady, and I didn't like to deceive her. I wondered how she had gotten involved with Harry Mapes. Maybe because it's a blue-collar, male-oriented town, I thought, where a woman's opportunities are limited. Regardless, I felt sorry for her.

I took Alafair back to the house, called the baby-sitter, then Tess Regan, but neither of them was at home.

'There's a dollar double feature at the Roxy. How about I take her to that?' Dixie Lee said.

Before I could hide it he saw the hesitation in my face.

'You think I'm gonna get drunk, I'm gonna run off and leave her alone?' he said.

'No.'

'Or maybe I ain't worked up to the step where you can trust me as good as that old woman down at the church.'

'I just didn't know what you had planned for today.'

'You want me to look after her or not?'

'I'd appreciate your doing that, Dixie.'

'Yeah, I can see that. But that's all right. I ain't sensitive. It all bounces off me.'

'I probably won't be home until late this evening,' I said. 'Can you fix her supper?'

'Show me a little trust, son. I'd be grateful for it.'

I drove back across town and parked on a side street behind the Heidelhaus so I could see the yellow Mercury. It was a long wait, but at eight o'clock she came out of the restaurant, walked to her car with her purse on her arm, started the engine, and drove south into the Bitterroot Valley.

I followed her twenty-five miles along the river. The light was still good in the valley, and I could see her car well from several hundred yards away, even though other cars were between us; but then she turned on to a dirt road and headed across pastureland toward the foot of the mountains. I pulled to the shoulder of the highway, got out with my field glasses, and watched the plume of white dust grow smaller in the distance, then disappear altogether.

I drove down the dirt road into the purple shadows that were spreading from the mountains' rim, crossed a wide creek that was lined with cottonwoods, passed a rotted and roofless log house with deer grazing nearby, then started to climb up on a plateau that fronted a deep canyon in the mountains. The dust from her Mercury still hung over the rock fence that bordered the property where she had turned in. The house was new, made of peeled and lacquered logs that had a yellow glaze to them, with a railed porch, a peaked shingle roof, and boxes of petunias and geraniums in the windows. But her car was the only one there.

I drove on past the house to the canyon, where there was Forest Service parking area, and watched the house for a half-hour through my field glasses. She fed a black Labrador on the back steps, she took some washing off the line, she carried a carton of mason jars out of the shed back into the house, but there was no sign of Harry Mapes.

I went back home and found Alafair asleep and Dixie Lee putting a new set of strings on his sunburst Martin.

I didn't have to call Dan Nygurski again. He called me at five minutes after eight the next morning.

'You beat me to it,' I said. 'I tried to catch you at home yesterday.'

'About Sally Dio.'

'That's right.'

'About your phone conversation with him.'

'That's right. So he did use the pay phone down the road from his house?'

'Yeah, he sure did. In fact, he was using it several times a day. Calls to Vegas, Tahoe, LA, Galveston. Notice I'm using the past tense here.'

I squinted my eyes closed and pressed my forefinger and thumb against my temples.

'I've sympathized with you, I've tried to help you,' he said. 'I took you into my confidence. I just had a conference call with a couple of federal agents who are very angry right now. My explanations to them didn't seem to make them feel any better.'

'Dan—'

'No, you got to talk yesterday. It's my turn now. You blew a federal wiretap. You know how long it took us to set that up?'

'Listen to what you've got on that tape. Solicitation to commit murder. He stepped in his own shit.'

'You remember when I told you that Sal is not Bugsy Siegel? I meant it. He did time for stolen credit cards. He's a midlevel guy. But he's connected with some big people in Nevada. They're smart, he's not. He makes mistakes they don't. When he falls, we want a whole busload to go up the road with him. Are you starting to get the big picture now?'

'All right, I screwed it up.'

'That doesn't bother me as much as the fact that I think you knew better.'

'He walked into it. I let it happen. I'm sorry it's causing you problems.'

'No, you wanted to make sure he thought he was tapped. That way he wasn't about to try to whack you again.'

'What would you do?'

'I would have stayed away from him to begin with.'

'That's a dishonest answer. What would you do if a guy like Dio was trying to whack you out, maybe you and your daughter both?'

I could hear the long-distance hum of the wires in the receiver.

'Did that Missoula detective get a hold of you?' he asked.

'He came out and left his card.'

'I hope he'll be of some help to you if you have more trouble there.'

'Look, Dan—'

'I have another call. We'll see you,' he said.

I went into the kitchen to fix a bowl of Grape-Nuts and spilled the box all over the floor. I cleaned up the cereal with a wet paper towel and threw it in the trash.

'I'm heading out for work,' Dixie Lee said.

'All right.'

'Who was that?'

'Nobody.'

'Yeah . . . well, what do you want to do after Wednesday?'

'What?'

'About Alafair. That job ain't but four hours a day. I can put them in any time I want.'

'What are you talking about?'

'School's out for the summer, ain't it? I can help look after her. What's the best time for me to be home?'

'I don't know, Dixie. I can't think about it right now.'

I felt him looking quietly at the side of my face, then he turned and walked outside to his automobile. I looked at my watch. It was eight-thirty. I locked the house, put the .45 under the truck seat, and drove south once again into the Bitterroot Valley.

This time the black Jeepster was parked right next to the Mercury, and when I pulled into the yard and got out of the truck woodsmoke was blowing off the stone chimney. Through the front window I could see the woman named Betty drinking coffee with a man at a table in the living room.

The porch rails and the lacquered yellow logs of the house were wet with dew. I stepped up on the porch, knocked on the door, and when the woman opened it I saw Harry Mapes stare at me with his mouth parted over his coffee cup. Then he got up and walked out of my line of sight into a side room.

'Hi,' she said, and smiled with recognition. 'You're—'

'I didn't tell you my name yesterday. It's Dave Robicheaux. I'd like to talk to Harry.'

'Sure. He's here. But how'd you know where I lived?'

'I'm sorry for disturbing you, but I'd appreciate it if you'd ask him to step out here.'

'I don't understand this,' she said, then turned and saw Mapes standing behind her. 'Harry, this is the guy I told you about.'

'I figured it was you,' he said to me.

He wore jeans and a flannel shirt, and a black automatic hung from his left hand. The chain scars on his face were almost totally gone now.

'Harry, what are you doing?' she said.

'This is the guy who attacked me in Louisiana,' he said.

'Oh!' she said. Then she said it again, 'Oh!'

'Come outside, Mapes,' I said.

'You don't know when to leave it alone, do you?' he said. 'My lawyer told me you might try something like this. He also told me what to do about it.'

'What's that?'

'You try to intimidate a witness, you just create more trouble for yourself. Figure it out.'

'So you're holding all the cards. Look, I don't have a weapon. Why don't you step outside? Nobody's going to eat you.'

His fingers were long on the sides of the automatic. I had seen only one or two like it since I had left Vietnam. It was a 7.62-millimeter Russian Tokarev, a side arm often carried by NVA officers.

I saw Mapes wet the triangular scar on his lip, his mouth tight, his eyes narrowed as though he were biting down softly on a piece of string. He wasn't a bad-looking man. He still had the build of a basketball player or a man who could do an easy five-mile morning run. You wouldn't pay particular attention to him in a supermarket line. Except for his eyes. He was the kind who was always taking your inventory, provided you represented or possessed something he was interested in; and sometimes when you studied the eyes in his kind you saw a hidden thought there that made you look away hurriedly.

'You're right,' he said, and set the pistol on the arm of a couch by the door. 'Because you're all smoke. A guy who's always firing in the well. A big nuisance who couldn't mind his own business.'

He opened the screen door and stepped out on the porch.

'You think it's going to come out different somehow at your trial?' he said. 'You think following me around Montana is going to make all that evidence go away?'

'You've got it wrong, Harry. I gave up on trying to nail you. You're too slick a guy. You've fooled people all your life. You burned two people to death when you were seventeen, you murdered the Indians, the waitress in Louisiana, your partner, and I think you raped and murdered Darlene. You got away with all of it.'

I saw the blood drain out of the face of the woman behind the screen. Mapes's chest rose and fell with his breathing.

'Listen, you asshole—' he said.

'But that's not why I'm here. You were at the school ground, in that Mercury there, looking at my daughter through field glasses, asking questions about her. Now, my message here is simple. If you come around her again, I'm going to kill you. Believe it. I've got nothing to lose at this point. I'm going to walk up to you, wherever you are, and blow your fucking head off.'

I walked off the porch into the yard.

'Oh, no, you don't,' he said. 'You, too, Betty. You stay out here and listen to this. My lawyer did some checking on this guy. He's a drunk, he's a mental case, he's got an obsession because he got his wife killed by some drug dealers. Then somebody threatened his daughter, and he accused me and my partner. The fact that he's an ex-cop with dozens of people who'd like to even a score with him doesn't seem to enter his head. Let me tell you something, Robicheaux. Betty's son goes to a Catholic school in Missoula. She and her ex-husband have shared custody. Sometimes I pick him up or drop him off for her. If that's the same school your daughter goes to, it's coincidence, and that's all it is.'

'You heard what I said. No warning light next time,' I said.

I got inside my truck and closed the door.

'No, Harry, bring him back,' the woman said. 'Who's Darlene? What's he talking about a rape? Harry?'

'He's leaving. Close the door,' he said to her.

'Harry, I'll call the sheriff. He can't get away with saying that.'

'He's leaving. He's not coming back.'

Then he walked toward the truck window just as I started the engine.

'You're going to prison,' he said. 'Nothing's going to change that. You can mess me up with my girl, you can say stuff about blowing me away if it makes you feel good, but in a few weeks you're going to be hoeing sweet potatoes in Angola.'

I put the transmission in reverse and began backing around in a half-circle. The wind blew his hair, and his skin looked grained and healthy in the sunlight. His eyes never left my face. My knuckles were ridged on top of the gearshift knob, and my thighs were shaking as I depressed the floor pedals.

It had all been for nothing.

But there was still time, the moment was still there. To pull the .45 from under the seat, to aim it suddenly at his face, knock him to his knees, screw the barrel hard into his neck and cock the hammer, let him experience the terror of his victims who clawed the inside of an automobile trunk while the metal heated and the flames spread to the gasoline tank. I could feel the .45 leap into my hand as though it had a life of its own.

I shut off the engine and stepped out of the truck. My face felt cool in the bright air. The yellow log house and the ponderosa and blue spruce on the hillsides seemed dazzling in the sun. His eyes dropped to my hands. I held my palms up.

'Did you ever go to the stake in Saigon?' I said.

'What?'

'Some ARVN and white mice would march them out to the stake, tie them to it, and put a round behind the ear. At least that was what I was told. I never saw it.'

'I think you had some head damage over there. You've got thirty seconds to be past Betty's property line, then we call the sheriff.'

'You'd better concentrate on my words, Harry. The executioner was probably a special kind of guy. He could kill people and go home and have lunch. He's somebody you can understand. You'd recognize each other in a group. But you know I'm not like you, and that's why you're not afraid of me. I can come out here and talk about cooling you out, but you know I won't do it. But how about Sally Dio?'

'Dio? You must truly be out of your mind. Get out of here, man.'

'He was talking about whacking you out. That's not a shuck. He's got some new guys up at the lake. They're the real article, genuine syndicate hit men. You can call Dan Nygurski at the DEA in Great Falls and ask him. Or, better yet, ask him to deny it. If that's not enough for you, I can give you Sal's unlisted number and you can talk with him about it. If I'm just jerking you around, you can clear the whole matter up in a few minutes.'

'What's Dio care about me? I only met the guy twice.'

'Ask him. Maybe you shouldn't have gotten mixed up in his and Dixie Lee's lease deals. He's probably a borderline psychotic. I doubt if he thinks too straight.'

His eyes looked like they were focused on a thought ten inches in front of his face. Then they came back on me.

'Where'd you hear this?' he asked.

'Stay away from my daughter. Don't come near that school. I don't care if your lady friend's son goes there or not,' I said, and I got back into the truck and drove out on the dirt road.

In the rearview mirror I saw him standing alone in the yard, staring after me, the woman holding the screen door wide behind him.

I went back home, walked down the street to a noon AA meeting, bought groceries for our supper that evening, then sat on the back steps in the shade and tried to put myself inside the mind of Harry Mapes. He was a smart man. He had killed a number of people over the years – his first when he was seventeen and God only knew how many in Vietnam – and he had never spent a day in jail for it. He wasn't compulsive; he was calculating, and he used fear and violence to achieve an immediate, practical end. Like any sociopath's, his emotions were simple ones and concerned entirely with desires, survival, and the destruction of his enemies. He remained passive, functional, and innocuous in appearance until he felt threatened. Then he rose to the occasion.

When he saw me east of the Divide, on the dirt road between the Indian beer joint and the home of Clayton Desmarteau's mother, I scared him in some way. He went to the school ground to keep my mind on other things or, perhaps, to provoke me into attacking him again. Somehow he had also concluded that Darlene had sent me east of the Divide, had put me on that dirt road south of the Blackfeet Reservation, and he feared that somewhere in that hardpan country I would discover what had happened to Clayton Desmarteau and his cousin.

In the last two days I had managed to turn it around on both Dio and Mapes, to use some smoke and their own frame of reference against them, so that in all probability they wouldn't come around me and Alafair again. But my legal situation remained the same as it had been when I left Louisiana. My victory had become the restoration of the status quo. I lay down on the living room couch in a funk, with my arm across my eyes, and fell asleep.

The image in my dream was brief, like needles of light in the afternoon haze. *Darlene kneeling by water, white-tailed deer thudding across the wet ground between the cottonwoods.*

I felt feathers brushing across my forearm and cheek. I opened one eye and looked at Alafair's grinning face. The other day she had found an old feather duster in the house.

'How you doing, you cute little guy?' I said.

'How you doing, you cute little Dave?' she said. She wore jeans and her Baby Orca T-shirt.

I sat up on the couch.

'How'd you get home?' I said.

'Dixie Lee walked down and got me. You was asleep. Dave?'

'What?' I rubbed my face and tried to make the afternoon come into focus.

'We only got two more days of school. We going home then?'

'Maybe so, little guy.'

'We better call Batist and tell him.'

'Alafair, when we go back home, it might be for just a few days. I might have to sell a few things and raise some money so we can take another trip.'

'Trip?'

'To a different place for a while. Down by the ocean, maybe.'

'We're not going to live at the house no more?'

'I don't know, Alf.'

I looked at the confusion in her face.

'Let's take things as they come,' I said. 'I just don't want you to be disappointed later if we move somewhere else for a while.'

I heard the phone ring in the hallway. Alafair picked

up her lunch box from the coffee table and started toward the kitchen.

'Miss Regan asked if we eat redfish,' she said. 'Why she ask that? What's she care about redfish? I got pushed down on the school ground. I threw a dirt clod at the boy that did it.'

I let her go and didn't say anything more.

'Dave, you better take this,' Dixie Lee said in the doorway, the telephone receiver in his hand.

'What is it?'

'St Pat's Hospital. They got Clete in there.'

We drove to the hospital on Broadway, left Alafair in the second-floor waiting room with a comic book, and walked down the corridor to Clete's room. A plain-clothes cop, with his badge on his belt, was just coming out the door. He had a blond mustache and wore a white shirt and knit tie. He was putting a small note-book in his shirt pocket.

'What happened?' I said.

'Who are you?' he said.

'A friend of Cletus Purcel.'

'What's your name?'

'Dave Robicheaux.'

He nodded slowly, and I saw the name meant nothing to him.

'Your friend got worked over,' he said. 'He says he didn't know the two guys who did it. But the bartender who phoned us said the two guys called him by name. Tell your friend it's dumb to protect people who'll slam a man's hand in a car door.'

He brushed past me and walked to the elevator. Dixie Lee and I went inside the room, which Clete shared with an elderly man who had an IV connected to his wasted arm. Clete's bed was on the far side of the partition, one end elevated so he could look up at the television set that was turned on without sound. One eye was swollen into a purple egg, and his head was shaved in three places where the scalp had been stitched. His right hand was in plaster; the ends of his fingers were discolored as though they were gangrenous.

'I heard you with the detective,' he said.

'He doesn't seem to believe your story,' I said.

'He's probably got marital trouble. It makes a cynic out of you. What's happening, Dixie?'

'Oh man, who did this to you?' Dixie Lee said.

'A couple of Sal's meatballs.'

'Who?' Dixie Lee said.

'Carl and Foo-Foo. I got Foo-Foo one shot in the rocks, though. He's not going to be unlimbering his equipment for a while.'

'What happened?' I said.

'I stopped at this bar off Ninety. They must have seen the jeep in the parking lot. They caught me with a baton when I came out the side door. When I thought they were through, they dragged me to a car and slammed my hand in the door. If the bartender hadn't come out, they'd have done my other hand.'

'Tell the cops,' Dixie Lee said. 'Why do you want to protect Carl and Foo-Foo?'

'What goes round, comes round,' Clete said. 'I ain't sweating it, mon.'

'You used to say "Bust 'em or smoke 'em." Let the cops bust them,' I said.

'Maybe they've got a surprise coming out of the jack-in-the-box,' Clete said. He looked at my face. 'All your radio tubes are lit up, Streak. What are you thinking about?'

'Why'd they do it?'

'Sal's running scared. He's got nobody but his old man and his hired dagos. Even the cornholers cut out on him.'

'That's not it,' I said.

'How do I know what goes on in his head?'

'Come on, Clete,' I said.

'When I left, he owed me fifteen hundred in back salary. Plus I'd already paid my rent to him in advance. So I went in his house and took a couple of gold ashtrays.'

'You crazy bastard,' Dixie Lee said.

'He didn't kill Darlene, then, did he?'

'I don't know,' Clete said.

'Yes, you do. Somebody shot at him. He thinks it was Charlie Dodds. If he had killed Darlene, you'd be the first person he would fear. Those two guys wouldn't have just broken your hand, either. They would have passed you on the road and taken you out with a shotgun.'

'Maybe,' he said.

'No maybe about it, Cletus,' I said. 'It was Mapes. He thought she sent me over by the reservation where he killed the two Indians. He found her alone, and he raped and killed her. You've got a beef with the wrong guy, and you know it.'

'I got a beef with Sal for all kinds of reasons,' he said. 'But that's all right. Our man's going to have a sandy fuck.'

'What?' I said.

'A fifties joke. Sand in the Vaseline,' he said. 'Forget

it. Hey, do me a favor. My jeep's still out at that bar. It's a log place, right where Broadway runs into Ninety. Take it to your house, will you? The keys are on the table. I don't want some local punks to clean it out.'

'All right.'

'Where's Mapes?' he said.

'You'll have to find him on your own, partner.'

'You know where he is, then.'

'Do you want us to bring you anything?'

'Come on, you think I'm going to get out of bed and scramble Mapes's eggs? You give me too much credit.'

'You'd find a way, Clete.'

He wet his mouth and smiled.

'Dixie, can you give me and Streak a minute?' he said.

'Sure.'

'It's just something from our First District days,' Clete said.

'I don't mind,' Dixie Lee said.

'Then come on back later,' Clete said.

'Don't be talking down to me. It hurts my feelings,' Dixie Lee said. 'I'll come see you tomorrow.'

He walked out of the room.

'He's not full of booze,' Clete said.

'What do you need, Cletus?'

'I screwed up a lot of things back there in New Orleans. Blew my marriage, took juice, knocked a girl up, got into the shylocks. Then I cooled out that shitbag in the hog lot. But I paid for it. In spades. I'd like to change it but I can't. I guess that's what remorse is about. But the big one that's been eating my lunch all this time is that I could have brought that guy in and gotten you off the hook. For ten grand I helped them turn you into toilet paper.'

'The lowlifes all took a fall one way or another.'

'Yeah, your fourteen years with the department went down the hole, too.'

'It was my choice, Clete.'

'You want to act like a stand-up guy about it, that's copacetic. But I don't buy it. I fucked you over. It's the worst thing I did in my life. I'm telling you I'm sorry. I'm not asking you to say anything. I'm telling you how I feel. I'm not bringing it up again. You were my best friend. I stuck it to you.'

'It's all right. Maybe you were doing the best you could at the time.'

His one open eye stared up at me. It looked like a piece of green glass in his battered face.

'It's time to write it off, partner,' I said.

'That's straight?'

'Who cares about last year's box score?'

He swallowed. His eye was watery along the bottom rim.

'Fuck, man,' he said.

'I have to go. Alafair is in the waiting room.'

'I've got to tell you something,' he said.

'What?'

'I've got to whisper it. Come here.'

'What is it, Clete?'

'No, closer.'

I leaned over him, then his good hand came up, clamped around the back of my neck like a vise, and pulled my face down on his. He kissed me hard on the mouth, and I could smell the cigarettes on his breath, the salve and Mercurochrome painted on his stitches and shaved scalp.

*

We drove out west of town to the bar where Clete had been beaten up by Sally Dee's goons and found his Toyota jeep in the parking lot. Dixie Lee drove it back to the house, parked it in back, and locked it. A few minutes later Tess Regan called.

'Can you come over?' she said.

'When?'

'Tonight. For redfish. Didn't Alafair say anything?'

'It came out a little confused.'

'I called you earlier, but nobody was home. It's nothing special, really. We could make it another night.'

'Tonight's fine,' I said.

And it was. The evening was cool and smelled of flowers and sprinkled yards, and she blackened the redfish on a grill in the backyard and served it in her small dining room, which glowed with the sun's reflection through the tall turn-of-the-century windows. She wore tight blue jeans and low heels, a short-sleeved blouse with tiny pink roses on it, and gold hoop earrings, but her apartment gave her away. The wood floors and mahogany trim on the doors gleamed; the kitchen was spotless; the hung pictures and those on the marble mantel were all of relatives. The wallpaper was new, but the design and color did nothing to remove the apartment from an earlier era. A Catholic religious calendar, with an ad for a mortuary on it, was affixed to the icebox door with small magnets. She had crossed two palm strangs in an X behind the crucifix on the dining room wall.

After supper we did the dishes together while Alafair watched television. When her leg bumped against me, she smiled awkwardly as though we had been jostled against one another on a bus, then her eyes looked at my face with both expectation and perhaps a moment's fear. I suspected she was one of those whose heart could be easily hurt, one to whom a casual expression of affection would probably be interpreted as a large personal commitment. The moon was up now. The window was open and I could smell the wet mint against the brick wall and the thick, cool odor of lawn grass that had been flooded by a soak hose. It was the kind of soft moment that you could slip into as easily as you could believe you were indeed able to regain the innocence of your youth.

So I squeezed her hand and said good night, and I saw the flick of disappointment in her eyes before she smiled again and walked with me back into the living room. But she was one with whom you dealt in the morning's light, unless you were willing to trust the nocturnal whirrings of your own heart.

She came to me in a dream that night, a dream as clear in its detail as though you had suddenly focused all the broken purple and tan glass in a kaleidoscope into one perfect image. Darlene's hair was braided on her shoulders, and she wore the doeskin dress she had been buried in, the purple glass bird on her breast. I saw her look first at me from the overhang of the cliff, then squat on her moccasins by a spring that leaked out of rocks into a tea-colored stream. She put her hands into the trailing moss, into the silt and wet humus and mud, and began to smear it on her face. She looked at me again, quietly, her mouth cold and red, her cheeks streaked with mud; then she was gone, and I saw a huge golden deer crash through the underbrush and cottonwoods.

I sat straight up in bed, my breath coming hard, my hands shaking. I looked at my watch. It was two in the morning. I shook Dixie Lee awake on the couch.

'I've got to go east of the Divide. You have to take care of Alafair until I get back,' I said.

'What?'

'You heard me. Can you do that? Fix breakfast for her, walk her to school, pick her up in the afternoon?'

'What's going on?' His face was puffy and full of sleep.

'I have to depend on you, Dixie. I'll be back by tomorrow evening. But you've got to take good care of her. Call in sick at work if you have to.'

'All right,' he said irritably. 'But what are you doing?'

'I think I'm going to nail Mapes. I think I'm going to do it.'

He sat up on the edge of the couch in his underwear, his arms draped between his thighs. He widened his eyes and rubbed his face.

'I hate to tell you, son, you still act like a drunk man,' he said.

Fifteen minutes later I stopped at an all-night diner on the edge of town, bought a thermos of black coffee, then I was roaring up the highway along the Blackfoot River, the tree-covered crests of the mountains silhouetted blackly against the starlight, the river and the cottonwoods and willows along the banks aglow with the rising moon.

It was dawn when I drove down the dirt road where Clayton Desmarteau had gone in the ditch. The hardpan fields were wet with dew, and the long rays of the sun struck against the thick green timber high up in the saddles of the mountains that formed the Divide. I took an army entrenching tool out of the back of my truck, jumped across the stream on the north side of the road, and walked up the incline into the lodgepole pine. It was cool and the wind was blowing, but I was sweating inside my shirt and my hand was tight on the wood shaft of the E-tool. Low pools of mist hung around the trees, and I saw a doe and her fawn eating the bear grass. Then I intersected the thin trace of a road that had been used as an access to a garbage dump, and walked on farther across the pine needles until I hit the stream that flowed under a heavy canopy of trees at the foot of a rock-faced hill, and followed it across the soft moldy remains of a log cabin, a rusted-out wood stove half buried in the wet soil, and carpets of mushrooms whose stems cracked under my shoes. Finally I saw the spring that flowed out of the hillside, glistened on the dark rocks and moss, and spread into a fan of blackened leaves and rivulets of silt at the end of the stream.

Annie and my father had tried to tell me in the dream, but I hadn't understood. It was winter when Vidrine and Mapes had murdered Clayton Desmarteau and his cousin. It was winter, and the ground must have been frozen so hard that a posthole digger could only chip it. My heart was beating as I unscrewed the metal ring under the blade of the E-tool, folded the blade into a hoe, and tightened the ring. I scraped away the layers of leaves and raked back long divots of silt and fine gravel, creating half a wagon wheel that spread out from the stream's edge back to the spring's source. My pants were wet up to my knees, my shoes sloshing with water. Then I reset the blade and began digging out a level pit in five-inch scoops and setting the mud carefully in a pile on the bank. I worked a half-hour, until my shirt was sweated through and my arms and face were streaked with mud. I had begun to think that maybe Dixie Lee was right; I was simply behaving as though I were on a dry drunk.

Then my shovel hit the toe of a work boot, and I worked the sand and mud off the edges, the congealed laces, back along the gray shank of shinbone that protruded from the rotted sock. I uncovered the other leg, then the folded knees and the collapsed, flattened thigh that was much too small now for the cloth that lay in strips around it. The second man was buried right next to the first, curled in an embryonic position, the small, sightless, tight gray ball of his face twisted up through the soil.

I stepped back from the pit into the middle of the stream, cleaned the shovel blade in the gravel, then knelt on the opposite bank and washed my arms and face in the water. But I was trembling all over and I couldn't stop sweating. I sat on the bank, with my knees pulled up in front of me, and tried to stop hyperventilating, to think in an orderly fashion about the rest of the morning. I hadn't hit the perfecta in the ninth race, but it was close, if I just didn't do anything wrong. Then, as I wiped the sweat out of my eyes with my thumb and looked across the stream at the glistening mound of mud and silt that I had dug from the bodies, at the nests of white worms that I had lifted into the light, I saw a corroded green cartridge that had been ejected from an automatic. It had the same bottleneck shape as the 7.62-millimeter round fired by a Russian Tokarev.

*

I had to drive three miles down the dirt road before I found a pay phone outside of a closed filling station. It had started to rain over the mountains but the sky in the east was still pink and blue, and the air smelled of pine and sage. When I got Dan Nygurski on the phone at his office, I told him all of it, or I thought all of it, but my words came out in a rush, and my heart was still beating fast, and I felt as if I were standing at the finish line at the track, my fingers pinched tight on that perfecta ticket, trying in the last thunderous seconds of the race to will the right combination under the wire.

'Let your motor idle a little bit,' he said. 'How'd you find them?'

'They were run off the road between the beer joint and Clayton Desmarteau's house. I think Mapes and Vidrine took them out of the truck at gunpoint and drove them into the woods. An old road leads off the main one and runs back to a garbage dump. They got out there and walked back to the stream. But the ground was probably covered with snow and frozen solid. I bet you could bust a pick on it in wintertime. Then they walked across a warm-water spring, where the ground stayed soft and wet year-round, and that's where they shot Desmarteau and his cousin.'

'Tell me about the shell again.'

'It came up in a shovelful of mud. I didn't even see it until I had stopped digging. It's bottlenecked, like a 7.62 round. Mapes has got a Tokarev. He had it in his hand at his girl's house down in the Bitterroot. I think he had it in Lafayette, too. He was trying to get to his open suitcase when I hit him with the chain. Look, it's enough for a search warrant. But it's got to be done right. You can bring the FBI in on it, let them coordinate it.'

'Oh?'

'They can use kidnapping and interstate flight, or depriving a minority of his civil rights by taking his life. The locals might blow it. If Mapes gets a sniff of what's going on before they serve the warrant, he'll lose the Tokarev.'

'I had to take a lot of heat because of that phone tap.'

'I'm sorry.'

'It hasn't quieted down yet.'

'I was up against the wall. I don't know what else to tell you. You want me to hang up and call the sheriff's office?'

He waited a moment.

'No, don't do that,' he said finally. 'I guess we've got a vested interest. This whole Indian thing started with Pugh, and Pugh's had a longtime involvement with Sally Dee. Give me the directions again.'

I told him in detail once more. The shower had moved eastward across the fields, and rain was now clicking on the roof of the phone booth. An Indian boy on an old bicycle with flat tires rattled past me on the road, his face bent down against the rain.

'I'll call the FBI and the Teton sheriff's office,' Nygurski said. 'Then I'll be out myself. I want a promise from you, though.'

'What is it?'

'Other people take it from here on in. You're out of it. Absolutely.'

'All right.'

'I want your word. You don't go near Mapes.'

'You have it, but you've got to get him with the Tokarev.'

'I think you've made your point. But are you sure that's what you saw in his hand? I wonder why he didn't get rid of it.'

'They were prize souvenirs in Vietnam. Besides, he always sailed out of everything he ever did.'

'Where are you going to be?'

'On the road where their truck went into the ditch. We can walk in from there, or find the access road that leads back to the garbage dump.'

'Did you hear anything more from Dio?'

'Nope. Except two of his goons broke Purcel's hand. He says he took a couple of gold ashtrays out of Dio's house.'

'Bad guy to steal from. Purcel must not have pressed charges, because we didn't hear anything about it.'

'He said something strange when I went to see him in the hospital yesterday. He said, "Our man's going to have a sandy fuck." Or maybe I misunderstood him. I think Dio has a girlfriend named Sandy. Anyway, it didn't make any sense to me.'

'Where is he?'

'St Pat's in Missoula.'

'Maybe it's time we have a talk with him. I'll see you a little later this morning. In the meantime, congratulations. You're a good cop, Robicheaux. Get your badge back.'

'You've been a good friend, too, Dan.'

'And, lastly, keep your name out of my paperwork for a while.'

I drove back up the road in the rain and parked by the stream where I had entered the woods at dawn.

Then the clouds moved eastward and the rain drifted away over the land behind me, and in the distance the sheer red cliffs of the mountains rose into the tumbling plateaus of ponderosa. When I closed my eyes and laid my head back against the seat I heard robins singing in a lone cottonwood by the stream.

The next morning I drank almost two pots of coffee and waited for the phone to ring. I had spent nearly all of the previous day at the murder site, the Teton sheriff's department, and the coroner's office. I watched three deputies finish the exhumation and put the bodies gingerly in black bags, I gave a statement to the FBI and one to the sheriff's office, I talked to the pathologist after we had opened up the brainpans of both Indians with an electric saw and had picked out the 7.62 slugs that had been fired at close range into the back of their skulls. I had them contact the St Martin Parish sheriff's office about Dixie Lee's deposition in which he claimed to have overheard Vidrine and Mapes talking about the murder of the Indians. I told them where to find Mapes in the Bitterroot Valley, where his girlfriend worked in Missoula, the kind of cars he drove; I talked incessantly, until people started to walk away from me and Nygurski winked at me and said he would buy me a hamburger so I could be on my way back to Missoula.

So I drank coffee on the back steps and waited for someone to call. Dixie Lee went to work and came back in the early afternoon, and still no one had phoned.

'Ease up, boy. Let them people handle it,' he said.

We were in the kitchen, and I was shining my shoes over some newspapers that I had spread on the floor.

'That's what I'm doing,' I said.

'You put me in mind of a man who spent his last cent on Ex-Lax and forgot the pay toilet cost a dime.'

'Give me a break on the scatology.'

'The what?'

'It's not a time for humor, Dixie.'

'Go to a meet. Get your mind off it. They got his butt dead-bang. You're out of it, boy.'

'You have them dead-bang when you weld the door on them.'

Finally I called Nygurski's office. He wasn't in, he had left no message for me, and when I called the Teton sheriff's office a deputy there refused to talk with me. I had become a spectator.

I sat down at the kitchen table and started buffing my loafers again.

'While you were gone yesterday I put all Clete's stuff in the basement,' Dixie Lee said. 'Was that all right?'

'Sure.'

'He'll probably get out in a couple more days. He's got one rib that's broke bad, though. The doc says he's got ulcers, too.'

'Maybe he'll go back to New Orleans and get started over again.'

'There was something funny in his jeep.'

'What's that?' But I really wasn't listening.

'A pillowcase. With sand in it.'

'Huh.'

'Why would he put sand in a pillowcase?'

'I don't know.'

'He must have had a reason. Clete never does anything without a reason.'

'Like I say, I don't know.'

'But it's funny to do something like that. What d'you think?'

'I don't care, for God's sakes. Dixie, cut me some slack, will you?'

'Sorry.'

'It's all right.'

'I just thought I'd get your mind off of things.'

'Okay.'

'I want to see you loosen up, smile a little bit, start thinking about Louisiana, let them people handle it.'

'I'll do all those things. I promise,' I said, and I went into the bathroom, washed my face, then waited out on the front porch until it was time for Alafair to get out of school.

But he was right. I was wired, and I was thinking and acting foolishly. In finding the bodies of the Indians I had been far more successful than I had ever thought I would be. Even if the FBI or the locals didn't find the Tokarev, Mapes would still remain the prime suspect in the murder because of motive and Dixie Lee's testimony, and he could be discredited as a prosecution witness against me in Louisiana. No matter how it came out, it was time to pack our bags for New Iberia.

And that's what I started doing. Just as the phone rang.

'Mr Robicheaux?' a woman said.

'Yes.'

'This is the secretary at the DEA in Great Falls. Special Agent Nygurski called a message in from his car and asked me to relay it to you.'

'Yes?'

'He said, "They found the weapon. Mapes is in

custody. Call in a couple of days if you want ballistic results. But he's not going to fly on this one. Enjoy your trip back to Louisiana." Did you get that, sir?'

'Yes.'

'Did you want to leave a message?'

'Tell him *Playgirl* magazine wants him on a centerfold.'

She laughed out loud.

'I beg your pardon?' she said.

'Tell him I said thank you.'

Five minutes later Alafair came through the front door with her lunch box.

'How'd you like to head home day after tomorrow?' I said.

Her grin was enormous.

We cooked out in the backyard that evening and had Tess Regan over, then Alafair and I climbed the switchback trail to the concrete *M* on the mountain behind the university. The whole valley was covered with a soft red glow. The wind was cold at that altitude, even though we were sweating inside our clothes, and rain and dust were blowing up through the Bitterroot Valley. Then the wind began to blow harder through the Hellgate, flattening the lupine and whipping grains of dirt against our skin. Overhead a US Forest Service fire-retardant bomber came in low over the mountains and turned toward the smoke jumpers' school west of town, its four propellers spinning with silver light in the sun's afterglow.

The thought that had kept bothering me all afternoon, that I had tried to push into a closed compartment in the back of my mind, came back like a grinning jester who was determined to extend the ball game into extra innings.

When we got home I unlocked Clete's jeep and picked up the soiled pillowcase that was on the floorboard. I turned it inside out and felt the residue of dry sand along the seams. Then I called Sally Dio's number at the lake. It was disconnected. I had reserved the next day for packing, shutting off the utilities, greasing the truck, making sandwiches for our trip home, and having a talk with Tess Regan about geographic alternatives. But Sally Dee was to have one more turn in my life.

'What time are you going in to work?' I said to Dixie Lee at breakfast the next morning.

'I ain't. The boss man said he don't need me today. That's something I want to talk with you about, Dave. With you cutting out, I don't know what kind of future I got here. Part-time forklifting ain't what you'd call a big career move.'

'Will you watch Alafair while I go up to the lake?'

'Why you going up there?'

'I need to talk with Dio. If he's not there, I'll leave him a note. Then I'll be back.'

'You're going to do what?' He set his coffee cup down on the table and stared at me.

I drove to Polson, then headed up the east side of the lake through the cherry orchards. I could have called Dan Nygurski or the sheriff's office, but that would have forced me to turn in Cletus, and I thought that a man with ulcers, a broken rib, a crushed hand, and stitches in his head had paid enough dues.

It was cold and bright on the lake. The wind was

puckering the electric-blue surface, and the waves were hitting hard against the rocks along the shore. I parked in front of the Dios' redwood house on the cliff, took off my windbreaker and left it in the truck so they could see I wasn't carrying a weapon, and used the brass knocker on the door. There was no answer. I walked around the side of the house, past the glassed-in porch that was filled with tropical plants, and saw the elder Dio in his wheelchair on the veranda, his body and head wrapped in a hooded, striped robe. In his hand was a splayed cigar, and inside the hood I could see the goiter in his throat, his purple lips, the liquid and venomous expression in his eyes. He said something to me, but it was lost in the wind, because I was looking down the tiers of redwood steps that led to the rocks below and the short dock where Sally Dee and his two hoods had just carried armloads of suitcases and cardboard boxes. Even Sal's set of drums was stacked on the dock.

The three of them watched me silently as I walked down the steps toward them. Then Sal knelt by a big cardboard box and began reinforcing a corner of it with adhesive tape as though I were not there. He wore a yellow jumpsuit, with the collar flipped up on his neck, and the wind had blown his long copper-colored hair in his face.

'What d'you want us to do, Sal?' one of his men said.

Sally Dee stood erect, picked up a glass of iced coffee from the dock railing, drank out of it, and looked at me with an almost amused expression.

'Nothing,' he said. 'He's just one of those guys who get on the bottom of your shoe like chewing gum.'

'I'll just take a minute of your time, Sal,' I said. 'I think somebody fucked your airplane.'

'Yeah?'

'Yeah.'

'My airplane?'

'That's right.'

'How'd they fuck my airplane?'

'I think maybe somebody put sand in your gas tank.'

'Who's this somebody you're telling me about?'

'That's all you get. You can make use of it or forget I was here.'

'Yeah? No shit? Fuck with my airplane.'

'If I were you, I'd check it out.'

'You see my airplane around here?'

'Well, I told you what I had to say, Sal. I'll be going now.'

'Why you doing me these favors?' he said, and grinned at the two men, who were leaning against the dock rail.

'Because I don't want a guy like you on my conscience.'

He winked at the two men, both of whom wore shades.

'Keep looking at that spot between those two islands,' he said to me, and pointed. 'That's it, right over there. Keep watching. You hear that sound? It's an airplane. You know whose plane that is? You see it now, coming past those pine trees? It sounds like there's sand in the gas tank? It looks like it's going to crash?'

The milk-white amphibian came in low between the islands and touched down into the dark blue surface of the water, the backwash of the propellers blowing clouds of spray in the air.

'Number one, I got locks on those gas tanks,' Sal said. 'Number two, I got a pilot who's also a mechanic, and he checks out everything before we go anywhere.' Then he looked at the other two men again and laughed. 'Hey, man, let me ask you an honest question. I look like I just got off the boat with a bone in my nose and a spear in my hand? Come on, I ain't mad. Nothing's going to happen to you. Give me an honest answer.'

I turned to go.

'Hey, hey, man, don't run off yet. You're too fucking much.' His mouth was grinning widely. 'Tell me for real. You think we're all that dumb? That we weren't going to catch on to all these games? I mean, I look that dumb to you?'

'What are you trying to say?'

'It was a good scam. But you ought to quit when you're ahead. Foo-Foo promised the florist a hundred bucks if he should see the guy who sent flowers and the note. So he came out yesterday and told us he seen the guy. So we found the guy, and the guy told us all about it. Charlie Dodds hasn't been anywhere around here.'

'It looks like you're on top of everything. I'm sorry I wasted your time.'

He tried to hold his grin, but I saw it fading, and I also saw the hard brown glint in his eyes, like a click of light you see in broken beer glass.

'I'll tell you what's going to happen a little ways down the road,' he said. 'I'm going to be playing cards with some guys in Nevada. Not Carl or Foo-Foo here. Guys you never heard of or saw before. I'll just mention your name and the name of that shithole you come from. I'll mention Purcel's name, too. And I might throw Dixie's in as a Lucky Strike extra. That's all. I won't say nothing else. Then one day a guy'll come to your door. Or he'll be standing by your truck when you come out of a barbershop. Or maybe he'll want to rent a boat from you. It's going to be a big day in your life. When it happens, I want you to remember me.'

His two men grinned from behind their shades. The sunlight was brilliant and cold on the lake, the wind as unrelenting as a headache.

chapter twelve

The story was on the front page of the *Missoulian* the next morning. The amphibian went down on the Salish Indian Reservation, just south of the lake. Two Indians who saw it crash said they heard the engines coughing and misfiring as the plane went by overhead, then the engines seemed to stall altogether and the plane veered sideways between two hills, plowing a trench through a stand of pines, and exploded. A rancher found a smashed wheelchair hanging in a tree two hundred yards away.

I wondered what Sal thought about in those last moments while the pilot jerked impotently against the yoke and Sal's hired men wrenched about in their seats, their faces stretched with disbelief, expecting him to do *something*, and the horizon tilting at a violent angle and the trees and cliffs rushing up at him like a fist. I wondered if he thought of his father or his lover in Huntsville pen or the Mexican gambler whose ear he mutilated on a yacht. I wondered if perhaps he thought that he had stepped into history with Ritchie Valens, the Big Bopper, and Buddy Holly.

But I doubted that he thought any of these things. I

suspected that in his last moments Sal thought about Sal.

I folded the paper and dropped it into the trash sack in the kitchen. Alafair was putting our Styrofoam cooler, with our sandwiches and soft drinks, on the front seat of the truck.

'How would Clete get into Sally Dee's house to steal those ashtrays?' I asked Dixie Lee.

'He probably just let himself in. Sal didn't know it, but Clete copied all his keys. He could get into everything Sal owned – house, boat, cars, airplane, meat locker in town. Clete ain't nobody's fool, son. Like the Wolfman used to say, "You got the curves, baby, I got the angles." I saw them in one of his boxes when I put his junk in the basement.'

'Would you mind getting them for me?' I said.

Dixie went down the basement stairs and came back with a fistful of keys that were tied together with a length of baling wire.

I walked out on the front porch into the morning, across the lawn and the street and down the embankment to the river's edge. The sun was not up over the mountains yet, trout were feeding in the current around the stanchions of the steel railway bridge, and the sawmill across the river was empty and quiet. I unfastened the looped baling wire and flung the keys out into the water like a shower of gold and silver coins.

Dixie Lee was standing on the curb, watching me, when I walked back up the embankment.

'Ain't that called destroying evidence or something?' he said.

'It's all just rock 'n' roll,' I said.

'How come Dixie always says "ain't"?' Alafair asked.

'Try not to say "how come," little guy.'

'Great God in heaven, leave that little girl's grammar alone,' Dixie said.

'I think maybe you're right,' I said.

'You better believe it, boy,' he said, then took a deep breath down in his chest and looked out at the ring of blue mountains around the valley as though he held title to them.

'Ain't this world a pure pleasure?' he said.

epilogue

Harry Mapes was sentenced to two life terms in the Montana state penitentiary at Deer Lodge, and the charges against me in Louisiana were dropped. I'm up to my eyes in debt, but it's late fall now, the heat has gone out of the days, and the sky has turned a hard, perfect blue, the way it does in South Louisiana after the summer exhausts itself in one final series of red dawns and burning afternoons. The water is now cool and still in the bays and coves, and the fishermen who go out of my dock bring back their ice chests loaded with *sac-a-lait* that are as thick as my hand across the back.

I invited Tess Regan to visit us, made arrangements for her to stay with my cousin in town, but when the time drew near for her to catch the plane, I knew she wouldn't be here. She said it was a sick grandparent in Bozeman. But we both knew better, and that's all right. I believe every middle-aged man remembers the girl he thinks he should have married. She reappears to him in his lonely moments or he sees her in the face of a young girl in the park, buying a snowball under an oak tree by the baseball diamond. But she belongs back *there*, to somebody else, and that thought sometimes rends your heart in a way that you never share with anyone else.

Clete moved back to New Orleans and opened a bar right down from Joe Burda's Golden Star on Decatur. I don't know where he got the capital. Maybe he came away from Sally Dee's house with more than two gold ashtrays. Dixie Lee worked with me in the bait shop for a month, played weekends at a Negro nightclub in St Martinville, then moved to New Orleans and organized a trio. They play regularly at Clete's place and one of my brother's clubs. One night I was down on Decatur, and I passed Clete's place when the door was open. I saw Dixie at the piano, way in back by the dance floor, his white rhinestone sport coat and pink shirt lighted by the floor lamps. I heard him singing:

'When they lay me down to rest,
Put a rose upon my breast.
I don't want no evergreens,
All I want is a bowl of butter beans.'

Three weeks ago I was deep in the marsh at first light. At that time of day you hear and see many strange things in the marsh: a bull gator calling for his mate, a frog dropping off a cypress tree into the water, the cry of a nutria that sounds like the scream of a hysterical woman. The fog hangs so thick on the dead water and between the tree trunks that you can lose your hand in it. But I know what I saw that morning, and I know what happened, too, and I feel no need to tell a psychologist about it. I was picking up the trotline that I had strung through the trees the night before, and just as it started to rain through the canopy overhead Annie and my father walked through the mist and stood on a sandspit right by the bow of my pirogue.

She was barefoot and wore a white evening gown, and she had strung together a necklace of purple four-o'clocks around her throat.

'It's good-bye for real this time, Dave. It's been special,' she said, then waded into the water, her dress billowing around her. She kissed me on the eyes and mouth, as perhaps my mother would have.

My father's tin hat was at an angle on his head, and he grinned with a matchstick in the corner of his mouth and held up one of his thumbs and winked. Then they walked deeper into the marsh, and the fog became so white and thick and cold that I had to reach out with the paddle and knock against the hard wood of a cypress to know where I was.

Neither sleep nor late-night thunderstorms bring them back now, and I rise each day into the sunlight that breaks through the pecan trees in my front yard. But sometimes at dusk, when the farmers burn the sugarcane stubble off their fields and the cinders and smoke lift in the wind and settle on the bayou, when red leaves float in piles past my dock and the air is cold and bittersweet with the smell of burnt sugar, I think of Indians and water people, of voices that can speak through the rain and tease us into yesterday, and in that moment I scoop Alafair up on my shoulders and we gallop down the road through the oaks like horse and rider toward my house, where Batist is barbecuing *gaspagoo* on the gallery and paper jack-o-lanterns are taped to the lighted windows, and the dragons become as stuffed toys, abandoned and ignored, like the shadows of the heart that one fine morning have gone with the season.